FELLOW TRAVELLERS

FELLOW TRAVELLERS

JESSE BETHEA

BELLWETHER

BELLWETHER

SINCE 2009

LCCN: 2020922395

Hardback ISBN: 978-1-63337-460-7
Paperback ISBN: 978-1-63337-461-4
E-book ISBN: 978-1-63337-462-1

1 3 5 7 9 10 8 6 4 2

For Melissa

1

THE OLD MAN

THE OLD MAN was unusual in several ways. He was American, for one thing—a rarity in rural India. He lived alone, just up the stony hill from the house where Bindra Dhar lived with her family. But he was not a recluse. He interacted with the others in the village. He went to the local pub on Mondays. He liked football and cricket. He spoke passable Hindi. And certain people in the village believed he was a sorcerer.

Most of the villagers dismissed these rumors. People in small towns like to natter, especially about newcomers and foreigners. And the old man was of African descent as well, and perhaps some of their neighbors held some prejudices about that. That was Vikram Dhar's assumption, in any case. He had grown up in the city before moving to the mountains to command the fire and rescue brigade in the nearby national park. He was a man of daily adventures, had lost count of how many lives he had saved, and he was content to accept the inwardness and backwardness of the rural villagers in exchange for the monotony of the mountains. Vikram Dhar was determined to raise safe and sheltered children, and so he accidentally raised a daughter determined to have adventures.

1

Bindra was always a thin girl, and she had always been shorter than most of the other girls in the village. She kept her hair shorter than most of the girls in the village as well, always cut just above her shoulders and parted just above her left eye. She was fond of sweaters and kept a collection of them, which she never seemed to outgrow. On colder days she would wear her father's old, forest green jacket with the symbol of his fire and rescue brigade. She preferred it in part because it smelled like him—a smell she would later learn was really just the aroma of burning wood. Her schoolmates teased her for wearing such a ratty, musty, smelly old jacket, but more often they teased her because of her name, which was neither a given name nor particularly feminine. Bindra was a family name, chosen for the purpose of honoring her mother's family. She once asked to be given a nickname to avoid the teasing, since none of her younger brothers or sisters were burdened with such embarrassment. But her mother explained this would be futile because bullies always find reasons to justify their bullying. Bindra's mother could always be counted upon for this sort of logical advice.

The Dhar household was one of quiet, humble, safe consistency. Every morning Bindra listened to her parents at the breakfast table. Her father, Vikram, would lean his chair away from the table, scratch his beard and tell farcical tales of foreign tourists who got lost in the park and needed rescuing, or who trampled on patches of rare flowers. Next to him would sit Bindra's mother, Amrita, devouring the political news and shaking her head.

"Cowards," she would mutter, reading about the latest foibles of Uttarakhand's legislature. "All of them, cowards."

To Amrita Bindra, herself a former politician, this was the harshest of insults.

Then it was off to school to be teased or, if she was very lucky, ignored. Then it was back home, passing the same people, the same houses, the same trees, the same mountains. Every day, the same. Bindra's only escape from the monotony was wondering about the old man.

She observed his movements, telling him "hello" whenever he passed on the road. The old man would nod and say "hello" in return. This went on for about ten years. When she was a teenager, Bindra set out to do more diligent research. She collected rumors about the old man from all the town gossips and tried to sort out their meaning. Some people said he could disappear and reappear at will. Others said he knew about things he couldn't know. Others said he studied the stars to learn about events that were going to happen.

But the most critical information came from the owner of the town market. She told Bindra she had once seen the old man shopping when he apparently ran into a friend. The two men immediately embraced and exchanged words the market owner remembered. "It's good to meet a fellow traveller!" exclaimed the old man, and his friend replied, "To make the road less lonely!"

The day after she heard this story, Bindra waited more than an hour for the old man to walk by her fence. He came walking up the road, hunched over in the cold with his hands in his jacket pockets. He wore a blue hat with a red Latin letter "C." For "Chicago," she had been told, the old man's faraway home.

"Hello, sir," she said to him as he passed. He smiled back at her.

"Hello there."

He continued up the road until he reached the stone steps that led up to his hill. When he got there, Bindra worked up the nerve to call out to him.

"It's good to meet a fellow traveller!" she yelled.

The old man stopped and turned. Bindra leaned against her side of the fence and wondered what his response would be. The old man started walking toward her with the sure footing and confident steps of a man who kept his physique strong even in advanced years. When he smiled, flecks of white, unshaven whiskers glistened in the sun, and when he arrived at Bindra's fence, he towered over her.

"To make the road less lonely," he replied. "But you're not a traveller, are you?"

"I don't understand," said Bindra.

"What do you know about that greeting?" asked the old man.

"I don't know anything about it," said the girl. "But I know it means something to you."

"And what do you know about me?"

Bindra didn't know how to respond. "I think," she began, "that you may be a sorcerer, sir."

The old man roared with laughter, deep, resonating laughter that echoed off the mountains. Bindra felt embarrassed and ashamed and sickened at the idea that her life's work was incorrect.

"I suppose," said the old man, "you might as well think of me as a sorcerer."

This raised Bindra's hopes back up, and she spoke before she could stop herself.

"I want to learn," she announced.

"Learn what?" said the old man.

"How to do magic."

"I can't teach you magic. I don't know magic."

Bindra's shoulders fell again.

"Let me tell you what I can teach you," said the old man. "If you're willing to work very, very hard."

"I am. But if you aren't a sorcerer and you don't know magic, what will you teach me?"

"May I see your bracelet?"

Bindra glanced at the bracelet on her right wrist.

"It's metal, right?" asked the old man.

Bindra nodded. "Silver. My grandmother gave it to me."

"It's important to you?"

"Yes, very."

"If I promise to give it back," said the old man, "may I borrow it?"

He held out his hand. After a moment's hesitation, Bindra took the bracelet from her wrist and gave it to the old man, who put it into his jacket pocket.

"Walk with me," he said to Bindra.

The old man and Bindra walked down the road for several minutes in silence. Bindra watched the old man as he admired the mountains and the landscape around them. Finally, he pointed to a tall, leafless tree and said, "There. That one should work just fine."

The old man and Bindra approached the tree.

"Do you think you can climb it?" asked the old man. "All the way up to the hollow at the top of the tree?"

"Of course I can."

He gestured for her to try. She approached the tree and surveyed it for a moment. She removed her father's jacket for better mobility and started to climb. It didn't take her long to reach the hollow.

"I found it," she called down to the old man.

"What's inside?" he asked, still admiring the mountains.

Bindra looked back into the darkness of the tree hollow and reached inside. Her hand soon found something that clearly didn't belong in the hollow of a tree. It was a small plastic bag, and when she pulled it out, she could see that sitting inside was her bracelet. She looked down to the old man.

"How did you do that?" she asked.

"Do what?"

"How did you get my bracelet all the way up here?"

"I didn't," said the old man, and he held up the bracelet for her to see.

"How is that possible?" she said, and she pulled the bracelet out for him to see in case he didn't understand.

The old man smiled. "It was always in the tree. Because I put it there. I will put it there. I am putting it there, right now. I'll put it in the hollow of the tree when the tree is barely taller than you are. For as long as you've been alive, your bracelet was in that tree."

The old man walked to the base of the tree trunk.

"What's your name?" he asked.

"Bindra Dhar."

The old man seemed almost startled. He cocked his head to the side and smiled before making a gesture that Bindra thought looked like a bow.

"Well, it's an honor to meet you, Bindra Dhar," he said. "My name is Walter Franklin Brooks, and I am a time traveller. If you really want it, and if you will work hard and study hard, you can be a time traveller too."

2

THE ELEMENTS OF TIME TRAVEL

FOR THE NEXT FEW YEARS, Bindra Dhar spent a majority of her time with Walter Franklin Brooks as he taught her how to time travel. Or at least that's what he said she was learning. For the most part, Bindra's studies involved a lot of reading and note taking. Mr. Brooks gave her books on physics, theoretical physics, quantum physics, metaphysics, mysticism, biology, geology, chemistry. She absorbed only pieces of it. Mr. Brooks also took the time to teach her English, some Arabic, and a little Latin, a language he called "surprisingly useful." She, in exchange, tried to help him with some of the finer points of Hindi, particularly youthful slang that mostly went over his head.

Eventually, astronomy became the thing Mr. Brooks wanted her to study most. He showed her his array of telescopes and ordered her to spend months tracking the planets and stars across the night sky.

"What does this have to do with time travel?" she finally asked him.

"It has everything to do with time travel," he said. "Because it has everything to do with navigation. All travel is navigation, including time travel."

She turned away from the telescope and looked to Mr. Brooks for an explanation.

"We are in India right now, right?" he said.

"Yes."

"But if I were to stand in this spot and travel back in time by three months, I would not be in India. I would not even be on Earth. I would be in space, suffocating! Don't laugh, many an inexperienced and reckless traveller has died that way. You must know where you're going as well as when you're going. This is essential, Bindra."

Bindra, of course, was expected to continue her conventional studies as a diligent Indian student. As far as her parents understood the arrangement, their strange American neighbor was tutoring their daughter in English, apparently for free, and they were grateful. And although she had learned a great deal of English, after a year of her studies with Mr. Brooks, Bindra had yet to time travel. But in that second year, the books she was told to read suddenly changed. Mr. Brooks now gave her books from his own, vast collection—books about time travel, written by time travellers, books she didn't even know existed.

Bindra started with a beaten, weathered copy of *The Elements of Time Travel*. Mr. Brooks instructed her to keep diligent notes in the margins, which she found difficult given the quantity of annotations already penned by other readers over the years. It seemed to her as if every stray thought a reader could have while reading the text had already been noted. Finally in the twelfth chapter, "Be Mindful of Changing Landscapes," she thought of something that hadn't yet been noted and started to write, "Maybe there are records of what rivers have been diverted, and where?" But just as she put her pen to the page, smooth cursive writing appeared next to the passage she'd been reading.

One ought to study engineering records, river diversion in particular!

Naturally, Bindra assumed the book was possessed and tossed it

8

across the room with a yelp. When Mr. Brooks arrived to ask what was the matter, Bindra explained what she had seen.

"Yes, that happens," he said. "It's nothing to be afraid of. It just means another traveller is reading the same book in the past and making notes. The notes will appear as the traveller writes them."

She asked him how that could be possible.

"If another time traveller made these notes in the past," she said, "shouldn't they have always been there?"

"Not necessarily. There are a lot of stray factors determining these things. Even we don't understand everything about how time works. In fact, the only thing we all agree on is that time doesn't work. It doesn't even exist."

So Bindra continued her attempt to annotate the book, all while fighting with what seemed like three or four other apprentice time travellers, all in different years, yet reading the same book at the same time. And though she did absorb some of the elements of time travel from the book, she suspected the old man's true purpose in making her read it was to make her feel like she was one of the nameless annotators, like part of a community—the community of people who had learned to break down the barriers of time.

But there were other books the old man had her read, such as *The Time Traveller's Companion*; *Stranded During the Plague*; *So You've Been Accused of Witchcraft*; and *Stop Visiting 1912!—A Guide to Overcrowded Years*. She labored her way through *A History of the Time Travellers' Guild*, as well as the far more interesting *A (People's) History of the Time Travellers' Guild*.

But nothing was worse than the intricate, twenty-five-volume *Time Travellers' Revised Code*. To acquire just the first of these volumes, Bindra had to accompany Mr. Brooks to one of the libraries in the next town over—a distance easily covered by car, but as always, Mr. Brooks preferred to walk because he "didn't trust robots."

"You've started to spend most of your free time with me," he said as they walked along the road.

"I guess so," said Bindra.

"It's really that important to you?"

"What do you mean?"

"Becoming a time traveller," said Mr. Brooks. "I told you it was hard work. You've devoted a lot of time to it, and I want to make sure you're still up to the challenge."

"I still want it," said Bindra, but she noticed Mr. Brooks didn't really seem to be listening.

"You have your friends, of course," he said.

"Yes, I've got friends."

"And boys, perhaps. You're at that age."

Bindra laughed. "No, no boys."

"And what about girls?" said Mr. Brooks.

Bindra became very silent. Mr. Brooks did something he was unnaturally good at—smiling at someone without looking at them.

"One thing you'll learn about time travellers, Bindra," said Mr. Brooks. "We know all sorts of things."

"I still want it," blurted Bindra, just to change the subject. "I still want to be a time traveller."

"That's good to know. We don't take a chronological life away from anyone who wants it. Nor do we instruct anyone who isn't ready."

"How long will it take before I'm ready?"

Mr. Brooks sighed and shook his head. "We have a saying, you know. 'One should not half-bake a time traveller.'"

"What?"

"It means it takes a long time, and it should take a long time. For you, two more years."

"It takes two more years?"

"It will take exactly two years, five months, and fourteen days," he replied.

"How do you know that?"

"I looked it up. The Guild keeps records of when a time traveller is admitted."

"So, it's already happened?"

"No," he said. "It will happen, has happened, is happening. When will you learn?"

As it happened, this visit to the library was the first time Bindra met time travellers other than Mr. Brooks. While she and Mr. Brooks searched for the first volume of the *Time Travellers' Revised Code*, they encountered a trio of foreigners—Bindra believed them to be English—who immediately recognized Mr. Brooks. The oldest was a tall woman with long, wavy black hair, brown eyes and a soft face and smile. The other two were children, a boy and girl, both with black hair and brown, intense eyes. Bindra guessed they must be a family.

The tall woman, upon seeing Mr. Brooks in the library, embraced him and then stood at arm's-length, squeezing his shoulders.

"It's good to meet a fellow traveller," she said.

"To make the road less lonely," said Mr. Brooks. "Bindra, I want you to meet Madolyn Listratta, and her, um…"

"Niece and nephew," said Madolyn Listratta. "This is Llewellyn and this is Ginnifer."

The children, with proper smiles, both shook Bindra's hand. Bindra was excited to learn more from these new time travellers, but soon she grew more interested in Mr. Brooks's expression. He was, perhaps, the most suspicious person she'd ever met in her young life, and he had a hard time hiding it. Whenever he didn't quite believe something, he would usually tilt his eyes upward and allow the corner of his mouth to wince as if lies physically stung him. Bindra observed this same expression many times as she watched him interact with Madolyn Listratta.

"What brings you to India?" he asked the tall woman at one point.

"Oh," she said with a wave of her hand. "Family business."

"Of course," he said. "Family business."

"And what are you doing, Walter?" said Madolyn with a laugh. "Taking in an apprentice at your age! She'd be the third, am I correct?"

Then she turned to Bindra. "He must be reading you to death. Like an old schoolmaster."

Bindra nodded.

"It's the only way he knows how to teach," replied Madolyn. "But of course, he probably hasn't given you any of his books."

"You've written books?" she asked Mr. Brooks.

"Of course!" said Madolyn. "He's one of our finest travel writers."

Then the two children took her by the hands and brought her to a dusty section of the library where they pulled out several volumes, giggling all the while. Each book they presented was written by Walter Franklin Brooks, and they all seemed to be about sports.

"This one's my favorite," said the boy. "*Encounters with Greatness.* That's the one where he interviewed Jackie Robinson and Babe Ruth. And here's *A Time Traveller's Guide to Football*—he means American football, not the real kind—and here's *The World Cup Every Day*, and *First Pitch: The Definitive Invention of Baseball.*"

Bindra picked up *First Pitch* and flipped to the back cover where she found a brief biography of Mr. Brooks next to a picture of him as, surprisingly, a much older man than the man she knew.

Walter Franklin Brooks is one of the Guild's most prolific travel writers, known for his exploration of sports history, his advocacy on the issue of overcrowded years, and as a founding member of the Society of Black Time Travellers. As of this publication, Mr. Brooks resides in the Twenty-Second Century.

"He's a fascinating man, your instructor," said Madolyn Listratta.

Bindra closed the book and turned. Madolyn stood in the dark alley of library books. In the dim light, her black dress gave her the appearance of being but a levitating face. Bindra sensed the two children behind her, stepping away from their aunt as she approached.

"You are really quite lucky to have him teaching you the profession," said Madolyn. "Walter Brooks will take you far."

Madolyn stopped and bent over to stare closer at Bindra, studying her face. The woman's eyes got thin and curious as she smiled a toothy, mischievous grin.

"Would you like to know how far?" said Madolyn.

Then she winked and Bindra nearly jumped.

"*Ghamud dayim*," said Mr. Brooks in a firm voice.

Madolyn Listratta stepped to the side and revealed Mr. Brooks standing at the end of the stacks.

"We still believe in that, don't we, Madolyn?" he said.

"Yes, yes," said Madolyn. "Ghamud dayim."

Mr. Brooks politely, but swiftly, bid farewell to his fellow travellers, and he and Bindra checked out their book from the library. Bindra held her tongue for as long as she could and waited until they were walking back to the village to ask Mr. Brooks what he'd said to Madolyn Listratta.

"I know it's Arabic," said Bindra. "But I don't recognize the phrase."

"Ghamud dayim," said Mr. Brooks, "means 'permanent mystery.' It's what a time traveller says to another when the other is about to reveal something about the traveller's future. Each of us has a right to some mystery in our lives."

"She was going to tell me my future?"

"I thought she might. So I gave her a gentle reminder of our rules."

"Why can't I know my future?"

"Because it might drive you insane, or into depression, or make you think you are invincible, or make you start killing people," said Mr. Brooks. "Or all of the above, like Macbeth."

"Who?"

"Never mind."

"Why would she want to tell me my future if it's against the rules?"

"I don't know."

Mr. Brooks stopped walking and looked at Bindra with tired eyes. "Bindra, it's important that you understand this. You must find in yourself a reason to time travel. You must find fulfillment in the profession, but it can't be selfish fulfillment. You'll come to encounter travellers who defile the profession for the sake of personal gain. There's a lot of power in knowing how to travel through time. But you must remember this—to travel is to better yourself, not to better your possessions. I write my books because I want to learn everything I can about sports and athletes, far more than anyone can learn living chronologically. And I want to share that knowledge with whomever wants to know it. But we never, ever travel out of selfishness."

With this last sentence, he stood up straight and stared back in the general direction of the library, and Bindra saw him tilt up his eyes and wince with the pain of a lie.

3 ANCHOR POINTS

ABOUT A YEAR LATER, Mr. Brooks took Bindra into the national park to a rocky outcrop not far from the road. He brought her to the center of the rocks and told her to stand in silence for a time. They stood among the rocks for about half an hour without speaking. Bindra did not see the utility of this exercise, and she told him so.

"What is time travel, Bindra?" he asked.

"Ummmm…" was all she could reply.

"Come on, Bindra. I tell you this all the time. When will you learn? Time travel is…"

"Travel!" she said. "Time travel is travel."

"Right, time travel is travel. It's no different than any other mobility. Time travel is no more mystical—"

"No more mystical than walking or running or swimming," she said, for she had heard this many times. "Time travel is simply travel."

"Exactly," said Mr. Brooks. "And all travel is…"

"Navigation?" she ventured.

Mr. Brooks sighed. "Yes, Bindra. All travel is navigation." He spread his arms wide and gestured to the rocks around them. "This, Bindra, is how you navigate."

Bindra looked around her at the outcrop. "I navigate with rocks?"

"Do you feel anything, standing here?"

"No."

"You don't feel anything at all?"

"Uh…confusion."

"Not an emotional feeling," said Mr. Brooks. "A physical feeling."

"No."

"Try."

"Okay," she said, and started strolling around the rocks. "I feel the wind on my face. I feel the ground. I feel this rock right here with my hand."

"You don't feel any kind of energy here?"

"No."

"Try to keep up with me here," said Mr. Brooks. "Beneath the ground in this spot is a sort of mineral anomaly. A geological accident that occurs almost everywhere on Earth. A spot where certain minerals in the ground interact with one another in strange ways and create a faint energy, almost like magnetism, that your brain, if you concentrate, can feel."

"I can feel…rocks?" said Bindra.

Mr. Brooks smiled. "All through time, animals have felt these spots in the Earth. It's how pigeons know where they are. Human cultures worship them as sacred places. In Britain and Ireland, the ancients build stone circles around them. People even think they have magical healing properties."

He approached her and put his hands on her shoulders. "But that, Bindra, is bullshit. It's not magic; it's science. It's a simple geological phenomenon that the laymen just haven't discovered yet."

He took his hands from her shoulders and sauntered around the rocks.

"But even though there's no magic here, these spots are very useful to time travellers," said Mr. Brooks. "We call them anchor points, and they will keep you from getting lost. You have to remember, time and space are intertwined. As long as you can feel that mineral energy, you can tether yourself to the closest anchor point. When you jump through time, your mind will take your matter to that spot whenever you want to go. It will help you navigate, and more importantly, it will keep you on the Earth's surface."

"But I can't feel any energy here," said Bindra.

"You will. I told you, this isn't magic, Bindra. You can't just do it. You must learn it."

So every day for several months, Bindra came to the outcrop alone and stood in silence, trying to feel the energy of the anchor point. Each time she would stand there and feel nothing. Sometimes she would get mad and storm off. Sometimes she would sit and fall asleep.

As the months went by, she eventually gave up. She did not return to the outcrop for a few weeks, instead spending her days reading or rereading the books that Mr. Brooks had given her. She was sure the old man noticed that she wasn't going back to the anchor point, but he never mentioned it. She scoured the books for more information about anchor points, and more importantly, why she couldn't feel them. She wanted a shortcut, but she knew there probably wasn't one. In desperation and anger, she scrawled in the margins of *The Elements of Time Travel*, "What is wrong with me? Why can't I feel the anchor points?"

Blue, cursive, English words materialized over her own. "Keep trying."

That was different. While she had gotten used to the other travellers' notes randomly appearing in the margins of the books, none of her annotations had ever received a reply. Now she knew enough about the profession to understand what was happening. A traveller in the future must have seen her notation and then gone back to before she had written it and replied to her in the same book. That would explain why the reply was written over her own notation—the replying traveller couldn't see her

17

words because they hadn't been written yet. It was, she thought, a long way to go to offer some encouragement, and therefore a very kind gesture on the part of this time travelling stranger.

So she took the traveller's advice. She returned to the anchor point with the intention of staying until she felt the magical energy, which, she reminded herself, was not magic because magic, as Mr. Brooks often said, was bullshit.

As soon as she arrived at the outcrop, she knew something had changed.

She walked over the rocks and felt a tingling sensation in her fingertips and the soles of her feet, not unlike when her legs would fall asleep after crossing them for a long time. That was, at the time, all the feeling was, and she couldn't be sure that it was The Feeling. But it was more than she had ever felt before.

She made subsequent sojourns to the anchor point, and as she did the feeling grew stronger. And as the feeling grew, so too did the distance she could be from the anchor point and still feel it. Asleep in her own home, she could tell which direction the rocky outcrop was. She could sense it like a magnet. She was tethered.

Bindra informed Mr. Brooks that she now felt the pull of the anchor point. Despite her excitement at this revelation, he seemed completely uninterested, and he told her it was time to move on to a new phase of her training. That phase apparently involved almost constant meditation and yoga, activities that Bindra, having always been a restless young lady, despised. Mr. Brooks insisted these lessons take place in the rocky shallows of the Dhauliganga River, explaining that the sound of rushing water would improve her focus.

"Yoga," said Mr. Brooks during one such lesson, "is how Indian apprentices have become Indian time travellers for generations."

She gave up on a difficult contortion and opened her eyes. Mr. Brooks sat on the banks of the Dhauliganga, ignoring her and reading one of his many volumes on quantum physics while she was on a flat rock in the middle of the stream.

"And how do Americans become time travellers?" she called to him.

He raised his eyebrows and flipped a page. "Brute force of will. And alcohol."

"That one sounds better."

"I agree. Now try again, from the beginning."

Bindra returned to the first pose and closed her eyes. She tried to remember Mr. Brooks's instruction that she meditate on another time, any other time, but with intense focus on the moment, not simply the year. But she didn't really know what that meant, and ambiguity tended to break her focus.

"When will I be a time traveller?" she asked, for perhaps the hundredth time that week.

For a while she didn't hear anything, only water rolling over the rocks. Then he finally spoke. "When you least expect it."

By this time, Bindra's grasp of English was strong enough that her parents were delighted at the wide range of international universities their daughter might be able to attend. They still appreciated Mr. Brooks and his tutoring, but Vikram Dhar couldn't help but notice how much time Bindra now spent hiking in the hills alone, and it worried him. At dinner one night, he demanded to know where she was hiking.

"In the foothills near Kedarnath," she replied. Her father furrowed his brow.

"In the park?" he asked.

"Yes," she said. "It's perfectly safe."

"Ha!" laughed her father. "Not the way I remember it."

"What do you mean?"

"Your father is being dramatic," said her mother. "Remembering glorious old fires."

"Which fire was this?" asked Bindra of her father.

"Some thirty years ago. There was a drought. The forest and grass-lands below Nanda Devi, surrounding Kedarnath, caught fire. It burned for fourteen days, but we beat it back and saved everyone in the villages, and the temple of course."

Her father continued to eat with silent pride.

That night, Bindra fell asleep thinking of her father's past heroism, a story like many she'd heard before, and as she slipped into unconsciousness, she was acutely aware of the energy she still felt from the nearby anchor point. Soon she was dreaming, and in her dream she was lying in the middle of the rocky outcrop she knew so well from her hikes, still in her pajamas. Only it was bright daylight above and the air felt different. It seemed thin, even for the high altitude, and smelled heavily of smoke. She looked around at the outcrop. Some of the rocks and boulders, each one she knew very well after visiting so many times, seemed to be in different positions. The two trees that grew at one end of the outcrop had disappeared completely. And as she looked to the west, she saw a thick, black column of smoke rising from the valley, blocking out the view of Nanda Devi completely.

Then she came to realize she was not dreaming. She actually felt the ground beneath her feet. The smoke from the fire burned her nose. The ground was real. The smoke was real. The fire was real. She was there, in the foothills outside Kedarnath, at the anchor point, and the fire was burning. This couldn't be happening.

"Oh no," she said to herself. "Oh no, no, no, no…" She stood up and walked to the road. With each step, the realness of her surroundings was too much to ignore. She came over a small hill and saw the road below. It was made of gravel. A bad sign. The road she took to the outcrop was paved.

"Oh no, oh no, oh no…"

She heard a noise on the road, something mechanized racing closer.

CHAPTER 3: ANCHOR POINTS

Around the bend she spotted three forest green trucks and instinctively hid behind a large boulder. From there she could see they were the trucks of the fire and rescue brigade, but much older than the trucks she had seen all her life. She had the awful feeling that her father was in one of those trucks, racing toward the monstrous drought fire beneath Nanda Devi.

Some thirty years ago.

"No!"

She had done it. She had time travelled. By accident. That wasn't supposed to happen. At least she didn't think it was supposed to happen. She always imagined when she first travelled it would be with Mr. Brooks guiding her. But here she was, thirty years back in time, alone.

She raced back to the outcrop wondering if she would be able to travel back. Surely if she could travel thirty years by accident, she should be able to travel thirty years on purpose. And going forward in time— downstream, it was called—that was always easier than going upstream, because people are always time travelling downstream. She remembered that from the books. So maybe she could do this. She stood in the middle of the outcrop, fully conscious of the anchor point's energy, and spread her arms wide.

"Hello!" she said to absolutely no one. "I really, really, really need to go back to my time now, please."

It wasn't working, and in the back of her mind she knew why. Panicking isn't how you time travel. She remembered that from the books too. She also remembered that travelling under stress or duress could have negative consequences, ending up when you didn't intend to be and so forth, and since she had already done that, she had to be careful.

So panicking wasn't the answer, she told herself, but it was hard not to panic at a time like this. She stood in the middle of the outcrop and tried to focus on her training. It isn't about years, she heard Mr. Brooks saying, it's about moments. What did that mean? She always thought that phrase was nonsense, but it kept popping up in her books in different variations. *It isn't about years…it isn't about numbers…it's about moments. Find a moment,* she thought, *not a year.*

She would concentrate, then, on the moment she left and not the year. She didn't want to go to the first of May 2117. She wanted to go to the time when the snow was melting and the foreigners started arriving to visit the national park. She focused on the kinds of flowers that were blooming at the time she left, the music that was popular in the time she left, the moments that made up the time she left. The moments, not the year. Moments, moments, moments…

As she stood there, the world around her went black and she stumbled onto the cold ground. The smell of smoke dissipated. The noise of the fire trucks on the road was gone, replaced by the silence of the night. Her eyes began to adjust to darkness, and she could see the stars above her. The constellations and planets were, after years of staring through Mr. Brooks's telescope, familiar to her, so much so that they appeared to her as a clock. The position of each celestial object told her without question when she was: the first of May 2117.

All travel is navigation, said Mr. Brooks's voice annoyingly in the back of her mind.

It had worked. It had worked just the way all the books said it would work. The anchor point had kept her in one geographical place while her mind carried her body through time and back again. She was, suddenly and without fanfare, a time traveller. She was also far from home, cold, and still in her pajamas. So Bindra Dhar, newly-minted time traveller, walked barefoot and shivering down the road in the direction of Mr. Brooks's house.

When she arrived at his home in the middle of the night, Mr. Brooks reacted as if such an occurrence was simply one of the quirks of mentoring a young time traveller. He welcomed her inside, gave her a seat by the fire, a blanket and some hot tea, and she told him what had happened.

"That's fantastic!" he exclaimed at the end of her story. "Bindra, I can't tell you how proud I am."

"It was not fantastic," she said. "It was terrifying. I didn't think it could just…just happen!"

"I know. It's very unusual, but you should be very proud."

"Why?" she demanded.

"Because, not everyone can do such a thing. It means you have an aptitude for this. You're a natural time traveller!"

"I thought it wasn't supposed to come naturally," she said, and began to mimic his American accent. "'This isn't magic, Bindra. You can't just do it. When will you learn?'"

"Well, yes, everyone has to learn. And you've spent four years learning. But just like every skill, some people take to it better and faster than others. It took much longer for me to figure it out myself, and I only travelled ten years in my first jump. You did thirty! In your sleep!" He chuckled. "I guess what I'm saying is, either you're a natural or I am an extraordinary teacher."

She rolled her eyes at him and sat back in the chair, gripping her forehead. "What's wrong with me? My muscles ache all over; my head is on fire. I felt like I was carrying a bag of bricks all the way here."

"Of course you did," said Mr. Brooks. "You travelled a total of sixty years in one night. Imagine walking sixty kilometers in one night. It's bound to wear you out."

"So I'm going to feel like this every time?"

"Not if you use a little moderation. Even an experienced traveller can only jump an average of thirty years in one go. You have to rest in between. Time travel is travel, and travel is tiring. Come along. I'll take you home and you can sleep."

She did sleep. She slept for what she thought was a night and what she learned from her family had been a day and a half.

After that, Bindra and Mr. Brooks travelled regularly. She learned that whatever matter she touched when she made her jump—her clothes, any object, even any person—would come with her through time. This allowed Mr. Brooks to take her through time without her feeling the tiring effects.

Mr. Brooks taught Bindra about the nuances of the anchor points, how they should be treated with respect, and he taught her some tips and tricks on how to use them. Each of these maneuvers had its own catchy American nickname. "Daisy chaining," for example, was when a time traveller jumped from one anchor point to another over a great geographical distance, but only a very short distance upstream or downstream. When daisy chaining, it was important to stay mentally tethered to both the departure and the arrival anchor point, Mr. Brooks told her, or she could die. There was also the "snapback" effect, meaning the tendency of a time traveller to arrive exactly at an anchor point, even if they had jumped from a certain distance away. Mr. Brooks explained that this had happened to Bindra the first time she time travelled, leaving her bed and arriving in the mountains, and she needed to be very careful with snapbacks or she could die.

There were, Bindra realized, a great many ways to die in time travel.

Together they went on trips through the decades. They attended cricket matches that Mr. Brooks insisted were important but that she had little interest in. She saw the world as it was before she was born. She saw her little village as it was built and grew into what she had known all her life.

In one long, tiring journey, Mr. Brooks took her a couple of decades upstream, and together they rode the bus to Delhi, a place Bindra had always heard of but never visited. It was, as one might imagine, a shocking experience. In Delhi she encountered more people than she'd ever seen in one place, all of them speaking what seemed like every language on earth. Above the teeming humanity loomed buildings that never looked so terrifying in photographs, but now seemed pressurizing.

Mr. Brooks sensed her discomfort but refused to coddle her. "You had better get used to it. We are only twenty-seven years in your past. Take this feeling and remember it's ten times stronger when you're in another century."

Bindra stayed in a daze as she followed Mr. Brooks through the crowded city streets. Though she was completely lost, he seemed to know exactly where they were going. They came to a town square, cordoned off by police officers and filled with people. Mr. Brooks guided her around the human mass to a place where she could see through to the center. There she saw that all of the people had gathered around a red truck, and standing in the bed of the truck was a woman in a yellow sari, pontificating into a microphone connected by winding wire to a large speaker. The woman seemed only a little older than Bindra and looked almost exactly as she would see herself in a mirror, but with the traditional dress and confidence she almost never wore. Bindra listened with the crowd.

"...corruption of the police, corruption of the courts, corruption of the legislature—at every level, the men you trust, the men you believe, the men who ask your praise, all of them care only for themselves and their wants and needs. The rest of us are tools or bystanders or obstacles to overcome or destroy."

The crowd applauded with righteous understanding.

"The India they believe in is a great game," said the woman. "It is a game where there can be only one winner, and each of them intends to be that winner. In time, they will all stab each other in the back, most certainly, but not before they have stabbed India in the heart!"

At this the crowd openly cheered.

"We believe in a different India," said the woman. "We believe in a fair India, an ambitious India, an India with plenty of room for the immigrant and the refugee, the sick and the poor, the lost and the down-trodden, the Hindu, the Sikh, the Christian, the Muslim, the Jain, the woman and the man and the woman who loves a woman and the man who loves a man!"

The crowd applauded, yes, but Bindra noticed apprehension in some of the audience at the woman's last statement. She felt a primal sort of uneasiness at their uneasiness.

"We believe in that India," said the woman in the bed of the truck. "We believe that is the only India, the only India for the future. I believe in that India. Those who do not believe, those who believe in the game instead of the people, you must point them out in the street! You must laugh at them and call them what they are—cowards! All of them, cowards!"

Bindra's thoughts were lost in the crowd's excited cheers.

"Who is she?" she asked Mr. Brooks, though she already knew.

"Amrita Bindra," he said. "She wins this election and serves two years in parliament before she's undone by the corrupt politicians she's spent her life fighting against. She'll move to the mountains, meet a firefighter, raise a family, but while she raises that family, she writes a book—*Thoughts on Indian Democracy*. Not the catchiest name, but when it's printed in English, they give it a better title—*Amrita's Revenge*. One of my favorites, actually, and the whole reason I travelled to your village in the first place. I'd like to write about her one day."

Mr. Brooks and Bindra turned their attention back to the square. Her mother was still finishing her speech, but her words, even amplified by the microphone, were drowned out by hundreds of other voices chanting.

"Bindra! Bindra! Bindra! Bindra!"

It was the first time Bindra had ever heard any sort of power, majesty, or force associated with her name. She liked it.

4

THE CLERK OF ADMISSION AND EXPULSION

EVERYONE KNOWS there are four anchor points under Washington, D.C.: Barracks Row, Anacostia, Dupont Circle and Mount Pleasant. Then there's the one that fewer people know about, under the building without significance or description where Mr. Brooks took Bindra Dhar. They had not left the Twenty-Second Century, but had flown to Washington after suggesting to Bindra's parents that they would visit some prestigious American universities where Mr. Brooks had connections. Instead, Mr. Brooks took her to Headquarters.

Naturally, the Headquarters of the Time Travellers' Guild must change physical locations from time to time, but from 1945 to 2170 you will find it at 2121 J Street, NW, Washington, District of Columbia, United States of America. According to the layman postal services, of course, J Street "doesn't exist" but, rest assured, the building is there if you know what to look for. It's blocky, whitish-gray in color and generally inconspicuous on the outside. On the inside, however, Headquarters is gorgeous with a great hall of columns and gold leaf, crystal chandeliers and enormous murals of such indescribable beauty. Truly, the Headquarters of the Time Travellers' Guild is a marvelous place and a privilege for any time traveller to visit. It's almost always empty.

"Why is it empty?" asked Bindra. Her words echoed through the haunting void of the abandoned Headquarters.

"It's almost always empty," said Mr. Brooks. "Travellers only have to be here for official Guild business. There's rarely official Guild business so there's rarely anyone here."

"Doesn't anybody work here?"

"Ha! No, no, no, not at all," said Mr. Brooks. "If any of us wanted to come to work at the same place at the same time every day, we wouldn't have become time travellers."

"Aren't we supposed to be meeting someone?"

"Yes," said Mr. Brooks. "The Clerk."

He stopped walking and turned to her with that look he had whenever he had to tell her something important. "Now, Bindra, I don't mean to imply that I think you would offend the Clerk. But it's very important that you don't offend the Clerk."

"Is the Clerk easily offended? Also, who is the Clerk?"

"He's not easily offended," said Mr. Brooks. "In fact, I don't think he's ever been offended in his life. But the Clerk of Admission and Expulsion is a man of considerable authority. He's a representative of the Commissioners of Time Travel, and though he's not a commissioner himself, he acts on their behalf. One should always try to stay on the Clerk's good side."

Just then, Bindra and Mr. Brooks heard heavy footsteps down the long hallway, walking toward them with purpose.

"There he is now," said Mr. Brooks.

Bindra looked down the hallway, expecting to see a man of considerable authority. Instead she saw a tall, slender, almost scrawny young man with messy brown hair and glasses. He wore a thin black tie and suspenders and carried a brown leather bag from a strap around his shoulder.

"I'm sorry I'm late," he said. "Bindra Dhar, I presume? And Walter Brooks, it's an honor to meet you."

CHAPTER 4: THE CLERK OF ADMISSION AND EXPULSION

The Clerk shook hands with both of them, lingering a while with Mr. Brooks.

"I'm a great fan of your books," said the Clerk. "When I saw you on the ledger as Ms. Dhar's instructor, I was so very excited to meet you. I hope you don't mind, when this is over, if you might sign my copy of *First Pitch*?"

"Of course," said Mr. Brooks.

"Thank you so much, sir," the Clerk said. He turned to Bindra and smiled. "And of course it's good to meet you, Bindra. I am the Clerk of Admission and Expulsion for the Time Travellers' Guild. If you'll follow me to Hearing Room 104, we will begin the ceremony."

Many time travellers will remember Hearing Room 104 from their own admission ceremonies. It is a dull, wood-paneled room kept in low light, with a courtroom bench at the front and a painting of a double parabola, resembling a Latin letter S, turned on its side and pierced by a horizontal line—the universal symbol of time travel. And in the corner, of course, is that single wooden chair.

The Clerk walked in behind Bindra and Mr. Brooks and closed the hearing room door. He brushed past the chair and motioned for them to stand before the bench, while he ascended a few steps to stand behind it, opening up a black leather book.

"Now," said the Clerk, taking a fountain pen from his shirt pocket. "Let us begin. Name of the traveller to be admitted?"

The Clerk raised his eyebrows at Bindra and she snapped to attention with an answer.

"Bindra Dhar."

"Country of origin?"

"India."

"Century of origin?"

"Twenty-Two."

"Wonderful," said the Clerk as he finished a notation and turned to Mr. Brooks. "Now then, name of instructor?"

"Walter Franklin Brooks."

"Instructor's country of origin?"

"United States of America."

"Instructor's century of origin?"

"Twenty."

"Ah, Twenty," said the Clerk. "A little wild for me, but I know some good folks there. Very well, Bindra, what I'm going to do now is write in this ledger that you have applied for admission to the Guild and that you have the recommendation of your instructor and myself. Some time in the future, the commissioners will review the application and send word of their approval or disapproval."

At that moment, there was a knock at the hearing room door. The Clerk stepped down from his bench to open it, revealing a woman who handed the Clerk a manila envelope before disappearing back into the hallway. The Clerk opened the envelope on the way back up to the bench.

"Very well, I have received word that the commissioners have reviewed and approved your application," he said as he sat down at the bench and picked up his pen. "It's a little rude of them to review and approve the application before I've written it, but commissioners do what commissioners want, I suppose."

Bindra and Mr. Brooks stood in silence and watched as the Clerk continued to write in his ledger. At one time or another Bindra realized there were other people in the room. She looked to see two women sitting in the rear corner of the hearing room. They smiled at her and one of them bowed her head.

"Who are they?" Bindra whispered to Mr. Brooks. He looked back at the two women.

"Must be people you know."

"I don't know them."

"You will."

"Now," announced the Clerk. "We can continue with the ceremony. And I see we have some attendees; welcome, everyone."

The Clerk nodded at the people behind Bindra. She looked again to discover even more people had arrived. In addition to the two women in the corner, three men were standing dressed in suits and ties, as if they were attending a wedding. She blinked and out of the corner of her eye, two more women appeared and found seats.

"We welcome guests to this ceremony, of course," said the Clerk to the audience. "But let us please keep things quiet until after the oath. Now, Bindra, we will proceed. I shall write in the ledger a summons for—"

The opening of the hearing room door again interrupted the Clerk. A short, round, Arab man walked into the hearing room. The Clerk quickly stood, and Bindra could hear the attendees behind her standing as well. When she looked again there were at least five more people in attendance, all of whom were strangers to her.

"I hope I'm not late," said the round Arab man. "Am I, Clerk?"

"Not at all, Your Honor," said the Clerk. "In fact, you're early. I haven't yet summoned you."

"Oh, gracious me!" said the Arab man. "I apologize for my rudeness. Please be seated, everyone. Clerk, continue your summoning."

"Bindra," said Mr. Brooks. "This is His Honor, Faisal Muhammad Raisuni, the Twenty-Second Centurion. He is the highest authority in Twenty-Two."

"It's an honor to meet you, Your Honor," said Bindra, shaking the man's hand.

"The honor is all mine," said the centurion. "Are we ready to begin, Clerk?"

"Go ahead, Your Honor," said the Clerk.

"Bindra," said the centurion. "Will you raise your right hand?"

She did so and the centurion raised his as well.

"Repeat after me," he said. "I, Bindra Dhar…"

"I, Bindra Dhar…"

"Do solemnly swear… To travel through time without selfishness or greed… To travel with integrity and honor… To uphold the laws and customs of my ancient and noble profession… To show respect for the ancient knowledge bestowed upon me… And to cherish and love my family of travellers."

"…And to cherish and love my family of travellers," finished Bindra.

"I have sworn this, I will swear this, I do swear this…"

"I have sworn this, I will swear this, I do swear this…"

"Always."

"Always."

The centurion lowered his hand and stood straight, staring into her eyes.

"It is good to meet a fellow traveller," he said.

She replied in a quiet voice, "To make the road less lonely."

Behind her, they all cheered. She turned around to find a room full of strangers. She didn't recognize any of them, but they all recognized her. They crowded around her and shook her hands, told her how proud they were and how they couldn't wait for her to meet them. She realized they were her people, her friends. They always had been. She was, apparently, someone important enough to them that they would travel through time, even when they knew she wouldn't recognize them, just to see her admitted into their noble ranks. They were, will be, are, her family. Always.

5

THE TIME TROOPER

ZELDA CLAIRING was a woman of few guilty pleasures, in that she felt no guilt about any of her pleasures. But there was one thing she kept hidden from most of her fellow travellers in the Nineteenth Century. It was a remnant of life before she learned the Knowledge, when she was still called Griselda. Within her remained an ancient rage, directed at nothing and no one in particular. She found odd happiness in bruised knuckles and broken bones. Fighting and brawling—and if need be killing—brought her pleasant reminders of a bygone life. With her body hung over the ropes of the boxing ring in the smoky din of the Hourglass, a San Francisco time traveller inn on the border between Nineteen and Twenty, she spat a glob of her own blood on the floor and smiled.

Zelda shook free of the ropes and bobbed back into the ring. Her white blouse was spattered with dirt and blood, though still tucked into her trousers, which hung from her hips at an angle since her left suspender snapped five minutes into the bout. Her hands were unprotected except for cloth strips she'd wrapped around her fingers. Her long, maroon hair was tied in a single braid that swung wildly around her neck and shoulders as she pranced around the ring.

She could just barely see her opponent through the smoke of a hundred pipes and cigars. Shirtless Davey Reilly, the grinning, side-burned Hourglass innkeeper, was big and solid and always nice to her even though he talked a little too much. Around them teemed a drinking, shouting, hollering crowd of time travellers, all of them "passing through" the year 1899 and eager to get a little gambling in before they had to travel on. Zelda Clairing's reputation as a trooper of the Nineteenth Century bolstered their excitement. They knew time cops like her fought hard and dirty.

"Tired, Zelda?" taunted Davey, lifting his fists for defense.

"Never been tired in my life."

"Yeah, but you know how it goes," said Davey. "Time always catches up with you."

"Yes, yes it does."

Zelda always scoffed at how time travellers would sometimes fetishize long distances, bragging about going forty or fifty years in one jump without collapsing. And of course, one cannot become a centurion without going one hundred years in a single leap. But Zelda found short-distance travelling—jumping seconds or even milliseconds upstream or downstream—to be just as strenuous and particularly useful in combat. As the Hourglass was built atop the Tenderloin anchor point, Zelda was free to use that skill to her advantage.

Her adversary could do short distance, but he was nowhere near as nimble. When Davey launched himself at her, she simply disappeared and reappeared after he'd landed. She leapt and gave him a good kick in the ribs before disappearing again. The crowd roared. Time traveller fights have few rules.

When Davey stood up, Zelda materialized, wrapped her arms around his neck and used her weight to suffocate him.

"Time catching up with you, Davey?" said Zelda.

"Wager," gasped Davey. "I've a wager for you."

"But we already have one, my friend," said Zelda, tightening her grip. "What else can you give me?"

"DuPree," grunted Davey.

"DuPree?"

Davey elbowed Zelda in the stomach and escaped her grasp, grabbing her braid in the process. He tugged it and spun Zelda to the side of the ring while she gave a bloodcurdling cry. The crowd whooped and cheered, hardly believing their luck at catching such a wonderfully violent spectacle. Zelda rubbed her scalp and spat ancient, guttural words that roughly translated to, "May the devil break your bones, Davey Reilly!"

With her remaining strength, Zelda spun her body around on the floor of the ring and disappeared. She reappeared behind Davey and swept her legs beneath his, knocking him to the ground. Before he could right himself, Zelda leapt onto his back, wrapping an arm around his neck. He attempted to escape her grasp by time travelling, but it was futile while she kept her grip. Whenever he went, he carried her. The referee called it.

"Tonight's champion!" he bellowed. "Zelda Clairing, trooper of the Nineteenth!"

The crowd cheered. Most of them were smart enough to bet on Zelda. She bowed and accepted her winnings from the bookies, then walked back into the ring and pointed at her beaten adversary.

"DuPree?" she said. "I want him."

"It's complicated," he said, nursing some ribs that were probably broken.

"Buy you a drink?" she said, holding up her winnings.

Zelda followed him into the back kitchen of the Hourglass Inn where they took turns cleaning themselves at the giant dishwashing sink. Davey had secretly installed a well and water pump, so that unlike every other building on that street in that century, visiting time travellers at the Hourglass would enjoy running water. Zelda alternated between dunking her hair beneath the rushing water and drinking gulps directly from the faucet. Eventually Davey nudged her out of the way so he could wash his own wounds, while Zelda searched the cupboard for the bourbon Davey kept only for special customers. She poured a glass and brought him some of his own whiskey.

"There you go, Davey," Zelda said, passing him the glass. "Now do your civic duty and tell me, when is DuPree?"

Most time travellers would know the name Francisco Pierre DuPree, the Nineteenth Century's most notorious time travelling jewelry thief. So notorious, in fact, that Her Honor Lupita Calderon, the Nineteenth Centurion, placed a bounty on his capture, dead or alive.

"DuPree fled the century," added Zelda, pouring herself a slightly larger share of whiskey than the one she'd given Davey. "You know when he is now?"

"I've seen a police report," said Davey. "From Twenty. January 1, 1947, someone steals the Sanguine Diamond."

"Where?"

"There's no telling it's him, Zelda."

"It's DuPree," she said. "He's obsessed with the Sanguine Diamond. Once stole it right off Marie Antoinette's neck. And, mind you, the neck was still in one piece at the time. Where is he?"

"Baltimore. Maryland, United States of—"

"I know where Baltimore is."

"Fine, fine," said Davey. "It's at a place called the Grand Republic Hotel."

Zelda nodded, thinking up a plan. Though muffled by the kitchen door, she could still hear the cheering crowd in the tavern. Another fight would start soon. She quickly downed her whiskey and pointed at the lockers by the kitchen sink.

"All right," she said. "You've got some clothes for me?"

CHAPTER 5: THE TIME TROOPER

"What?"

"Clothes. 1940s. I've a long way to travel."

"You can't just go to 1947," said Davey.

"Of course I can. I'm a time traveller."

Davey rolled his eyes and nursed his wounds. "You have to go through the proper channels, Zelda. The troopers of the Twentieth, the Twentieth Centurion—"

"You really think I'd trust Solomon Christie with something like this? I won the bout, so give me some proper clothes for Twenty or I'll start telling people you reneged on a wager."

Davey opened one of his lockers and pulled out some women's clothes—things he kept and lent out to passing travellers as a common courtesy. He tossed them to Zelda and turned his back as she disrobed. She quickly dressed and remembered cheerfully that when she was going there was no need for a corset.

Davey turned to see her off. "Safe travels, Zelda. Once again, I think this is a bad idea."

"Well, that's the only sort of idea I have."

With that, she pushed through the back door into an alley. As the door closed behind her, she emerged some years later. She would take it a few years at time, conserving energy until she reached 1946. From there she would need to board a train for the East Coast. She glanced over her shoulder but saw nothing; the building she'd just left was gone. Of course, she remembered. Davey's Hourglass Inn was destroyed in the earthquake.

Time always catches up with you, she thought.

6

MIDNIGHT AT THE GRAND REPUBLIC

IN 1946, few buildings in America were as spectacular as the Grand Republic Hotel in Baltimore, Maryland. And few could argue there was any hotel more splendid than the Grand Republic on New Year's Eve. The Christmas trees, decorated bright green and red all through the month of December, were readorned in pure white and silver. The finest bands on the East Coast were commissioned to play through the night. It was said that at least one great hotel in New York City was always without their best chef on New Year's Eve, for the Grand Republic in Baltimore would pay for the best, and only the best.

In 1946, New Year's Eve at the Grand Republic had been a tradition for fifty years and the staff was determined to welcome 1947 with style, class, and a dedication to an older and finer sense of civilization. Civilization, after all, had nearly collapsed in the preceding years. It was an age when people wondered if civility, and civilization in general, was even worth preserving. It was a time when the guests of the Grand Republic needed a little familiarity, a little grace, a little bit of the time before atom bombs, before civil defense, before rationing, before Nazis, before assassins, before the wars, before the Depression, before the whirlwind that was the first part of the Twentieth Century. What the Grand Republic Hotel offered on New Year's Eve was a sense of the old fashioned.

Zelda appreciated the old fashioned. She did not feel at home in this century, largely because she wasn't. As a trooper of the Nineteenth, Zelda was forty-six years into a century when she wasn't supposed to be. Not only is it illegal for a trooper to venture into another century and operate there, it is considered the highest offense to a centurion to enter his or her realm without invitation or permission. While other travellers can easily pass through a century without having to seek the reigning centurion's blessing, for a trooper to enter unannounced and chase a criminal traveller suggests that the centurion and troopers of that century are incapable of doing their jobs. Protocol and tradition dictate that instead of chasing a criminal across century lines, a trooper should send a message or courier and allow their colleagues to handle things on their own.

Zelda had little patience for protocol. Francisco DuPree crossed century lines on the assumption that she would not follow. He likely believed he was safe from her in 1946, and she needed to prove him wrong although it meant risking whatever cruel punishment the Twentieth Centurion favored for trespassers. She had to make an example of DuPree. It was the principle of the thing.

So Zelda walked through the ballroom of the Grand Republic, trying to appear natural while scanning for her quarry. She wore a sparkling blue gown, which she'd stolen. Instead of braided, her maroon hair was free tonight and curled. Her pale skin shimmered under the lights of the ballroom, and if anyone had spent enough time observing her, they may have noticed her fidgeting after long periods of stillness, or that wine glasses and other things sometimes shivered in her hands. She was well aware of this constant simmer—a hint of the ancient rage.

Zelda did not care much for the future. To an ancient like her, the sights, smells, and accents of 1946 were overwhelming. The music was awful. She despised automobiles. But she enjoyed the natives. It was her first visit to Twenty, and of course she had heard all the rumors, but her illicit sojourn confirmed the century's reputation for barbarism. Soldiers just home from war had dressed in their finest uniforms, only to sully them by brawling with anyone willing to do battle. The women smoked and drank and flirted, quite in public. These, more than the rigid residents of Nineteen, were her kind of people. She'd once been a barbarian herself, after all.

But there was a dark side to it all. The wars, the genocides, the atrocities. Of course, such things happened in her resident century, but the scale of Twentieth Century cruelty was legendary. The blame for this likely rested with the local centurion, Solomon Christie. It was her assumption, and the assumption of many travellers, that Solomon's recklessness, carelessness, and hooliganism were showing quite clearly in his governance of the century. He was said to have a list of the very best parties, balls, bashes, parades, festivals, and gatherings in Twenty and spent the majority of his reign travelling to every single one of them. It was said he has attended Woodstock more times than he attended his own court.

It was a fallacy, Zelda conceded, to believe a centurion was totally responsible for the character of their century. Centurions rule only the travellers, of whom there are far fewer in each century than there are laymen. It is understood that non-travellers determine history; time travellers simply experience it. But then again, the primary job of a centurion is to prevent time travellers from interfering with history. Twenty attracts villains, pirates, and time criminals like DuPree, people who have no compunction about interfering. Who, then, could say that Twenty's reputation for lawlessness and wanton destruction wasn't the result of Solomon's disregard for his sacred duty?

Zelda pushed her way through the grand ballroom, hunting for DuPree, but saw him nowhere. She came to the edge of the revelers and saw, between two sparkling Christmas trees, the small hotel bar through a side corridor. She had learned through hundreds of investigations like this that, no matter the year, tavern keepers remembered their customers. She approached the bar and hoped this quality was held by the bartenders of Twenty.

This particular bartender seemed unoccupied. His only customers at the bar appeared to be a sailor, slumped over and dragging his finger among the ice cubes in his empty glass, and a taller, more cheerful, and much more alert man who'd undone the tie beneath his tuxedo. She arrived at the bar and the barkeep approached her with a smile.

"What'll you have, ma'am?" said the bartender.

"Nothing, for the moment, thank you," she said. "I was wondering if you've seen someone."

"Seen a lot of people tonight," said the bartender. "Who're you looking for?"

"He's a Frenchman. A blond gentleman, but he has a slender mustache of a slightly darker color."

The bartender shook his head, frowning. "Wish I could help you, ma'am. But I ain't seen any Frenchies tonight."

"Well, thank you anyway."

The young man with the undone bowtie set down his drink. "I do hope this Frenchman hasn't stood you up, madam," he said. "The French are notoriously untrustworthy."

She turned to find him smiling at her, and she studied him closer, as she would a criminal. His clothes were rather fine, but he wore them loosely, and purposefully so. He'd undone his tie, but he hadn't put it away in his pocket, as if he wanted to show off how much he didn't care if he wore it or not. His white shirt shimmered beneath his black tuxedo jacket. His hair was deep, dark brown, but the electric lights of the ballroom seemed to illuminate certain golden strands here and there.

His eyes were bright green, and they beheld her with a combination of confidence and mischief.

She did not like him.

"Don't worry about it," she told him. "My friend is probably just late."

"Or perhaps you're just early."

His accent was one Zelda couldn't quite place. Certainly English, but with an odd lilt she did not recognize. She nodded at his remark and stood from her barstool, turning to walk back into the throngs of ballroom dancers. Then she heard his voice again.

"He's a thief, isn't he?" said the man. "Your Frenchman?"

She turned and walked back to the bar, lowering her voice.

"Why do you think that?"

"Just this very night I observed a person quite like the man you described, picking pockets hither and thither."

He glanced at her in celebration of his lucky guess and returned to his drink.

"Perhaps it was another person," she told him, "with similar features."

"I have observed you too," said the man. "You are watching and appraising, but certainly not waiting for a man. And of course, what sort of man would dare break a date with a woman like you? A criminal in every sense, I should think."

He finished his drink. The bartender quickly replaced it with another.

"No, I should think you are some sort of—what do the Americans call it? A 'G-Man.' Or a 'G-Woman,' I suppose. The FBI perhaps? Certainly not a hotel detective."

"Certainly?"

"I have never met a hotel detective with eyes like yours," he said.

"Flattering me will not convince me to find you charming, sir."

"I never flatter, m'lady. Just as your eyes never stop looking to the doors, taking stock of who enters and exits. Eyes like those belong to an investigator, not a common hotel dick. And I am charming whether you find it so or not."

For their part, his own eyes were piercing hers and she found their perceptiveness almost as annoying as their shimmering green glow. But as smug as the man at the bar was, he'd demolished her cover only to replace it with a perfectly usable alternative. She was a detective, as he presumed, and so she could easily play the part without revealing that she was also a time traveller.

"If you were right about me," she said, "and about my Frenchman, perhaps you might be so kind as to trade me some information as to where you saw this person?"

"Trade?" he repeated. "Trade for what?"

"A dance."

"A dance?"

Zelda smiled. The man at the bar was insufferable, but she could suffer a dance to get further along the road to DuPree. Here was yet another similarity between her resident century and this one—the men were just as feeble-minded, easily tricked by their own delusions of grandeur and charm.

So the man at the bar joined Zelda for a dance around the ballroom. She was, admittedly, unsure about her ability to follow the ridiculous music of this century, but she kept up fairly well. Likewise, the green-eyed man also seemed to have some mild difficulty keeping pace. He took close interest in the hand he was holding.

"Your hand is buzzing," he told her.

"Buzzing?"

"Yes. Not shaking, nor shivering. Buzzing, like the top of a boiling kettle."

She issued a little shrug. "I burn a little hotter than most people," she said, and decided to change the topic. "Do they dance to this sort of music in England?"

"I am quite certain they do. Just not at the parties I've attended. And what of your home? I take it English is not your first language?"

"You've an ear for dialect," she said.

"Perhaps that's why I remembered your Frenchman."

"For his accent and not his thievery?"

"His thievery I found notable, but I thought I'd keep it to myself 'til a beautiful woman should ask about it."

"One is asking now," she said. "Where did you last see this man?"

"Let me think." They twirled around the ballroom. "I last saw him in the grand dining room on the second floor, with his hand invading a good lady's purse. But perhaps you would be more interested to know where I see him now."

Zelda resisted the urge to look around the room for DuPree. "He's here?"

"Seated in the northwest corner of the room," said her dance partner. "He's hidden by the band, quite on purpose, which is why you couldn't find him."

Zelda's partner swung her around before she could get a good look at the northwest corner.

"I do believe he is waiting and becoming most impatient," he said. "If his glances are any indication, I should think he will soon depart to the Great East Corridor."

A thought came into Zelda's mind. Her dance partner was doing more than playing investigator.

"I've never met a hotel detective with eyes like yours," she told him. He turned those eyes away from the northwest corner and back to hers.

"You still haven't," he said.

"Well, sir," she said. "I think our dance has come to an end."

"I am afraid not. We have some things to discuss."

"Of course, I understand, you want custody. American police, British police, or whoever you are. He can spend the night in your jail, and we can work it out in the morning."

Zelda knew that, for a time traveller, plucking someone out of a layman jail was easily done.

"That is not what I mean," said her dance partner. "There is something I have to say…"

Zelda caught a glimpse of the northwest corner behind the band. DuPree had disappeared.

"There's no time," she said. "I have to go get him."

"We have time. And I cannot let you get him."

"What are you talking about?"

"There is something I have to say."

"Then say it."

Her dance partner leaned in close and whispered in her ear.

"'Tis very good to meet a fellow traveller."

Zelda had never been so angry in her life.

● ● ●

About five minutes later, Zelda swept into room 505 of the Grand Republic Hotel. It was the sort of extravagant hotel room where someone might take a mistress, she thought, or perhaps a spouse who found out about a mistress. A crystal chandelier hung from the ceiling above a crisp, ivory bed with tasseled pillows. The scarlet drapes over the window were pulled ajar, revealing the city of Baltimore blanketed with snow. On the bedside table sat an ice bucket with an unopened bottle of Champagne, and Zelda imagined beating her green-eyed fellow traveller with it, right in that pretty, smug face.

It did not improve her mood that he hadn't spoken a word since he pulled her from the ballroom, directed her to the elevator and brought her down the hallway to this room. She seethed with every passing moment he remained silent. And on top of everything else, she was angry most of

46

all at the fact that she, not him, and not Francisco Pierre DuPree, was in the wrong this time. DuPree was at large, perhaps having already stolen the Sanguine Diamond, and yet, for no other reason than archaic traveller custom, she was the criminal of the night. The trespasser. Whatever punishment was to be hers—humiliation, torture, banishment, expulsion— all of it paled in comparison to the punishment of knowing DuPree had escaped her. And the architect of her ignominious downfall? This oily, foolish, smiling, too-clever-by-half imbecile who used the profession to charm ladies instead of catching genuine criminals. What was wrong with this century?

He closed the door and walked into the room, locking eyes with Zelda. She sat on the bed with her arms folded, fuming and waiting for him to speak. He did not. Nor did she. Finally, he made a face that indicated it was her who should speak. She rolled her eyes, throwing her arms in the air.

"To make the road less lonely, all right?" yelled Zelda.

"Thank you," he said with exasperation. "Custom keeps us civil in uncivilized times."

He pulled a chair away from the desk and sat across from Zelda. "Now. What is your name?"

"Zelda Clairing, trooper of the Nineteenth," she answered through pursed lips. "Clairing" was not really her surname, but more like a modern equivalent. She'd chosen it to keep things simple at times like this.

"Nineteen?" he repeated. "That would make you a trespasser. Do you know what they do to trespassers?"

"Yes," she mocked. "I know what they do to trespassers."

"In the B.C.s they would draw and quarter you. Katherine the Iron Heart, the Twelfth Centurion, is partial to cutting off an offender's toes. When I grew up, in Sixteen, they would throw you in the pillory for a week. Children would throw things at you until your banishment."

Sixteen. That explained the accent. He was neither an ancient, like her, nor was he quite a modern.

"Yes, and what tortures does the Twentieth Centurion prefer for nefarious trespassers like me?" asked Zelda.

Any torment would certainly be less excruciating than this lecture.

"You may ask him yourself," replied the man.

"Is he coming now?" She hadn't expected Solomon Christie to be the sort of man who doled out punishment personally.

The man closed his eyes and shook his head. "That was my fault. I should have been more specific. You are asking him. It's me. I'm him."

"What?"

"Zelda Clairing, trooper of the Nineteenth," he said, in an annoyingly calm voice. "I am Solomon Christie, the Twentieth Centurion."

Zelda felt all sorts of emotions, most of them rage adjacent. But she shoved all of those feelings and urges deep down into herself as she stood, rigidly and defiantly, and bowed to the seated centurion.

"No," said Solomon Christie. "No, no, no, no, stop that."

"I sincerely apologize to Your Honor."

The word "apologize" made her want to vomit.

"Stop it," he said. "Stop, stop, stop. I command you, stop."

Zelda abruptly stood to full height.

"I have disrespected Your Honor and the entire Twentieth Century," she said, though inside she held almost no respect for His Honor or his century. "An apology is required, as is a punishment."

The centurion rolled his green eyes. "There will be no punishment. You have done nothing I wouldn't do. But you have threatened my own intentions for our mutual French friend. Please sit down and we shall calculate what to do next."

This was confusing. The centurion spoke to Zelda as an equal. Solomon's reputation, of course, was for unorthodoxy, but she assumed he was the sort of self-centered leader who would demand all customary honors be observed in his presence. The only solid ground she appreciated about the situation was the notion that Solomon had "intentions" for Francisco DuPree. Perhaps there remained a glimmer of hope that she would finally catch the thief. Suspicious, she sat back down on the bed and faced him.

"I suspect you are here," he began, "because of the bounty your centurion, Lupita Calderon, has placed on DuPree's head. That's why I understand your desire to cross century lines as you have done. But I am afraid he means too much to Twenty to let you apprehend him just yet."

"What does that mean?"

"I believe that your Frenchman, Francisco Pierre DuPree, is in league with a criminal my troopers and I have feared for quite some time. A man named Thurmond."

Zelda straightened up and—though she would not admit it to herself—shivered. "Thurmond is a myth, Your Honor."

"I wish he were."

The centurion stood and started tapping on the wall of the hotel room as if he were looking for something on the other side.

"I am sure those who say he is a myth are led to that conclusion by similar wishful thinking," said Solomon. "But I am afraid Thurmond is very real. Though I know not what he looks like, nor his true identity, the stories about him are too consistent, too detailed. Thurmond is real and he is out there, travelling and scheming as we speak."

"I've chased DuPree across nearly a hundred years. He is a loner by design. What use would he have for a partner in crime? And what use would someone like Thurmond, if Thurmond really exists, have for a diamond thief?"

"That is what I have come to find out." He concluded his tapping and departed to the bathroom. "Right about now," he shouted from the bathroom, "our friend Mr. DuPree has his diamond, but he hasn't yet fled, which I found odd the first time I travelled here."

Zelda heard a metallic snap inside the bathroom.

"But on my third journey here, I saw DuPree standing by the west loading dock," continued the centurion. "He will be there in seven minutes. I believe he is meeting someone, and I intend to find out who."

"Wait," said Zelda. "How many times have you travelled here and now?"

Solomon emerged from the bathroom carrying a metal towel rack.

"This is visit number eight."

"Eight? Are you mad?"

All time travellers know, of course, that it is incredibly dangerous to visit the same location in spacetime over and over again. On the one hand, you run an enormous risk of encountering your past or future self, which is illegal (*Time Travellers' Revised Code 11.33.03[b]: Communication with one's future or former self is forbidden*) but also practically dangerous—there are few better ways of driving yourself insane than learning secrets of the future from yourself. There are also physical laws to consider. The universe does not much like it when matter doubles itself while occupying the same limited region of spacetime. For that reason, every traveller has a physical limit on how many instances they can jump to a particular time and place. Once a time traveller has travelled to the same hotel on the same night enough times, they physically cannot make that trip again. It's spacetime's way of saying, "You don't have to go home, but you can't stay here."

"You must be nearing your limit," said Zelda.

"I'm sure I've reached it. Which is why tonight may be my last chance, and you may be my last hope."

He returned to the wall and smashed a hole through it with the towel rack. Zelda stood to watch as he expanded the hole and reached inside.

"Now," said Solomon, "do you happen to know how to use one of these?"

From the hole in the wall, Solomon Christie retrieved a dusty handgun and held it out with his finger and thumb as if he found it distasteful. It looked like a typical revolver, but it was a model Zelda had never seen. She noticed an engraving on the gun's silver barrel.

A gift from the Family Listratta to the Family Christie.

"I live in Nineteen," said Zelda. "I know how to use a six-shooter."

"Good." He handed her the gun. "I never learned to use a pistol, but I thought it prudent to make a stop during the hotel's construction and leave one just in case."

"We can't risk hurting laymen in this century, you know that."

"Of course not," said Solomon. "This is a lightning gun from Twenty-Three. It fires electric rounds, nonlethal and bulletless. No dead laymen, no artifacts from the future and no interference. Now, are you ready?"

"Do you have a plan?"

"I don't need a plan," he said. "I've seen the future."

7

THE TIME TRAVELLING JEWELRY THIEF

JUST ABOUT MIDNIGHT, while the laymen revelers of the Grand Republic Hotel arrived in 1947 and began singing, Zelda Clairing and Solomon Christie stood on the balcony above the crowds in the Grand Ballroom and waited.

"Which way to the west loading dock?" said Zelda.

"Through the north corridor or the south corridor," said Solomon. "But we cannot go either of those routes."

"Why not?"

"Because I am in both of those corridors right now."

Zelda rolled her eyes. "Avoiding your past really makes things complicated."

"'Tis no matter," he said. "I never caught him in either hallway. He must get there another way, and I think I know how. We just have to wait."

"Wait for what?"

"For this," he said. "Cover your ears."

"What?"

The centurion managed to cover his ears, but Zelda missed her opportunity before a severe crash echoed off the ballroom walls. She looked down and saw a server had dropped a stack of plates on the dance floor.

"There is me, distracted," said Solomon

Zelda scanned the crowd and spotted Solomon, wearing a different tuxedo, looking over the heads of the revelers toward the source of the commotion. Then Zelda noticed someone else in the ballroom.

"And there is DuPree," she said. "Seizing the opportunity."

DuPree, clearly aware of Past-Solomon's presence, scurried through the ballroom as everyone focused on the noise and mess. Zelda and Solomon watched from the balcony as DuPree slipped through the doors to the kitchen.

"I knew it," said Solomon as he left the balcony. "Come along, we haven't much time."

Zelda followed Solomon as he rushed down one of the corridors. He came upon a door with a "Staff Only" sign and furiously twisted the handle, but it wouldn't budge.

"'Tis locked," he announced.

"Yeah," said Zelda. "'Staff Only' typically means—"

"Staff only." Then he snapped his fingers and turned his head, shouting "Cakes!"

Solomon started down the corridor in the opposite direction and Zelda followed.

"Cakes?" shouted Zelda. "What does that mean?"

Ahead of Solomon, Zelda saw another "Staff Only" door swing open as two chefs emerged, rolling a cart stacked with tall, ornate cakes. Solomon sped up and managed to catch the door before it closed, ushering Zelda in behind him. The two chefs with their cakes shouted after the two time travellers, "Hey, guests aren't allowed back there!"

Zelda caught up to Solomon as he pushed past busy servers and chefs who stared and shouted at them. They were in the secret hallways between the hallways of the hotel, which allowed the maids and chefs and janitors to make discreet entrances and exits wherever they were needed. This was, Zelda reflected, certainly the most hands-on work she'd ever seen a centurion do alone. As they raced through the secret bowels of the hotel, Zelda heard Solomon muttering to himself, "Right, then right, then stairs…right, then right, then stairs…"

Solomon guided them to the right down the kitchen hallway, right again down a hallway of hanging towels, then down two floors through the stairwell. They pushed through a pair of double doors and turned right down a hallway that was empty except for a single laundry cart. The air in this particular hallway was crisp and cold. One of the light bulbs was on its way out and flickered on and off intermittently. They kept running until Solomon looked at his wristwatch and shouted, "Stop!"

The pair of time travellers stood still and looked down the flickering, empty corridor. After a moment, Solomon pushed Zelda behind the laundry cart and the two of them crouched against the wall.

"What are we doing?" said Zelda.

"He arrives at the west loading dock in forty-five seconds."

"Where's the west loading dock?"

"Directly behind us."

Zelda turned. The hallway behind them ended with another pair of double doors. Through the windows she could see the snow drifting in the streetlights. She pulled the lightning gun from her purse. It felt light without bullets. She turned back around and watched Solomon watch the hallway for DuPree.

"Your Honor?" she said.

"Please stop calling me that. Call me Sol, or nothing."

"Excuse me?" grumbled Zelda. "You are the Twentieth Centurion. You are the pillar of what all travellers should aspire to be. You are the living symbol of law and order in the Twentieth Century and the commander of all time travellers therein. And I am to call you by your forename?"

"If 'twould make you feel better," replied the centurion, "as the commander of all time travellers herein, I command you, you shall call me Sol."

"Fine, Sol. How long before we—"

Both of them looked over the laundry cart to see Francisco Pierre DuPree staring back at them. Sol stood up slowly.

"Hello, Francisco," he said.

"How..." stuttered DuPree. "How did you..."

"Come now, Francisco, we're all time travellers here," said Sol. "I'm sure you can figure it out, and I do not feel like explaining."

Sol grabbed the edge of the empty laundry cart and shoved it toward DuPree, hoping to catch the thief off-balance. DuPree, however, was able to catch it and shove it back toward Sol, a reaction the centurion was not prepared for. He dove out of the way, but the cart caught him in the ankle and he fell over. With Sol out of the way, Zelda lifted the lightning gun and aimed for DuPree.

For whatever reason, Zelda did not expect a lightning gun from the Twenty-Third Century to produce a literal bolt of lightning. But that was exactly what happened when she pulled the trigger. A jagged lightning bolt sprang from the barrel and shot down the hallway. DuPree ducked and the bolt hit the wall, sending electricity in every direction. The weak light bulbs in the ceiling shone bright for a moment and then exploded in a shower of sparks. Zelda dropped to the floor to avoid the sparks and landed, somewhat embarrassingly, on top of Sol, who yelped in pain.

"Yeah," he said. "It does that."

Zelda felt a rush of air above her and saw the shadow of DuPree going for the door to the west loading dock. She aimed the lightning gun in the darkness as Sol tried to stop her.

"Please do not just blindly pull the trigger."

But Zelda ignored him and just blindly pulled the trigger. The lightning bolt smacked into the corner of the hallway and electric currents spidered across the ceiling. In the moment of brilliant white light, Zelda caught a glimpse of DuPree slipping into the snowy night.

As her eyes adjusted to the darkness, Zelda managed to stand up. She gave a hand to Sol.

"Any chance you've seen any more of the future?" she said. He grabbed her hand.

"I'm afraid we've arrived at the present."

• • •

At about the same time on January 1, 1947, a young man named Nathan Hocking sat in a parked car around the corner from the Grand Republic Hotel. Hocking was twenty-seven, with a handsome, boyish face and greased blond hair. His fur overcoat hid a shimmering blue tuxedo, for he was taking an extended break from another New Years party across town. No doubt his father, high lord of the industrial empire the young man was to inherit, would take notice of his absence and scold him accordingly. But it didn't matter. Or else, he hoped it didn't matter. When the old man was dead and Nathan Hocking inherited the family business, he hoped to have a new advantage—the strange little Frenchman who promised fantastic things in exchange for an odd task.

Hocking watched a familiar figure emerge from the swirling snow and unlocked his passenger door for Mr. DuPree.

"Start driving," said DuPree.

"Where?" asked Hocking.

"It doesn't matter." So they started driving around the block as the Frenchman caught his breath. Then he turned to his driver. "Have you looked over the designs?"

"Yes," said Hocking. "So have my engineers."

"Can you build it?"

"Yes, in theory. But they tell me we'd run into problems with the metallurgy, problems with the weight, problems with hunting oscillations, with harmonic vibrations, and even then it would take years."

"Years we have. Years are of no concern to my employer. We will provide you with the necessary materials."

"I still haven't agreed to this," said Hocking. "This is a strange thing you're asking me to build. I don't understand it, I don't understand you and I don't understand your employer, this Mr. Thurmond."

"It is not *Mr.* Thurmond. His name is Thurmond," said DuPree. "And what you are really asking is what is in it for you, no?"

Hocking chuckled. "Why, indeed I am, Mr. DuPree."

"Aside from what we're willing to pay, there are plenty of things we can do for you. Impossible things."

"Like what?"

DuPree reached into his jacket pocket and pulled out a rolled-up napkin. He pulled back the folds of the napkin to reveal the Sanguine Diamond. Hocking parked his car to examine the gem. It was beautiful, amazing and, indeed, impossible.

"How?" said Hocking. "How did you do this?"

"It is what you said you wanted in return, no?"

"That was a joke. I never thought you could deliver the Sanguine Diamond, of all things."

"Nothing is impossible for people like my employer," said DuPree. "The diamond is nothing. We can give you so much more. Trends in the stock market. What to buy and what to sell. The outcome of elections, of wars. If you can build this thing, whatever you want, whatever you can dream, it does not matter. With Thurmond, all things are possible."

CHAPTER 7: THE TIME TRAVELLING JEWELRY THIEF

The young man in the driver's seat was at a loss. None of this could be possible. These people couldn't possibly be able to do the things they promised. It was witchcraft or sorcery. Yet he held the Sanguine Diamond itself, and all he had to do in exchange was promise to build something unusual. Unusual, but certainly not impossible.

"We will be in touch," said Hocking.

"I'm afraid my employer will need a more direct answer."

"Yes," said Hocking. "I will build this for you."

They were ready to shake on the deal when another car, driven by Solomon Christie, smashed into theirs from behind.

• • •

As Zelda followed Sol from the loading dock to the place where he'd parked his automobile, she assumed he must know how to operate one of the infernal machines. While Sol apparently understood the acceleration and brake systems, all other facets of automobile driving seemed foreign to him. He swerved and swung the vehicle through the snow and ice as they hunted for the mystery car that picked up DuPree and ultimately slid into its rear end. Sol then began pushing the other car across a parking lot and then across a city street.

Nathan Hocking managed to start his engine and accelerate away. Sol gave chase while Zelda rolled down the passenger side window and retrieved the lightning gun.

"Please be careful with that," said Sol.

"Please keep the car steady," she replied.

Zelda leaned out of the window and tried and failed to keep aim while Sol tried and failed to keep the automobile on a steady track. Her first shot hit the rear bumper of the fleeing car with no effect. On the second try, Sol veered the car in a wildly unexpected direction and Zelda's lightning bolt hit a streetlamp, extinguishing power in a small wedge of Baltimore.

"Mórrígan's name!" shouted Zelda as she re-entered the vehicle. "Will you keep this thing steady?"

"I think I'm starting to remember how to do this."

"I've only got two shots left. You have to get me in front of them."

"Why?"

"The car battery and engine," she replied. "They're located in the front of the automobile. If I can hit it, it might stop them."

"You cannot operate a horseless carriage, but you can disable one?"

She shot him an annoyed look and he hit the accelerator. As he pulled up along the left side of DuPree's vehicle, the front of the car inched closer into Zelda's view. She took aim and waited for her clearest opportunity, wondering if there was any conventional wisdom about where best to strike a car with lightning. She almost felt ready to fire when the driver of the other car veered to the left. He crashed into their vehicle and they screeched into a snowbank. The car carrying DuPree continued for a few yards before sliding to a stop.

Sol was the first one out of the crashed car and rushed to aid Zelda. He wrenched open the passenger door and pulled her out of the car.

"Zelda?" he shouted, shaking her awake. "Zelda!"

Zelda's eyes opened and flicked to something behind him. She shoved him away, lifted the lightning gun and fired. Sol turned to see the lightning bolt just barely miss DuPree as he leapt from his vehicle and started running. The driver of DuPree's car drove in the opposite direction and quickly disappeared into the snow. Zelda started after DuPree but paused and turned to Sol.

"Mind if I keep this?" she said, holding up the gun.

"'Twill be more useful in your hands than mine."

"Well then," said Zelda. "Farewell, Your Honor. It wasn't so terrible to meet you."

Sol nodded.

"'Til we meet again, Zelda Clairing, trooper of the Nineteenth."

She gave him a short smile and ran down the alley after DuPree. Sol walked back to the crashed car, repeating to himself the license plate number of the mystery man DuPree had spoken to—ZTF-0066.

Much later that night, when the first police officer to arrive at the snowy accident scene wrote his report, he mentioned that at first he thought he saw a man standing next to the crashed car, but that this man spontaneously disappeared into thin air. The officer concluded in his report that this must have been an illusion created by the drifting snow.

• • •

Several streets away, Zelda rounded a corner to find Francisco DuPree in the process of throwing a taxi driver out of his own cab. As DuPree started the ignition, Zelda took careful aim and shot a white-hot bolt of lightning into the front of the taxi. The cab's dashboard exploded into flames and DuPree forced his way out of the car, falling onto the road in a fit of coughing. He looked back only to get a glimpse of Zelda before running through the swirling snowflakes in the opposite direction. Zelda knew where he was headed; the Camden Street anchor point was close. She could feel its influence growing stronger. If he felt a strong enough connection with the anchor point, DuPree could snapback and escape her. But if she caught hold of him before he did, she was sure she had a strong enough connection to take him out of the century.

Zelda watched as he tried two different doors in an effort to escape her. Then she saw him leap onto a metal ladder on the side of one building. Though he was still coughing and out of breath, he managed to climb most of the way to the top by the time she reached the bottom of the ladder.

"This has been a delightful adventure, Francisco," she shouted. "But it's time to come on down and settle this like adults."

"I didn't think you had it in you, Zelda," he panted. "Following me to Twenty like this. But I am afraid you are out of your depth."

"Where is the diamond?" said Zelda.

"I do not have it. I have given it to a worthier cause."

"You expect me to believe that all the centuries you've rooted through for that diamond, you would just give it up? For the sake of a myth?"

DuPree laughed through his coughs. "That's what he wants," he shouted down to her. "He wants you to think he isn't real. But he has planned everything to perfection. Of all time travellers, he is the greatest who ever walked the Earth. He's going to lead us now. No more rules, no more troopers, no more Guild. He will save everyone."

"I'm sure Her Honor will love to hear all about it, Francisco," said Zelda.

"I'm not going to bow before Lupita. You will have to come get me."

It's common knowledge that iron is an excellent conductor of things such as heat, cold, electricity, and the effects of time travel. Perhaps Francisco Pierre DuPree had forgotten about this, but Zelda had not. She touched the cold metal of the ladder, closed her eyes, and travelled forty-eight years into the past, across the border into 1899, carrying Francisco Pierre DuPree with her.

She had not anticipated, however, that the building with the ladder might not exist in 1899. At the moment of arrival, she felt the cold metal evaporate from her grasp and opened her eyes right as DuPree's body fell to the ground in front of her with a yelp, a thud, and a couple of snaps. Zelda slumped to the ground next to him. Time travelling forty-eight years can really take it out of a person, and it was more of an effort than she was used to. DuPree let out a moan and Zelda saw bones protruding from two or three of his limbs. His head was twisted almost all the way around and blood gurgled from his mouth.

"I know I'm supposed to feel bad about this, killing a fellow traveller and all that," said Zelda between deep breaths. "But you really could've avoided this, and I can't bring myself to care all that much."

By then DuPree wasn't moving or moaning or breathing anymore. Zelda felt a trickle of blood rush from her nose. Sudden pressure changes are a common hazard with time travel. But still she smiled as the smells and sounds of Nineteen welcomed her. She took in the subtle clatter of the carriages rolling on cobblestones and the shouting of the newsboys on the streets. As she sat next to Francisco Pierre DuPree's dead body, she said to herself, "It's good to be home."

8

TIME BOMB

AS A TEENAGER, Henry Zoller spent a lot of time alone, wandering through his neighborhood late at night. It was not the wisest choice of activity for a boy of Henry's age, for his quiet, suburban neighborhood of Jackson Park, Virginia, was kept quiet through frequent patrols by the police and by neighborhood watch members, who could be even more nosy than the police. Henry knew during his late-night walks that if he were ever stopped by a police officer and asked where he was going, he would not have a good enough answer, or really any answer at all. But these nightly walks were the only consistent opportunities the young man had to think. School was not a good place for thinking; there were too many distractions and performances to put on. At home, he was commanded to keep company with his mother, who, having recently divorced her second husband, demanded even more attention than usual.

Henry Zoller was convinced that if he didn't take an hour every night to wander in the darkness, he would most likely go insane.

Most of the time these walks would transpire without incident. But it happened that one night in 1999 he noticed someone else walking the neighborhood, a girl just a few years older than him. She had black hair and dark skin, and she wore a green military-style jacket over a pink sweater. It was weird. Never had Henry encountered another person on his walks. He knew the girl hadn't seen him, and he filed the incident away, expecting never to see the young woman again.

He saw her again the very next night.

Again the girl did not see him, and she wore the exact same clothes as she had the first night. Henry saw her walk down Collins Street, beneath an overhang of tree branches, and then she disappeared. She did not come back onto the sidewalk, and Henry would've thought she had simply entered a house on that side of the street if he hadn't known there were no houses there, only trees. But Henry did not want to investigate and be a young man following a young woman in the dead of night.

The next night, the young woman returned. Again, she wore the same green jacket and pink sweater. Again, she disappeared into the trees on the right side of Collins Street. Again, Henry did not want to follow but instead resolved to investigate the area during the day. The next afternoon he walked down Collins Street to the spot where the girl kept disappearing. There, hidden in the brush, he found the entrance to a long-forgotten concrete path.

Henry followed the broken path through the trees and came to a bridge over a deep ravine. The bridge opened up into a flat, decaying compound of concrete, brick, and chain-link fence. Henry realized he was looking at an abandoned pool and beyond that, an abandoned tennis court. The pool's water was green and covered with algae. The tennis court walls had vines hanging over them, giving it the appearance of a jungle ruin.

Henry never knew such a thing was there, hidden in his neighborhood, and he found it fascinating. But he still could not understand why the young woman he kept seeing would want to come here late at night.

That would be the night he decided to find out.

CHAPTER 8: TIME BOMB

•••

As it happened, that was also the night when a young time trooper named Bindra Dhar came looking for a man named Randall. Bindra knew very little about Randall, only that he had committed some horrendous crime for which he was expelled from the Guild. His travelling abilities were stripped, through what means no one would tell her, and he was marooned in the late Twentieth Century. Now, for some reason, Randall had passed a message through the time travel courier network that he wanted to talk to her.

In his brief message, Randall requested her presence at the Jackson Park anchor point some time during the last week of September in 1999. Since he had frustratingly given no specific date, Bindra was forced to take a whole day and make four trips to the Jackson Park anchor point, located beneath an abandoned tennis court and pool in Jackson Park, Virginia, on the 27th, 28th, 29th and 30th of September, 1999.

On the first three jumps, Randall was nowhere to be found. On the last jump of the day, Bindra arrived at the anchor point and did her typical walk around the moonlit neighborhood. She saw no signs of Randall, and so she walked back to Collins Street and departed down the cracked pathway back to the anchor point. But as she came to the bridge, she heard something below in the ravine. It sounded like a man hacking, coughing, and mumbling to himself.

She looked over the railing of the bridge and in the moonlight saw the figure of a man crouched on a large boulder in the middle of the stream, hunched over the water. She climbed down into the ravine and approached the man on his boulder. She was careful about which rocks she stepped on as she came toward him, but all the while she kept watch on the hunched-over man shadow. As she already knew, Randall was a dangerous man.

The shadow heard her and stopped mumbling to itself. He looked up and turned his head toward her.

"Bindra," he said slowly. "Bindra Dhar."

Bindra did not feel comfortable with the way he said her name.

"It's good to meet a fellow traveller," said Bindra.

"Oh, Bindra Dhar," said the shadow. "Treating old Randall like he's still a traveller. Oh, sweet Bindra Dhar, thank you for coming, gracious Bindra Dhar, for Randall wants to make your road less lonely."

Randall climbed down from his rock, and Bindra could fully see his face in the moonlight. It was ragged and beaten and his eyes were wild. Bindra held up her hand.

"Keep yourself there."

"Oh, yes," said Randall. "Oh yes, madam Bindra Dhar, trooper of the Twentieth. Still a trooper, aren't you? A nasty time cop? Or do you want old Randall to tell you what comes next?"

"Ghamud dayim," she hissed.

"Of course, of course," said Randall, winding away from her and walking among the rocks of the ravine. "Randall was wrong to spoil the mystery, wrong to spoil the future of Bindra Dhar. Even though Randall guesses all that's changed now anyway…"

"What do you want, Randall? Why did you summon me here?"

"What does Randall want?" said the old man. "Randall wants to go home, is what Randall wants. Randall wants to travel again."

"I don't think I can do that. You're a criminal time traveller, and you've been expelled from the Guild."

"I know I've been expelled!" roared Randall, startling Bindra. "I was there! Do you know what happens when they expel you!? Do you, Bindra Dhar!?"

His outburst over, Randall smiled a wicked smile and continued his wobbling around the ravine.

"Randall knows he was expelled," he said through laughter. "Randall remembers. Randall's just gone a little out of it, that's all. Man wasn't meant to live chronologically. Makes a man crazy. No, Randall doesn't want you to fix him; no one can fix him. Randall just wants good Bindra Dhar to return him to civilization."

"Civilization?"

"Yes, yes. Anywhere but Twenty."

"You'll soon be in Twenty-One," said Bindra, though she regretted tempting the crazed man's patience with a joke.

"Twenty-One is even worse, and Bindra Dhar knows it. Take Randall to his time, good Bindra, and he'll behave himself. He swears he will."

Bindra had not been a trooper for very long, but even to her inexperienced mind, this trip seemed like a waste of time.

"Randall cannot return to his time," sighed Bindra, "until Randall has repaid his debt to his community of travellers."

The old man's face grew blank, and Bindra turned her back on him and began walking back to the bridge.

"I've met a ripple," murmured Randall.

She turned to face him.

"You did?" said Bindra. "Or did Randall?"

"No," he sneered. "You idiot. I did. I met a ripple. He was here. Just the other day."

"Ripples are not real."

That is what Mr. Brooks had always told Bindra about ripples, of course—people who are supposedly born as a result of time traveller interference, allegedly possessing true free will, living independent of fate, able to change history in unpredictable ways, and all of that nonsense. Bindra knew that a time traveller announcing that he'd met a ripple was similar in many respects to a layman announcing she'd had brunch with a leprechaun.

"Oh, this one was very real, Bindra Dhar, Randall knows it. He can do things. Things most travellers have only dreamed of. He told me his plan, Bindra Dhar. His plan for all of us. And it was beautiful."

"The ripple had a plan?" laughed Bindra. "What was the magical ripple's plan?"

"He has a plan to save everyone."

Bindra lost her smile. She had heard this language before.

"What was this man's name, Randall?" she said in earnest.

"Aha!" laughed Randall. "I thought Bindra Dhar might never ask the man's name! She knows who I'm talking about, of course Bindra Dhar knows. She's the one he's so worried about. So I sent my message to Bindra Dhar."

The broken old man launched himself toward her and fell to his knees, grabbing her hand and pleading with her.

"Please take old Randall back to his time. Old Randall will help you get him, if he can be got. But Bindra Dhar should hear his plan, she really should. Bindra would like him if she met him, Randall thinks."

"His name, Randall," ordered Bindra. "What was the name of the man you talked to?"

Randall's eyes went glassy. He launched a deep, haunting laugh and spread his arms wide. He spoke with a whisper from the back of his throat.

"His name is Thurmond. And he's going to save everyone."

Bindra dipped her head and stared at the old man. She tried to make her voice sound as serious as she could. "You spoke to Thurmond? When is he?"

"Oh, he's everywhen. He's everywhen and nowhen. Randall believes in his plan, he really does. And Randall is terrified of Thurmond, and Bindra Dhar should be too. But Randall wants so very badly to go home. Randall will help Bindra Dhar find Thurmond if it means going home."

"How can I trust you?" She pulled away her hand as the old man prayed to it.

"Oh, Bindra Dhar must trust old Randall. She has to trust him. Because Randall knows. Thurmond told Randall, he did. He told Randall he would kill Bindra Dhar."

Bindra's stomach sank. She felt her hands go hot with sweat and fear. If Thurmond, of all people, wanted to kill her, she had reason to worry. And what could she possibly have done to piss off a psychopathic, time travelling enigma so badly?

"Why?" asked Bindra of the old man kneeling before her. "Why does Thurmond want to kill me?"

"Oh, Bindra Dhar doesn't understand. Thurmond doesn't want to kill her. Thurmond has killed her. Will kill her. Is killing her."

Bindra's eyes widened as the old man shrugged.

"Oops," said Randall. "Ghamud dayim, I suppose."

Bindra had every intention of answering him, but the old man's chest exploded and he slumped over into the water. Bindra wasn't entirely sure what happened as she felt a warm mist drape over her face and neck, blown about by the wind. She soon realized it was Randall's blood. His face was inches deep in the water. He was not breathing.

"What?" was all she could sputter.

Bindra's first inclination was to escape, but as a good investigator, she needed evidence of what just happened. So, reluctantly, she crouched over Randall's body and embraced it. From the bridge over the ravine, Henry Zoller watched as the mysterious young woman and the old man disappeared, as if they'd never even been there.

9

THE PARADOX

THE COURTS in the B.C.s are something to behold. Any time traveller who's gone that far upstream would tell you. Not because you need to know, but because they'd want to make it clear that they've travelled that far. Edward Tullery was such a traveller. He insisted that he'd been everywhen and seen everything, and nothing compared to the grand courts of the B.C. centurions. His Honor Darius Bey, the Seventeenth B.C. Centurion, for example, sits upon a golden throne and hunts mammoths for recreation. Her Honor Delilah the Fair rules the Eighth Century B.C. from the back of an elephant, said Tullery, marching up and down the banks of the Nile River. But after all of the places and centuries he'd travelled to, after all of the centurions he counted among his friends, Edward Tullery was still a lowly trooper assigned to an uncivilized, backwater, hellhole of a century—Twenty.

Twenty, with its drunken, moronic centurion, Solomon Christie III. The III was important, of course, as it reminded everyone that King Sol came from an illustrious time travelling family, the noble Christies. Sol's father was the Sixteenth Centurion. His grandfather was the Tenth. But while the other two Christie kings ruled their centuries from what,

73

in Tullery's mind, were courts befitting of their rank, King Sol ran the Twentieth out of a smoky bar in Philadelphia.

The Paradox Tavern is still a popular time traveller inn and safe house built atop the Passyunk Avenue anchor point. In the four floors above there are rooms for weary travellers to rent as they pass through Twenty. On the first floor is cheap alcohol from throughout spacetime. On some occasions you may find genuine, freshly-made Viking mead. On other occasions you'll find beer that won't even be invented until Twenty-Three.

It was in the back room of the Paradox where three troopers of the Twentieth gathered for court at an old poker table. There sat Trooper Fergus Reed, with his long beard and fringe jacket, fresh from 1920s Alberta. Trooper Oscar Castagnola was also there, and he told the others about his latest mission, breaking up a ring of wildlife smugglers attempting to extract soon-to-be extinct animals from the Amazon rainforest and sell them in the future. But all Trooper Tullery wanted to talk about was who wasn't there.

"It is most inappropriate for a king not to attend his own court," sniffed the indignant trooper. "Most inappropriate indeed. And where are the others?"

There were, of course, ten troopers of the Twentieth—one for each decade.

"Soo-Yin needed help in the Teens," said Fergus Reed. "Some trouble with historians observing the first war. She asked Jordan to help, so that's when they are."

"Abobo's still working that robbery in 1965," offered Castagnola. "And Massoud and Fay both said they're not coming to court anymore."

"Ha!" said Tullery. "Doubtless because our own king doesn't come to court anymore. And what about the new girl?"

"Who?" asked Castagnola.

"He means what's-her-name," said Reed. "Bindra."

"Oh her," said Castagnola. "I don't know. She comes and goes."

"What are we supposed to do, then?" said Tullery. "Hold court between the three of us? Ha! The outrage. No wonder this century is a laughingstock."

The back room door opened and interrupted Tullery. The troopers of the Twentieth all stood at attention as the Clerk of Admission and Expulsion, with his bow tie, sweater vest and brown leather bag, strolled in. This was unusual. The Clerk rarely attended the meetings of court in any century. The troopers of the Twentieth were, of course, terrified by the Clerk's presence; it signaled only ominous things. He was unlikely to be pleased by the absence not only of the centurion, but also a majority of the troopers.

"Oh," said the Clerk. "Have I interrupted something?"

"Not at all, Clerk," said Fergus Reed. "We're holding court."

"Ah, of course, my apologies," said the Clerk. "I always forget 1980 is the capital."

"Were you not here for court, then?" said Tullery.

"No, no," said the Clerk, looking at the clock on the wall. "It seems I'm a little bit early."

"Early for what?" asked Reed.

"Oh, I'm here for the body."

"The body?"

Before the Clerk could answer, Bindra Dhar and the bloody body of Randall popped onto the poker table and sent the troopers of the Twentieth scattering. Bindra tried to right herself but slid off the table with a limp thud. Fergus Reed was the first one to reach her and started shaking her awake.

"Bindra?" he said. "Are you okay?"

"I'm fine," said Bindra, rubbing at her forehead. "I'm a little dizzy."

"Where were you?" said Fergus.

"The border," said Bindra. "1999."

"The border?" said Fergus. "How did you get here?"

"Daisy chain," said Bindra. "Jackson Park to Dupont Circle, Dupont Circle to Cumberland, Cumberland to Passyunk."

"All the way from '99?" said Fergus. "Bindra, that's a hell of a daisy chain."

Reed called out to the Paradox barkeep, "Hey, get her some green tea, will you?"

"What is the meaning of this?" demanded Tullery. "Why is Randall here? And why on Earth is he dead?"

"Thurmond," said Bindra.

The room paused. Even the barkeep let out a tiny gasp before retreating back to the bar to get the green tea.

"Thurmond?" said the Clerk, still examining Randall's body. "How can you be sure?"

Bindra tried again to get up off the floor, but she collapsed back down again, closing her eyes. "Randall contacted me with information about Thurmond," she explained. "He wanted to buy himself a ride out of the century."

"Let's go then," announced Castagnola. "We'll go to '99, stake out the place and nab Thurmond when he shoots Randall." Trooper Castagnola threw his jacket on with a flourish. "Reed, you're with me. We'll finish him once and for all."

"I don't think that will work, Oscar," said the Clerk.

"Why not?"

"Because Randall wasn't shot," said the Clerk, poking around Randall's deadly wound. "It was a time bomb."

"A what?" said Reed.

"A time bomb. A small one. Someone slipped it in his jacket. We'll never know when, exactly, which is the point. He wasn't there when Randall died."

"Still," said Castagnola. "We go find Randall, follow him, see who slips the bomb in his pocket. Reed, c'mon."

"I'm coming too," said Bindra.

"Eh, Bindra," said Fergus, holding up his hand. "You're not recovered yet."

"I'm going," she insisted, and tried again to stand up.

"I don't think any of this is a good idea," said the Clerk, as Bindra finally pushed herself off the floor and immediately grabbed the back of a chair to steady herself.

"We have to try," said Bindra. "This could be our only chance."

The Clerk frowned and pondered her words as he pulled out his notebook. "I'll write a message for the commissioners. We'll see what they think."

As the Clerk wrote the message in his book, the barkeep returned, bringing a cup of hot green tea for Bindra.

"And there's also a message for you," said the barkeep. She handed Bindra a small, tightly bound scroll of parchment.

She unrolled the parchment and read it aloud.

To Ms. BINDRA DHAR, Mr. OSCAR CASTAGNOLA,
and Mr. FERGUS REED, Troopers of the Twentieth Century—

IN REFERENCE to your request to pursue an unknown assailant
in the year 1999, made on April 3, 1980, The Paradox Tavern,
Philadelphia, Pennsylvania, The United States of America—

OUR ANSWER is herein—

No.

SO ORDERED.
Commissioners SUTTON, LEE, and LONG

"I suppose that settles it," said the Clerk.

"It doesn't settle anything!" shouted Bindra. "We can't just sit here while Thurmond is out there." She looked around the room. "Where is Sol?"

"That's actually a very good question," said the Clerk, scanning the room with a frown.

"I am very glad you've asked that, Clerk!" said Trooper Tullery. "In point of fact, our centurion is—"

Bindra cut Tullery off and marched up to face the Clerk. "This is as close as we've ever been to him. He's out there somewhen, and he is planning something big."

"What did Randall say about him?" said the Clerk. "About Thurmond? What does he plan to do?"

"'Thurmond is coming to save everyone,'" said Bindra.

"Well," said Castagnola. "That certainly doesn't sound too terrible."

Bindra frowned at him.

"He also said Thurmond was going to kill me."

10

THE TIME TRAVELER CONVENTION

IN MAY OF 2005, a student at the Massachusetts Institute of Technology came up with a clever way to test whether time travel is physically possible. Amal Dorai and his friends organized what they called the Time Traveler Convention on MIT's campus, on the premise that if time travel was ever invented in their future, some of the travelers might stop in for a visit. They placed invitations to the convention in time capsules and obscure books in Cambridge libraries that were unlikely to be opened for some time. But despite Amal's best efforts, no time travellers came to his convention on May 7, 2005.

Their failure to show up was not for a lack of trying.

Visiting the MIT Time Traveler Convention of 2005 is explicitly outlawed in section 21.203.99(d) of the *Time Travellers' Revised Code*. Despite this, travellers from all across spacetime are constantly trying to get in, and the troopers of the Twenty-First are constantly apprehending them and sending them back to their native centuries. For some time, the Guild considered making the entire state of Massachusetts, for the entire year of 2005, a forbidden zone. The commissioners ultimately rejected that proposal and instead left the security of the Time Traveler

79

Convention in the hands of the Twenty-First Century troopers and their centurion, Akande the Gallant. Working security at the 2005 MIT Time Traveler Convention is a nightmare assignment for any time traveller.

That was the nightmare that Sean Logan, trooper of the Twenty-First, woke up to morning after morning. Every day was May 7, 2005. Every day he was expected to go stop dumbass time travellers from trying to get into this dumbass convention at MIT. Sean Logan was compelled by law to spend every day in Cambridge on May 7, 2005, until he reached his limit. He would not argue that he didn't deserve this sentence. The Guild could have been much more punitive, given his crime. Sean believed that his friendship with Akande the Gallant had something to do with his lighter sentence, though Akande denied this. Sean wasn't complaining. But the problem was that he'd been living in May 7, 2005, for a month and still hadn't reached his limit. Normally that sort of talent would be reason for pride in a traveller. But Sean was miserable.

He was letting himself go. He could see it in the mirror. He had never thought of himself as being particularly handsome, but he had at least once been moderately attractive. (Or so he'd been told by people who had no reason to flatter him.) But that was pretty much over now. He was getting pudgy, fast. He had at one point decided to use his sentence to experiment with growing a beard, but it turned into a scraggy, unceremonious display. After another month, he looked like he was deteriorating, like May 7, 2005, was eating away at him, and it probably was. He knew every story on the morning news, every song that would come on every station, every person he would see on the street. He knew every sight, smell, and sound; he knew every minute, insignificant event that occurred in Cambridge, Massachusetts, on May 7, 2005. The only things that were ever different were the time travellers.

The upside to living in purgatory was the other time travellers were extremely easy to spot. They kept coming, and Sean kept snagging them and sending them home or to a safe house if they were too tired to travel. One time he caught four Romans headed for the Time Traveler Convention—actual Romans, in togas and everything. He found it particularly offensive that they hadn't even bothered to dress for the century. He confronted them and they made up some lame excuse—came to see the great universities of the Twenty-First Century, or something like that—and when he told them to get back on the road, they cursed at him.

"*Ede faecam!*" shouted one of the Romans, and then she spit on him. He looked it up when he got back to the hotel. Latin for "eat shit."

"Well, ede faecam to you too," he said to his computer screen and took another swig of beer.

One thing that did change with every day was Sean's living situation. It had to; he couldn't occupy the same space as his day-old former self. Every night at the stroke of midnight on May 8, he travelled back twenty-four hours and looked for a new place to sleep. He kept a duffel bag with essential supplies—clothes, money, laptop computer. At first he slept outdoors, then he moved around to different hotels before eventually breaking into apartments and houses, because by that time he knew which ones were unoccupied for the day.

To keep his mind sharp, Sean used his unlimited free time in May 7, 2005, to keep up with the red books. Downstream of Twenty, with the advent of mass communication, it's easy enough for time travellers to communicate with each other when they're in the same time period. There are inconspicuous internet forums and secret radio frequencies. The numbers stations are popular, but they do attract some layman attention. For communicating across time, however, the red books remain the Guild's preferred system, even though it's a tricky system. For one thing, you have to stash a red book in a place where the laymen aren't likely to find it, preferably close to an anchor point. If you want to communicate with the future, you simply leave messages in the book to be found later. But if you want to send a message to the past, you have to note this request in the red book and hope that some traveller in the future brings your message back to its recipient in the years long gone. There are few guarantees in this system.

There are two primary red books in Boston—one stashed in an old tree near the harbor waterfront and another hidden in a false brick in the Old North Church. By reading the red books every day, Sean was able to keep track of what all the other travellers in centuries past were up to. It was in the red books that he first started to read the scattered reports about the time traveller who called himself Thurmond.

Most of the dispatches seemed to be appearing in the Twentieth Century sections of the red books. There was a general report of concern from the centurion Solomon Christie, and another disturbing note that Thurmond had not only killed an expelled traveller but had also threatened the life of a trooper. Soon he began to see reports in the Nineteenth Century sections—something about Thurmond's connection to Francisco Pierre DuPree, the jewel thief.

In his third month living in May 7, 2005, Sean noticed a distinct drop in the number of travellers attempting to crash the MIT convention. Perhaps the message was spreading that there was a trooper stationed there (semi) permanently. At first he was pleased not to have to deal with all of those morons, but the luster soon wore off and he was more bored than ever. He did everything he could to stop himself from going insane. One night, on May 7, 2005, he rented and watched the movie *Groundhog Day* because he thought it would be fun, given his situation.

It was not. It made him very sad.

When he entered the fourth month of May 7, 2005, he still hadn't reached his limit. *I must be really, really good at time travel*, he thought. Sure, this was an awful way to find out just how good he was, but still. Take that, laws of physics. Bow down.

CHAPTER 10: THE TIME TRAVELER CONVENTION

On the first day of the fifth month of May 7, 2005, Sean Logan noticed someone who didn't belong. He had placed himself on MIT's campus, waiting on a bench and watching for troublesome time travellers, when he noticed her—a woman, maybe sixty or seventy years old, walking toward the building where the Time Traveler Convention was held. By this time, he knew the faces and movements of every person in Cambridge, hell, every person in Boston on May 7, 2005. This woman had never shown up on MIT's campus before. She had to be a time traveller.

Sean stood from his bench and called out to her as she walked by.

"It's good to meet a fellow traveller," he shouted, full of the arrogance and sarcasm that had become his calling card in purgatory.

The old woman turned to face him. Her hair was long and brown. Her blue eyes were shielded by half-moon glasses. Sean was not prepared for the feeling in her eyes. It was longing, more than any other emotion, and he had not expected to see it in some traveller just out to have a good time. She looked him over, appraised him, and stared him in the eye, utterly confused.

"I'm sorry?" she said softly.

Sean realized he must have gotten it wrong.

"I'm sorry, ma'am," he said. "Continue on your way."

He turned, and walked away from MIT's campus, convinced that he would never see the old woman again. Until, that is, he heard a soft voice behind him.

"You're one of them, aren't you?" said the woman. "You're a time traveller."

Startled, he turned and faced her. He considered his options for a moment and decided to try and shrug the comment off. He produced a weak, unsure laugh.

"Why would you say that?"

83

"That's how they talk to one another," said the old lady. "'Fellow traveller' and all that."

"You're for real, lady? Do you know some time travellers?"

She frowned at him. "I am not a crazy person. I don't believe in crazy things. But I met a time traveller. A real one. Almost a year ago. I'd very much like to speak to him again, and I was hoping that perhaps he would be here."

Sean didn't know what to think of the old woman. On the one hand, it wouldn't do any damage to let her through to the convention. They might think she was crazy and send her to a home, but the laymen probably wouldn't believe her. On the other hand, he should have seen her there the day before, or the day before that, or every day he spent in May 7, 2005. Such a change in spacetime suggested the influence of a time traveller, and if a traveller was out there running his mouth to laymen like this, he needed to know.

"Well," said Sean. "Maybe you'll find your time traveller in there. What did you say his name was?"

"Thurmond."

He must have made some sort of face because the old lady noticed. "Is he a friend of yours?"

Now it seemed that Sean would have something to add to the Twenty-First Century section of the red books—the story of the lay-woman who introduced herself to him as Nevie Brown. As delicately but firmly as possible, Sean redirected Nevie to a nearby coffee shop where they could talk privately. Sean admitted to her that she was right; he was a time traveller. He then took out a notebook and pencil, ready to take notes for his red book report.

"So, Nevie," he said when they had settled down at a table. "What can you tell me about Thurmond?"

She squinted her eyes at him as if she were suspicious of the question. "He was very nice. A perfect gentleman. Very normal, for a…well, you know…a time traveller."

Sean smiled at her. "We try to seem as normal as possible." Except, apparently, for the Romans. "Can you tell me, why did Thurmond seek you out? What did he say to you?"

"He wanted to know more about my train crash. And about my husband Robbie."

"There was a train crash?" said Sean. "What train crash?"

Nevie sighed and braced herself to tell the story. "Robbie and I were on the *Appalachia Arrow*. It was the Continental Railways passenger line, the one that went off the rails in 1984. That was at Rosbys Rock, West Virginia. Seventy-two people were killed, including Robbie."

"I'm very sorry to hear that, ma'am."

"It's okay." She nodded and a couple of tears streaked down her face. "It's okay. Thurmond is going to make it okay. He said he was going to save everyone."

Sean looked up from his notepad. "He said what?"

"He said he was going to save everyone," repeated Nevie, smiling through her tears. "He said he has a plan to save everyone on the train, including my Robbie. He's going to go back in time and he's going to stop the train from ever crashing."

Sean put down his pencil and stared at his notebook. How was he going to explain this to her?

"Sir," said Nevie. "Why are you so concerned about Thurmond? Is he some sort of criminal?"

"He…" said Sean, trying to think of how to explain. "Yes, he is a very, very bad man. And if this man really was Thurmond, you might be the only person I know of who's actually met him. Some people wonder if he really exists, or maybe he's a group of criminals pretending to be one. That's why what you've told me is so important and so disturbing. What he's told you he wants to do is a crime among our people. We call it 'interference,' and it's one of our most serious crimes."

"It's a crime to save people's lives?"

"It's a crime to change the outcome of events," said Sean. "Little things can change. But big things like wars or disasters or train crashes— basically all the things every time traveller wishes they could stop—those things have to happen. It's a crime to interfere with fate."

"What's so wrong with changing how things turn out?"

"Because we don't know everything. We don't know what will happen because of our actions. We don't know that if we stop a bad thing from happening yesterday, the trade-off won't be something worse happens tomorrow."

She pushed her coffee away and folded her arms, looking at him the way his instructor once looked at him whenever he disappointed her.

"I don't believe that for a moment, Sean," she said. "And frankly, I don't believe you believe it either."

He'd never been a great liar.

"I do believe it," he said defiantly. "And even if I didn't, and even if it wasn't the law, the person who would presume to know how to control fate is always a dangerous sort of person."

The old woman nodded and seemed to lower her defenses. "Are you from the future?"

"No," he said. "I was born in 1905."

"Oh my. You were born thirty years before I was. And how old are you?"

"Biologically, I'm thirty."

"Well," she laughed. "You never know what to expect out of life. I certainly never expected to meet a time traveller. Now I've met two." She shook her head and sipped a little more of her coffee. "I'll tell you this, Sean," she said, smiling. "I think you're a good boy. You've been very kind to me, and I know you've got a job to do, but I hope you fail. I hope you're wrong about the laws of your people, about fate and whether or not you can change it. I hope you're wrong about Thurmond. And even if you're not wrong, I hope you fail. I don't care about your laws or fate or whatever. Maybe I'm wrong not to care, but I don't. Maybe if you were like me, maybe if you had to live life at regular speed, forward only, you would understand. I like you, Sean, but I hope you fail."

Sean felt touched by her sincerity. He rarely had encounters with laymen, and when he did, it was all the same. Go back and fix this, go back and fix that. He had never bothered to explain the law until now. What had he expected?

Oh, I'm sorry, Mr. Time Traveller, I didn't realize it was against the rules for you to save my beloved husband. I will carry on with my chronological life as if nothing ever happened.

No layperson would ever believe that. How could they without understanding the world the travellers lived in, the world apart from time, the world without time? He couldn't expect Nevie to believe it.

That night, when the clock struck midnight, Sean found an anchor point and prepared to return to the beginning of May 7, 2005, but quickly found that he couldn't. It had never been hard to turn back the clock twenty-four hours; that's basically nothing for a time traveller. But now it was proving impossible. Travellers sometimes liken the act of time travelling to opening a door that had always seemed locked. Now, however, Sean found his door to Cambridge, Massachusetts, on May 7, 2005, was permanently locked. He had finally reached his limit.

11

THE ALARINKIRI

THE KEY TO RULING A CENTURY, Akande often said, was style. One must be of the right mind, of course, to be centurion. One must be a true and honest leader for his travellers. There was no doubt about that. And the Guild had their requirements too—a centurion had to be able to jump one hundred years without getting tired, and so forth. But what really sealed the deal for a king, what made your every word the law of the century, in Akande's mind, was style. And style was something he knew.

It helped that he was bookended by some fairly unfashionable kings. Faisal, the Twenty-Second Centurion, was far too bookish in Akande's opinion. He spent most of his time in his libraries, never making royal appearances. Travellers in Twenty-Two must think they're stuck with a professor for a leader. And Twenty? Under Sol Christie's rule? Don't even start. No, no, no. Akande liked to have a good time himself, but he knew there was a line. King Sol certainly did not. Akande knew himself to be a king among kings because he ruled his century with equal parts responsibility and style.

His name was part of that style. He was born in a time and place where single names were the fashion, so he was free to attach an honorific, just like Roland the Clever, Wong the Victorious, Rebecca the Slayer of Traitors, and all those other centurions who commanded the utmost respect. So he became His Honor, Akande the Gallant, the Twenty-First Centurion. It suited him, and it gave his people an idea of what sort of ruler he was, or at least what sort of ruler he thought he was.

Akande's physical style was yet another crucial part of his sovereign appearance. He made absolutely sure, no matter what year of his century he chose to visit, that he was dressed to impress. He patronized the finest tailors in every decade and kept a prized collection of three-piece suits. Every detail of his wardrobe was given close attention in an effort to reflect the diligence with which he commanded Twenty-One. He took equal care of his body, conducting intense fitness training every day so that anyone who wished to encounter the Twenty-First Centurion would be met with ninety kilos of pure Yoruba muscle.

Then there was the *Alarinkiri*, Akande's gleaming white yacht, his court, his palace, his "ship of mysteries." The most important mystery, of course, was how it was possible that time travellers were able to arrive onto the *Alarinkiri* at all without an anchor point. Time travellers had long tried to figure out a way to travel onto and off of vessels and moving objects, but these attempts usually ended in failure, injury or spontaneously appearing in the vast vacuum of space. Akande and his closest confidants had clearly figured out a way to do it, but he wasn't telling. It was all part of the mystique, he would say. Part of the style, part of the appearance, part of ruling.

As he cruised the ocean aboard the *Alarinkiri*, Akande played a quick match of billiards against himself (a worthy opponent, indeed). In the midst of this competition, he was joined by an old friend.

As soon as Sean Logan was freed from May 7, 2005, he travelled to the *Alarinkiri* to seek an audience with Akande the Gallant. He was not sure how his friend would react to his return, whether his crime, though it had been atoned for, would be totally forgiven by his centurion. Still, the anticipation of seeing his closest friend after months of May 7, 2005, was almost more than Sean could handle. His hands shook as he entered Akande's billiards room and saw the tall centurion chalking up his favorite pool cue. Akande looked up and his face immediately seemed to lighten when he saw Sean.

"Sean, my friend," he said. "Back so soon?"

Sean thought this must be a joke.

"Ha, yes. Feels like I saw you only yesterday."

"It was yesterday," said Akande. "But it's no matter. I need a friendly face today."

The centurion approached Sean, shook his hand tightly and pulled him into a firm hug. Sean felt a rush of relief. His friendship with Akande had always been somewhat tense, at least on Sean's end of things, ever since the centurion had appointed him a trooper of the Twenty-First. It was difficult to balance his friendly devotion with his knightly devotion. He had feared that his crime against the law of the Guild would cost him both Akande's trust in him as a trooper and Akande's love of him as a friend. Learning that he'd lost neither was almost more liberating than his freedom from purgatory.

"I am actually here on business, Your Honor," said Sean.

"Business? Here we are, in the middle of a reunion, and you must speak of business? Fresh out of imprisonment, and you must speak of business? You enjoy working too much, my friend."

"I'm afraid it's urgent, Your Honor. Have you read the dispatches from Nineteen and Twenty about Thurmond?"

"I have," said Akande as he finished his chalking and aimed his cue. "He cannot possibly exist."

"I think he can, Your Honor. I think he does."

"You've seen him?"

"No, Your Honor. But a picture is coming together. A trooper in Twenty, Bindra Dhar, reported that she believes Thurmond has marked her for death. And another trooper in Nineteen, Zelda Clairing, reports that he had some sort of an arrangement with a diamond thief. He is real, Your Honor, the evidence is mounting."

"Even so," said Akande. "Twenty is wilderness. And one can never be certain of what exactly is going on in Nineteen. This Thurmond fellow, if he exists, is too much of a puzzle to spend much worry on, my friend."

"I think I may have a piece of that puzzle, Your Honor. A laywoman in 2005. He seems to have been careless and told her about his plans."

"What are his plans? According to this laywoman?"

"Interference," said Sean. "He's supposedly going to stop a train crash that killed seventy-two laymen."

"Ah, Sean," said Akande. "We deal with interference all the time. You know that better than anyone. When is this train crash supposed to occur?"

"1984," said Sean.

"So it's Sol Christie's problem."

"Yes, if he knew about it."

"Send him a message in a red book," offered Akande. "Or send a courier. That's all your duty requires of you."

"I can do more than that. And so can Your Honor."

"What do you want from me?"

Sean took a deep breath. "Call for a conference. Aboard the *Alarinkiri*. Yourself, Solomon Christie, Lupita Calderon. Nineteen, Twenty and Twenty-One, all in the same room in a show of strength, law and order."

"Ha!" said Akande. "I do not want them on my ship."

"Why not?"

"Sol will drink through all of my liquor. And Lupita scares me."

"Right, yes, very valid points," said Sean. "But I want you to consider how this will affect your image."

"My image?"

"Well, just think about it. A conference like this would show the Guild you take the matter seriously, especially if Lupita and Sol do not. If Thurmond is dealt with, swiftly, under your leadership, it would be widely spoken of across the centuries."

Akanda stood his cue on its end and began to rub his chin. "I suppose it would."

"And the more dangerous Thurmond turns out to be, all the more glory to you, Your Honor. Not only would you be stopping a dangerous criminal traveller, you would be enforcing law and order in Twenty, where it's not even your responsibility. Imagine how embarrassing that would be for Sol Christie—"

Akande waved him off and picked up his cue, rounding the corner of his billiards table and lining up on a new shot. "I see what you are doing."

"You do?"

"Yes, and I like it," said Akande. "Embarrassing the other centuries is always a worthy cause. You may make contact with Twenty and Nineteen, and I mean you alone. I do not want to be involved at all. I will host this conference, if there is to be a conference. But I will not go begging Lupita and Sol to come disturb my peace and quiet."

"Yes, Your Honor. Is this a command, then?"

"Yes. Happy?"

"Yes, Your Honor," said Sean, smiling. "I will contact the other centuries."

12

TUG-OF-WAR

BINDRA DHAR'S PARENTS believed she left home to become some sort of police officer. This, Bindra felt, was the easiest way to explain things to her father and mother, who of course did not know she was a time traveller and could not possibly understand what a time trooper was. When Bindra Dhar told Mr. Brooks she intended to become a trooper, he was proud, of course—"a noble public service" he said—but he was also a little bit surprised. He asked her how she came to this career choice, and she talked about wanting to give back to the community of time travellers, wanting to serve the Guild, which was kind of a lie, but it was what she thought Mr. Brooks wanted to hear. She didn't think he would like the real reason.

The real reason was that reading about the work of time troopers had sparked her ambition. It wasn't so much the job of keeping law and order across a century, but the rigorous training a trooper must go through. She read about how troopers test themselves and push their skills to the limit. Bindra was surprised to find within herself an insatiable ambition to be a better time traveller than most time travellers. She found this ambition frightening, almost a little bit shameful, but mostly it was exhilarating.

95

In the years following her admission to the Time Travellers' Guild, from age eighteen to twenty-three, Bindra put herself through trooper training. She identified her limits and pushed against them. She read about the famous troopers and the fugitives they chased. Bindra wanted to be the best. Or at least, one of the best. With every book she read, Bindra hungered to prove herself. She ached for a challenge.

The challenge she wanted came from the Time Travellers' Guild. A courier arrived at her family's home one day and delivered what appeared to be a telegram, something she'd read about but never actually seen.

BINDRA DHAR

APPLICATION FOR TROOPER ASSIGNMENT RECEIVED (STOP) APPLICATION FOR TROOPER ASSIGNMENT APPROVED BY COMMRS (STOP) HEREBY ASSIGNED TO TWENTIETH CENTURY PER COMMRS (STOP) REPORT TO HIS HON SOLOMON CHRISTIE IN YEAR 1980 (STOP)

CLERK OF ADMISS AND EXPULS

END

She had learned from her books, from Mr. Brooks, from other travellers, that Twenty was a wild and dangerous century. There were world wars and riots and genocides there, and that was just the laymen troubles. Mr. Brooks told her countless time criminals made Twenty their home. The troopers there were disorganized and discontented. The centurion, Sol Christie, was a buffoon. "All he knows is selfishness," Mr. Brooks said of him. Enforcing the law in a lawless century would be hard, Bindra knew, and that was exactly what she wanted.

Her experience in the Twentieth Century had been something of a duality. On the one hand, she encountered all the typical challenges a time traveller faces in a new century—the music, the customs, the language, the society, the technology (or lack thereof). This was compounded by the fact that Twenty was truly lawless. Thieves and cheats thrived there, and interference was common. Time travelling gamblers cheated laymen at every major sporting event in Twenty, knowing, as they did, the outcome of every match. Bindra marveled at the inability of the laymen to notice that time travellers had rigged nearly every single Kentucky Derby of the century. Her fellow troopers of the Twentieth were not that bad. Well, Trooper Tullery was pretty terrible, but the rest were not incompetent. They were all stretched too thin, however, and they were suspicious of Bindra and her youth.

On the other hand, she discovered that the common description of the Twentieth Centurion was not completely accurate. Sol Christie was an informal ruler, and yes, he liked to dabble in all the hedonistic pleasures the Twentieth Century had to offer. But over time, Bindra discovered that underneath the veil of apparent recklessness, there was a mind at work inside Solomon Christie and an unexpected degree of sadness. The life of a time traveller could be a lonely one, especially for a new traveller like Bindra, but she could tell that Sol had, on occasion, gone out of his way to be her friend.

He favored her so much, it would seem, that he assigned her to investigate the rumors about a mysterious time criminal called Thurmond. So Thurmond became her biggest obsession and her biggest challenge. And perhaps it was her pursuit of a challenge that led her to be marked for death by Thurmond's hand.

All the more reason to get better at time travel.

To that end, whenever she could, Bindra found a lonely place in the wilderness and met with Lumen. Lumen was a young traveller from Twenty-Three, and yes, Bindra would admit, she had any number of feelings for him. But the core of their relationship was the fact that both of them had the same interest—an extreme time travel exercise that many consider too dangerous to try even once.

A few days after her encounter with Randall, Bindra was aching for a training exercise. She needed something to make her feel like she could confront Thurmond if the time came. She walked alone through the Pennsylvania woods, searching for one of their designated meeting spots near a little-used anchor point. She found Lumen sitting atop a green, fungus-encrusted boulder.

"It's good to meet a fellow traveller," he called down to her.

"To make the road less lonely," she replied.

"What took you so long?" he said.

"I had some things to take care of. Trooper business."

"Ah, of course." He gave her an exaggerated salute. "Trooper business."

Lumen leapt down from the boulder, letting his messy black hair flop around his head as he landed. He was about Bindra's height, which meant that he was relatively short, and this was made even more apparent by his preference for oversized knit sweaters. It was the gray one that day. Bindra's favorite.

"Are you ready?" said Lumen. "I found a really nice spot."

"Let's go," said Bindra.

She chased him up a leafy hill and down a ridge toward the waters of the Schuylkill River. All around her she felt the presence of the anchor point growing stronger. He stopped at a rocky ledge overlooking the river with a single tree growing overhead. They stood opposite each other and Bindra took a moment to enjoy Lumen's eyes. They were icy blue, full of adventure and wisdom. Part of it was his origin from a downstream century, his knowledge of events she knew nothing about. Part of it was that his need to push the boundaries of his skill was equal to her own. A much larger part was that she wanted him, badly.

CHAPTER 12: TUG-OF-WAR

A young time traveller has needs, after all.

"How far are we going?" he asked her.

"Let's do fifty."

"Fifty? Are you sure?"

"We don't have to," she said, "if you're too scared."

She gave him a flirtatious look. Besides, she thought, fifty years was no more dangerous than having a time travelling super villain after you.

"All right," he said, smiling. "We'll do fifty."

He held out his hands with his palms upward. Bindra held out her hands with her palms facing down to his and inched them closer. As they closed the distance, Bindra started to feel something like static electricity jump between his palms and hers. She looked again into his eyes.

"I'll go downstream," he said.

"I'll go upstream," she replied.

Bindra felt as if she were holding her palms over two small, silent firecrackers. The energy between them crackled as they clasped their hands together.

The practice of long-distance counter-travelling, commonly known in English as "tug-of-war," is an ancient time traveller sport. In a tug-of-war session, the two parties will agree on how many years they will travel against each other. One traveller will attempt to pull the other however many years into the future, and vice versa. Tug-of-war is commonly used as a test of skill between travellers, but also as a form of exercise, for it should theoretically increase the ability of an individual to travel decades without needing rest.

It cannot be emphasized enough that you should not try this at home.

While tug-of-war is not technically illegal, it is highly dangerous. Even conventional time travel is mentally and physically exhausting. Counter-travelling is doubly so. It's not uncommon for reckless travellers to overextend themselves during a tug-of-war and die, or worse, lose the ability to time travel. It's also dangerous for the fact that if the two travellers in a tug-of-war are evenly matched in their skills, they will exist neither in the past, nor the future, but the present, a terrifying and little-understood dimension of spacetime.

As soon as she clasped hands with Lumen, Bindra's world appeared to pinch and stretch like an enormous wormhole through space, because that's what it was. The world became a fifty-year tunnel that disappeared behind Lumen's head, as if she were looking into a mirror facing another mirror in a never-ending reflection. She knew the same tunnel was stretching behind her head, leading fifty years into the past. The atmosphere around them shifted and spun in a swirling storm. The temperature and pressure flew up and down depending on who held the upper hand in the exercise. Bindra felt herself losing strength to him. She felt Lumen tugging them both into the future. She looked down at her feet and remembered.

It's about moments, not numbers.

She would have to take it slow.

All she needed was snow. It was mid-spring when they started, so she would take them back into winter. It was a small step to start a fifty-year journey, but she'd done this before. All she needed was a little push to get going. She concentrated only on stabilizing the weather, the temperature, the pressure, on going back to the time when it was cold, snowing, and the pressure was low. Back to winter. Back to winter. Back to when there was snow on the ground.

Cold snow enveloped her feet and Lumen's. She kept going. Back to autumn. Back to autumn. Back to autumn. Their shoes, icy and wet, were covered now in brown and golden leaves. She kept going. Back to summer. Back to summer. Back to spring, back to spring, back to...

Then it was dark. She squeezed Lumen's hands and pulled him close to her as her eyes adjusted to the night. Whenever they played tug-of-war, Bindra and Lumen aimed to arrive at night so the stars could tell them who was the victor. Bindra wrapped her arms around Lumen and rested her head on his chest while they both searched for constellations in the sky.

"Can you see anything?" she asked him.

"I don't have to. It's you. You've won. I can feel it."

She looked back to him. His features were starting to show themselves in the moonlight.

"We're fifty years upstream," he said. "Bindra, that's incredible. You travelled fifty years, and with my fifty years on your back. How do you feel?"

Bindra pushed away from him and spun around the ridgeline. "I feel great. I feel amazing. I feel…powerful."

She leapt onto a rock at the edge of the water and shouted over top of it. Her voice echoed off the rocks on the other side.

"Come and get me, Thurmond!"

Lumen laughed behind her. "He's no match for you."

Bindra turned away from the water's edge and tackled Lumen to the ground. They both tumbled into the grass, laughing all the way down. When they stopped rolling, Bindra crawled on top of him, pulled her dark hair back and kissed him. She no longer thought of Thurmond and Randall and the prospect of being killed or the prospect of having already been killed. She wasn't even totally sure what year they were in. All she knew was that Lumen was so much better, so much easier than time travel. She wanted him more than she wanted the challenge. So she kissed him, closed her eyes, and hoped with everything she had that when she opened them back up again, he would look pleased.

And perhaps he would have, but Bindra did not get the opportunity to find out. As she kissed him, she went limp and slid off his body. Lumen watched her roll down the ridge and plunge into the Schuylkill River.

13

THE ROYAL SUMMONS

AS SOON AS BINDRA WOKE UP, she knew she had been shivering for a long time. Her jaw hurt from chattering teeth. She was lying on an old sofa, naked but wrapped in several layers of blankets like a human burrito. Above her was a ceiling of concrete and steel beams. From one of the beams hung her clothes, shoes, and her father's green jacket. She recognized this place. It was the top floor loft above the Paradox Tavern. Orange sunlight streamed in from a window somewhere above her, splitting her brain in two. The room smelled like stale cannabis.

She shifted around, hoping to find Lumen waiting over her. What she found was infinitely worse.

Solomon Christie sat in a rocking chair across from her sofa, dressed in a red bathrobe, sipping coffee. "Good morning," said Sol.

Bindra retreated under her array of blankets, crushed with embarrassment. "This can't be happening," she groaned.

"I am afraid it is, Trooper Dhar," said the Twentieth Centurion. "Believe me, I am just as surprised as you."

"What happened?"

"Your gentleman friend came looking for me, very distraught. He pulled you out of the water but was too weak after your exercise to carry you. So of course, I had to heroically come retrieve and take care of you."

Bindra shuddered. "Did you undress me?"

"No, of course not," said Sol. "I left that to one of the girls."

"Girls?"

Behind Sol, Bindra saw another figure peek into the room. It was a slender woman with bleach-blond hair, completely naked and holding a bottle of whiskey.

"Are you doing better, sweetie?" asked the naked woman.

"Yes," said Bindra, wide-eyed.

The blond woman retreated back into the other room. She heard giggles.

Bindra lifted her body and peered through the window. Beneath a rising, golden sun she saw the familiar features and skyline of Philadelphia, the American city Sol had declared his Century Seat for no apparent reason at all.

"When are we?" she said.

"Back in 1980."

"Where is Lumen?"

"That is a difficult question," he said.

She swung her head around to look at him. "Where is Lumen?"

"Now, Bindra," he said. "You must understand, what you do with your skill is your own business. I will not pretend I haven't pushed my own limits from time to time. But tug-of-war is a dangerous exercise, and that young man ought to know better."

"Where is Lumen?"

"Once it was clear that you would survive," he continued, "I lost my temper. I admit I may have been harsh, but 'twas also warranted."

"Where is Lumen?"

"I gave him a very stern lecture with metaphors and cautionary tales and then I banished him from the Twentieth Century."

"You banished him?" said Bindra. "You can't possibly do that!"

"I assure you, I can."

Bindra shot up off the couch and stood over him, clutching the blankets around her. "You had no right to do that, Sol," she shouted. "You are not my father."

"No, I'm afraid 'tis much worse," he said, standing to confront her. "I am your centurion. I am the pillar of what all travellers should aspire to be. I am the living symbol of law and order in the Twentieth Century and the commander of all time travellers therein."

"You make speeches now?"

"The point is, I can banish whomever I wish, and I will certainly banish anyone who would dare put one of my troopers in danger." He took a breath. "I made an example of him, yes. Setting examples is an important part of governance."

"What would you know of governance?" she shot back at him.

"Again, I will warn you, Trooper Dhar," he said with an outstretched finger. "You are talking to your centurion and you shall show him the respect he is due."

"We're leaving," said a voice behind Sol. Bindra watched as the bleach-blond girl and two other women walked out of Sol's bedroom and out of the apartment, giggling all the while.

"Fare thee well, ladies," he said over his shoulder, never taking his eyes off Bindra.

"It wasn't just his idea, you know," she said when she heard the apartment door close. "I was the one who found Lumen; I was the one who went looking for a partner."

"Why? There are safer ways of improving your skills."

"But none better. All of the books say it. Nothing improves your travelling like counter travelling, precisely because of how risky it is."

"But why must you put yourself through it? This boy, Lumen, told me you started at five years, ten years. Then suddenly you wanted to go fifty years. Why are you pushing yourself so hard?"

"Because of Thurmond," she said, and then sat back down on the sofa. Sol likewise relented in the argument and sat in his rocking chair.

"Yes, I heard about your report from the border," said Sol. "Travellers kill other travellers from time to time, Bindra, 'tis true. But a time traveller does not simply murder another time traveller in cold blood. There are so few of us, and we are, for all of our faults, a community."

"He had no trouble killing Randall," said Bindra. "I can't trust the better nature of a traveller who's already murdered another traveller in cold blood."

"I can help you. I can keep you safe."

"How can you keep me safe from something that's already happened? Besides, I'm not interested in hiding from him, that would be cowardice."

"If the choice ever comes between cowardice and death, please, pick cowardice," said Sol. "I command you, pick cowardice. But if you feel as though you must confront Thurmond directly, would you consider confronting him with others by your side?"

"What do you mean?"

Sol reached into the pocket of his bathrobe and retrieved a scroll of paper. "I was going to assign this to one of the other troopers," he said, handing her the paper. "Fergus or Castagnola or someone. But I suppose, since this is now of personal interest to you, it might as well be yours."

"What is it?"

"A royal summons. To the Realm of the Twenty-First Century. His Honor Akande the Gallant has invited myself and Her Honor Lupita Calderon of Nineteen to discuss the Thurmond problem."

"You're going to Twenty-One?" said Bindra.

"I am not. I have no interest in being lectured by Lupita nor made to marvel at Akande's damned silly boat. That's why you shall go in my stead."

"Won't it be insulting to Akande if you don't attend?"

"Oh yes," he said. "'Tis the point."

"What about the evidence you gathered from 1946?"

"I think you can relay that information just fine without me," he said.

"And the other troopers?"

"I don't trust them."

"But you trust me?"

"No," he said. "But I like you more."

14

THE COURT OF THE NINETEENTH

AS HER CARRIAGE rolled through the Mexican country-side, Zelda reflected on the fact that there were, in her opinion, only two good things that came out of the Twentieth Century—women's suffrage and Tupac Shakur. The latter she enjoyed via the speaker system discreetly installed inside the carriage; she was careful to turn the volume down whenever they passed laymen on the road to Lupita's seaside villa in 1857.

Lupita's mansion was an imposing structure fit for the ruler of a century. The walls were the color of the sand on which they were built, held together with a series of white columns that wrapped around the entire villa. The mansion was constructed on a rocky peak hanging over the Pacific Ocean in such a way that three of its four sides had perfect views of the white, rough seas. Some said that if a traveller displeased Lupita, or if a trooper ever dared trespass in her realm, she would simply have them tossed from her throne room into the ocean. Zelda knew these rumors were untrue, but she also knew that Lupita liked them.

Zelda opened the carriage door and thanked her driver. "California Love" briefly sounded over the ocean. Then she proceeded to climb the one hundred steps that led up to the villa's grand entrance, followed by the symbolic nineteen steps that led into the villa itself. The building's interior was a remarkable display of open space. In every direction stood a geometric forest of columns and arches with the ocean beyond. The floor was all one enormous Roman mosaic, and her every step upon it sent echoes throughout the chamber.

After walking through the colonnade, Zelda arrived at the throne room of Lupita Calderon. Ten chairs stood in a semicircle around Lupita's throne, with its back to the ocean. Other troopers of the Nineteenth had already taken their seats, prepared for court. Zelda sat with the others and waited for the arrival of the centurion. Soon, after all the seats were filled, two of Lupita's stewards arrived, dressed in the regalia of the old conquistadors. One of the stewards stabbed the ground three times with his halberd.

"All rise!" he shouted.

The troopers of the Nineteenth did as they were told.

"Fellow travellers!" bellowed the steward. "We stand in the glorious presence of Her Honor, Lupita Calderon, the Nineteenth Centurion!"

The troopers remained standing as a dark figure swept past the columns from the right of the throne room, accompanied by loud, purposeful footfalls. Draped in a flowing black dress, the Nineteenth Centurion whisked herself before her throne and surveyed her troopers. From afar, one might be forgiven for momentarily thinking Lupita Calderon was a walking skeleton. It was as if time had withered away every excess and defining feature from her appearance and left only the very basic structure needed to carry a human body. She scowled as she looked out upon her court, and those who knew her best recognized this scowl as the sign of a good mood.

"It's good to meet a fellow traveller," she said.

"To make the road less lonely," replied the troopers.

"Be seated," she ordered.

Her troopers obeyed.

"We will start with the Crimea," declared Lupita. "Mikhail? Report."

Zelda watched as Mikhail Szevka, a large, bearded Ukrainian who wore perhaps too many layers for the hot Mexican climate, stood to deliver his dispatch.

"The war is proceeding as it should. But a group of four, maybe five travellers from Twenty-One came to observe. History students from the University of Toledo, they said. I'm afraid they made quite a mess."

"Interference?" asked Lupita.

"Not intentional, Your Honor," said Mikhail. "Reckless kids is all. Wanted to take selfies with the Russian soldiers."

"What is a selfie?"

"It is a photograph, Your Honor," explained Mikhail. "You hold the camera facing yourself."

"Nonsense," said Lupita. "Have they been banished?"

"They shall be, if that is Your Honor's wish."

"So ordered. Tell them they can make their apologies through Akande. Allison, what do you have from the '60s?"

Mikhail sat and Allison Rosey, a pale, raven-haired trooper from the United States, stood up. Zelda turned away and tried to contain a smirk. Allison Rosey was Lupita's Captain of Troopers, but Zelda was always Lupita's favorite, which was why she was given special assignments like chasing Francisco DuPree. Both women were keenly aware of Lupita's preferences, of their silent competition for her favor, and of their mutual disdain for one another.

"The Society of Black Time Travellers would like special permission to observe the assassination of Abraham Lincoln," said Allison.

"Remind me who that is," said Lupita.

"The sixteenth president of the United States."

"Yes, yes, I remember. That event is a protected zone. They know this, yes?"

"They do, Your Honor," said Allison.

"And I will not tolerate the collection of relics," said Lupita sternly. "We will not have a repeat of that business with King George's head."

"They know, Your Honor. The Society is typically very respectful. Can I tell them they have your permission?"

"So ordered. Now to Francisco DuPree. Trooper Clairing, report."

Zelda stood even though it seemed like Allison Rosey wanted to say more. Zelda nodded at her competitor and smiled.

"Yes, thank you, Trooper Rosey, for that thrilling report," said Zelda.

Allison bit her lip and sat down. Zelda turned to face Lupita and drew in a deep breath. Even after all her years of service to Lupita, Zelda still felt nervous, reverent, and mildly fearful in her presence.

"Francisco Pierre DuPree is no longer with us," she announced.

"Hear, hear," said Trooper Williams. The other troopers joined him in applauding her.

"What of the diamond?" asked Lupita.

"The diamond escaped," said Zelda. "It appears that DuPree was employed to steal the Sanguine Diamond and use it as leverage for an unknown deal with a layman."

"Employed by whom?"

"Evidently by the criminal traveller called Thurmond."

From the corners of her eyes, Zelda could see the other troopers exchange quick glances. She knew how it must sound, discussing Thurmond during a meeting of court. They probably all thought Thurmond was a myth, just as she had before she chased DuPree deep into Twenty. She wondered what Lupita must think of this development. She held a glimmer of hope that perhaps Lupita's love for her might lend itself to believe in the ominous reality of Thurmond. She looked for signs that might confirm her hopes in Lupita's expression, but her face gave nothing away.

"Be seated," was all the centurion said. Zelda obeyed.

CHAPTER 14: THE COURT OF THE NINETEENTH

The rest of the court session flew by with Zelda paying only minimal attention. The seven other troopers reported the mischief in their parts of the century and Lupita delivered curt orders or admonishments here and there. Finally Lupita rose from her throne and the troopers followed.

"Steward, please adjourn," she ordered.

"Fellow travellers," shouted the steward. "The Court of the Nineteenth Century now stands adjourned."

"Trooper Clairing," said Lupita. "Please walk with me."

Zelda solemnly joined Lupita as the other troopers shuffled out of the throne room, glancing at her over their shoulders. Together they strolled down the centurion's private colonnade with the ocean to their left.

"This Thurmond business disturbs me," said Lupita. "I am not in any mood to be tricked."

"You believe Thurmond is a hoax, Your Honor?" asked Zelda.

"I have believed that since I first heard of the man."

"May I ask why, Your Honor?"

"Perhaps I simply do not want to believe such a fiend might travel among us," replied the centurion. "Nevertheless, I want to tell you something. There is to be a conference in Twenty-One regarding this man Thurmond. Akande the Gallant has asked that I join him and Solomon Christie to assess this danger. I want you to represent me, Zelda."

"You will not go yourself, Your Honor?"

"Goodness no. I will give neither Akande, nor Solomon, nor Thurmond the honor of my presence."

Lupita stopped and stared out over the ocean. Only the crashing of the waves below broke the silence between them.

"I have been thinking," she said. "In light of these events, perhaps we should revisit activating the Machine."

Zelda sighed, as she usually did when Lupita's thoughts turned to the Machine. "The Machine is a waste of Your Honor's time. When we last sought it out, we found it still didn't work. Even if it did work, it isn't proper."

"Perhaps not. But these are dark times. The time may come when the Machine is necessary."

Lupita turned her gaze from the ocean and leaned in close to Zelda. "Know this, Zelda," she whispered. "This man, if he exists, he is not a problem for Nineteen. This is a civilized century. We have control over our travellers, Francisco DuPree notwithstanding. This fellow is a product of Twenty. He is a product of Solomon, the immature little brat-king. You will investigate this conference and report back to me on its findings, but you will make it clear to Twenty and Twenty-One that Nineteen will not be drawn into their mess."

"I understand, Your Honor."

"So ordered," said Lupita Calderon, and she continued on through the colonnade.

15

THE CONFERENCE

BINDRA FELT A LITTLE SORRY for the crew on the airplane. When they landed they would certainly panic over the fact that one of the passengers on their manifest never made it.

She was following the detailed instructions of Sean Logan, a trooper of the Twenty-First, sent to her by courier along with a cell phone. When her plane reached a specific point over the Pacific Ocean, she was to travel to December 1, 2010. Sean instructed her to make the jump even though she would not feel the presence of an anchor point. Bindra did not care for that. She did not understand how she could expect to arrive anywhere without feeling the draw of an anchor point. Logically she would either end up in the middle of the Pacific Ocean or in the middle of open space—in the year 2010, but that would be of little consolation. Sean seemed to understand she would have these reservations, and in his instructions he assured her many times that the snapback effect would kick in, and she would arrive at the right place at the right time.

Sean's instructions said he had timed out her flight and scheduled a message to the cell phone for the exact moment when she needed to jump. The phone presented a few challenges. Since she was on a plane in the year

115

1980, she had to keep it hidden in order to avoid awkward questions. She also did not completely understand how the device worked, having been born in a century when cellular phones were primarily found in museums. Perhaps this was why she didn't realize the volume of the phone's ringer was turned all the way up.

When the message did arrive, the rhythmic beeping from Bindra's pocket was impossible not to hear. Heads all up and down the plane perked up in her direction as she fumbled to pull the device out and get it to stop making that noise. She looked up and saw the stewardess staring at her, confused and a little horrified. Bindra, too, was a little horrified. *This is it*, she thought. *This is how you end up the subject of internet rumors and conspiracy documentaries.* But there was nothing she could do now. It was time to leave.

"I'm really sorry," she said, before vanishing.

The stewardess fainted. The pilots heard the screams from the cockpit. The police reports were interesting, to say the least.

Bindra, thankfully, did not end up in the middle of the ocean. Instead, when she materialized, she found herself in a white room that reminded her somewhat of a hotel lobby without a receptionist. Everything seemed very clean and welcoming, in particular the giant sign in front of her that said, "Welcome!" In smaller letters the sign said, "You are a prized guest of His Honor Akande the Gallant, Twenty-First Centurion! Make yourself at home!"

She felt a brief rush of air and a mild change in pressure, the signs that another traveller had arrived. She turned and saw a woman, older by a few years, with creamy pale skin and dark red braided hair. The newly arrived traveller spied Bindra up and down with interrogative blue eyes and a scowl. Then she met Bindra's eye line.

"Hi," she snapped.

A noise came from the hallway outside the welcome room. Bindra and the new traveller looked to see a third person enter, a bearded, tired young man carrying what looked like a white dishrag.

CHAPTER 15: THE CONFERENCE

"I'm sorry, I'm sorry," he said as he entered. "That was my fault."

"What's your fault?" asked Bindra.

As she said the words, she felt a pop and release inside her nose. Blood came rushing down her lips.

"That," said the bearded man. "That's my fault. I should've thought about the pressure change."

He put the dishrag to Bindra's face and she took hold of it, keeping it pressed against her nose.

"Anyway," said the man. "Welcome to Twenty-One. My name is Sean Logan, I'm a trooper of the Twenty-First. You must be Zelda Clairing from Nineteen."

Sean shook the hand of the woman behind Bindra.

"And Bindra Dhar from Twenty," said Sean, taking Bindra's hand. "If it's okay with you two, I think we should get going to the throne room so we can, you know, get it over with."

Sean left the welcome room and Bindra and Zelda followed him into the hallway.

"Where are we?" Bindra heard Zelda ask.

"This is the *Alarinkiri*," said Sean. "This is the home and century seat of Akande the Gallant."

"It's a ship?" asked Zelda.

"Yes," said Sean. "He likes to call it his 'ship of mysteries.' Feel free to make fun of the name, we all do."

"How is that possible?" said Zelda. "How do you make a moving object into an anchor point?"

"That's one of the mysteries," said Sean. "There's a rumor that Akande got a scientist in Twenty-Five to build him a machine that recreates the effects of the natural anchor points and he keeps it hidden somewhere on the ship."

"Is that true?" asked Zelda.

"Telling you would ruin the mystery," said Sean.

"What did you mean when you said we had to 'get it over with?'" asked Bindra.

"Akande is under the impression that this'll be a conference between centurions," said Sean.

"And you did not tell him that our centurions refused to attend," said Zelda.

"No I did not," said Sean. "Because then there would be no conference."

"Isn't Akande going to be mad when he finds out?" asked Bindra.

"Very mad," said Sean. "So let's get it over with."

They arrived at a set of tall, wooden double doors. Sean shoved the doors open and revealed to them the grand throne room of the Twenty-First Century. The three troopers walked down a warmly lit corridor toward the throne itself. The floor beneath them was one long, red carpet. On either side of the corridor hung giant tapestries depicting the major events of the century, and intermittently they walked past bronze statues of Akande the Gallant.

Akande himself stood waiting with his right hand on the back of his throne, dressed in a gleaming white suit and vest and his official red centurion's sash. As his guests approached, Akande smiled wide, clapped his hands together and walked in front of his throne to greet them.

"Welcome, my wonderful guests, welcome!" he said, opening his arms wide. "My food shall be your food, my cup shall be your cup, my century shall be your century! Together I am certain we can confront the troubles that worry us—"

The centurion's expression turned from gracious to puzzled to annoyed as the faces of his guests came close enough to study.

"Where the hell are Sol and Lupita?" he demanded after a moment's pause.

CHAPTER 15: THE CONFERENCE

Sean stepped aside and looked to Bindra and Zelda to explain themselves. Bindra stepped up and delivered a short bow.

"Your Honor," she said. "My name is Bindra Dhar, trooper of the Twentieth. I've come to represent His Honor, Solomon Christie, the Twentieth Centurion, in Your Honor's court."

"And what reason does Solomon Christie have for not travelling here himself? Too drunk?"

"Does Your Honor want an honest answer?"

Akande rolled his eyes and then cocked his head toward Sean. "Honesty would be a nice change of pace. Wouldn't you agree, Sean?"

"His Honor Solomon said he did not want to be lectured," said Bindra. "Neither by Your Honor nor by Her Honor Lupita Calderon."

"Ha!" said Akande. "What am I, his schoolmaster? And you, what is your excuse?"

Bindra retreated and Zelda took her place. The trooper of the Nineteenth gave a swift bow and spoke.

"My name is Zelda Clairing, trooper of the Nineteenth. Her Honor Lupita Calderon sends her regards, but she did not believe her presence at this conference was necessary."

"In that case, I suppose neither is mine," said Akande. "Carry on as you wish. Stop Thurmond, don't stop Thurmond, oh, make Thurmond the Twenty-First Centurion for all I care. My ship is yours, but I will not be insulted like this. You ladies can express my displeasure to your rulers, I trust? And Sean, my friend, if you come up with another delightful way to embarrass me, keep it to yourself, won't you?"

The spurned centurion turned to leave, but Sean interrupted him. "Your Honor?"

Akande stopped and stared at his friend.

"Manners?" Sean reminded his centurion.

Akande sighed and rolled his eyes.

"It is good to meet a fellow traveller," he said to the two women.

"To make the road less lonely," they replied in unison.

Akande the Gallant looked once more, flaring his eyes and biting his lip as if to contain all his anger. Then he left, slamming the door of the throne room behind him.

Sean looked to Zelda and Bindra. "That went about as well as it could have."

He turned and walked to Akande's throne with Zelda and Bindra following.

"You couldn't possibly have thought our centurions would lend their prestige to this conversation," said Zelda. "And you can't blame us for your presumptions."

"Exactly," offered Bindra.

Zelda turned and again appraised Bindra up and down with narrowed eyes. "That's funny. I don't remember asking for your opinion."

Sean leaned against the throne. "I'm sure you agree, at least, that Thurmond is definitely real?"

"How are you so sure of that?" shot Zelda.

"Why else would you be here?"

"I am here because my centurion sent me to represent her," said Zelda. "And to deliver a message. Thurmond could be the most dangerous time traveller who ever existed. Or he could be a figment of some very active imaginations. Either way, he is none of Nineteen's concern. Nor should it be any of your concern, Trooper Logan."

"How do you figure that?"

"Because," said Zelda, gesturing at Bindra. "It's her problem."

"Me?" said Bindra.

"Thurmond, if he's even real, befriended a diamond thief in Nineteen and talked to an old woman in Twenty-One," said Zelda. "But he murdered a man in Twenty. He's been most active in Twenty, hasn't he? And is that any surprise? Your man-child centurion has allowed lawlessness to fester and now he is reaping the rewards."

"Thurmond is real," said Bindra. "He's real, he has a plan and it's a plan that apparently involves killing me, so I'd appreciate a change of attitude from you, Trooper."

"A change of attitude?" said Zelda. "Allow me to express my sympathy, but time travel is a messy business. And if Thurmond does manage to kill you, that'll be two dead from Twenty and none from Nineteen. We take care of our own. It's not our fault if Solomon can't take care of his."

"Thurmond is real," said Sean. "I believe he's real, anyway, and I believe that whatever his plan is, it clearly involves Nineteen, Twenty and Twenty-One. Which means we need all three hundred years on the same page."

"On the same page?" said Zelda. "Do you see any centurions standing here? You can't even get three hundred years on the same boat. And I know all about you, Trooper Logan. As far as I can tell, the only reason you haven't been expelled from the Guild is because your best friend happens to be Akande the Gallant."

"What are you talking about?" said Bindra.

"Nothing," said Sean.

"Nothing?" said Zelda. "Is that what they call interference these days?"

Bindra looked at Sean with her mouth agape, holding it like that for a few moments too long before closing it. He must have seen her shock anyway because his face turned red, and when he met her eyes, he looked away in shame. The idea of a trooper committing interference—the highest of time traveller crimes, save for murdering another time traveller—was unthinkable. Many of the deeds the Guild considered crimes were disregarded and mocked by even the most upright of time travellers, even people like Mr. Brooks. But interference was a different story. Changing the past to make one's life better was the height of selfish time travelling. It was abhorrent to cause unpredictable ripples in time, to put untold lives at risk, for one's own benefit.

Finally, after a long silence between the three troopers, Sean spoke up. "Maybe I was naïve for thinking this would work. You two are welcome to stay, if you would like, or if you'd rather you can go back to Lupita and Solomon and tell them the conference has failed, we'll keep ourselves to our own centuries."

Sean stepped away from Akande's throne and started to leave. Zelda shrugged and started for the door. Bindra twisted her head, watching the two troopers go their separate ways, and Sol's voice flashed through her head.

If you feel as though you must confront Thurmond directly, would you consider confronting him with others by your side?

"Zelda," called Bindra. "Just wait."

Zelda and Sean paused. Zelda folded her arms and cocked her head to the side. "Yes, Trooper?"

"Don't you want to know what Francisco DuPree was doing in 1946 before you killed him?" said Bindra.

Zelda kept her arms folded and stared into the distance above Bindra's head, softly clicking her tongue in her open mouth.

"Ummm," said Zelda, before returning Bindra's gaze and shaking her head. "No, not really."

"I'm sorry?" said Bindra.

"I never really care what someone is doing before I kill them, save for the fact that they did something that got them killed," said Zelda. "Nice try, though."

"Trooper Clairing," said Sean. "Trooper Dhar is my guest and I want to hear what she has to say."

Zelda threw her hands in the air. "Fine. Let's hear it, then."

"Solomon investigated the license plate number of the man DuPree talked to in 1946," said Bindra. "His name is Nathan Hocking. The future president and CEO of Continental Railways."

"Thurmond wants to buy a railroad?" said Zelda.

"It's the train crash," said Sean, and the two other troopers looked to him. "The laywoman in 2005. She said that Thurmond told her he would stop a train crash in 1984. The *Appalachia Arrow* crash. She said he would save her husband."

"Save everyone," said Zelda quietly. Her eyes snapped up when she realized Sean and Bindra were staring at her. "Something DuPree said before his fall. He said Thurmond would 'save everyone.'"

"Randall said something like that too," offered Bindra.

"But it wasn't the train crash," said Zelda. "At least that's not what I thought he meant. I thought he was talking about us."

"What do you mean?" said Sean.

"Ah, I don't know," said Zelda, annoyed. "I just didn't think he was talking about saving laymen. DuPree said something about 'no more centurions, no more troopers, no more Guild.' I felt like it meant he was going to save all of the time travellers."

"From what?" asked Sean.

"Who knows?" shot Zelda. "It was the ramblings of a crazy person. How is anyone supposed to stop a train crash anyway? Especially after running his mouth to everyone about what he plans to do?"

"He's a ripple," said Bindra. "Thurmond is, anyway, or at least that's what he told Randall."

"A ripple?" asked Sean. "That's like a…" He twirled his hand in the air trying to remember time travel mythology.

"They're people who are born because of time traveller interference," said Bindra. "Supposedly."

Sean put his hand on his forehead and nodded. "Right, right. So because they're ripples in time then, what, physics don't apply to them?"

"Supposedly," said Bindra.

"Wonderful," said Zelda. "He's a time traveller, a psychopath, and he thinks he's magic." She shook her head laughing and began a dramatic march from the throne room. "You two can sort out all that nonsense," she said as she left. "But until you can show me something that proves any of this, the Nineteenth Century will stay in the past, thank you very much."

16

THE BLINDFOLD WALLY

HENRY ZOLLER stood frozen atop a boulder in the middle of the creek bed, right where the mysterious girl had stood and argued with the old man, right on the spot where they had both disappeared into thin air. It had all happened just a few seconds earlier. He stood waiting—waiting for them to come back, waiting to wake up from whatever strange and vivid dream he was having, waiting to realize he had hallucinated the whole thing and was probably going crazy. The cool of the night air wrapped around him, and he listened to the sounds of the crickets in the grass. It wasn't a dream; he was certain of that. He was really there, in the ravine next to the ruins of the abandoned tennis court. And he didn't think he was hallucinating. After all, he never had before, so why should he start now? So he tried to think of other explanations. Perhaps the two people had just run away in the darkness and he didn't see where they went. Maybe they were aliens, or angels.

More than anything, Henry Zoller felt overwhelmed with joy. The stress and monotony of teenage life, compounded by near-constant familial disappointment, melted away with the knowledge that here, in this spot, in his neighborhood, he'd found mystery in the world. He started to take notice of things he had previously ignored on his twilight walks. The smell of the night air, the dancing of the bats across the moonlit sky. And in particular, he noticed the fireflies. He had never truly appreciated them before. They swirled around the tennis court, though it was still mostly concrete without much foliage. They seemed, for whatever reason, to innately like this place. And so did Henry Zoller.

For the next few years, Henry made constant pilgrimages to the bridge, the ravine and the tennis court ruins. It became his place of celebration and his place of refuge. He took a girl he was dating there at midnight to see the fireflies. He spent hours there sitting and thinking on his eighteenth birthday when he came home to find his mother already asleep after a couple bottles of wine. When it came time for him to leave for college, he made sure to go and say goodbye, and rejoiced in the fact that the tennis court continued to deteriorate, that the bridge and concrete path were still cracked and broken, that the whole place remained so much of an eyesore that no one ever passed him by and he could enjoy the fireflies in peace.

Henry reveled in his first year at college. He was free from just about everything that troubled him as a teenager—the relentless immaturity of his peers, the droning of his teachers, the pressurizing tests and projects, and, though he still loved her deeply, his mother. But when his freshman year ended and it came time for him to return home to Jackson Park for the summer, he looked forward to returning to the spot in the woods, his place of mystery and discovery.

Henry Zoller was not one for emotionality, but it was still indescribably painful to arrive at the end of the broken concrete path and find that the tennis court ruins had been dug right out of the ground. The bridge had been demolished and the ravine and creek bed were choked up with concrete rubble. A temporary sign was posted nearby.

CHAPTER 16: THE BLINDFOLD WALLY

Future Home of James W. Robinson Park
By Order of the Fairfax County Park Authority

Devastated, Henry waited for nightfall. It came, eventually, but the fireflies did not.

●●●

Three years later, on almost the exact same spot where Henry Zoller waited for the fireflies to appear, Sean Logan looked out over an empty park and said, "I can't believe it's gone."

Like Henry Zoller, the trooper was shocked that the spot in the woods near the neighborhood of Jackson Park had so drastically changed. He, of course, was not waxing nostalgic for the ruins of an old tennis court. But the mineral deposit beneath that tennis court that made the anchor point an anchor point was itself missing. That was not supposed to happen.

"Maybe it was an accident," offered Bindra. She stared at a wooden sign in the amber glow of the setting sun.

James W. Robinson Park, Est. 2003
Fairfax County Park Authority

"Maybe the laymen destroyed it when they built the park," she said.

"That's not possible," said Sean. "Laymen build on top of anchor points all the time. It doesn't make a difference so long as they don't disturb the bedrock. Only a geological event could destroy an anchor point so totally. At least by accident."

"Maybe in the construction they dug the rock out of the ground."

"It doesn't happen," said Sean. "We have ways of making sure it doesn't happen."

They had left the *Alarinkiri* weeks ago searching for someone Sean knew and trusted, an old time traveller who could give them information on the obscure train crash that seemed to hold Thurmond's interest. He finally replied to Sean's messages in the red books with a request to meet in Fairfax City, Virginia, in 2003.

"There's supposed to be some sort of flood in June of '03," explained Sean. "He doesn't want to be pulled away from his work."

Together, Sean and Bindra made their way across the United States and back in time, daisy chaining between anchor points from the West Coast to northern Virginia and from 2010 to 2003. They conserved their health and energy by jumping only a few years at a time, from one anchor point to the next. Jackson Park in 2006 was the last anchor point on the way to Fairfax City in 2003. But somehow, it was missing.

"We have to steal a car," said Bindra. Stealing from laymen is, of course, discouraged among time travellers, but it is usually forgiven when necessary. And in this case, it was necessary. "We'll just drive to Fairfax City, find the anchor point there and get to 2003."

"Can you drive?" asked Sean.

"No."

"They don't have cars in Twenty-Two?"

"Not ones you're expected to drive yourself," said Bindra. "What about you? Can't you drive?"

"Sort of…" He looked back out on the empty James W. Robinson Park. "This is Thurmond's doing."

"How do you know that?"

"Because this is insane," he exclaimed. "Deliberately destroying an anchor point is a crime against time travel itself."

"You don't know that's what happened," said Bindra, though she secretly agreed with him. "We have a job to do."

"This is part of it. Stopping Thurmond. We need to find out how this happened. Besides, it's on our way. Now, take my hands."

CHAPTER 16: THE BLINDFOLD WALLY

"Are you crazy?" said Bindra. "We can't just jump without an anchor point. We could end up in China, or space!"

"Relax. You did it when you jumped onto the *Alarinkiri*."

"I knew when I was going," said Bindra. "We don't even know when the anchor point was last here."

"Sure we do," he said, pointing at the sign. "Established 2003."

"We have to be more specific than that."

"Exactly. Which is why you're going to take us."

"What?"

"Don't worry. American travellers do this sort of maneuver all the time," said Sean. "We call it a Blindfold Wally. It's how you get to an anchor point that existed in the past but doesn't anymore. Instead of focusing on the moment, focus on the anchor point, and you'll snapback to the moment when the anchor point was still here. Usually. I'm surprised Walter Brooks never taught you this."

"Why would he?"

"Because he invented it. That's why it's called a Blindfold Wally. It's perfectly safe, I promise."

"Why don't you take us?" said Bindra.

"Because I'm not very good at the Blindfold Wally, and I don't want to kill us."

"You said it was safe."

"It's not. It's really, really dangerous," said Sean. "But I believe in you."

"Why?"

"Because you've been to this anchor point before when you met Randall in 1999. And, from what I hear, you've practiced much more dangerous forms of time travel than this."

Sean reached into his jacket pocket and Bindra wondered how many people Sol had told about her tug-of-war sessions. Was he warning everyone like a paranoid parent?

Sean pulled out two small notebooks, one black and one red. He handed both to Bindra.

"What are these?" she asked.

"In case we get separated. I have that one," he said, pointing to the red book, "from when it was new. Anything I write in my red book will appear in yours. You have the black book from when it was new. Anything you write in there—"

"I get it."

"Much more reliable than cell phones, trust me. Now take my hands."

Reluctantly, Bindra took his hands, much as she'd taken Lumen's on the Schuylkill River. She sensed the same electricity from Sean's hands as she had from Lumen's, but it felt different. Where Lumen's hands buzzed with firecracker energy, Sean's felt more subdued. Perhaps it was because he was older, a more practiced time traveller, his temperament more relaxed compared to the spirituous ambition that sparked between Lumen and Bindra whenever they travelled together. Or maybe it was simply that Bindra didn't feel for Sean what she felt for Lumen.

"Bindra," said Sean quietly, his eyes closed.

"Yes," she replied.

"We've been standing here for a while now."

"I am working on it."

"Okay," said Sean. "It's just, any minute now—"

"Do you want to do this?"

"No."

"Okay, so hush."

Instead of focusing on the moment, focus on the place.

It was almost the exact opposite of the instructions Mr. Brooks had once given her. In common, run-of-the-mill, everyday time travel, the moment was all that mattered. Which made sense—it was time travel, after all. The whole point of the anchor points was that a time traveller didn't have to think about place at all. Just keep your mind tethered to the mineral energy under the ground, focus on the moment when you want to go, and you should be fine, in theory. But now she had to focus on the place.

How hard could it be? She'd been here before. She knew what this place felt like. She knew what all anchor points felt like. None of them really felt that much different from each other. What was so special about this one? The trees? The sounds? The seclusion? She searched for that part of her mind that let her time travel. Come on, she said to it. We've done this before. Just take me to the last time this place was still an anchor point.

"How do I find the moment for this place?"

"Uh, Bindra," said Sean.

"Hush," she said. "I'm not talking to you."

"Are you talking to…yourself?"

"You have your methods. I have mine."

She returned to her mind.

"Sorry about him."

We're really not supposed to be doing this.

Long ago, the voice in her mind which guided her travelling had annoyingly taken on Mr. Brooks's American accent. There seemed to be no way of fixing it now, and she had tried.

"I know. But there has to be a way."

We need a moment. We can't just go to a place. You're a time traveller, not a teleporter.

"I know, I know. But there must still be a moment."

Yes, a moment, Bindra. Not a year. Not a number. Stop looking for a number. When will you learn?

"Fine, then show me a moment."

You show me the moment. That's how this works. Give me the moment you want to go to, and I'll give you the place.

"I can't give you a moment, I've only been here once before."

Yes, that's good. Tell me what was happening when you came here last.

"What does that mean?"

You know what it means. You've been to this anchor point before. You've been to all kinds of anchor points. What happens there? What do you feel? What do you see?

"I feel…energy. Tingling. Buzzing. A little noise in my ear sometimes."

What else?

"Animals seem different. Friendlier. Birds especially."

What else?

"Fireflies."

"Bindra?" said Sean. "Who are you talking to?"

"Shut up," she snapped. "It's the fireflies."

"What?"

"That's when we want to go," she said. "Take us to the last time the fireflies came here."

Knew you'd get it eventually.

The trip was rockier than usual, in that Bindra literally hit her head on a rock. As she tumbled down the rocks, she worked out what went wrong. Whoever destroyed the anchor point had left some pieces behind, debris scattered around the area. Most of this rubble must've disappeared by the time Bindra and Sean arrived, but once upon a time each piece was still an active, miniature anchor point. Bindra arrived atop a big chunk of it on the side of a steep ravine and started tumbling down into the creek bed below. As she fell, she was aware of two immediate challenges. The first was that it was night and pitch black in the woods. The second was that Sean wasn't with her.

She landed on the rocks of the creek bed with her face looking up to the night sky. It was a clear night, and before she lost consciousness, her astronomy skills kicked in. The planets and stars were in the right place for 2003.

"Well at least I got that right," she said before the world went black.

17

THE LAYMAN'S DUE

IN HER ADDLED STATE, Bindra imagined she was being carried through the woods by Lumen.

"Lumen?" she mumbled airily. "Lumen, guess what. I just did a Blindfold Wally and it worked… I hit my head on a rock, but it's 2003, so it worked… I am the greatest traveller who ever lived… I am invincible…"

"What?" said a voice above her. "Listen, just hold on. I can't get a cell signal down here. When we get to the road I'll call an ambulance."

It was not Lumen's voice. Time travellers do not call ambulances. She was being carried by a layman.

"No, no," she said. "No ambulance."

"Are you joking?" said the voice. "You just hit your head on a rock. After appearing out of nowhere."

"Just, just take me somewhere. I just need to rest."

"Look, I don't know what's going on. But you need to see a doctor."

"I'll explain," she mumbled. "But I can't see a doctor."

Not one in this decade, anyway. She remembered chapter 4 of *The Elements of Time Travel*, How to Avoid Bloodletting (And Other Medical Perils).

She wasn't sure if the voice that carried her would follow her instructions, but it didn't speak again. Through half-closed eyelids she saw the tree branches above give way to streetlamps and sky beyond. Mild bursts of lightning illuminated rolling clouds. The air was humid and electric. A storm was coming.

Whoever carried her didn't stop to call an ambulance, which was a good sign. Hanging in the man's arms, she saw the tops of houses and basketball hoops pass by until she crossed beneath a doorway. Warm yellow lights came on. She was gently placed onto a soft surface, and her vision grew softer as well. She was slipping back into hazy darkness, but at least now she was inside and she felt certain she was somewhere safe. And that, she noted before falling out of it completely, meant she had a new obligation: the layman's due.

Bindra slept for a little while, maybe an hour, by her own estimation. When she woke up, she found herself on a soft couch. She twisted her head to examine the room. American history had not been taught in her girlhood school, but she'd seen American movies from that time and recognized some of the items around her: incandescent lamps, a television, an electric vacuum in the corner. Heavy rain pounded the roof above her. She felt dizzy enough to vomit but did her best to hold it in. She heard frantic steps walking toward her and turned over to see who was coming.

"Oh my God, are you okay?"

It was the voice that had carried her out of the woods, only now it had a face. It was a boy, or young man, near to Bindra's age but white, with sandy hair and brown eyes. To say he looked worried would be an understatement. His hair was mussed up from where he'd been pulling at it while Bindra slept.

"I'm..." started Bindra. "I think I'm okay. Do you have green tea?"

She felt like her exhaustion had less to do with her fall and more to do with the dangerous time travel maneuver she'd just performed—a maneuver she worried Sean may not have survived. Fergus Reed had given her green tea the last time she'd almost collapsed with time travel exhaustion.

"Green tea?" asked the young man. "Are you serious right now?"

"It helps. I'll explain, I promise."

The young man rolled his eyes in a universal sign of acquiescence.

"I think my mom has some in the kitchen," he said, walking away.

"Is your mother here?" she asked.

"No," he shouted from the kitchen. "She's probably clubbing downtown. She'll be back after sunrise."

Bindra heard a series of strange beeps and noises from the kitchen. The young man came back with a cup of steaming liquid, which he handed to her and she gratefully drank. It sort of tasted like green tea, but it was a bit weak and oddly cool. Then she remembered: Americans hate tea and don't know how to make it.

"This is great," she lied. "Thank you."

The young man kept his arms folded and shook his head at an ever-increasing rate. "This can't be happening. This just absolutely can't be happening."

"Look, I know this doesn't make a lot of sense, but I appreciate everything you've done for me—"

"This is crazy!" he said. "It's you!"

"I'm sorry?"

"Four years ago!" he shouted. "You…you…you were there! In the woods! It was you! You talked to that old guy and then he fell over and then you just…you just poofed! You disappeared!"

Uh-oh, thought Bindra.

"And then you showed up again tonight!" he continued. "I just…I can't…what the hell is happening?"

There was no helping it now. "My name is Bindra Dhar, and I am a time traveller," she blurted. She had never had to explain herself to a layman before, and so she copied Mr. Brooks's first words to her.

It's a common misconception that telling the laymen about time travel is illegal. A time traveller is forbidden from making a concerted effort to reveal him or herself to a large group of laymen—you can't go to CNN or a Hearst newspaper or something and announce it to the world, for example (for a more thorough explanation, please consult *Time Travellers' Revised Code 08.41.41*). That's why events like the Time Traveler Convention are off-limits. But there is, in fact, nothing in the *Revised Code* that forbids outing oneself to a layperson. Keeping a secret that big would be highly impractical, and of course, time travellers must reveal themselves on occasion in order to teach certain laymen the Knowledge and thus create new time travellers. Besides, there's no real need to keep the existence of time travellers a secret from the laymen, as they typically disregard obvious evidence of time travel as nonsense or coincidence. They routinely ignore books about the profession that sit in their public libraries. When they see travellers on the street dressed in odd clothing from the past or the future, they are content to dismiss such people as insane.

"You're a time traveller," said the young man. "Of course you're a time traveller."

He slowly collapsed on the floor, in the space between Bindra's couch and the coffee table. He leaned his head back, let out a deep breath and seemed to be searching the ceiling for something that wasn't there.

"I know this must be very confusing for you," said Bindra. "And probably difficult to believe."

"It's..." began the boy quietly. "It's a little much."

He kept staring distantly at nothing, and Bindra wasn't sure what would happen next. Revealing yourself to a layman was always a toss-up. Twenty-One wasn't one of the centuries with witch-hunts, right? Not in the United States anyway, she was pretty certain.

"Are you okay?" he said suddenly. "You fell a long way and you seem a little dazed."

"I'm fine. Thank you for taking me in. What is your name, by the way?"

"Henry Zoller. And you said…what did you say your name was again?"

"Bindra Dhar."

"Bindra," he repeated. "That's a really pretty name."

"No it's not," said Bindra.

"Why do you say that?"

"It's not really a name. A first name, anyway. It was my mother's family name, but she wanted to honor my grandparents so she insisted that I be named Bindra. I got made fun of a lot in school—the girl with two surnames."

"I think it's cool," said Henry. "Like Harrison Ford."

"Who?"

"Never mind," he said quickly. "So, are you from the future or the past?"

"I'm from the Twenty-Second Century."

"Really? What's it like then?"

"About the same. But with different music."

"So, do you have, like, a time machine somewhere?"

She laughed as much as the pain would allow. "No. Time machines don't exist."

"But time travel does?"

"Of course it does," she said. "You can travel without a machine, can't you?"

He smiled. "I guess so. So you just decide a time you want to go to and you go?"

"Something like that."

"Can you go back in time or forward in time?"

"Both."

"Are you the only one there is?"

"Not at all," she said. "There are…well. I don't even know how many of us there are. Anyone can time travel; you just have to learn."

Bindra adjusted herself and slowly sat up on the couch. Bites of pain shot from wildly unexpected places all over her body.

"Every time traveller starts as a layman," she continued.

"What's a layman?"

"It's what you are. It's a person who doesn't know how to time travel. Which reminds me, I have to explain something to you that's a little complicated."

"More complicated than this?"

Bindra took a deep breath. "Time travellers..." she started. "We have a lot of traditions. One of them is something called the layman's due. It means that when a layman, like you, helps a time traveller, like me, we are obligated to do that layman a favor. We actually think it might've been how the legends about genies got started."

"Are you trying to tell me I get three wishes?" he said, only half-serious.

"No," said Bindra, firmly. "I can't grant any wishes. And I can't change the past for you, so don't even ask me. But if you'd like, I can show you things. Things that have happened, or things that will happen. I will warn you that you may not want me to show you what happens to you in the future. Sometimes it's best not to know. Trust me. But there are still a lot of experiences only we can have, and I'm obligated to share them with you, if you so wish. I owe you the layman's due."

Bindra knew, of course, that the layman's due does not appear in any section of the *Time Travellers' Revised Code*. Travellers are routinely saved by laymen and feel obligated to do nothing for them in return. But Mr. Brooks had always taught her that should she ever be indebted to a layman, paying the layman's due was right and proper.

She tried to read Henry Zoller's reaction to what she told him. He was staring again into nothingness, thinking with a slight, disbelieving, gentle smile. Everything about him seemed gentle. His mere presence felt comforting. His voice had no edge, no detectable meanness to it at all.

"This is a tough decision," he said finally. "I mean, you probably know best."

"Me?"

"Of course. You're the time traveller here. You tell me, what's the best thing to go back and see? Did you ever go hang out with Marilyn Monroe and JFK?"

"Ha," she said. "No, unfortunately."

"Really? Huh. What about...what about Hitler? Everyone wants to go back in time and kill Hitler."

"Oh, I know they do," she said, nodding. "It's actually a huge problem."

"What about movies? Did you ever go back to 1977 and watch the premiere of *Star Wars*?"

She gave an embarrassed smile and a painful shrug. "Nope. Sorry."

"What?" His faux-offended face made her laugh. "Are you messing with me right now?"

"Nope."

"You're telling me that you are a time traveller and you have never gone back to 1977 to watch the premiere of *Star Wars*?"

"I have never actually seen *Star Wars*," she admitted. "My grandfather tried to show it to me once, but old movies always make me fall asleep."

"I gotta say, Bindra, you are really disappointing me as a time traveller right now."

She laughed. He laughed with her.

"Well, would you like to do that then?" she said. "Not now, unfortunately. I still have some things to take care of. But tomorrow night for you—who knows when for me—I'll come take you to 1977, and we'll go to the movies together."

"Wow, a date with a time traveller. It's tough to pass that up." Then he shook his head. "But no. I don't want that."

"I'm sorry?"

"I don't want to go back in time with you," he said. "I want you to teach me."

Her face fell slightly. He must have noticed.

"I mean, I know I just met you," he said. "And this is all insane, and, you know, probably not real. But when a person tells you they're a time traveller, what else are you gonna say?"

He was right, of course. She knew nothing about Mr. Brooks when she asked him to teach her the Knowledge. How could any sane person pass up such an opportunity? But she knew becoming the instructor for a new time traveller was serious business. Mr. Brooks once called it a "sacred duty," though, to be fair, Americans often describe things in such grandiose terms. But she knew this wasn't one of his exaggerations. The bond between a traveller and her instructor was iron. Travellers gushed about their instructors, they boasted about the accomplishments of those they had once instructed, and they shunned instructors who failed their apprentices. "One should not half-bake a time traveller," as Mr. Brooks liked to say.

Bindra Dhar was not ready to be an instructor. She knew an instructor had to be patient, kind, dedicated, and not distracted with hunting and being hunted by a pseudonymous criminal mastermind. She knew herself to be equal parts underdeveloped and reckless. In short, she had no time to instruct a new time traveller. And yet, he was owed a layman's due.

"That might be a little harder to do," she said. "Instructing a new time traveller is very complicated. And I—I'm not sure how to explain this—let's just say I have a lot on my plate right now, and a long way to travel."

He nodded. "It's okay. But maybe one day, if you ever get the chance—and, of course, if this isn't an amazing dream—I sure would like to learn."

"Not one day," she said, smiling. "Tomorrow night. I'll be here tomorrow night, and if I am able, I'd be happy to be your instructor. And if I am unable, then we'll go see *Star Wars* in 1977. Do we have a deal?"

He smiled back at her. "It's a date. Are you feeling better, by the way? Can you time travel again?"

"I think I'm okay," she said, reaching into her back pocket, searching for the notebooks Sean had given her. "But I don't think I can travel just yet."

"Why not? Is something wrong?"

"It's fine. Sometimes, after we travel so many years, we get tired and we need a while to rest. If you walked ten miles, you'd need to rest. It's the same with time travellers and years. Do you have a pen?"

Henry stood up to fetch one, and she pulled the little black notebook from her pocket. She had to remind herself it was the one she was supposed to write in to communicate with Sean—outgoing calls, she thought. The problem was the red book—the one for incoming calls—was missing. She realized it must have fallen out while she was rolling down the rocks. That was a problem. On the one hand, travellers are expected to avoid recklessly leaving artifacts from the future in the past (*Time Travellers' Revised Code 02.34.13*). But a mere notebook probably wouldn't cause too much trouble. On the other, much more important hand, she had no way of receiving messages from Sean, if he was still alive.

Henry returned with a pen. He handed it to her and looked down at the black book. "What's that?"

"It's how we communicate with one another. Phones don't exactly work across time. We are, however, very active on the internet. What's your address, Henry?"

"305 Pickering," he said.

She wrote in the first page of the notebook: *Sean—survived the jump. With a layman. Cannot travel yet. Am at 305 Pickering Street, Jackson Park, 10:51 PM, June 17, 2003. Really, really, REALLY hope you're still alive. —Bindra.*

As Bindra finished her last letters, someone knocked at Henry's front door. Henry and Bindra looked at each other and he went to answer it. Bindra stood up for the first time, got over some brief dizziness and limped into the hallway after him. She watched as he unlocked the front door, which then flew open. Sean Logan seized Henry by the arm and shoulder and flipped him onto his back in the middle of the hallway. Henry gave out a brief, pained shout.

"Sean, wait!" said Bindra.

Sean looked up at her. "Did he hurt you?" he demanded.

"No no, not at all," she said. "He saved me."

"Oh," said Sean. He looked down at Henry. "Sorry about that."

"S'okay," gasped Henry. Sean freed him and he rolled over and staggered to his feet.

"Are you okay?" Bindra asked Sean.

"Yeah, yeah, I'm fine. I landed on some rocks out there at the anchor point two weeks ago."

"Two weeks ago?" said Bindra. "What have you been doing since then?"

"Made my way to D.C., hid out at one of the safe houses there. Finally found a car I understand, so we are good to go."

"Now?" she said, taking a quick glance at Henry. Sean nodded vigorously.

"Yeah now. We're supposed to be in Fairfax City," he glanced at his watch, "two hours ago."

"Okay," said Bindra. "Okay, let me just say goodbye."

"Oh," said Sean. "Of course. Thanks, um…"

"Henry," said Henry.

"Thanks, Henry, for helping Bindra. I'm sorry for the, you know, for that."

"Don't worry about it," said Henry.

Sean turned and started to walk for the door, but he quickly returned to Henry's side, carefully thinking about his words.

"By the way, we're time travellers," he said, gesturing between Bindra and himself.

"I know," said Henry.

"Okay, good," said Sean. "Wasn't sure if that was made clear."

Sean left Bindra and Henry alone.

"Thank you for everything, Henry Zoller," said Bindra.

"Thank you, Bindra Dhar," said Henry. "For everything."

"I really don't know how I can repay you."

Henry shrugged. "Maybe I'll see you tomorrow night."

Bindra smiled. "I hope so. I cannot say how old I'll be tomorrow night, but I hope so."

"Me too."

Henry offered her his hand. Bindra ignored it and kissed him on the cheek.

18

INTERFERENCE

THE MODERN VEHICLE seemed to give Sean a lot of trouble. He swerved and skidded at times, struggling to pierce through the fierce wind and rain. Luckily, it was deep into the night, and no one was on the roads. With Bindra in the passenger seat, Sean sped through the winding forest roads of northern Virginia, away from Jackson Park and toward Fairfax City.

"Something very bad is happening this year," he told Bindra while he drove through the storm.

"What did you find out about the anchor point?" she asked eagerly. "How did it get destroyed?"

"None of the time travellers around here seem to know. Or at least they don't want to talk about it."

He explained how he came down hard on a patch of rocks two weeks before Bindra arrived. He surmised, as she had, that the anchor point had been scattered into rubble, but most of it was definitely gone and not simply destroyed.

"What do you mean?" she asked.

"It's been taken."

"Taken?" said Bindra. "You mean stolen?"

"That's what it looks like." ·

The resident time travellers who visited the discreet safe house on Capitol Hill gave Sean few answers as to who would've destroyed or stolen an anchor point. Some advised him to stop asking questions about it. Others advised him not to stay too long in 2003 but to simply "pass on through." Nobody was sticking around here too long.

"It's like everybody got a memo and we didn't," he said. "Like everyone knows the Twenty/Twenty-One border is a bad place to be right now. Everyone's scared."

Slowly, Sean became more comfortable with the car. He loosened his grip on the wheel. Both he and Bindra relaxed a little bit, though not for a lack of concern about the events taking place around them. They simply had no more evidence to discuss and there was no sense in worrying about something if they couldn't needle their way through it any further.

"The kid back there," said Sean, breaking the silence. "You said he saved you?"

"Yeah, he saw me fall. I don't know why the jump took so much out of me; it was only three years."

"Well, three years carrying me. And without an anchor point. Most people can't do that. I mean, honestly, I was pretty sure you were gonna kill us both."

Sean smirked at her.

"Have you ever had a layman save you?" she asked him.

"Myself? No. But it happens. Did you tell him about the layman's due and all that nonsense?"

"Yeah, I told him," said Bindra.

"You don't have to do it. It's just a dumb tradition."

"I know, I know. It's what's right, though. But he wants me to teach him."

146

"What do you mean?" said Sean. "He wants you to teach him the Knowledge?"

"I don't know that I can. I've never taught anyone anything before and I still don't know…anything, really. About time travel or anything else."

"You know plenty," said Sean. "You're a trooper, after all."

"Of the Twentieth."

"Being a trooper of the Twentieth is nothing to be ashamed of."

Bindra frowned sideways at him.

"Okay, so it's something to be a little ashamed of, but it's not that bad," said Sean. "Most laymen, if you tell them what you can do, they always want what you can't give them. Fix this, fix that, make someone love me, make me rich. It's like they think time travel is only good for interference."

Sean's mention of the word returned the car to silence. Bindra had tried, with a lot of success, to put Zelda's revelation of Sean's crime out of her mind. But now she'd been reminded that the person next to her, the person driving her to Fairfax City, the person she'd come to somewhat admire and trust, had once been convicted and sentenced by the Guild for interfering with spacetime. In her mind, she tried to rationalize what it was Sean might have done. Perhaps whatever it was he tried to change about the past was minor. Maybe he had a good reason. Like a really good reason. A totally non-selfish, good person reason for committing the highest of time traveller crimes. But whenever she thought this way, she heard Mr. Brooks's voice advising her, "The only way to know for sure is to ask him." Now was a perfectly good time.

"Can I ask what you did?" said Bindra.

Perhaps not the most tactful way to introduce this topic to the car.

"What now?" he said.

"I'm sorry," said Bindra. "It's just, I've been thinking about…on the ship, what Trooper Clairing said…she's incredibly unfriendly."

"She certainly has a way about her."

"Anyway," said Bindra. "What she said about you almost being expelled because you interfered. I just wanted to ask if it was true or if she was just being…what do Americans say? An asshole?"

Sean laughed but kept his eyes far ahead on the road. "She wasn't being an asshole. She was telling the truth. I interfered and came close to being expelled."

"But you weren't," said Bindra. "Obviously."

"No, but there was punishment. We'll leave it at that."

"What did you do?"

"It's a long story."

"I'm sorry, it's just…" started Bindra. "It's just hard to believe you would do such a thing."

Sean rolled his eyes and shook his head. "It's not that simple. It's not just 'such a thing.' What do you know about interference?"

"Just what Mr. Brooks taught me. That it's selfish, always selfish. And one should never travel out of selfishness."

"Yeah, that's fair," said Sean.

Silence returned to the car. A bright blue sign materialized out of the rain: *5 miles to Fairfax City*. The sign also noted the onramp for Interstate 66 was approaching. Abruptly, Sean swerved the car to the right and sped up the ramp onto the highway. He kept speeding for about a mile, passing only a couple of other cars on the road in the night before stopping at the shoulder of the highway. The rain snapped at the windshield, and Sean leaned on the steering wheel staring straight ahead.

"It happens about a mile up that way," he said, nodding down the dark interstate. "A few years from now, there will be an ice storm, and thirteen cars will slide into each other on this highway and seven people will die, and I know that it's gonna happen just like that because I made sure it happens just like that."

Sean looked at Bindra.

CHAPTER 18: INTERFERENCE

"When Akande assigned me to it, the case seemed simple. The first car has to slide, the second car brakes in time but the truck behind him can't and it slips over. The next few cars slide, another car flips. Seven people have to die. It's an event that has to happen. But there was this guy—a new traveller, it seemed like. He was a little shaky with his jumps. I think what it was is he had someone important to him who died in the crash and he did everything, I mean, this guy tried absolutely everything to stop it from happening. He tried over and over and over again. Reliving the day, day after day. I was there waiting for him every single time, I stopped him every single time. It was insane. He was so determined. He must've known he couldn't beat me. He must've known I'd always be there to stop him, but he kept trying. It took him twenty days to reach his limit. On the twentieth day, I stopped him for the last time and the pileup happened just as it was supposed to—slide, brake, slip, flip, crash.

"On the twenty-first day, I showed up, but he wasn't there. There was nothing left to do but let the crash happen. But after twenty days of watching all those people die, over and over again, I just couldn't leave without giving it a try. Maybe I lost it a little bit. It's certainly possible. Living the same day for too long can really make you…anyway. There was one thing the guy never tried, so I thought, why not? And so I stole a state highway maintenance truck and tried to shut down the highway for the hour when the crash happens."

"Did it work?" said Bindra.

"Of course it didn't work," said Sean. "The troopers were waiting for me. The Guild sent some guys from Twenty-Three—I guess they didn't trust the other Twenty-First troopers to arrest one of their own. Akande intervened on my behalf, like Zelda said. I got an easy sentence. Well, easier.

"But my point, Bindra, is that it's not as easy as saying that interference is selfish. No disrespect to Walter Brooks, but what he taught you, what the Guild teaches you, is that time travel is about knowledge only.

It's about learning from the past, or the future, but not trying to change either one. But to me, that's what's selfish. We gather knowledge, but really we hoard it. We may share it between ourselves, like Walter and his books. But we don't use it for good. We don't use it for evil, or at least we're not supposed to, and I'm fine with that. But we don't use it for good either. We have power that no one else has to help people, to save lives, and we deliberately refuse to use it. I spent twenty-one days learning every angle of that crash, learning how each one of those people died, and I did nothing to help them. How is that not selfish?"

He sighed and stared back out into the storm.

"I don't know what Thurmond wants. I can't imagine it's anything good," said Sean. "But I'm not surprised that people would agree with him."

"Are you saying you might be one of those people?"

Sean started the car again. The headlights shot through the storm and lit up the individual raindrops.

"I'm saying that's why he scares me," said Sean.

He slowly pulled the car back onto the highway and drove to the nearest exit to Fairfax City.

"Coincidentally," he said as they turned onto the exit. "That pileup is when I first met Mr. Disaster."

19

MR. DISASTER

DISASTERS AND MASS TRAGEDIES are natural magnets for time travellers. The sinking of the *Titanic* is an obvious example, and the primary reason why 1912 is the most widely cited example of an overcrowded year. But no time traveller has visited, studied, autopsied, and explained more tragedies through spacetime than Mr. Disaster. His nickname eventually became so common that his real name has been totally lost to most time travellers. And his scholarly investigations of disaster are not limited to the major, household names. It's not all earthquakes and hurricanes and plane crashes for Mr. Disaster. He will devote just as much attention and analysis to car accidents and sudden sinkholes. It is said that as long as more than one person died unexpectedly, Mr. Disaster will be there.

When Bindra and Sean arrived at Fairfax City, the northwest corner of the town was lit up with red and white lights. Ahead of them on Old Lee Highway, the police had blocked off the road.

"We are definitely too late," said Sean.

He turned the car into a suburban neighborhood and parked it next to the sidewalk. They abandoned the car there, and Bindra followed him between the houses. The red lights silhouetted the rooftops, but there were no sirens. The streets were all still in the early morning darkness. A dog barked from one of the backyards, and helicopter blades beat rhythmically in the distance. The rain was still steady but no longer so harsh and unforgiving.

Sean and Bindra came to the top of a slight hill, stopped by a chain link fence. There, Sean stopped to take a breath.

"You feel that?" he asked.

"Yeah."

She'd been feeling the anchor point even as they drove down Interstate 66 approaching Fairfax. *It must be enormous*, she thought, *spread out beneath the entire city.*

Through the fence, Bindra could see the scene they had been driving to all night. Across the highway was a square, brick building, about five stories high. Bindra could see, however, that it had once had six stories. The entire building had apparently sunk into the ground and was sagging curiously at one of the corners. Fire trucks and ambulances surrounded it, each one flashing brilliant red lights through the storm.

"That's why he's here," said Sean. "The floodwater washed out the drainage tunnels beneath the city, and there was a weak point beneath that building. The whole tunnel collapsed and the building came down with it. Three people dead, I think? But anyway, that's where Mr. Disaster is. Or was, anyway."

Sean turned to Bindra. "Can you travel?"

"I don't think so. Not yet. Can you?"

"I think so," he said. "It's just a few hours, right?"

Sean and Bindra joined hands, and Bindra was blinded by the returning daylight. Her eyes adjusted and she looked back across the highway. The collapsed building was at its rightful height with all of its windows above the ground. The sun was just starting to set behind it. Bindra heard a rumbling behind her and looked to see dark clouds billowing in the east, roped with lightning and coming ever closer.

"Come on," said Sean. "He's this way."

•••

In a neighborhood not too far away, a green van pulled along a cul-de-sac and parked there. The man called Mr. Disaster left the van and gathered up everything he had brought with him. He looked out across the neighborhood and spied two houses: one pastel yellow, the other pastel blue. Between those two houses, he knew, was the way in.

Squat, round, and bristled with a white beard, the man called Mr. Disaster had made a career and a science out of studying how and why things went wrong, as only a time traveller could. In every catastrophe he observed, he was able to learn the point at which everything fell apart and the point at which everything could have been fixed if only the right people had paid attention to the right signs. Right here, in this neighborhood, he knew what the local teenagers knew: that between those two houses was something the kids called the "gates of hell." In reality it was a gated entrance to an intricate series of tunnels beneath the city, meant for heat venting and electrical conduits. Mr. Disaster knew that since the late 1970s, teenagers had gone down into those tunnels to smoke weed or screw around. Mr. Disaster also knew that by the late 1990s, the local kids had stopped going down there because they realized something the adults didn't: the structural integrity of the tunnels had been compromised. When a severe summer storm flooded the city in June of 2003, the tunnels would collapse and take a building with them, killing three people. Mr. Disaster planned to observe it all from every angle.

The man called Mr. Disaster trudged through the lawn between the two houses toward a small hillside overgrown with tall grass.

153

"It's good to meet a fellow traveller," said a voice nearby. Mr. Disaster pushed through the brush and saw the concrete "gates of hell," rusted and cracking in the tall grass. On one side of the entrance was a young woman he didn't recognize. On the other side was an old friend.

"To make the road less lonely," said Mr. Disaster. "I didn't think you'd make it, Sean. Who is this?"

"We almost didn't," said Sean Logan. "This is Bindra Dhar, trooper of the Twentieth."

"Twentieth?" said Mr. Disaster, frowning.

"Don't worry, sir, she's not trespassing," said Sean. "We have an agreement. It's a shining moment for intercentury diplomacy."

"Uh-huh," said Mr. Disaster. He shook Bindra's hand and smiled. "Well, I suppose you're here for a tragedy, Sean?"

"That's right, sir."

Mr. Disaster nodded to the gates of hell. "Come on in."

Beyond the gates of hell, three of the underground tunnels converged in a central chamber where Mr. Disaster had secretly established his base of operations for observing the building collapse that night. Weak orange lights barely illuminated the tunnels. The old man darted around the chamber switching on several of his own portable industrial lights while Bindra and Sean looked through the papers, maps, blueprints and newspaper articles, all chronicling the impending building collapse, scattered around a card table left in the middle of the room. Every scrap of paper was colored with notes and highlighter marks.

"What is it you want to talk about, Sean?" said Mr. Disaster.

"A train wreck. Something called the *Appalachia Arrow*."

"Ah, yes," said Mr. Disaster, his voice echoing off the chamber walls. "February 23, 1984, Continental Railways Train Number 202, the *Appalachia Arrow*, derails at Rosbys Rock, West Virginia. Seventy-two dead, hundreds wounded."

"Have you studied it?" asked Sean.

"Indeed," said Mr. Disaster. "I've watched it happen many a time."

"So what happens?"

"What happens?" repeated Mr. Disaster. He pulled a metal folding chair from the wall and sat down at his card table. "What happens, what happens, what happens. What happens is what always happens. The thing you learn doing this job is that disaster always follows the same pattern. Like anything else, it's bound to the laws of physics and chemistry and just a little bit of unpredictable human nature, but even that follows a pattern. And there's always a point of no return, and it's usually a point no one notices."

The old man started sifting and shuffling through the maps and blueprints littering his card table until he pulled out a brown, accordion-style folder. From the front of the folder he whisked out a thick packet of papers held together with brass rings.

"What's that?" said Sean.

"That is the NTSB report on the *Appalachia Arrow*," said Mr. Disaster. "Written by Shaw and Kim, two of the best disaster investigators the US government ever produced. Personal heroes of mine."

Bindra picked up the report and flipped through its pages. They were full of maps, diagrams, and black-and-white photos of destroyed train cars lying in a forest, each of them labeled with curly, inviting letters—"Site A," "Site B," "Site C," "POD—Point of Derailment," and so on. More of the photos showed the inside of the wreck, with twisted metal and crumpled walls. One photo of the overturned control compartment included the grotesque sight of the engineer's dangling body stuck between his crushed seat and the dashboard.

"Shaw and Kim liked to work separately," continued Mr. Disaster. "They always liked to come up with competing theories of a catastrophe. Kim's *Appalachia Arrow* theory revolved around something called harmonic vibrations."

"Harmonic vibrations?" said Sean. "What are those?"

"Dramatic weight differences between railcars can sometimes cause these tiny vibrations," said Mr. Disaster. "If the vibrations build up on each other, they start shaking a train like waves on the ocean and eventually push the wheels off the tracks. The effect is especially dangerous around curves like the one at Rosbys Rock. Amtrak had the same problem with their SDP40F locomotive in the '70s, and since the Continental Railways DMX90 locomotive was really just a knockoff—"

"Um," said Sean. "Maybe we don't need all the details."

"Right," said Mr. Disaster. "Of course. What was I saying?"

"Harmonic vibrations," said Bindra.

"Yes," said Mr. Disaster. "The problem was Kim couldn't account for the necessary weight differences to produce harmonic vibrations on the *Appalachia Arrow.* But by that time it didn't matter."

"Why not?" said Sean.

"Because of Shaw's theory. Shaw found out Continental Railways had reports that one of their engineers—the same engineer on the *Appalachia Arrow*—was drinking on the job, but they never removed him. Shaw's theory had a simple poetry to it, which is why Kim agreed: the engineer was drunk and crashed the train."

"That's all it took?" said Sean.

"Oh, most definitely," said Mr. Disaster. "That's all it ever takes. A speed reduction of just fifteen miles per hour would've brought Number 202 around Rosbys Rock just fine, but if the man was drunk at the dynamic brake he easily could have pushed the train too fast, hit the curve too hard and thrown the whole thing into the valley."

"Was there ever any question of interference?" said Sean.

"You mean travellers?" Mr. Disaster pondered this a moment and shrugged. "There were rumors. There are always rumors, you know, in our community, whenever there's a disaster, that time travellers caused it somehow. Some of the survivors did say they were pulled from the wreckage by people who were never identified among the other survivors, but there was a lot of confusion and commotion, and not necessarily a reason to think our people are there meddling. I believe Shaw and Kim's verdict. The engineer was drunk at the time and hit the curve too fast."

The orange tunnel lights flickered several times, interrupting them. Bindra could feel the faint rumble of thunder above them.

"The storm is getting worse," said Mr. Disaster. "It won't be long now."

He stood up and gathered some of his maps, twirling them into scrolls and putting them under his arm.

"If you don't mind, I have to get ready," he announced, disappearing into the darkness of another tunnel. His voice echoed back to them: "You're welcome to join for the main event, but it won't be pretty."

Sean and Bindra remained in the chamber and closed in for a whispered meeting.

"If it's just a drunk engineer, that's not too complicated at all," said Bindra. "If Thurmond wants to stop the crash, all he has to do is keep the engineer off the train. Kill him or just delay him."

Sean shook his head. "Even if he manages to keep him off the train, too much could still go wrong. Or right, I guess."

"Still, we have something we can use," said Bindra. "I'll get a message to Sol, and he can send troopers to 1984 and make sure the engineer gets on the train."

"We'll do that. But not yet."

There was another rumble of thunder far above ground. Bindra looked to her right and saw water leaking from between the bricks in the tunnel walls. The rain was soaking the ground, its weight straining the tunnels. Sean stared down the tunnel where Mr. Disaster disappeared. "I'm going after him. You stay here."

"Why?"

"Because," said Sean. "Something's not right."

"What's not right?" Sean pointed at the thick *Appalachia Arrow* disaster report still clutched in Bindra's hands. "He didn't even have to look for it. It was right at the top."

So Bindra remained in the chamber and Sean disappeared into the darkness.

•••

The man called Mr. Disaster walked slowly through the flickering orange light of the tunnel, approaching the roaring noise at the end of the line. He came out to a short concrete balcony overlooking a storm drain. Angry torrents of water rushed from one opening of the drain to another, but Mr. Disaster knew that for all the water's rage, it was not the reason the drain's ceiling would soon collapse, dropping the apartment building right in front of him. Up above he could see streams of water leaking from the ceiling, a testament to how degraded the brick tunnel was after decades of neglect. *This is where it happens. This is where it all could have been stopped if someone had just given a damn.*

"Mr. Disaster?" said a voice behind him. He looked and saw Sean emerge from the tunnel onto the overlook.

"Sean, my boy," he said. "Where's our friend?"

"She stayed behind. And I think maybe we should go back too. It's getting pretty bad."

"So it is," he said, returning to his observations.

"I wanted to ask you," said Sean. "You've been in this year a while. You must've noticed what happened to the anchor point in Jackson Park."

"Yes, yes. Quite an inconvenience."

"Not just an inconvenience. It's a very serious crime. Have you heard anything about who might be responsible?"

"Well, I thought that would've been obvious," said Mr. Disaster. "Thurmond."

Sean stared at the old man. "You know about Thurmond?"

"Everybody knows about Thurmond."

"Why would he do such a thing? Why would anyone destroy an anchor point? Why here, why now?"

"I have no idea," said Mr. Disaster. "I suppose it has something to do with the plan. Everyone likes to talk about Thurmond's plan, but few actually know what it is."

A chunk of brick dropped from the ceiling and crashed into the water.

"Do you know why I do this, Sean?" said Mr. Disaster. He left his maps on the ground and walked to the edge of the balcony. "Why I study disasters like this? I suppose I started out like most time travellers. I wanted to know the truth of things. I wanted to know the exact truth of how and why bad things happen. After all, only we can know the real truth of things. Memories betray the laymen, but we always know the truth.

"But here's the real truth of it, Sean—I study disaster so I can stop it. That's always been the goal, even when I didn't admit it to myself."

Sean watched as the old man edged closer to the rushing water, staring all the while at the ceiling.

"Listen, why don't you come back over here and we'll talk about this up top," said Sean, reaching out for his friend. He was ignored.

"I want to know, Sean," said Mr. Disaster. "I always want to know the point at which everything went wrong. I want to know so I can reverse it. I want to save them, those people in the building up there who are about to die. I want to save everyone. Even though they say it's wrong, even though they made it illegal, I've waited so long for someone who would lead us on the true path."

When he turned around at the edge of the balcony, his eyes were wild.

"Interference is the only way, Sean. The Knowledge is a gift. Time travel is a gift. We can't squander it anymore."

"I understand," said Sean. "I understand, I know what you're talking about, and I feel the same way. But why don't you come back up with me and we'll figure all this out?"

"Are you going to arrest your old friend, Sean? Haul me in to the commissioners?"

"We don't have to do that. You can take me to Thurmond, and I can sort it out with him."

"You don't need to do that," said Mr. Disaster. "I've played my part."

"What?"

"I told him how to stop it." A smile crawled across his face. "I told him how to save everyone."

Behind the old man, bricks and chunks of concrete started raining down at an alarming pace. Mr. Disaster lifted his arms and leaned his head back in joy.

"It's time!" he announced.

"Step back from the edge," shouted Sean. "We can figure this out! Come back here—"

Cracks and snaps echoed off the walls of the storm drain. Wind and dust swept into Sean's face as the ceiling collapsed. Sean fell back into the tunnel and watched Mr. Disaster disappear as a building fell on top of him. As the old man vanished, his final words echoed through the tunnel.

"Praise Thur—"

• • •

It was minutes before the collapse when Bindra started to feel something wasn't right. Her stomach felt uneasy and her heart picked up its pace. She felt the familiar buzzing in her ears and the prickling along her skin she'd come to associate with the presence of an anchor point. These tunnels must have been cut alongside the giant anchor point under the city. But the feeling was different than usual. It felt as if the anchor point itself was trying to warn her about something. Something dangerous.

She felt her senses telling her that whatever the dangerous thing was, it was in the tunnel to her right, not the tunnel they had followed into the chamber from the surface and not the one down which Sean and Mr. Disaster had disappeared. She peered down this tunnel, but the weak orange lights didn't allow her to see anything beyond a couple of meters.

"Hello?" she said into the tunnel. She got no response. Her eyes adjusted to the darkness more and she saw there was nothing but tunnel. But still, the feeling persisted. The dangerous thing wasn't there, her senses told her. But it would be.

From the other tunnel she heard shouting. The words were indistinct, but it sounded like Sean. She turned around and returned to the chamber.

"Sean!" she called down the other tunnel.

She didn't hear a reply, but she also didn't listen carefully for one. She was distracted by a feeling, a very real and physical feeling, of the air moving ever so slightly. The pressure had changed suddenly in the tunnel where the dangerous thing was supposed to be. She walked back through the chamber and approached the dark opening of the tunnel. The orange lights were of no help. The tunnel was dark. But she knew he was there.

"Thurmond?" she asked the darkness.

"Bindra Dhar," the darkness replied.

White-blue light cut through the blackness of the tunnel. Bindra yelped, not at the light, but at the severe and painful force that knocked into her chest and stole her breath. The noise was so sharp in the tunnel, and the ringing in her ears disoriented her as Thurmond shot her three more times. She collapsed against the card table in the middle of the chamber and felt the air pressure change again. He was gone. Her head felt heavy and rolled to the side. She heard shouting and rumbling from the other tunnel and felt the wind from the building collapse rush into the chamber. She lost feeling in her hands and feet, and as more and more blood left her body, she closed her eyes.

20

THE WAYFARING STRANGER

TIME TRAVELLER FUNERALS, like everything else associated with time travel, involve ancient and intricate rituals. The first thing that happens when a time traveller dies is the cremation of their body. This tradition comes from the firm conviction of time travellers never to leave artifacts from one era behind in another, including themselves. For similar reasons, the ashes of a time traveller are always buried in the year of their birth, in part so that no piece of a traveller is left when it's not supposed to be, but also to symbolize the never-ending cycle of life and time.

On June 18, 2003, the time travellers who happened to be staying at a safe house in Clifton, Virginia, received a grave request—to cremate the body of a murdered time traveller. Though they did not know the deceased traveller, and though they knew they would not be paid for their efforts, they dutifully obliged, for that is the nature of the time travelling community.

All day they searched for brush around the lonely farmhouse in the hills, far from any laymen, and though dry wood was difficult to come by after the storm on the night before, they gathered enough for a proper funeral pyre. That evening, the body of the murdered traveller arrived and it was gently laid upon the wood. The pyre was lit, and with his fellow travellers, including Bindra Dhar, looking solemnly on, the body of Sean Logan was consumed by the flames.

• • •

Bindra Dhar felt water dripping onto her forehead. She was lying on the floor with the wind knocked out of her and something heavy on her chest. She opened her eyes slowly and saw the ceiling of the main chamber with rainwater dripping down from in between almost every brick. She tried to push herself off the floor, but as she did, the weighty thing on top of her coughed.

Bindra pulled herself out from under Sean. His eyes were closed and four bloody holes peppered his chest.

"Sean?" she said in a hoarse whisper. "Sean, what happened?"

"Thurmond," he whispered in reply. "Thurmond happened."

"I saw him," said Bindra through a cough. "He was there, in the tunnel."

"He's gone now."

"I don't understand," she said, cradling Sean's head. "You were in the other tunnel."

"I came back," rasped Sean. "I watched you die, and I came back, right in front of you. Pretty good aim if you ask me."

He laughed and coughed up some blood.

"You time travelled?" said Bindra. "You interfered."

"Yeah. Don't tell anyone or else I might be in some real trouble."

He stopped talking as his breathing slowed and he settled his head into Bindra's lap. Blood spilled out of the wounds hidden behind his back, creating a black, expanding pool around them. Bindra held his hands and felt how clammy and cold they were as more blood drained from his body. His face became paler and paler until he smiled weakly at her and finally died.

CHAPTER 20: THE WAYFARING STRANGER

• • •

The residents of Matawan, New Jersey, certainly noticed a sudden influx of strangers on August 9, 1905. Scores of them passed through town, stopping for food or to briefly take in the sights. Many of them spoke with odd accents or languages the townsfolk didn't recognize. Some carried strange devices with them. All were dressed bizarrely, but the women were most scandalously dressed with ankles and shoulders showing in quite inappropriate ways. Among the strangers were a fair number of black men and women—more, indeed, than many of the younger residents of Matawan had ever seen at once. The strange conclave peaked around lunchtime, and by mid-afternoon they had all disappeared. Some townsfolk saw them walking into the woods toward the creek.

In keeping with tradition, the three jars containing Sean Logan's ashes were brought not only to his birth year, but also to his birth home. His funeral was to take place on the Matawan Creek where his ashes would be scattered. While it is typical for laymen to mourn in black, time travellers have long chosen white as the proper mournful attire, and so a hundred of Sean Logan's fellow travellers formed two white-and-cream-colored lines on either side of the Matawan Creek.

Bindra was there, of course, and though she did not weep openly that day, her eyes were in a constant state of welling. Inside her she hid a dreadful and consuming sense of guilt for the fact that Sean had traded his life to Thurmond in exchange for hers.

From her perch between two trees, she saw three very young mourners standing at the creekside, each of them carrying a jar of Sean's ashes. Leading the trio was a spindly young woman with soft brown skin standing with her toes at the water's edge. Behind her was a pale girl with freckles so prominent Bindra could count nearly every one from the other side of the creek. The last mourner was a tall, sandy-haired boy with glasses. All three held their portion of Sean at their stomachs with both hands and waited.

Bindra saw Zelda leaning against a tree on the other side of the creek. Her face was contorted in a determined scowl. Near Zelda stood Akande the Gallant. He wore his red centurion's sash, of course, but his three-piece suit was gone and his white shirt was wrinkled and shabby. He was not crying, but his face looked broken and weary. And not far from Akande, she saw Sol Christie, also wearing a simple white shirt, climb atop a boulder where he would be making remarks as the sovereign of the deceased traveller's native century. Sol had also donned his red sash for the occasion.

"'Tis good to meet a fellow traveller," Sol declared.

A chorus of voices from both sides of the creek replied, "To make the road less lonely."

Sol scanned the line of mourners on the opposite end of the Matawan Creek and squinted in the glistening sunlight.

"We are gathered here today," he continued, "to settle the matter of Sean Joseph Logan. His matter, which has burned to ash, we shall consign to this river in space, which is finite. His memory, which cannot be burned, we shall carry with us as we travel upon the river of time, which has no end. So it was, so it is, so it shall be."

It was the simple prayer every centurion read at every funeral. Everyone knew it, for it had been written centuries earlier (or later) and never changed, except for the language in which it was read. When Sol was finished speaking, those mourners who had been praying raised their heads, ready for the next part of the ceremony. Indeed, the three mourners who carried Sean's ashes briefly stirred, expecting to go on with their part in the funeral. But they stopped when Sol kept speaking. "I want to say one last thing."

Heads on either side of the creek darted in Sol's direction. Bindra saw Akande's face twist into a glare.

CHAPTER 20: THE WAYFARING STRANGER

"I want to say one last thing," repeated Sol. He looked up from his stammering and Bindra felt embarrassed for him. She wanted to tell him to stop and she imagined probably a lot of the mourners wanted to do the same thing, but no one would dare speak over a centurion in his own century. Sol started fumbling around in his pocket. As the faces in the crowd grew more and more confused, he pulled out a piece of paper and unfolded it.

"I want to read you this," said Sol. "This is a message Sean sent me not long ago. This is the message that convinced me to send one of my troopers to help Sean stop the criminal time traveller named Thurmond. As it happened, Sean sacrificed his own life to save that same trooper. I thought it was important to tell you all that, and to read just this one part of Sean's letter to you:

"'We have shackled ourselves to tradition, Your Honor. We have made centuries into possessions instead of homes. We have injected time travel with arbitrary pomp and circumstance, and none of it is necessary except to affirm the pride of the centurions, the troopers, and the Guild. We cling too tightly to the traditions that divide us, and we let slip the traditions that would bind us together. I am speaking not only of our customs, but our laws as well. Including the law that forbids interference.'"

Bindra's stomach felt hard. What reason would Sol have to embarrass Sean at his own funeral, revealing his private views on the most heinous of time traveller crimes, the crime so embodied by the very man who had murdered him?

"'I intend to stop Thurmond,'" Sol continued with Sean's words, "'but not because of interference. I have nothing against a time traveller who wants to change the past. I will not stop Thurmond because of my allegiance to Akande's century, or to your century, because to tell you the truth, I feel no real allegiance to either century. I've never really believed much in centuries. But I do believe in moments. For the laymen, moments can only be experienced once before they become memories, but for us

167

they are real, and tangible. Moments are our landmarks, our mountains and forests, our rivers and lakes. Moments are our sacred lands, and a person can't bulldoze through a moment because it's inconvenient. This is how Thurmond made an enemy out of me, Your Honor. And no breaking of a petty rule or law or custom could have made a bigger enemy out of me.'"

Sol looked up from his paper.

"Sean is far more eloquent than I, I'm afraid," he said. "Which is one reason why I thought he should say some words at his funeral. The other reason is that I want you all to think over his words and his service to this community. He died for a trooper not of his century. He died for a fellow traveller, for all his fellow travellers."

He held up the paper for all to see.

"Perhaps now we know why."

Sol folded up the paper and returned it to his pocket. Then he nodded at the first mourner who carried Sean's ashes. She acknowledged him and waded into the creek. As her feet touched the water, the forest surrounding the rest of the mourners echoed with her angelic, melancholy voice.

> *"I am a poor, wayfaring stranger,*
> *A-traveling through this world of woe.*
> *But there's no sickness, toil, or danger,*
> *In that bright world to which I go..."*

The other two mourners followed her into the water, and as they did, their voices joined with hers. They strode into the center of the creek and lifted their jars into the sky. Then the jars came down and were opened, and each mourner reached into their jar and pulled out a handful of ash, drifting it into the brown water, singing all the while.

"Sometimes I wonder what they'll sing at my funeral," said a voice not far from her ear.

She looked over to see the Clerk standing next to her wearing his white checkered shirt and brown bow tie accompanying his thick glasses and moppish black hair. As always, he carried his brown leather satchel around his shoulder.

"Ghamud dayim," she said to him in a vague, detached huff.

Below them, in the water, the song of the mourners came to an end, each of their jars empty of Sean's ashes. On the other side of the creek, people began to disperse.

"We should go," said the Clerk behind her.

"What about them?" asked Bindra, nodding to the three mourners in the water. They remained motionless with their heads bowed, empty jars still cradled in their arms.

"They won't leave until the ashes have all gone downstream."

Reluctantly, still eyeing the angelic mourners, Bindra followed the Clerk as he climbed back up the embankment into the lush green forest. The other mourners in white fluttered past them but said nothing beside the occasional respectful nod to the Clerk. They walked together, and Bindra expected that before long he would depart and go his own way. She would find the nearest anchor point and return to 1980, perhaps to beg Sol for direction, perhaps to confer with the other troopers about the next move. Maybe she'd find Lumen whenever he'd gone. Maybe she'd go to Henry Zoller and teach him the Knowledge, cap off a brief and volatile time travel career by becoming an instructor. Maybe she'd disappear into time and hope Thurmond never found her. Maybe she'd return to her parents in India and hide. *Hide.* The word sickened her.

None of those things involved the Clerk, but still he did not leave her side. Together they wandered through the woods. Neither one acknowledged the other, and yet they both seemed resigned to each other's presence. When they came to a narrow path between two boulders, the Clerk stepped aside and gestured for Bindra to go ahead of him. When their meandering path brought them to a difficult hill, Bindra took the Clerk's arm and helped him up. Bindra started to believe perhaps they'd go on like that forever, walking alone together. Then, when they came to a thick range of trees, the Clerk gestured ahead.

"It's this way," he muttered.

Bindra watched him walk ahead. She had no idea what "it" was or that they were walking toward something for all that time. The Clerk seemed to examine each of the trees until he found one that looked no different from the others. He stuck his arm into a hole in the tree and Bindra realized he must be expecting a message.

"There's a red book all the way out here?" she asked.

"It's not exactly for public reading."

Bindra came closer as the Clerk fished out a small silver cylinder. He twisted the top of the cylinder and it released a high-pressured hiss. From inside the cylinder the Clerk pulled out a yellowed scroll of parchment. He read it quickly and passed it to Bindra.

"The commissioners are very worried," said the Clerk. "None of this was supposed to happen."

Bindra looked down at the parchment and read.

To Ms. BINDRA DHAR, Trooper of the Twentieth and
THE CLERK OF ADMISSION AND EXPULSION—

IN REFERENCE TO The killing of Mr. SEAN LOGAN, Trooper of the Twenty-First, and the continued threat posed by the criminal time traveller known as THURMOND, and the apparent unpredictability of events surrounding HIM and HIS activities—

OUR INSTRUCTIONS for further action in this matter are located herein—

Do nothing. Await further instructions.

CHAPTER 20: THE WAYFARING STRANGER

SO ORDERED.

Commissioners SUTTON, LEE, and LONG

Bindra crushed the paper and tossed it to the ground.

"Who are these people?" she said to the Clerk. "Sutton, Lee, and Long?"

"They're commissioners."

"The only commissioners?"

"Of course not," he replied. "There are thousands of commissioners. Sutton, Lee, and Long are just the ones assigned to monitor these events."

"And what makes Sutton, Lee, and Long so special? Why do they get to decide it's over, that we're letting Thurmond go?"

The Clerk sighed. "It's difficult to explain. Let's just say the commissioners are the only ones who are allowed to see the whole picture."

"Good for them," said Bindra.

She rarely thought about the commissioners, but when she did, she imagined them, Sutton, Lee, Long, and however many more there were, all old and gray, gathered in a dark room somewhen discussing a fate only they could control.

"Not at all," said the Clerk. "It's actually a horrific burden knowing everything. Not everyone can handle it. Not every commissioner can handle it."

"If they know everything, why don't they just stop Thurmond? Why didn't they stop him from killing Sean?"

"They don't know what's going to happen," said the Clerk. "Only what's supposed to happen. But that's why interference scares them, especially on a scale like what Thurmond has planned. Whenever you change the past, it disrupts spacetime a little bit. Usually spacetime can handle it. Toss a rock into the river and the river doesn't care. Sean changed the past to save you, and I mean no disrespect, Bindra, but whether you lived or died was not a big enough rupture in the fabric of spacetime that spacetime couldn't figure it out. But stopping seventy-two people from dying in a train crash? That's not tossing a rock into a river; that's putting up a dam."

"But if they know everything, why didn't the commissioners see him coming? Why don't they just go back and kill him or arrest him when he's a kid?"

The Clerk just shrugged. "I could lie to you, Bindra, and make the commissioners look good. But the truth is they don't know how he snuck up on them. Lee and Long think they just missed it somehow, but Sutton thinks he could genuinely be a ripple."

"Ripples are myths," Bindra said instinctively.

"Not necessarily. Some would even argue they're a statistical likelihood. And if someone is born as a result of time traveller interference, anything they do in their lifetime would probably not appear within the commissioners' scope of things that are supposed to happen."

The Clerk walked over to her and picked the balled-up parchment off the dirt.

"All this to say, Bindra, the commissioners don't know who he is or what he's going to do next, and they are devastated about Sean. They don't want to put any more travellers at risk, so they're calling you off the hunt. You and Zelda, Sol, Akande and Lupita as well. Everyone involved is expected to back off while the commissioners regroup and try to figure out what to do next."

"And what if they decide the thing to do next is nothing?"

"That's definitely an option. And in that event, we will all carry on and see if spacetime can mend itself."

"That may work for you," said Bindra. "But when Thurmond figures out he didn't actually kill me, how long do you expect I'll be able to carry on and see what happens?"

The Clerk paused and looked into the tree canopy.

"I am here to represent the commissioners and convey their wishes," he said. "Thurmond must face justice. He must be stopped. But it's my job to tell you not to stop him. Have I done that?"

"You have."

"Good," said the Clerk, as he started walking away. As he disappeared through the foliage, he called back to her in a slightly melodic voice.

"But still, he must be stopped…"

21

SOLOMON'S TALE

AS SOON AS SOL CHRISTIE staggered back up off the ground, he felt two powerful hands grab his shoulders and throw him against a tree. Once more on the ground, he saw Akande the Gallant's powerful frame coming toward him.

"This is your fault!" said Akande as he kicked Sol in the chest. "You let Thurmond fester! You did nothing to protect your native! And at his own funeral, you had to make your little speech? When all that's expected of you is to say the words, to respect him! To mourn him! But no!"

Akande started kicking Sol between each of his words.

"Because it always…has…to be…about…you!"

With the last kick, Sol regained enough strength to reach out and grab Akande's leg. Akande fell hard on his back and Sol gathered himself off the ground. As he rose, Sol became aware of the circle of onlookers around them. None of them would dare intervene, unwilling to draw the anger of either centurion. But none could resist the sight of the Twentieth and Twenty-First Centuries doing battle right before their eyes.

"How dare you?" growled Sol. "You are a guest in my century."

"Your century? Yes, most definitely your century. Full of criminals and scoundrels, and now you've let one of them grow into a killer, a menace to us all!"

"You have no way of knowing he came from Twenty," countered Sol.

"Where else?" shouted Akande. "Thurmond lurks in your realm, Solomon Christie, in your years, because he knows he is safe here, safe from civilization, safe from you! Who here can deny it? Who here defends you? Where are your troopers, Sol Christie? What's a king who cannot even command his knights? No king at all. What's a realm under such a king? No realm at all. Your century, indeed, King Sol."

Sol rushed Akande at a speed that surprised the onlookers. In this new clash of centuries, Twenty quickly gained the upper hand. Sol was faster and more maneuverable and despite his muscles and bravado, Akande had never cultivated an enjoyment of single combat, and his bulk was cumbersome in a fight.

The battle between the two kings soon devolved into a messy and unattractive wrestling match in the dirt, yet the other travellers remained transfixed. This group was a mix of residents from both Twenty and Twenty-One, and though both sides found the clash between their leaders embarrassing and juvenile, decorum dictated that they could not interfere in what were, after all, courtly matters.

Akande managed to push and roll Sol off of him and stood back up, readying himself for another attack. Sol stood as well and again rushed at his opponent. But this time, a slim figure darted into the fray. Zelda knelt at Sol's knees and he tripped over her, flipping over her back.

She straightened back up and turned her attention to Akande. The Twenty-First Centurion was momentarily stunned by the sudden defeat of his opponent, but he quickly took advantage of the situation. He approached Sol, who remained flat on his back, gasping for air, but was stopped when Zelda punched him across the face.

CHAPTER 21: SOLOMON'S TALE

Akande stepped back and massaged his jaw. He glared at Zelda and started marching toward her.

"Are you mad?" he shouted. "You have no part in this, Trooper! As the Twenty-First Centurion, I command you—"

Akande's march ended when Zelda twirled gracefully to the ground, sweeping her legs beneath his before effortlessly returning to her feet. He, too, fell onto his back not far from Sol, trying to regain his breath.

"I answer to another century," she said in an airy voice. She looked at the crowd of gawking travellers. "It's been a hard day," she announced. "Emotions are a little high. We all express grief in our own ways, don't we?"

A few of the gawkers nodded.

"All right," sighed Zelda, waving her hand. "Now go the hell away."

The dazed gawkers shuffled away to begin the long hike out of the woods. Zelda turned around and stood over the vanquished kings. She lowered her hand to Akande.

"I am very sorry, Your Honor," she said. "For your loss."

Akande seemed to calm down as he looked up at her, but still he swatted her hand away and pushed himself up. He tried half-heartedly to brush the dirt off himself. Then he looked to Sol and spoke with a softness that was somehow even more jarring than his anger had been.

"Sean deserved a proper funeral," he said to Sol. "That was all you had to do."

With that, Akande began his slow walk out of the forest.

Sol did not stand up but instead pushed himself along the ground until he could sit with his back on the trunk of a tree. Zelda sat next to him, worrying that he might interpret this as a sign of affection, friendship, or tolerance. In reality, she felt exhausted and needed a place to rest. Zelda had, of course, attended a number of funerals and had brought about a number of funerals as well. If she was being honest with herself, and she almost always was, Sean Logan meant next to nothing to her. And yet, her feelings, which she normally kept so effectively in check, were bursting just behind her eyes. It was, she knew, a result of having spurned Sean and Bindra Dhar at the conference aboard the *Alarinkiri*. Clearly neither of them had been prepared to face Thurmond on their own. Sure, she had been ordered to keep her distance from this matter. Sure, Thurmond was a problem for Twenty and Twenty-One, and so it made sense that Bindra and Sean should bear the consequences. Sure, she hadn't liked either one of them. But they were her fellow travellers, and she allowed them to go into battle without a warrior.

All of this she knew as she sat against a tree next to Sol Christie, and so she also knew why she'd broken up the fight between the centurions, and it became annoyingly clear that she owed Sol an explanation.

"Akande was wrong to say what he did," she said to the centurion.

Sol drew a deep breath and swung his head. "I have never had a friend I loved as much as Akande loved Sean. He is in more pain than you can imagine. And, moreover, he may be right."

"What do you mean?"

Sol refused to answer. Instead he let his head fall back against the tree bark and closed his eyes. Zelda watched shadows from the tree canopy dance on his face.

"I was born in London," he said finally. "That's where my father holds court as the Sixteenth Centurion. No one would question that he is a true commander of his century."

Sol opened his eyes and straightened up, turning his attention to the pebbles on the ground and throwing them in random directions.

"'Twas a certainty that I, like my father and my grandfather, would become a centurion. Never a question. I received my training from a number of instructors every day of my childhood. If it was necessary that my father should send troopers to pull me from the Boar's Head so that I could receive lessons for the day, then so be it.

"And so when the day came when I was to complete my test for the commissioners, travelling from one end of a century to the other without stopping, it required almost no effort on my part. I appreciated neither how easy it was for me nor how hard it was for most other travellers. I simply opened the door to my house in 1500 and stepped outside into 1600. My father and family, all my father's friends, troopers, commissioners, other centurions, all standing there cheering. Because I opened a door."

He glanced over at Zelda.

"Not a good lesson for a seventeen-year-old boy to learn," he said with a smirk. "And so suddenly I had a red sash and a whole century to play in. And I'm sure you have heard more than enough about how I've spent my time as centurion. One thing they cannot say about me is that I haven't travelled far and wide in this century. I've seen a great many things in a great many places in a great many years. The one place I never felt any need to visit was London. Not until just before I first met you, Zelda, did I decide I wanted to see what my childhood home had become in this century. I wanted to see all the old landmarks, all the places I used to go, chasing a good time like there was no tomorrow. God knows why. It's likely I was drunk. Do you know what I found when I finally did go?"

Zelda said nothing.

"Fire. Smoke. Rubble," he said. "Fate decided, I suppose, that I would visit London in the year 1940. Strange as it might seem, that really was the first time I…"

He let his words trail off. He met Zelda's eyes and gave her a shamed, painful smile.

"I haven't taken very good care of this century, have I?" he said before looking away.

"You can't think of things that way," she said. "You can't blame yourself for what the laymen do to each other. Non-travellers determine history.

Time travellers only experience it. Centurions aren't totally responsible for everything that happens in their centuries."

"Come now, Zelda. No one actually believes that."

"That doesn't mean it's not true," she lied. "You have no reason to believe any of this is your fault. You have no reason to believe Thurmond is your fault."

"No. But it certainly seems like something that would be my fault."

22

THE INDEPENDENT INTERCENTURY INTERFERENCE TASK FORCE

LATER, as she walked out of the forest, Zelda was determined not to feel sorry for Sol Christie. She found it wasn't difficult in the slightest. She felt no sympathy for Sol Christie, and despite her polite protestations, she agreed with everything he said. He had neglected his solemn duties, and it was more likely than not he was responsible for the unparalleled disaster that was the Twentieth Century.

No, Zelda was not sympathetic. Instead she was furious—furious not with Sol Christie, but with herself. Furious because Solomon Christie, of all travellers, of all people, had found it in himself to give a damn about stopping Thurmond, and somehow she had not. But no, she corrected herself, it wasn't that she didn't care. She cared a great deal. She cared for the reasons Sean had cared, apparently. She cared because interference was not a game or some noble enterprise. Changing the past was always selfish. She knew this in her very soul. And yet, she had been instructed not to care. She had been ordered to let this be somebody else's problem. And that, more than anything else, made her furious.

She was furious that duty mattered more to her than the things that mattered to her.

And perhaps it was the anger that distracted her so completely that she didn't notice the automobile coming up the road behind her as she walked back to town. The car slowed and pulled alongside her and the driver honked the horn twice.

"Trooper Clairing?" said the driver.

She looked and saw the car was operated by a thick-bearded man. In the passenger's seat sat another man with shiny black hair and a thin mustache.

"What do you want?" she said to them.

"Someone needs to talk to you."

"Yeah," said Zelda. "I think I need to talk to someone too."

• • •

As the sky grew dark, the automobile glided to a stop at the door of a secluded white church and Zelda could see a line of people, bags and things slung over their shoulders, snaking around to the other side of the building.

"Who are they?" she asked the bearded driver as they left the vehicle.

"Refugees from Twenty," said the driver. "This is the only anchor point for several miles. They're all getting out before it's too late."

Zelda clenched her teeth and shook her head. The driver and his partner opened the church doors for her and she walked down the pew aisles. Lupita Calderon stood at the altar with Trooper Allison Rosey, reading through a scroll of parchment. Rosey wore a green military coat and a leather belt across her chest bearing the gold seal of the Nineteenth Century. Lupita said something to Rosey in rapid Spanish and the trooper walked off, giving Zelda a curt nod as she left. Lupita turned her attention to Zelda with a maternal smile.

CHAPTER 22: THE INDEPENDENT INTERCENTURY INTERFERENCE TASK FORCE

"Trooper Clairing," said Lupita. "I'm very glad you are safe."

"I see we are to wear the uniforms," said Zelda.

"Yes, I'm afraid it's necessary," said Lupita. "I'll send someone to fetch yours."

"Never worn it before," said Zelda. "Who are these men, Your Honor?"

"This is Oscar Castagnola and Fergus Reed, troopers of the Twentieth."

"These men work for you now?"

"All the troopers of the Twentieth have renounced their allegiance to Solomon," said Lupita. "All except for…who is the young one? Bindra something."

"It isn't proper," said Zelda, "for a century to have more than ten troopers."

"Yes, but this is a time of emergency," said Lupita. She stepped down from the altar and gestured for Reed and Castagnola to leave. Then she approached Zelda. "The people outside are the last ones to make it out of Twenty. I will welcome any refugees who wish to escape Thurmond until midnight tonight. Then we are closing the border with Twenty. No one in, no one out. We shall enact new security protocols, and we shall monitor the anchor points for trespassers."

"You can't possibly guard every single anchor point in Nineteen," said Zelda.

"That is the reason for the additional troopers," said Lupita. "I will take any measure necessary to protect my century and my travellers, even if I must raise an army."

Lupita gently folded her hands over the corner of a pew, drew in a deep breath and gave Zelda a polite smile. "I am afraid the time has come for us to obtain and activate the Machine. I am told by Trooper Rosey that there may be a way to trace its location—"

"You cannot do that, Your Honor," said Zelda. "It isn't right."

Lupita tilted her leathery face. She was unused to such firm disagreement, especially from her most loyal trooper. "Who are you to tell me what is right? What you say is right may not be as easy as you think. The Machine is the only way to keep our century completely safe."

"You would turn Nineteen—our home—into a battlefield?" said Zelda.

"I will protect our home from the battlefield," snapped Lupita. In the darkness, the centurion's eyes almost seemed to glow with rage. "Thanks to Sol Christie, Twenty has become a war zone. Now the violence has spilled into Twenty-One. It shall not come in the other direction. I will not lose any of my people as Akande has."

Zelda had never seen such passion from Lupita when the centurion spoke broadly of all her fellow time travellers, but now the older woman was twirling her hands and nearly bursting with tears. Perhaps, thought Zelda, Lupita had begun to contemplate losing a trooper as special to her as Sean Logan was to Akande the Gallant.

"Your Honor, what has happened..." started Zelda. "What happened to Sean Logan is more horrific than any of us can contemplate. It is the ultimate corruption of our community. But, Your Honor, we are still a community, and the Machine—the way you want to use it—it's a violation of that community—"

"Thurmond is a violation of our community," interrupted Lupita.

"Then we should fight him. We should join in with Sol and Akande and hunt him down. If the time has come for extreme measures, direct those measures at him and his followers, not at your own people."

"I will not put my travellers in danger because of Sol's incompetency and Akande's adventurism," said Lupita. "I told you before you left, Thurmond is a mess of their making, and it is their job to clean him up."

Softly, Lupita approached and placed her hands on Zelda's shoulders. "I know that you are always ready for a fight. But you must back down from this one. You want to take action—that is good. Take action and bring me the Machine. Then help me secure our borders. But, I beg you, Zelda, you must not risk your life to solve problems that are not your own."

Zelda felt a tear roll down her cheek. "Please, Your Honor. I know how deeply you care for me, how you've always cared for me. But you are a good woman. Do not lose yourself because of me. Do not become a tyrant because of me."

Lupita's eyes narrowed and her bony grip on Zelda's shoulders became tighter before she let go altogether. She turned her back and walked to the altar.

"You want me to treat you as if you are not special to me?" said the centurion over her shoulder.

"Yes," said Zelda.

"You want me to treat you as I would treat all of my time travellers?"

"Please, yes."

"Then hear me, Trooper Clairing. You will bring me the Machine. You will return to Nineteen and secure the border. You will hunt down and expel trespassers. You will investigate and snuff out anyone who spreads the message of Thurmond in our century. And you will obey me so long as you owe allegiance to the Nineteenth Century. Do you understand, Trooper Clairing?"

Zelda stared into Lupita's eyes before she gave a slow, fuming nod.

"Good," hissed Lupita before turning back to her papers at the altar.

Zelda stood rigid, yet she already felt her ankles weakening. She already felt what she needed to do. Her ankles bent first, then her knees, and then she was kneeling on the cold church floor. Lupita looked and saw her trooper there on her knees, dressed in white, illuminated by moonlight made multicolor by the stained glass windows. With a quiet, trembling voice, Zelda started to speak.

"I renounce my allegiance to the Nineteenth Century," she said before gasping with tears.

"What are you doing?" snapped Lupita. "Stand up!"

"I renounce my allegiance to its centurion, Lupita Calderon," sobbed Zelda.

"This is nonsense," said Lupita, waving her hand. "Stand up this instant."

"I renounce my position as trooper of the Nineteenth…" said Zelda.

"I command you!"

"I travel on no one's behalf."

Her voice echoed off the church walls, and it seemed to keep ringing in the brass of the organ at the altar. Through blurry, tunneled vision, she saw Lupita's face, horrified, shocked and breathless.

"I am nothing," said Zelda, "but a fellow traveller."

• • •

Bindra Dhar sat at the bar of the Paradox Tavern on May 9, 1980, when she felt as if she wasn't alone. She was surrounded by the trash and discards left behind by the retreating troopers of the Twentieth. The capital, it seemed, had been abandoned. She had waited for Sol to arrive and give her any sort of guidance, but he never came. So then she waited for a good idea to come, and when it didn't, she waited for no reason at all. And then, something in the back of her mind told her a time traveller had joined her.

Cautiously she walked to the door of the back room where Sol used to hold court with his troopers. She lifted her hand to open the door, but instead the door came to meet her with stinging force. She winced and tried to shake the pain out of her hand as Zelda blew into the room.

"All right, Trooper, if we're doing this, we'll have to go over a few things," she announced. "First thing—I want to be very clear about this—I am not your mother, I am not your sister, and I am definitely not your instructor. I am a professional time traveller, and as far as I am concerned, you are still an amateur. Got it?"

"What?"

"Second thing," said Zelda. "We don't take orders from Sol or Akande or Lupita or even the Clerk. I'm officially declaring this here, the two of us, an independent, intercentury, interference task force. Understood?"

"What?"

"What am I talking about?" said Zelda, starting toward Bindra. "I'm talking about doing what nobody in either of our centuries wants to do. I'm talking about stopping Thurmond."

"Oh, well," said Bindra, tossing her arms in the air. "I wish I'd thought of that. It sounds so easy."

"I am aware that it's hard to do the right thing. But it is so goddamn easy to not do the wrong thing. So are you staying here, or are you coming with me?"

"Oh, I'm with you," said Bindra as she approached Zelda with burning anger. "But let me explain some things as well. First, I'm the one Thurmond wants to kill, not you. Second, I'm the one who has actually faced Thurmond, not you. And third, I was the last person Sean ever saw before he died, not you. So I don't want to hear you question my dedication ever again. Understood?"

Zelda looked Bindra up and down before speaking. "If you keep showing me that kind of attitude I might start to find you tolerable."

Zelda rolled onto a stool and reached over the bar for a beer bottle. Bindra sat next to her. "Do you have a plan?"

"Of course I have a plan," said Zelda, opening the bottle. "I'm going to find Thurmond and then I'm going to kill him."

"That's the whole plan?"

"Yes," said Zelda. "It's a two-part plan."

"And how do you expect to find him?"

"Ah," said Zelda, pointing at Bindra. "For that, we have to steal something."

"Steal what?"

Zelda looked sideways and sort of shrugged with her whole body while she brought the bottle up to her smiling lips.

"Oh," she said. "Just a machine."

23

THE TIME MACHINE

ON JUNE 18, 2003, Henry Zoller woke up wondering if everything that happened the night before had been an incredible dream. No evidence was left in his house to indicate a time traveller had been there. In fact, the only new item in his home was his mother, whom he found asleep in her bed. In the living room, he found the empty cup he'd used to make tea for Bindra Dhar. Or had he made tea for himself? It seemed unlikely, but then so too did the alternative.

Around noon, with his mother still asleep, he left the house and walked down the street toward the secluded path to the construction site. The pavement was still soaked from the overnight storm, but the sun was baking the rainwater into steam. As he walked down the concrete path, he became more and more convinced that what he'd experienced the night before had really happened. Bindra Dhar was real, and her existence confirmed for Henry his most cherished memory.

Just as on the night he first saw her, he longed to revisit the place where she had arrived. It was as if her arrival and return had made the construction site a holy place, a portal into a different world just beneath the surface of his own—the world of time travellers. And if Bindra Dhar was true to her word, he would see her again that night, and perhaps she would even take him into that world.

But Henry Zoller could not escape his own self-awareness. There was, as there always had been, the possibility, or maybe even the likelihood, that none of it was real. That it was a hallucination or a delusion, that he was mentally ill, a high-functioning schizophrenic or something like that. Even beyond the fantastic nature of the things he had encountered on this bike path, he still had no physical evidence that time travellers had ever visited him. And that's when he spotted the book.

He'd come to the hillside of rocks and rubble, the remnants of the abandoned tennis court the construction crew had demolished and tossed into the ravine. The rockfall was, for the most part, barren and stark except for a small square of red lodged in between two of the rocks. He climbed the short distance up the hill and plucked the little red book from the rocks. Even before he opened it, he had a feeling the notebook must be something belonging to Bindra. She, like the notebook, stuck out in the stark monotony of his memories.

For whatever reason, he expected the notebook to be empty, but when he opened it, he found a series of handwritten messages in faded ink.

Bindra—Arrived two weeks early (June 2, 2003) but alive. Reply in black book as soon as you read this. Sean.

Bindra—Safe in D.C., June 5, 2003. Hoping you'll arrive on date intended. Please reply ASAP. Sean.

Bindra—Still in D.C., June 10, 2003. I'm safe, but worried about you. Please reply in black book. Trying to pick a movie to rent. Have you ever seen Congo?

Bindra—Congo was okay. Also, are you alive? Pls reply in black book. Now here's the plot of Congo, in a nutshell...

CHAPTER 23: THE TIME MACHINE

So it was real. Bindra, Sean, time travel. It was all real, and now he had the physical proof. In that instant, the red book became Henry Zoller's most cherished possession. It became a promise to him from the universe that his world was not stark and inescapable, that nothing was impossible, that beauty and wonder existed. He would carry the red book with him all through college, through adulthood, through everything. Henry Zoller would carry that red book until the day he died.

•••

Right around midnight on May 10, 1980, the party really took off. Marc Kurtzman couldn't believe how well it was all going. He and his roommate had never thrown a party at their house before, choosing instead to keep a low profile during their brief time as Ohio University students. But recent developments necessitated celebration, and what a celebration it was. Marc's newfound wealth made sure the beer flowed freely and the weed was plentiful. He and his roommate had managed to get the entirety of the marching band to attend the party, and while any loser could get the football team at their party, it took a certain prestige to attract the marching band. And now one of the flute players had challenged one of the clarinet players—the two of them being more than gorgeous women—to a playful wrestling match in which hair-pulling, tickling and other such fouls were not only welcomed but encouraged by the enthusiastic crowd.

Yes, Marc Kurtzman was on top of the world and could not believe his luck. And then he heard the most annoying words a college student—even a fake college student—can hear at a party.

"Cops!" someone shouted. "The cops are here!"

Marc had never seen a room clear out so fast. The two beautiful musicians ceased their scuffle and grabbed their things. He followed the evacuating crowd into the living room where two figures stood just inside the doorway, shouting at everyone who passed them on the way out. One was a dark-skinned woman in a green jacket, about his age, shoving what appeared to be nothing but a foldout wallet into random faces. The other was a taller, older woman with dark, braided red hair, shining a small flashlight in various directions.

"Everybody out!" yelled the red-haired woman. "This is perfectly acceptable police behavior under the Constitution of the United States or something."

"Leave, all of you leave, right now!" shouted the dark-skinned woman. "You're all in violation of so many very real laws!"

"Oh, come on!" said Marc, as he tried in vain to convince the fleeing partygoers that the police officers barking at them weren't actual police officers. When everyone had left and Marc found himself alone in the living room with the two ladies who'd ruined his evening, the young man could do nothing but shake his head.

"Goddamn time travellers," he muttered.

The red-haired woman put her flashlight away while the dark-skinned woman breathed a sigh of relief and pocketed her wallet. The taller woman was the first to speak. "Name, resident century, native century, let's go."

"Excuse me," said the dark-skinned woman. "I have jurisdiction here."

"Fine," said the red-haired woman. "Go ahead."

"Name, resident century, native century, let's go," said the dark-skinned woman.

Marc rolled his eyes. "Marc Kurtzman. Resident century, Twenty. Native century, Twenty-Two."

"Hey!" she said. "Another Twenty-Twoer. Good to meet you!"

She held out her hand, and in his drunken politeness, Marc shook it.

"Anyway, this," she said, gesturing at the taller woman behind her, "is Zelda Clairing, trooper of the Nineteenth."

"Nineteen?" said Marc. "What the hell is she doing here?"

"It's a shining moment for intercentury diplomacy," she said. "And my name is Bindra Dhar, trooper of the Twentieth."

"I know," he answered.

"Excuse me?" said Bindra. "How do you know who I am?"

"Everyone knows about Bindra Dhar and Thurmond," said Marc. "And if this visit has anything to do with Thurmond, I don't want to be involved."

Bindra and Zelda exchanged silent, worried glances.

"What do you know about me and Thurmond?" said Bindra.

Marc leaned against a ratty sofa and folded his arms. "Oh, you know how it is with time traveller rumors. Stories come from one place and go back in time, suddenly little kids are hearing about it back in the Middle Ages or whatever, they grow up and tell their kids the same stories, maybe with some exaggeration—legends pop up kinda suddenly in the community."

"You're saying I'm a legend?" said Bindra.

Marc shrugged. "Well, you know. Some people say you're the only one who could defeat Thurmond. There's a story where you fought him off in a four-hour duel. Some people say you tricked him by letting him kill you and then somehow coming back to life. Some say you beat him by shouting his real name. I'm not sure why that would beat him, but you know how myths are."

"I am not a myth," said Bindra.

"Yeah, well," said Marc. "Neither is Thurmond. But I've got nothing to do with him or any of his people, so if that's what this is about—"

"That's not what this is about," said Bindra.

"Then what is it about?"

"Okay, that's a little bit what it's about—"

"Where is the Machine?" interrupted Zelda.

"What Machine?"

"Where is your partner?"

"What partner?"

"Trooper Dhar," said Zelda. "Do I have permission to torture a resident of your century?"

"You do," said Bindra.

Zelda briefly lunged at Marc, who flinched and held up his hands.

"Okay, okay," said Marc. "I'll cooperate."

"See how easy that was?" said Zelda. "Now where's your partner?"

Marc looked down the hallway at the bedroom doors.

"Shit," he muttered.

Zelda and Bindra followed Marc through the house, shuffling through piles of discarded beer cans. Marc came to a closed door with a sliver of pink light shining through the bottom and Bindra could hear muffled voices on the other side of it. Marc knocked on the door but received no answer. He reached out to knock again, but Zelda shoved him aside and pushed the door open. Then she reeled back when a wall of marijuana smoke washed over her.

Walking into the bedroom, the three time travellers saw in the light of a single lamp tinted pink by a repurposed scarf a circle of hazy bodies piled on top of each other. Each of them had the same look of dispossessed happiness, singing along with the record player.

"The future of America," said Zelda.

"Explains a lot," said Bindra. "Get them all out of here."

"Fine," said Marc. "Hey guys, I'm sorry but it's time to leave."

"Booo," shouted one of the girls in the pile, who then threw an empty beer can at him.

"Hey!" said Marc. "We've got business to take care of."

The pile groaned and started to separate into individual people. One by one they filed out of the bedroom.

"Screw you, Marc," said one of them on the way out.

"You ruin everything," said another.

"Yeah, yeah," said Marc.

He walked toward the last remaining body, a young man in a dark blue shirt nearly passed out on the bed.

"Hey," he shouted, kicking the person's knee. "Get up."

"What do you want?" said the body.

"We have a problem. Time cops. They want to see the Machine."

"How do they even know about the Machine?" said the body as it sat up and looked at Marc, Zelda and Bindra.

"Bindra?" said the body.

"Lumen?" said Bindra.

"You know each other?" said Zelda.

"What is happening?" said Marc.

"I thought Sol banished you," said Bindra.

"He did," said Lumen. "But then his troopers abandoned him, so no one's left to enforce his laws."

"I'm still here." Bindra was offended at the mere suggestion that she would abandon Sol.

"Why are you here?" said Lumen. "It's not safe in Twenty, especially not for you."

"Especially not me? What does that mean?"

"I just meant..." stammered Lumen. "Because of Thurmond, and how he's trying to kill you...and then he almost killed you—"

"I'm a trooper of the Twentieth, I don't back down from a fight. It's not safe for you either, but here you are. And you didn't even bother to contact me? We're in the same year!"

"I am starting to worry that we're straying a little too far from the point," said Zelda, just before she grabbed Marc by the arm and tossed him onto the bed next to Lumen. When Marc angrily tried to stand back up, Zelda shoved him back down.

"What do you want?" said Marc.

"We want the Machine," said Zelda.

"We already told Lupita," said Marc. "She can't have it."

"Lucky for you, I don't represent Lupita," said Zelda. "Unlucky for you, Lupita doesn't care what you have to say about it. She'll just come and take it."

"She would never do that," said Lumen, shaking his head. "She can't just invade another century."

"These are desperate times, boys," said Zelda. "I can't promise what Lupita will do to you both when she comes for that Machine, but I can promise you this—she will come for that Machine. I can also promise that if you hand it over to us, we, at the very least, won't kill you."

"It's not just Lupita," said Lumen. "We agreed when we built the Machine it wasn't for any centurion to use. We're not interested in helping tyrants."

"Then you're still in luck," said Zelda. "We do not represent any centurions. We are travelling on our own behalf, as an independent... intercentury...interference...um..."

"Task force," said Bindra.

"Right, task force," said Zelda. "The first of its kind."

"Probably the last of its kind," said Bindra.

"How do you expect to stop Thurmond with our Machine?" said Marc.

"Leave that to us," said Zelda. "Now, I think it's about time you lads brought the thing out, don't you?"

"It's not here," said Marc.

"Where is it?" said Zelda.

"You can't make us tell you," said Lumen.

Zelda giggled. "Is that a challenge?"

"Let's not take it that far just yet," said Bindra.

"Oh, sorry," said Zelda. "Did you want the first go at this one?"

"No, I just think he'll take us to the Machine of his own free will," said Bindra.

"Why is that?" said Lumen.

Bindra's head spun, and she glared in his direction. "To avoid prosecution."

"What?"

"On the authority of the Twentieth Century and its centurion, Solomon Christie, I'm placing you under arrest," said Bindra. "For trespassing, illegal immigration to the Twentieth Century, violating the edict of the Twentieth Centurion and offering illegal substances to underage laymen."

"What!?" said Lumen and Marc in unison.

"You have the right to remain silent," Bindra continued. "You have the right to a fair trial before the commissioners, you have a right to a full and thorough defense, and you have the right to a punishment proportional with your crimes."

"You can't do that!" said Lumen. "You just said you're an independent task force!"

"The task force rules are a little fuzzy," said Zelda. "And also unwritten."

"All of that can be avoided, of course," said Bindra. "If you take us to the Machine."

Lumen and Marc exchanged glances, and Marc buried his head in his hands.

"This party sucks."

• • •

Lumen and Marc led Zelda and Bindra on a walk through the little city of Athens. Bindra felt the odd and omnipresent sensation of several anchor points sitting all around her. She narrowed her vision and turned in the direction of each anchor point they passed. The group walked in tense silence, broken only by the chirping of bats in the air and the distant hum of a dozen different house parties. A thought was nagging at her. There was something Marc had said that bothered her, something she was dwelling on in the night silence as Lumen slowed his gait to walk next to her.

"You feel that?" said Lumen. "There's dozens of anchor points in just this one town. The laymen have a lot of ghost stories about this place. They call it one of the most haunted towns in the world, but they don't know it's all because of what's under the ground here—"

"Why are you talking?" said Bindra.

"I…" stammered Lumen. "I don't know, I just wanted to say something."

"Isn't saying something just to say something the same as saying nothing?"

"Um. I guess?"

"Why don't you think about that for a while?" said Bindra. "Quietly."

"Okay. But, really, I just meant to—"

"Or if you insist on talking, maybe you can tell me something."

She stopped walking, which made the whole group come to a halt. Lumen looked at her with wide, fearful eyes.

"How long did you know?" said Bindra.

"What?" said Lumen.

"The legend. The myth about me and Thurmond. Marc told us. This whole mythology thing where I'm the only one who can stop him—"

"It's just rumors, Bindra. You know how time travellers like to—"

"I know about time travel, Lumen, that's not what I'm talking about. But before we met, did you know about it? Did you hear those stories about me before you knew my name? Did you agree to tug-of-war with me…did you spend all this time with me…was it all just because I'm a legend?"

Lumen gently opened and closed his mouth several times without saying anything, searching the ground and sky and all around her just to avoid making eye contact.

198

"I didn't know all of it," he said finally. "I knew your name. I knew bits and pieces. I mean, everyone knows bits and pieces. But what was I supposed to do, tell you myths about yourself? Ghamud dayim, remember?"

Bindra's heart sank. Stray memories flashed through her mind. When Mr. Brooks seemed to bow the first time they met. When Madolyn Listratta almost whispered her future that day in the library. When Lumen told her Thurmond would be no match for her, and at the time, she didn't even stop to wonder how he even knew about Thurmond. Did he care about her at all, or did he just care about her legend? Had he only associated with her because he grew up with stories of Bindra Dhar? Was that the only reason Mr. Brooks decided to teach her time travel? Did she owe all her accomplishments to a myth?

She was suddenly aware that Lumen, Marc and Zelda were all staring at her. She shook her head and tossed her arms in the air, letting the loose-fitting sleeves of her father's jacket flutter as she brought them down again.

"I don't know what to tell you. I'm sorry to ruin the story, but I haven't defeated Thurmond, and I haven't figured out how to do it yet. So if that's the only reason any of you are with me right now, it might be time to find a new savior, because I don't know what I'm doing."

Lumen let his head fall to his chest. Marc winced and backed away from the tension of the group. Zelda smiled and put her hand on Bindra's shoulder. "Don't worry, Bindra. I've never been under any illusion that you know what you're doing. Now, lads, I think it's time for you to show us the Machine."

"It's in here," said Marc.

Zelda watched as Marc and Lumen climbed the steps of an imposing grey-and-red brick building lined with long windows.

"What is this place?" said Zelda.

"It's the university library," said Marc.

"You keep it in the library?"

"We have to," said Marc. "You'll see."

Marc opened the door and the group walked through the library lobby, taking on the quiet detachment time travellers embody when they don't want to be noticed by laymen. The library was dead with only a handful of students scattered at different tables, heads in books and notebooks, absorbed in overnight studies.

Marc and Lumen led Zelda and Bindra to the elevator and up to the sixth floor where they emerged to find nothing but endless stacks of books. There were no laymen in sight, and Marc felt comfortable speaking.

"The university lets us keep it up here. They think we're building a computer. Which we are. Sort of."

The group moved through the stacks of books until Marc stopped at a door along the wall. He pulled a key from his pocket and unlocked the door, leading the others into a small storage room. Lumen flipped the light switch, and all four of the time travellers looked upon the object in the middle of the room.

To Bindra, the Machine seemed like nothing more than a black box about the size of an overturned refrigerator. Looking closer, she saw the box sat on four wheels and had a silver, metal seam running along the side. Lumen and Mark stood at either side of the box and pulled it open at the seams. As it opened, a jumble of wires gushed out in a controlled mess of multicolored strands. At the center of this wiry nest sat a keyboard and a boxy, cream-colored computer monitor with a black screen.

"Well," said Lumen. "This is it. This is the Time Machine."

"Time machines don't exist," said Bindra.

"We know. We just thought it was a funny name," said Marc. "It's clever."

"Not that clever," said Zelda.

"What does it do?" said Bindra.

"Well, basically," said Marc. "It knows things."

CHAPTER 23: THE TIME MACHINE

Bindra watched as Marc reached his hand through the jungle of wires to flip several switches inside the Machine. As he did, Bindra saw what looked like a mirrored cube wrapped in a copper coil deep inside the nest of wires. As Marc flipped the last switch, the cube started rotating.

"Down here is the omni-spectrum, data-document scanner," said Marc, "which Lumen invented. And it's gathering data and sending it to the AI translating software, which I invented."

"Great," said Bindra. "What does it do?"

"It gathers information from whatever location you put it in," said Lumen. "Right now it's reading every book, record, document, newspaper, magazine and photograph in this library. Every scrap of information in close proximity, it can read."

"Is it reading our minds?" said Bindra.

"No," said Marc. "It can't do that. It can't even hear what we're saying. It can only scan historical records. Anything a human being consciously created and preserved for posterity."

"What's the purpose for something like this?" said Bindra.

"Lots of history is forgotten," said Lumen. "But not necessarily lost. If you're time travelling, forgotten history is like having a map with half the cities and roads missing. A person can't read every book in this library, and even if they could, a person can't remember or comprehend every single piece of information it holds. But the Machine can. This is the library's mind."

"It's a navigation tool," said Marc. "It can give you the where-and-when of anything. Information that may seem insignificant to the laymen, but important to time travellers, this Machine can find in an instant. It's the most detailed time travel roadmap ever devised."

"Time travel is travel, all travel is navigation," said Bindra quietly. "Why does Lupita want a navigation tool?"

"Because," said Zelda, "the catch is the Machine knows when and where everybody is. If you wanted to, say, illegally enter the Nineteenth

Century, you could probably avoid being detected by the troopers. You could even avoid other travellers who might report you to the troopers. But eventually you'd have to sign something, or pay for something, and then there would be some record, somewhere, of you being in a certain place and time, and that's all Lupita's troopers would need."

"Even if you used a fake name," continued Marc. "The Machine's software has facial recognition. If you show up in a photograph, even the background of a photograph, the Machine knows when and where you were, are, will be."

"It's a tracking system," said Zelda. "Every time tyrant's dream, and you two idiots built it."

"Hey now," said Marc. "We agreed when we came up with the designs that we'd never sell it to a centurion. Which is why when Lupita's troopers came asking about it, we said no."

"Yeah, and who did you sell it to?" asked Zelda.

"Walter Brooks," said Marc.

"Mr. Brooks?" said Bindra. "Why would he want this thing?"

"It wasn't for him personally," said Marc. "It's for the Society of Black Time Travellers. Lots of history is forgotten. In a lot of places, black history gets forgotten first. This Machine will revolutionize the way SBTT plans its research expeditions."

"And more importantly," said Lumen, "it's incredibly difficult for black time travellers to know when and where exactly they'll be safe, with lynchings and cops and all."

"Yes, please," said Bindra. "Continue explaining how being a time traveller of color can be complicated."

"Anyway," said Marc. "Mr. Brooks thought this might give them more of an advantage. He paid us to build the thing and paid us again to destroy all of our designs. He didn't want to help a tyrant either. Now do you get it? The Machine doesn't belong to Lupita."

"Lupita doesn't care," said Zelda. "Now show me how this contraption works."

"What are you going to do with it?" said Marc.

"I'm going to find out when Thurmond is," said Zelda.

"Are you crazy?" said Marc. "That is not what the Machine was built for."

"Times have changed," said Zelda. "As I understand it, you're both still under arrest."

"He's under arrest," said Marc, gesturing to Lumen. "What did I do?"

"Aiding and abetting," answered Bindra. "Now talk to your Machine."

Zelda insisted that she be the one to communicate with the Machine since she didn't trust Lumen, or Marc, or Bindra, really, or, in fact, anyone she'd ever met. But she was slightly confused when confronted with the Machine's keyboard. English was not her first language, and to complicate matters even more, her first language did not, strictly speaking, have an alphabet. She could read and write, of course, but typing had always been a challenge. But she worked through it, methodically punching each letter.

T-H-U-R-M-O-N-D.

"That's not how it works," said Marc behind her.

"Not how what works?" As she said this, Zelda saw green letters fade onto the black computer screen.

Question.

"You have to ask it a question," said Marc.

"Why did you make that rule?" said Zelda.

"We didn't," said Marc. "The Machine makes the rules."

Annoyed, Zelda started typing again.

When is Thurmond?

The time travellers hunched over the Machine waiting for it to respond. Slowly, the green letters materialized once again from the blackness.

Specific.

"It wants you to be more specific," said Marc.

"Oh, is that what 'specific' means?"

"There are a lot of Thurmonds in the world," said Lumen.

"And also," added Marc, "remember, the only things the Machine will know about Thurmond is whatever is written about him in this library."

Zelda typed again.

When is the time traveller named Thurmond?

"Does the Machine know about time travel?" said Bindra.

"Of course," said Marc. "It sees our people pop up in so many different eras of history, it's not hard to put the evidence together."

Once again, after a much longer pause than before, the green words materialized.

Thurmond the time traveller is dangerous.
Thurmond the time traveller is deadly.
One should not seek Thurmond the time traveller.

The attitude of the room became heavy and cold.

"Well," said Marc. "I think that should settle it."

Zelda ignored him and returned to typing.

"Trooper—" said Marc.

"It hasn't told us anything we don't already know," said Zelda as she finished her writing.

Do you know when I can find Thurmond the time traveller?
Yes.
When is Thurmond the time traveller?
Thurmond the time traveller is dangerous.
Where is Thurmond the time traveller?
Thurmond the time traveller is deadly.
Will you tell me how to find Thurmond the time traveller?
One should not seek Thurmond the time traveller...
But if one did...
Here is when one may find him...

24

THE GATHERING
IN THE WILDERNESS

ON AUGUST 20, 1866, a steamboat left port at Marietta, Ohio, sailing down the Ohio River for Cincinnati with the intention of making stops at Racine, Pomeroy, Gallipolis and Ripley. The steamboat's registry with the names of all 144 people who boarded and disembarked during the voyage would eventually be filed away with a number of other logbooks from that same steamship, the collection of which ultimately ended up in the library at Ohio University where it was scanned and read by the Time Machine. The Machine found that one passenger had bought his ticket under a single name.

As the man called Thurmond sat on the deck of the steamboat playing a game of solitaire and enjoying the view of the passing countryside, he did not know at that moment, more than a century later, a Machine was determining his whenabouts. If he had, he would not have worried much about it. Though he blended in with the laymen, as is the custom of time travellers, he made no attempts to conceal himself from other time travellers. In fact, he took steps to leave subtle hints about his true nature that any other passing traveller might recognize. He wore, as many time travellers do, a small pin on his lapel depicting a Latin letter S turned on its side and pierced by a horizontal line—the universal symbol of time travel.

He did not expect any of his fellow passengers to be fellow travellers. But as the woman with maroon hair started to approach his table, he saw in her eyes a flash of recognition—the sort of recognition that renewed his pride in his community every time he saw it.

"It's good to meet a fellow traveller," said the woman.

"To make the road less lonely," he said, smiling. "Please, join me."

• • •

Already Thurmond was not what Zelda expected. He was young, mid-thirties, she estimated. He wore round glasses over his brown eyes. He had on a black hat, and thick dark hair fell all around his head in contrast with the short controlled beard that clung tight to his face. Though many travellers usually failed in their attempts to wear clothing accurate to the decade they were visiting, Thurmond blended in perfectly with the laymen of Nineteen. Only the lapel pin gave him away.

"I'm Thurmond," he said, holding out his hand.

Zelda shook it. "I'm Zelda. When are you coming from, Thurmond?"

"Oh, I've been in Twenty a while. My birth century."

"Ah," she said with a smile. "A native of Twenty?"

"Yeah, yeah," he said, laughing. "Don't hold it against me."

"Is this your first time in Nineteen then?"

"Oh, no. I'm a resident."

Shit, thought Zelda. With Lupita's new security measures, Nineteen was perhaps the most isolated century in the A.D.s, and yet Thurmond could come and go as he pleased.

"Me too," she replied. "Things have become a little tense here though."

"I've noticed. But I don't think it'll last for too long."

He winked at her, and not knowing what to make of this gesture, she smiled and laughed it off.

"So you're a resident of Nineteen," said Thurmond. "But your accent sounds a little foreign. When's home?"

Zelda shifted in her seat. She didn't always enjoy talking about her native century, but she felt she needed to be honest with him if she expected to learn anything useful. "One."

"One?" he said with surprise.

"B.C.," she added.

"Oh," said Thurmond, leaning forward. "I don't think I've met anyone from the B.C.s before."

"Not many of us come this far downstream."

"Please, tell me about it. Where were you born?"

"On an island," she started. "I understand people in this century call it 'Ireland.' I was born to a tribe of…well, we didn't have a name for ourselves. From what I can tell, we apparently didn't leave many artifacts behind either, so no one really knows anything about us."

Zelda was content to leave it at that, but she could tell from his face Thurmond wanted to hear more. What's more, and more surprising to her, was that she wanted to tell him. Being in his presence felt oddly comforting. In the back of her mind, she remembered the Time Machine's neon green writing—*Thurmond the time traveller is dangerous.* And yet there was something about him—perhaps the assumption that she would eventually kill him anyway—that made her feel as if it was acceptable to tell him her most closely guarded story.

"My tribe lived on the coast surrounded by forest," she said. "My father was a chieftain, and he refused to let anyone, especially any of the children, go into the forest alone, because there were stories from some of the traders that a witch lived deep in the woods. My father was…he was a very feared man. He was a skilled warrior, and he defended our tribe for years against the other kings and tribes. Once, just after I was born, a great warrior king from the continent arrived on our coast with an army bigger than anyone had ever seen. But my father rallied the tribes against them, and before he killed the king on the battlefield, he asked the man the name of his favorite wife. The king answered 'Griselda,' and so that's what my father named me."

Thurmond smiled as he listened. "Sounds like a charming man."

"He trained all of his children," said Zelda. "All of my brothers, and me, how to fight. He taught us how to enjoy it—fighting and killing, I mean. But eventually, all of my brothers died, on the battlefield or in brawls, until it was just me. And I thought, since I was all that was left, he would name me as his heir. But he grew older, he became sick, and I learned that he planned to trade me to a rival chieftain as a wife while he took the other chieftain's son as his own heir. So I ran away."

"To the witch," guessed Thurmond.

Zelda nodded and noticed that while he was taking in everything she told him, he was no longer looking at her. He was staring to the side of their table.

"She was hard to find," said Zelda. "But when I finally found her, I asked her to teach me her magic."

"The witch was a time traveller," said Thurmond.

"Yes. She taught me the Knowledge, brought me to Nineteen, gave me a proper surname for the century. She taught me to be civilized."

She felt her hands shaking as she said the last word. *Buzzing*, as Sol Christie put it. Thurmond nodded, still looking away from her. She finally glanced over to what he was looking at. Two laymen sat at a table nearby, silently, without regarding each other or anything else for that matter. Both of the men wore blue wool uniforms, and it took Zelda quite a long moment to realize that one of them was missing both of his arms while the other was without the left side of his face.

"Civilization is hard to come by," said Thurmond. "No matter the century." He turned in his chair to face her again. "Do you miss your brothers?"

"Yes," she said. "Sometimes."

"Do you wish they hadn't died? I mean, if just one of them had lived, maybe your father wouldn't have tried to sell you, and you wouldn't have had to run away from your family."

"If my brothers had lived, I may never have learned how easy it was for my family to betray me. And I never would've become a time traveller."

He smiled, rubbing his bearded chin. "Ah, yes. A paradox. You could save your brothers, but then you'd never learn the Knowledge you need to save them."

"One thing always leads to another."

"It does, doesn't it?" said Thurmond. "Little things lead to bigger things, butterflies flap their wings and make hurricanes. But you know what I've never quite understood?"

"What?"

"Butterflies aren't that hard to kill," he said. "So what are we so afraid of?"

Zelda nodded.

"Where are you headed to, Zelda?" asked Thurmond.

"I suppose I'll sail all the way to Cincinnati."

"How would you feel about getting off with me at Pomeroy? There's a little gathering I'm expected to be at and maybe you'd get something out of it too."

"Gathering of what?" said Zelda.

"Just some travellers like us. People looking for a new way of thinking."

"I don't usually go to time traveller parties," she said. "You know how we can get when we're all together."

"Yeah, I know. Always showing off…"

"'I hunted a woolly mammoth,'" she mocked. "'Look at my pictures with Barack Obama…'"

"As if we're all going to be jealous that you watched the *Titanic* set sail," he said, shaking his head. "Who hasn't? But, community is still community. All we have is our fellow travellers."

Zelda seethed. *Fellow travellers like the one you murdered, you son of a—*

"I guess you're right," she said. "It can be lonely on the road."

"Then why not get off at Pomeroy? I think you'll find it interesting. If you have the time, of course."

"All the time in the world."

• • •

When the riverboat docked at Pomeroy, Zelda and Thurmond discreetly left the town and began walking through the woods. It was nearly black in all directions, yet Thurmond clearly knew exactly where he was going. Ahead of them, through the trees, Zelda started to see an orange glow accompanied by the sounds of guitars and harmonicas and rough singing.

Soon the encampment came into view. The gathered time travellers had propped up an enormous canvas tent in the middle of a clearing. All around the tent were scenes of friendly reunions, with old travellers hugging and laughing with each other, telling fantastical stories and, of course, bragging to one another. Most had dressed for the decade, but as you would expect for a time traveller gathering, many had brought anachronisms with them. Several travellers sat playing music in the bed of a Ford pickup they had apparently driven, undetected, through the Nineteenth Century. Zelda noted the orange glow flooding the clearing was not from candles or torches or gaslights but was instead created by electric lamps that floated, like glowing bubbles, just above their heads. She spotted a young woman rubbing one of the glass orbs between her palms until it lit up, at which point she tossed it gently into the air where it stayed afloat. Zelda was fairly certain such a device was not native to Nineteen.

As they passed, people broke off from their conversations to shake Thurmond's hand, greeting him in hushed but reverent tones—"It's good to meet a fellow traveller... So good to meet a fellow traveller... Good to meet a fellow traveller..."

Thurmond smiled at everyone who greeted him but never stopped on his march to the canvas tent. He pushed through the entranceway, and Zelda saw the tent was full of empty seats in front of a wooden stage. A red curtain hung behind the stage, and when Thurmond walked behind this curtain, he was immediately greeted by a young girl of no more than twelve.

"Thurmond!" she said. "It's so good to see you!"

The girl rushed up to Thurmond and hugged him around the waist. Thurmond, looking embarrassed, held his arms out above her for a moment before returning her embrace.

"It's good to see you too," he said. "Are you excited? It's going to be a big night."

"Very excited! Thank you ever so much for bringing me here."

"Of course," said Thurmond. "Sarah, this is my friend Zelda. I want you to stay close to her while I'm with the others, okay?"

Zelda's eyes bulged at the thought that she was supposed to babysit someone at this gathering. Thurmond gave her an apologetic glance.

"May I go outside and talk to the people?" said the girl. "I want to meet them."

"You'll meet them later," said Thurmond. "But right now you must stay here behind the curtain."

The girl nodded and walked backstage. Thurmond turned to Zelda and shrugged. "By the way, I have a favor to ask."

"Take care of her?" said Zelda.

"I'm sorry, I should've mentioned it before."

"It's fine," said Zelda. "She didn't say the greeting."

"What's that?"

"She didn't say it was good to meet a fellow traveller."

"No, she didn't," said Thurmond.

"Because she's not a traveller," said Zelda. "She's a layman."

"Yes," he admitted.

"Why is she here?"

"You'll see," said Thurmond. "Soon."

25

THE GOSPEL OF THURMOND

LESS THAN AN HOUR LATER, time travellers had filled the tent, all of them fidgeting in their folding chairs, sweating beneath the thick canvas and bathed in the hazy orange glow of the floating light bulbs. Zelda stood at the edge of the red curtain and watched as Thurmond strolled out onto the stage. With every step his boots creaked against the plywood stage and kicked sawdust into the air. With tense anticipation, the audience of time travellers awaited Thurmond's first words. He looked over the audience and smiled with almost twinkling eyes.

"It's good to meet a fellow traveller," said Thurmond.

"To make the road less lonely," replied the audience, more or less in unison.

Thurmond looked down and laughed to himself. "I love hearing that. My name is Thurmond, and I'm here to save everyone.

"Community always has more value for the outsiders," he declared. "I myself was once an outsider, and I think most of you were as well—one does not become a time traveller because they like when they live. I love this community. I love all of you. And because I love you, I have to tell you this—we have all been lied to.

213

"We have been told that knowledge—and more specifically, the Knowledge—is power, and that power must be used responsibly. This is not incorrect. But we have also been told that to use our powers responsibly means to not use them at all. We have been told not to interfere in the past. We have been told not to correct errors, we have been told to let terrible things happen as they may, we have been told to let others suffer and die. We have been lied to."

Zelda saw heads in the crowd turn to one another, reactions being whispered. She noticed a wave of squirming in the seats at his mention of the high crime of interference.

"Fellow travellers, I ask you, how can we continue like this? How can we continue to behave as if refusing to do what only we can do to end human suffering is not only acceptable, but noble? Lawful? What right does anyone have to call themselves centurions if they stubbornly ignore the horrors of their century? What right do the commissioners have to keep time travel for the time travellers alone? Who among us does not mourn the preventable loss of a layman? And is that truly mourning, or is it, in fact, guilt? The guilt that we have done nothing to help them, that we will do nothing, that we are doing nothing. Because, my friends, we have been lied to.

"I believe there is a higher power than the commissioners. There is a higher power than the *Revised Code*, a higher power than the Time Travellers' Guild. And being time travellers, we know we are not permanent. Time travel does not grant immortality. Everyone here will die. Everyone here is dying. Everyone here has died. And because you have already died, you have already met your creator. You have already had to explain to that higher power why, when it gave you a gift, you hoarded it. When that higher power gave you power, you squandered it. When that higher power gave you knowledge, you kept it to yourself. I wonder how you explained yourselves."

CHAPTER 25: THE GOSPEL OF THURMOND

Thurmond paused, for he knew his audience could not look away.

"And perhaps," he continued, "perhaps you do not believe in a higher being. In that case, you only have to explain to yourself why you allow the suffering to continue. All you have to do is find a way to sleep at night. All you have to do is live with yourself. You have help, of course. The centurions and the commissioners and the Guild all tell you that what you're doing—or, rather, what you're not doing—is good and noble. But I wonder if that's enough to silence the voice in the back of your mind telling you every night," his voice came down to an audible whisper, "*No. You could have saved him. You could have saved her. But you did nothing. This isn't right.*

"It isn't right, my friends," he declared. "It isn't right at all."

And then, when Thurmond had reached his most captivating peak, a lone figure stood in the audience. The figure held his hand up at the side of his face as if to signal Thurmond to pause his passion. For a moment, though Zelda knew all that Thurmond had said was a twisted and reckless philosophy, she couldn't help but feel offended that anyone would disrupt the vigor and momentum of his speech.

"Forgive my interruption," said the man. "But I'm not much for rhetoric. Let's say, for a moment, that you are right. Let's say that interference is not the crime the Guild makes it out to be. And let's even say that your speech convinced me—though it certainly has not—but let's say I'm open to the suggestion that we should change our ways, and perhaps change the past if we can, indeed, ease human suffering without causing even worse suffering. That would still leave me with a serious question—how?"

The interrupter looked familiar to Zelda. He was a slender and stoic black man, just about her age, wearing a simple linen suit and waistcoat, appropriate for the century.

Thurmond smiled at him. "First of all, let me just say, it's an honor to have Walter Brooks with us. I've long admired your work. Now, the question that Mr. Brooks has proposed just now is a very real one. If we decide that we must change the past, how do we do it? How do we do the very thing that we time travellers have set up an entire system of law and governance to prevent?

"How do we get around the troopers, for example? In my experiments with interference, I've run into this problem firsthand. Troopers can be tenacious, perhaps even zealous, in their enforcement of the corrupt *Revised Code*. But the troopers are our fellow travellers. I believe when they have heard the true word they will be enlightened.

"And if they will not be enlightened," he added, "they will be overwhelmed by those who are."

"I will put aside that threat of violence," snapped Walter, "against our fellow travellers. I will also put aside the assumption, on your part, that we here have all been convinced that the *Revised Code* is, as you say, 'corrupt'—a clever rhetorical trick, driving hard on a minority narrative as if it's already been decided by the majority, but as I said, I'm not much for rhetoric."

Murmurs of uneasiness spread through the crowd. Some of the travellers frowned and shook their heads at Walter. Others continued to shift uncomfortably in their seats, perhaps unsure of whether to love Thurmond or fear him. Zelda could see that young Walter Brooks was undeterred by all of this. So too, it seemed, was Thurmond.

"My point was less about the troopers and more a question of fate," continued Walter. "We change little things about the past every day. Time travellers can't help it. But we have found time and time again that we cannot change big things about the past. Usually it is because the troopers are there to stop the would-be interferers like yourself, but some would attribute this failure to manipulate time to something one can only describe as fate. How, then, do you plan to undo what's already been done?"

"Yes," said Thurmond. "Fate. The goddess of time travel."

He turned away from Walter and started pacing the stage, eager to return to his speechmaking.

"The laymen are governed by fate," said Thurmond. "We time travellers may dance with fate, but she always leads. But there are those to whom neither fate nor the physical laws of spacetime apply. You see, when you make one of those little changes to the past, which Mr. Brooks says you do every day, sometimes that little change can evolve. It can lead to certain events, and it can even lead to the birth of a person. And then you have an entire human life, an entire human mind, thrown suddenly onto the fabric of spacetime when the fabric of spacetime wasn't prepared for it. And what you have done there is not just a butterfly flapping its wings to make a hurricane—a single human mind is far more powerful than a hurricane. No, what you have created there is an enormous wrinkle in time, a ripple in the river unburdened by the current.

"Fellow travellers, I am here to tell you," declared Thurmond. "I am a ripple."

The audience didn't know what to make of this pronouncement. Some of the travellers clapped their hands over their mouths in shock. Some fell into a kind of nervous laughter, though never quite taking their eyes from the stage. Walter Brooks, however, knew exactly how to handle the news. Zelda could see he was barely containing a laugh.

"Oh my," he said. "I had no idea we were in the presence of a true ripple."

"I assume you'll want evidence, Mr. Brooks," said Thurmond.

"Well, seeing as you have just announced to us all that you have magical powers—"

"Of course," said Thurmond. "I would expect nothing less from a scientific mind like yours. Tell me, my friends, is there anyone here by the name of Caldwell?"

217

The heads of the time travellers turned left and right looking to see if anyone would answer to Thurmond. Soon, a single woman stood in the middle of the crowd.

"My name is Caldwell."

"Susan Caldwell?" said Thurmond.

"Yes, sir."

"Would you mind, Susan, coming up here to the edge of the stage?"

Susan Caldwell looked to Walter as if searching for advice. Walter gave no nod or shake of his head, and so Susan Caldwell walked up to the stage. Walter stood still and watched her pass, then narrowed his vision to Thurmond. The speechmaker came to the edge of the stage and knelt down to meet Susan when she arrived. Then he held out his hand and waited for her to take it. When she did take his hand, she pulled up her skirt as if to climb on the stage with him, but Thurmond made no move to help her up. Instead, he simply held her hand and spoke.

"You had a sister," he said.

Susan Caldwell looked up at him. "Yes, sir."

"You were both natives of Eighteen. But you both grew up here in Nineteen."

"That's true, sir."

"She was much younger than you," he said. "But you loved her. Very much."

"Yes, sir. Very much."

"And when you became a time traveller," said Thurmond, "you went back to that day, didn't you? You went to July 21, 1810."

"Yes, sir," said Susan Caldwell, and she started to cry.

"You went back to the barn," said Thurmond. "Do you remember what happened at the barn, Susan?"

"I opened the barn door," said Susan. "And there was thunder."

"The thunder spooked the horse. And your sister was right next to you. You went back to that moment. You saw yourself open the barn door. The thunder cracked, and you tried to push her out of the way."

"Yes, sir."

"You tried to push her out of the way. Before the horse came through the door."

"Yes, sir," she cried.

"But you couldn't reach her in time," said Thurmond. "No matter what, you couldn't reach her in time."

"No sir."

"You can't reach her in time. You won't reach her in time."

"No, sir."

"And so the horse always tramples her. And she lives for three days. And on the third day the doctor thinks things are looking better. But that night she dies. And you're the first to notice when she stops breathing."

"Yes, sir," said Susan Caldwell. Then she took his hand with both of hers and buried her face into it. He knelt even closer to her and whispered in her ear, and even though he whispered, the time travellers all heard, for they could be distracted by nothing else.

"No," he said.

Susan Caldwell looked up at him with red and purple eyes. "No?"

Thurmond released her hand and stood back up. "No, Susan. You didn't see her stop breathing on the third day. Do you remember?"

Susan Caldwell shook her head.

"On the third day you watched her sleep peacefully in her bed," he said. "The doctor didn't come to your house that day. You saw the doctor walking by the house while you stood on the porch. Do you remember what he said?"

Zelda watched as Susan Caldwell's eyes grew wider and her breaths grew heavier. She started to back into the crowd.

"He pointed to the sky," she said. "And he said things were looking better."

"Because the rain had stopped," said Thurmond.

"Yes."

"He wasn't talking about your sister. Because there was nothing wrong with your sister."

Thurmond, too, slowly backed away from the edge of the stage. As he did, his voice grew louder and his arms gradually lifted at his sides.

"You and your sister stayed inside all day," said Thurmond. "You stayed inside all day the day before, and the day before that."

With his arms almost completely outstretched, Thurmond lifted his head so that the floating orange light danced on his face. He closed his eyes.

"And the day before that, there was thunder and lightning, but the horse wasn't spooked that day. The horse didn't trample your sister that day, Susan. Do you remember why?"

"I…" she said. "I opened the barn door."

"Yes," said Thurmond. "You were the first to notice."

"When the horse stopped breathing," said Susan Caldwell.

Thurmond abruptly opened his eyes and startled Zelda when he turned and looked toward her offstage.

"Sarah," he said. "Why don't you come on out now?"

From the corner of her eye, Zelda barely saw the small figure of Sarah Caldwell flutter by and scamper onto the stage. The little girl waved at her sister.

"Hi, Susan!" said the girl.

Susan Caldwell clutched her stomach and stared at her sister with horror. "What?" was all the elder Caldwell could muster.

"On the third day," said Thurmond, "after you watched your sister sleep in peace and safety, you fell asleep, Susan. And a new friend came to visit her."

"Mr. Thurmond said he'd show me what you look like when you're grown!" said Sarah Caldwell. "He said you might be surprised to see me. But I'm safe! I promise!"

CHAPTER 25: THE GOSPEL OF THURMOND

Susan Caldwell collapsed and wailed. Walter Brooks darted toward her to help, but he was blocked by the other time travellers crowding around her. Sarah Caldwell jumped down from the stage and ran to her sister, who grabbed her and clasped her tight, wailing all the while. When Susan Caldwell had cried all that Zelda believed a person was capable of crying, she looked back up at Thurmond, who remained motionless on the stage. With a trembling, whispering voice, Susan Caldwell began to speak.

"Praise Thurmond," wailed Susan. "Praise Thurmond. Praise Thurmond!"

The chant spread from Susan Caldwell through the rest of the crowd. One by one the time travellers joined in, until only a shaken Walter Brooks remained silent.

"Praise Thurmond!" trembled the tent. "Praise Thurmond! Praise Thurmond!"

Thurmond allowed this to continue for a number of minutes before he lifted his hands over the crowd. They returned to silence.

"What you have seen here is what I can accomplish on my own," he said. "But there is greater work ahead of us for which I will need your help."

"What is there that a traveller like you could not accomplish?" said a man in the crowd.

"The tragic death of one person is not significant enough to the Guild for the troopers to preserve the event," he said. "But if we are to stop larger tragedies from taking place, we will have to face opponents on two fronts. As you have seen, I know how to confront fate. But I will need numbers to go up against the troopers."

"Larger tragedies?" said another man in the crowd. "Where do we start?"

"A plan is already in motion," said Thurmond. "More than a century from now, a train will derail not far from where we're standing. Seventy-two people will die because of a sharp curve and a drunken engineer."

"Sounds easy enough," said one of the time travellers. "Just stop the train from ever leaving."

"It is not simple," warned Thurmond. "Interference must be performed with a scalpel. One must get as close as possible and change as little as possible to stop a disaster. No, my friends. If we are to stop this disaster, we must remove the responsible factor at the last possible moment. We must kill the horse just before the barn door opens. We must remove the engineer before he hits the curve. We must board the train."

Again the time travellers nervously looked to each other, but no one was willing to express their confusion. No one except, of course, for Walter Brooks.

"That is impossible," he said. "You need an anchor point to time travel anywhen, and I've never known an anchor point to keep speed with a train."

Thurmond appeared to have an answer to this, but he was interrupted by a shout from the front of the crowd.

"Haven't you been listening, Walter?" said Susan Caldwell. "With Thurmond, all things are possible."

The crowd cheered. "Praise Thurmond" made a resounding return.

26

FOREST FIRE

ZELDA AND THURMOND trudged through the night. The hills beyond the clearing became steep and the chatter and music of the time traveller gathering disappeared even while the orange glow of the tent still lingered behind them.

"I think maybe that wasn't really what you were expecting," said Thurmond.

"How could you tell?" said Zelda.

"I don't really, I mean…" he struggled with his words. "I don't necessarily like the chanting and everything. I'm not a god. I'm not magic."

"You really are a ripple, though?"

"Yes."

"How can you tell?"

"I know it. I feel it. I know my family well enough to suspect it, in any case. And besides, I don't have another explanation for why I can do all the things I can do.

"I meant everything I said," he continued, walking ahead of her. "I love the community, and I don't want to force anyone to do something they don't believe in or that they aren't comfortable with. But I want people to see

223

the truth as I see it. I want them to believe in that truth, and be convinced to join us. I especially hope, Zelda, that you will be convinced."

"Why is that?"

"Because, as I said, I want the troopers to be convinced as well."

Thurmond looked up into her eyes, softly biting his lower lip. Zelda searched his face for signs that he knew less than he claimed. Finding none, she took the safest course of action and dove into the forest. He called after her, but she ignored him and kept running in a random pattern, dodging in between trees until she was sure she'd lost him. Behind the protection of a wide oak, she drew Sol Christie's lightning gun. Her hands stopped shaking.

"Please, Zelda," she heard him call out. "I don't want there to be violence here tonight, not between us."

"Why not?" she said, moving to a different tree. "Didn't you say if the troopers can't be convinced, they would be overwhelmed?"

"Are you not convinced?" said Thurmond into the darkness. "You saw for yourself what's possible with interference. Lives can be saved. This is a mission, Zelda, and it's bigger than any time traveller. Bigger than me, and bigger than you."

Zelda peeked around the tree trunk and saw Thurmond's shadow slowly—and, to his credit, reluctantly—drawing a pistol from inside his coat.

"I'm not very good with this thing," he said into the darkness. "But if I fire a shot, the others will come to my aid. We are fellow travellers, Zelda. There should be no violence between fellow travellers."

Zelda darted to another tree. "You have already murdered fellow travellers."

Thurmond's shadow appeared to deflate. The hand holding his pistol slumped to his side and he let out a deep, painful sigh.

"I did not want to kill Trooper Dhar," he said. "It was the hardest thing I've ever done."

CHAPTER 26: FOREST FIRE

Dhar? thought Zelda.

"Then why would you do it," she said, "if you love the community so much?"

"She's the only one who defeats me. My plan is perfect, Zelda, I know it will work. I know every factor that derails that train. The one thing I could never fix was Bindra Dhar. So I had to remove her. I regret it, I can't—"

His words cut off and Zelda thought he might be crying.

"I can't get through a day without seeing her," he said. "I will regret it for the rest of my life, but it needed to happen. For the travellers, for the laymen. I will save everyone. And to do that, Bindra could not survive."

Zelda rolled her eyes in the darkness.

"I don't want to do it again, Zelda," said Thurmond. "No more travellers need to die. We have to stick together. Will you please come out and join me? If you don't believe now, one day I think you will. Please, Zelda. Come out and join me, or else I can't promise what will happen next."

Zelda closed her eyes and her heart fluttered at the opportunity for a fight. "Thurmond, I'm placing you under arrest for interference, conspiracy to commit interference and murder. You have the right to remain silent. You have the right to a fair trial before the commissioners, you have the right to a full and thorough defense, and you have the right to a punishment proportional with your crimes."

"Zelda—"

"You are no longer welcome in my century," she said.

Zelda swung around the tree and fired the lightning gun at Thurmond. He dodged and the tree behind him burst into flames. As he leapt to the side, his gun went off, echoing over the hills. She heard distant shouts from the tent.

Zelda crouched toward another tree, but Thurmond's gun cracked two more times and his bullets whipped over her head. From the corner of her eye, she saw his shadow hurrying through the brush back toward the tent. She wheeled around a tree and shot a lightning bolt in front of him, cutting off his escape and setting another tree on fire. Then she swung around the other side, cutting him off with another lightning bolt. By now the small fires lit by her gun were creeping their way into one big fire.

She lost sight of Thurmond and went after him, pushing through the brush until a new figure came into view. It was not Thurmond, but a traveller with a head so bald it reflected the dancing firelight. He came with his gun drawn and spotted Zelda, but she was faster. Her lightning bolt left a black mark on his shirt and he thumped to the ground.

A gunshot snapped to her left and she dodged behind a tree. Another member of the tent gathering aimed a rifle at her, and she replied with the lightning gun. This time the lightning bolt was more interested in the metal rifle than the shooter. The bullets still inside the gun all exploded at once, and Zelda saw the man stumble away, dazed, with fewer fingers than before.

By now, the noise of the fire overwhelmed most of the other sounds in the forest, but Zelda could still hear faint voices shouting to one another. She pushed through the smoke and trees, staying out of the firelight until she reached the edge of a hill. Between the branches of a tree, she saw three figures huddled together talking. One was Susan Caldwell and another was Thurmond.

Zelda cupped her left hand under her right and aimed her lightning gun at Thurmond. She waited for him to stand still enough to guarantee a hit. But before she could fire, a commotion rose above the noise of the forest fire from the direction of the tent.

"Troopers!" someone shouted. "Troopers of the Nineteenth!"

Thurmond and his compatriots dispersed before Zelda could shoot him. She listened and heard the sound of galloping horses. She trudged back up the hill and from that perch saw a legion of troopers on horseback crashing through the tent and chasing the time travellers through the hills. There were far more than ten of them. Obviously Lupita had reinforced her troopers with Sol Christie's and probably some mercenaries as well. All of them wore olive green uniforms and brandished long sabers.

Zelda heard the galloping coming nearer and saw one of the troopers breaking off from the rest and charging up the hill toward her. She ran along the ridgeline before tripping on the undergrowth. She flipped on her back and fired the lightning gun at the charging trooper. The bolt hit the trooper's horse in the chest and it collapsed, throwing the trooper to the ground.

As more troopers flooded into the forest, chasing the time travellers in every direction, Zelda bitterly gave up on pursuing Thurmond and turned instead to survival. She knew she had to get out of the forest before the fire consumed it completely, and she needed to find the nearest anchor point and start the long journey back to 1980. Lupita had fully militarized the Nineteenth Century. Invading Twenty and hunting for Bindra and the Time Machine would be the next step.

Zelda felt confident about the direction of the river, but the smoke was too thick to see much of anything. She pushed through the trees with the fire raging at her heels, but soon she became aware of the blue splotches appearing in her line of vision. Her brain wasn't getting enough oxygen and she was starting to hallucinate. She retained enough of her faculties to stave off panic, knowing that panic would just make her inhale more smoke. Instead, she took a moment to catch her breath and then hold it, but in that moment the fire started to catch up with her. Zelda tried to push ahead but kept getting weaker with every step until she couldn't hold her breath anymore and took in a gulp of smoke. She leaned against an unburned tree and tried to crouch beneath the smoke layer. She started coughing and hacking and she felt her knees buckle. Then she felt a hand on her shoulder.

Zelda swatted at the hand, but she was too dazed to retrieve her lightning gun fast enough. The hand, instead of accosting her, passed her something limp and cold. She realized it was a wet piece of cloth and pressed it to her mouth, breathing in several mouthfuls of smokeless air.

Regaining lucidity, Zelda watched as the figure who'd come to her aid, masked with a dark handkerchief, gestured for her to follow. As she regained strength, the figure picked up the pace until they had left the oppressive orange light of the fire behind and emerged into a world of dark blue. She slid behind the figure down a muddy slope to the edge of the river that was shimmering in the moonlight. A small wooden boat bobbed along the water's surface, tied to a nearby tree.

Walter Brooks removed his mask and turned his attention to Zelda. "Are you okay? Do you need any water?"

Zelda nodded, and he went to retrieve a canteen but she ignored him and waded into the river, scooping water into her mouth and pouring it over her soot-blackened face. She looked back at Walter Brooks who was silhouetted by the raging fire atop the hills.

"Why did you help me?" demanded Zelda as she trudged out of the water.

"I heard them shouting. I didn't want them to hurt you."

"Do you believe in all this?" said Zelda. "In Thurmond?"

"Of course not; I spoke against him."

"Then why come at all?" said Zelda.

For a reply he nodded to the boat. "Get in and you'll see. We have to get out of here."

Zelda walked to the boat and peered over the edge. In it she found a teenage boy with tousled, curly hair, apparently unconscious.

"Thurmond's message holds a lot of power in the mind of a young time traveller," said Walter behind her. "He's a good kid. I couldn't let him get caught up with this nonsense."

"He's your apprentice?" said Zelda.

"My first," said Walter.

"And you drugged him?"

He shrugged. "I didn't know what else to do. I've never been an instructor before. You won't wake him, don't worry. But you and I both need to get out of here."

Zelda nodded and climbed into the boat, careful to avoid Walter's sleeping apprentice. Walter tossed his things into the boat and untied it from the tree. He pushed off from the shoreline and let the dark Ohio River pull them away from the firelight. For several minutes while they awaited the disappearance of the smoke and the glow, they kept silent. Zelda took in deep breaths of fresh air while Walter rowed the boat across the water. Every so often, Walter would check on his protégé to make sure the boy was still alive and unconscious.

"Are you an instructor?" said Walter.

"No," said Zelda. "Never had the time."

"It's harder than I thought," said Walter, shaking his head. "I liked my instructor, but she could be stern at times. Even after I was admitted to the Guild, I'd hear her voice all the time and hated it. *Restrain your feelings, Walter. Never travel with excess emotion, Walter. Your reputation is everything, Walter. When will you learn?*' But now..." He nodded to his unconscious ward. "I think I get it. Did you get along with your instructor?"

She hadn't been prepared for the question, and the answer she had to give was painful. "I loved her very much."

"Has she passed on?"

"We've all passed on. But she is, for lack of a better term, out of the picture."

"May I ask what her name was?" said Walter.

"Lupita." She quickly wiped away a tear.

"I see," said Walter. "I'm very sorry, I didn't mean to—"

"It's fine. I'm here because of her. I'm now because of her. She isn't herself anymore, but when she was, she was an excellent instructor."

Walter nodded. "I worry I'm not any good at it."

Zelda laughed. "How is that possible? You're Walter Brooks! You invented the Blindfold Wally!"

"Well, sure, but that was easy. I was the only one in danger. Now I'm responsible for a young time traveller, and I almost lost him to a cult. And then I had to resort to drugging him to get him out of it. That doesn't seem like proper education."

"I wouldn't worry if I were you," said Zelda. "I happen to know one of your future apprentices."

"Ghamud dayim," said Walter, then quickly changed his mind. "That one turns out okay, though?"

"Bindra?" said Zelda. "She's incredibly annoying. Naïve, clumsy, a slow learner, if you ask me. Not enough confidence, too much of a rule follower, an all-around bore, really…"

"And I trained this person?"

"Despite all that. She's got a good head, I suppose. And I need to get back to her as soon as possible."

"Why is that?"

"Because for some reason," said Zelda, "your apprentice is the only one who can stop Thurmond."

"Well," said Walter. "That sounds like something to be proud of."

27

BATTLE OF THE CENTURIES

HENRY ZOLLER'S second year of college felt even lighter and freer than the first. He did not dwell or obsess over Bindra Dhar and the time travellers. And of course, he did not tell anyone about the extraordinary things he had witnessed that summer and over the course of his life. He knew no one would believe it. But the world of the time travellers remained ever present in the back of his mind. He appreciated the world more. He found himself behaving a little kinder to strangers—especially the weird ones who gave his friends pause—because who knew if they were one of them? When he walked places at night, he felt the faint, electric sensation of magic in the world.

From time to time, he pulled the red book, his most prized possession, out of its hiding place and skimmed through it, hoping to one day find a message. Maybe not a message for him, but a message of any sort that might offer another glimpse into the community of time travellers. But there was never any writing other than Sean's, searching for Bindra. In this regard, he felt a sort of kinship with Sean, for he too was always waiting for the day when he would see Bindra again.

It was in this second year that Henry met Will. Almost every day, Henry saw Will working behind the counter of his favorite coffee shop.

Almost every day, the two of them would trade smiles. Smiles became winks, and winks became long conversations that made the people in line behind Henry annoyed and late. Then came the day when Will briefly kept his hand in Henry's as he gave over his change. It was just a millisecond, but it nearly stopped Henry's heart. Will smiled at him and leaned over the counter. "So what's it gonna take for me to get your number?"

Henry could have easily melted there at the counter, but he somehow kept the composure to summon the smoothest flirtation he'd ever attempted.

"More than that," he said with a wink.

He left Will with disappointed longing—or at least he hoped he had. As for Henry, he left with shivering hands and insides, feeling more excited than the day he discovered time travel.

• • •

"So once we figured out the best metal for the scanning coil," said Marc Kurtzman, "then we had a new problem, which was the motor had to spin at such a rapid pace that it was literally overheating."

"Uh-huh," said Bindra.

"So Lumen is staying up all night thinking up cooling systems," said Marc. "Like a ventilation system, or liquid coolant or something like that. But then ventilation would just make the whole thing too heavy, and we couldn't figure out the right coolant to use, and then also the tubing would be a mess in there."

"Uh-huh."

"So then I was like, 'Duh, we don't need to cool it down, we just need to get it to rotate slower,'" said Marc. "So I looked at the software, and I was like, 'How can I make you do the same thing without being so hard on the hardware?' So you know what I did?"

"Marc?" said Bindra.

"Yeah?"

CHAPTER 27: BATTLE OF THE CENTURIES

"Stop talking."

Zelda hadn't been gone for more than a minute when Bindra started to feel nervous. True, they hadn't set a time for Zelda to return, exactly, and maybe it would be more convenient to come back to 1980 by way of a different anchor point. But still Bindra expected Zelda to time her return accordingly. She was perpetually annoyed by how time travellers possessed the ability to show up everywhere on time but generally lacked the inclination to actually do so.

"This is taking too long," said Bindra.

"She just left," said Lumen.

"I wasn't talking to you."

"Maybe she forgot what time she left," said Marc. "It happens sometimes."

"I wasn't talking to you either," said Bindra.

Her annoyance with Marc and Lumen was so powerful she almost didn't notice the wave of discomfort draping over her. Her stomach became hard, and her senses felt a jolt the way they had just before Thurmond arrived in the tunnels the night he killed Sean.

"Did either of you feel that?" she asked the two boys.

"Actually," said Lumen. "Yeah."

Lumen was standing, looking absently into space as if trying to sniff out some unseen danger. Bindra gestured to the Machine.

"Does that thing move?" said Bindra.

"Yeah," said Lumen. "Slowly."

"Okay," said Bindra. "We need to start pushing."

Bindra begrudgingly accepted Lumen's assistance in closing the Machine back into its black box. Marc watched both of them with annoyed confusion.

"What's going on?" he asked.

"We have to leave," said Bindra.

"Why, what's wrong? Where are we gonna go?"

"I don't know," said Bindra. "And I don't know."

"Well what the hell are we—"

"Marc," snapped Lumen. "Shut up and help us move the Machine, now!"

The Machine did move, slowly. The three young time travellers managed to push it out of the room and down through the stacks of books to the elevator. But it was big and awkward and tough to maneuver. A troublesome wheel had it swerving continuously to the left, and Bindra had to keep pushing it back into position. As they rode the elevator down six floors to the library lobby, Bindra grew increasingly nervous. Her senses kept telling her something was coming, something dangerous. But she didn't know what or when or from what direction. When the elevator doors opened she leaned slightly forward, almost in an attack position, expecting whatever it was to pounce. But it did not. The only people in the lobby were the same half-sleeping college students as before.

With some effort, they managed to guide the Machine down through the main doors and down the ramp to the lonely street. It remained a dark and remarkably still night. Even the distant sounds of house parties uptown had died away. Whatever it was that her subconscious thought was so dangerous, Bindra's eyes could not see it.

Then, as they started to push the Machine up the street—to where, exactly, none of them knew—the wave of dread returned to Bindra's nerves. She turned and in the cool light of a streetlamp saw an unnaturally tall silhouette at the other end of the street atop the crest of a dark hill. After staring at the figure for several seconds, she realized it was the shadow of a person sitting on an imposing horse. Lumen and Marc stopped as Bindra did and followed her eyes. They too were stunned by the sight of the horseman.

"What?" said Marc, breaking the night's silence.

And then, without noise or light, the horseman became six horsemen. The three young time travellers all jolted. Bindra yelped. In unison, the line of horsemen made the same movement, a movement that gave off the distinct sound of metal scraping on metal. Together the shadow cavalry lifted their sabers high, their blades shimmering in the streetlight. Then the shadows jumped forward and charged.

"Run!" shouted Bindra as she slammed her body against the back of the Machine. The boys followed her lead, and together they pushed the Machine into a much faster speed than any of them thought possible. But there was simply no way they were going to outrun six galloping horses. So Bindra stopped pushing and wrapped her arms around Marc and Lumen.

"What are you doing?" shouted Lumen.

"Is this metal?" yelled Bindra.

"Mostly."

"Then hold on!"

Bindra touched her fingertips to the edge of the Machine and shut her eyes. She felt her ears pop and the air around her went from hot and humid to cool and crisp. Her eyes opened to blinding sunlight, and she immediately fell to the ground. She felt as if she'd been hit by a small car.

"Who was that?" said Marc behind her.

"Troopers," answered Bindra between heavy breaths. "Of the Nineteenth."

"How do you know?"

"Educated guess."

A few passing students on their way to class paused to gawk at the three people with a giant black box in the street.

"Excuse me," said Lumen to the passing students. "Could one of you tell us what year it is?"

"Uh," said one girl. "It's 1986."

"Oh good," said Lumen. "We are…this is…we're doing a social experiment for, um, class. You've been very helpful to our…data."

Lumen walked back to the Machine, and Marc stood angrily over Bindra.

"You only took us six years?" said Marc.

"I was carrying you, and him, and that!" snapped Bindra. "Not exactly a light load." With some effort she stood up, put her hands on her hips and bent at the waist, trying to catch her breath. "How did they find us?"

"It's the Machine," said Lumen. "The scanner produces a faint but very distinct electromagnetic frequency. There's no frequency in this century like it."

"In that case, we can't stop here," said Bindra.

"Why not?" said Marc.

"If they have the ability to track this thing, all they'd have to do is station troopers in this town and wait for our signal to show up. We have to keep going."

"Going where?" said Marc.

"Downstream. Fourteen more years. Don't you get it? Lupita Calderon just invaded the Twentieth Century looking for this thing. We have to get somewhen she won't chase us."

"Twenty-One?"

"Exactly."

"How do you know she'll stop at the border?" said Lumen.

Bindra shrugged. "Another educated guess. Stay here. Protect the Machine."

"Where are you going?" said Lumen.

"1980."

"You're going back!?"

"We need Zelda. The plan was for her to return to 1980, so I've got to go back and get her."

CHAPTER 27: BATTLE OF THE CENTURIES

"You can't! It's not safe—"

Again Bindra's ears popped and disorienting darkness fell around her.

She deliberately daisy chained to a different anchor point in the city, and she had plenty to choose from. She arrived in 1980 behind a small grouping of university buildings. Making herself flat against one of the buildings, Bindra listened to the galloping time traveller cavalry as they searched the area for Lumen, Marc and herself. She moved to the edge of the wall and peered through the dark branches of a shrub as the horsemen rode by with their glinting sabers aloft. As the galloping faded, she crawled back toward the library, where she assumed Zelda would return when she was done in 1866.

When she emerged from the edge of the wall, standing upright in the darkness, she heard a whoosh cut through the air and saw a silver flash swipe at her waist. Bindra shouted and jumped back just as the saber sliced a short tear in her jacket. She righted herself and saw her attacker more clearly—a helmeted horseman wearing the green uniform of the troopers of the Nineteenth. He swung his saber again, this time at her neck, but she dropped low and dove at his stomach.

The two of them tumbled into the dirt, and Bindra heard the saber fall just above her head. She stretched out trying to reach the sword but felt something at her ankle. The trooper clasped his hand around her leg and she felt time start to shift. He was trying to drag her back to Nineteen. Instinctively she counter-travelled, launching into an impromptu tug-of-war session. The ground went from hot to cold, dry to wet to ice, all at once. Ghostly figures danced around her—people throughout spacetime whose dimensions they were passing through. The pressure changes were harsh enough that she felt her nose pop and release a trickle of blood.

Bindra twisted her head around and saw the trooper she was fighting. He, too, was bleeding from the nose, but his face was also white and sickly. It seemed as if the tug-of-war with Bindra was crushing him.

"How are you doing this?" he said in a struggling whisper.

It was then Bindra realized she was remarkably stronger in this area of time travel than her adversary. She looked forward again and dedicated all of her strength to returning the both of them to 1980. Slowly, time started to move downstream. The ground froze and then thawed again. The sun went back over their heads, then again, and again, until night returned and Bindra saw the sword on the ground just above her head. The trooper of the Nineteenth still clutched her ankle, but his hand was limp.

Angry footsteps approached and she snatched up the sword, swinging it over her head and bringing it down hard against another saber slicing at her face. The two swords made a sharp clang, and Bindra pushed the new trooper away before stumbling to her feet. She saw this new trooper was a woman with wavy, raven hair falling from underneath her cavalry helmet.

With both hands clutching the saber, Bindra swiped wildly at the trooper's midsection. The woman simply stepped back, one foot at a time, easily avoiding the swinging blade and grinning all the while. Finally the trooper lifted her own sword against Bindra's and slid it, blade against blade, until her hilt knocked Bindra's saber to the ground. Bindra stumbled and fell against a tree. The trooper lifted her sword above her head, prepared to deliver a decisive slice through Bindra's neck.

A blinding light flashed over them. The trooper shouted in pain and tossed her saber to the side. Bindra saw smoke rising from her hand. The trooper wobbled for a moment and then collapsed.

Zelda, wearing a mud-stained dress from Nineteen, stepped out of the shadows. Bindra grimaced at her. She smelled like her father.

"You're late," grumbled Bindra.

"I went to the library, right where I left you, like we agreed," said Zelda. "No you, no Machine, no annoying schoolboys... Are they dead?"

"No, unfortunately," said Bindra.

Zelda rolled her eyes and grabbed Bindra's arm. "When to, Trooper?"

CHAPTER 27: BATTLE OF THE CENTURIES

"1986," said Bindra.

The darkness turned once again to blinding sunlight. Bindra heard galloping hooves in the distance and yanked on Zelda's arm.

"This way," she said. "We need the Machine."

With Zelda close behind, Bindra ran around the side of the brick building, quickly spotting the Machine still sitting in the middle of the street with the two boys cowering behind it. As Bindra stepped into the street, she saw a horseman charge past the Machine, swiping just above Marc and Lumen's heads with his sword. The horseman slowed and spun around for another attack, this time leaving Lumen and Marc with no protection.

Zelda pushed Bindra to the side and aimed her little silver pistol at the horseman. Just before she could fire, the same raven-haired trooper they'd just escaped appeared in front of Zelda and pushed her gun toward the sky. Zelda fired anyway, and a white lightning bolt shot into the clouds. There was a sharp clap of thunder, and Bindra saw the horseman thrown from his animal, his saber skittering over the bricks in the street.

While Bindra ran toward the Machine, Zelda scooped up the horseman's saber, spun around and blocked the raven-haired trooper's blade with a nasty clang.

"Get the Machine out of here!" shouted Zelda.

Bindra reached the Machine just as Marc and Lumen threw their weight behind it, pushing it at a higher momentum toward the unhorsed trooper who was beginning to right himself. The trooper, seeing the large, black machine wheeled ever faster at his head, vanished into time.

Zelda and her opponent fought their way down the street, with Zelda placing herself between the increasingly frenzied trooper and the Machine. As Bindra, Marc and Lumen pushed the Machine up the street, Bindra knew she was in no condition to time travel, let alone carry three others and the Machine.

"It's your turn," she shouted at Lumen. He nodded.

"When?"

"I don't care," said Bindra. "The future. And daisy chain us to a different anchor point, somewhere more private."

Bindra, Marc and Lumen all touched hands to the Machine. Bindra looked behind her and saw the trooper knock Zelda's saber from her hand. Zelda grabbed the trooper's wrists with both hands to keep the blade away from her face. They became locked in an angry, grunting shoving match.

"Zelda!" shouted Bindra.

"I'm a little busy!"

Suddenly Bindra heard neighing and galloping behind her. Three more troopers on horseback had appeared, attacking from the opposite direction.

"Now!" she shouted to Zelda.

"Ah, fine!"

Zelda tugged her opponent around and forced the trooper's sword down onto the metal edge of the Machine.

"Go!" she shouted. Lumen closed his eyes.

Bindra's next breath sucked in a cloud of dust and she started coughing. They were inside a small room, surrounded by bookshelves, boxes and cleaning equipment. The only light was the soft orange glow of a dangling bulb. The Machine took up most of the room, with Marc, Lumen, Bindra and Zelda pressed against the walls. Lumen collapsed from the weight and Marc propped him up.

"When did you take us?" said Marc.

"1995," he gasped, gingerly touching his bloody nose.

"That's good," said Bindra. "Just five more years. We might have a moment to rest."

"I'm afraid not," said Zelda. "We've got a hitchhiker."

Zelda slowly stood over the Machine. Bindra looked and saw the raven-haired trooper rise and lift her blade, pointing it at Zelda's heart with only the Machine between them. The trooper pulled off her helmet and shook out her black hair. Her shoulders rose and fell with heavy breaths.

"Hi, Zelda," said the trooper.

"Hi, Allison," said Zelda. "Quite a day we've had."

"You're going to Twenty-One, then?" taunted Allison. "'Just five more years.' You expect Akande to save you?"

The trooper gingerly stepped around the corner of the Machine, never breaking eye contact with Zelda, never lowering her blade.

"What makes you think you can trust him?" said Allison.

"I don't," said Zelda. "But the Machine can either be Lupita's or Akande's, and I know Lupita will use it to make herself a tyrant."

"Every ruler becomes a tyrant, eventually," said Allison. "Do you really think Akande is any different?"

Allison stopped circling the Machine and bobbed on her knees and ankles as if on springs. Bindra watched the trooper's eyes grow restless, looking Zelda up and down, flashing to the Machine and back again.

"You disgust me, Zelda Clairing," spat Allison. "Turning your back on your century—on all of us—just because you're no longer mommy's favorite—"

The trooper rushed at Zelda who again grabbed at her wrists. Zelda growled as she pressed Allison against a bookshelf, knocking a few boxes to the floor. Bindra pulled Marc and Lumen to the Machine.

"Marc!" said Bindra. "It's up to you, now."

Marc nodded.

"Five years," he said over the sounds of Zelda's struggle. "I can do five years…"

Bindra heard the sound of meat smacking meat and turned to see the trooper Allison dazed and slumped against the wall and Zelda shaking out her bloodied fist.

241

"Grab on!" said Bindra, reaching out her hand.

But as soon as Zelda touched Bindra's hand, she screamed in pain. Bindra looked down to see that Allison had stabbed her sword through Zelda's leg, just above the ankle.

Then the room froze. Marc and Lumen's shouts went silent. Bindra looked back at them and saw their mouths frozen open like screaming statues. Even the dust particles in the air stayed motionless, levitating in the orange glow of the light bulb. Bindra could feel the energy of the trooper holding the sword in Zelda's leg—frenzied, electric, and determined to drag them back to her territory. The trooper's eyes were closed and Bindra watched her yell in a sustained howl while she tried to turn back the clock. But as hard as Allison tried, Bindra had a firm grasp on time, and the three of them travelled neither upstream nor downstream.

"Bindra," said Zelda in a trembling whisper. "What's happening?"

"We're in the present," said Bindra.

"Bindra," said Zelda again, and this time Bindra looked at her. Zelda's face was pale and her eyes were wide and bloodshot. "I think I'm going to die."

Of course, thought Bindra. She and the trooper were engaged in temporal tug-of-war, but Zelda was just the conduit, bearing the brunt of the struggle between the past and the future. If Zelda was going to live, Bindra had to either give up the fight or she would have to…

With an audible grunt, Bindra pulled, both physically and temporally, until the sword slid out of Zelda's leg. Dust once again flew about the room, and Bindra could again hear Marc and Lumen shouting. She collapsed and then Zelda, with blood pouring from her leg, collapsed on top of her. Bindra grabbed Lumen's hand and held fast to Zelda. The trooper Allison lifted herself off the ground and made a screaming lunge at the Machine, jabbing her sword into its side just as Marc brought them all into the future.

CHAPTER 27: BATTLE OF THE CENTURIES

Bindra came to rest against a small gravestone. They were outside again in the moonlight. Marc had evidently daisy chained them to a new anchor point. Two tug-of-war matches in such a short period had left Bindra nauseous and dizzy. She twisted around, peering over her gravestone, and saw Marc and Lumen lying on their backs with the Machine next to them.

A moonlit shadow swept over her gravestone and Bindra heard an angry grunt. She twisted around to see a silver blade dropping over her. But the saber was stopped when a bare hand reached out and clasped it. Zelda was almost hopping on one leg while she squeezed Allison's sword, spilling drops of blood onto Bindra's face. With her free hand, she grabbed the trooper's throat. The trooper resisted by grasping Zelda's wrist, and the two women glared into each other's eyes.

"Drop it, Allison," said Zelda.

"I'll cut off your hand," gasped the trooper.

"I'll wear a very nice bandage to your funeral. Now drop it."

"Do as she says, Trooper Rosey," said a stern voice in the distance.

In the blue darkness, Bindra saw dozens of enormous shadows approach from the trees—the Troopers of the Nineteenth, all on horseback, led by Lupita Calderon herself. Bindra glanced up at the sky, trying to spot the constellations that would tell her when they were, but the full moon blocked everything out. All she could do was pray that Marc had gotten them to the Twenty-First Century. If they were short by even a few hours, Lupita could slaughter them all right there and snatch the Machine.

Lupita rode her horse into the graveyard, right up to Bindra. The Nineteenth Centurion stared down at her with dead, expressionless eyes and the leathery face of a reanimated Egyptian mummy.

"Relinquish your sword, Trooper Rosey," said Lupita without taking her eyes from Bindra's. "And unhand that woman."

Trooper Allison Rosey dropped her sword and shoved Zelda away. Lupita let the silence hang in the air before she spoke.

"We are, after all," said the centurion, "guests in this century."

Bindra shivered with relief. Marc had gotten them into Akande's realm.

"You are Trooper Bindra Dhar, I presume?" said Lupita.

"Yes, Your Honor," said Bindra.

"I suppose you know that all of your fellow Troopers of the Twentieth have pledged their allegiance to me," said Lupita.

"Cowards," said Bindra. "All of them."

Lupita smiled. "I rather admire your audacity, Trooper Dhar. I shall give you this opportunity, and this opportunity alone, to renounce Solomon Christie and pledge your allegiance to me and to the Nineteenth Century."

"I will not, Your Honor," said Bindra.

Lupita's eyes rolled as she nodded. "Very well. In that case, I will accept your surrender of the Twentieth Century, hereby annexed by the Nineteenth Century as a subordinate vassal state."

"I cannot surrender the Twentieth Century, Your Honor, as I am not its centurion," said Bindra. "And if I could surrender the Twentieth Century, Your Honor, I would never surrender it to you."

"Very brave of you," said Lupita. "And very loyal to your centurion—a quality I value."

Lupita's eyes darted to Zelda before returning to Bindra.

"Nevertheless, the Twentieth Century is mine," said Lupita. "And I intend to find its centurion, for the purposes of a formal surrender, of course. But I would also be inclined to return him to your custody in exchange for that Machine."

"Holding Sol hostage will not get you the Machine, Your Honor," said Bindra. "And Sol would agree."

"I think it will not be his decision, nor yours, but Akande's. He is your ruler now, it would seem. Perhaps he will think a brand new century—with the old centurion in chains—is a fair price for the Machine."

Lupita kept up her cold stare, waiting for Bindra to waver.

She did not.

"If you have anything at all to say, Trooper Dhar, now is your last opportunity," said Lupita.

Though she felt sick and quite small, sitting on the cold ground against a gravestone, looking up at a conqueror who seemed a thousand years older, Bindra summoned her courage and nodded dismissively at Lupita's cavalry. "You're trespassing."

Again, Lupita smiled. "So we are." She spun her horse and faced her troopers. "Let us inspect our new century."

Lupita and her troopers vanished with their horses. Bindra heard stirring behind her and looked over the gravestone to see Marc finally waking up.

"What happened?" he mumbled.

"You saved everyone's life," said Bindra.

Marc nodded and his eyes closed again.

"Of course I did."

28

THE KNOWLEDGE

HENRY ZOLLER was a cautious young man who had never believed that taking his time was the same as wasting it. And so his courtship of Will the barista drew itself out over the course of his second year at college. It wasn't until the beginning of his third year that he and Will first hooked up—an event that occurred without any sort of prior planning, which Henry found rattling and slightly embarrassing.

The following week they went on their first date, and they agreed that whatever was to exist between them would be a casual affair. And so that date followed several others that petered out as fall turned to winter. By Christmas they had fallen apart and gravitated toward others. But when the New Year came, with their friends singing "Auld Lang Syne" around them, they kissed once again. They spent the first morning of that year in Will's bed talking until the sun came up, and when it did, neither of them could deny that what was to exist between them was more powerful than they'd once imagined.

It would be easy to say their relationship was perfect, but Henry knew that wasn't always the case. They could be unkind to each other. They fought, sometimes bitterly. They would spend weeks apart, emotionally if not physically. They both came close to cheating on one another. But they found each other again and again, as they had in the first place. Nothing about their relationship was easy, and that made it perfect.

As a side effect of this new phase in his life, Henry lost almost all interest in Bindra Dhar and the world of the time travellers. They remained, as they always had, in the back of his mind, but he no longer waited for the day when he might be reunited with Bindra, and he no longer skimmed the red book every other day looking for new messages. Instead it gathered dust beneath his bed. He never even tried to explain it to Will.

There was one ritual with which Henry Zoller kept the memory of Bindra Dhar alive. Whenever he visited home, he always made time to hold a brief vigil at James W. Robinson Park in case that happened to be the night when Bindra made her return. It never was.

In the summer after he started dating Will, Henry Zoller returned home to visit his mother before returning to his university. He found the park empty as he watched the sun go down. The sign at the park entrance said it would close at dusk—an inconvenience the previous abandoned tennis court didn't force upon Henry—but regardless, he didn't plan to comply. Instead, he sat there listening to the crickets, remembering the time when Bindra Dhar was a part of his life.

But when it became dark and when it became clear that the only ones joining him that night would be the crickets, he made his way home to his mother. She had declared, to his surprise, that this would be a rare night when she would not go out to the clubs downtown with her friends or with any of her boyfriends. Instead she made the two of them dinner at home.

Henry had never expected much from his mother, and she had never delivered much in return. He accepted that she longed for a time to which she could not return. He looked the other way when she went out partying, sometimes disappearing downtown for a few nights in a row. In exchange, she rarely invaded his personal life, leaving him with freedom his peers didn't have and allowing him to avoid the awkward and often dramatic family reactions many of his other gay friends described. He found the arrangement most agreeable.

But on that particular night, his mother was unusually motherly. They ate dinner together, drank wine together—her far more than him—and she asked questions about his life at college with a degree of interest she had never before taken. To Henry it seemed as if she was reveling in his college life, perhaps feeling the pull of youth she had always fervently clung to, sometimes at his expense.

And then, without any warning, she said something that at first Henry thought he must have misheard.

"So I should probably tell you," said his mother. "Stephen is dead."

Henry squeezed his wine glass to keep from dropping it. There was no question about which Stephen she meant, but the abruptness of her words made him think it must be someone else. The harshness also shocked him. "Stephen is dead" instead of "Stephen died." As if his step-father had always been dead.

"When?"

"A few weeks ago," said his mother.

"Why didn't you tell me?"

"It just didn't seem that important," she said. "I haven't seen him for ten years."

"How did he die?"

"Cancer," said his mother, waving her hand. "He had it off and on for some time."

"I…didn't know…" stammered Henry. "You never told me."

"Oh, I just didn't see a reason to. There was nothing anyone could do."

"I would've visited. We should have visited. Was anyone with him?"

His mother was already staring into space, hand against her temple, swishing her wine glass around. "Elliot took care of him," she said with a twirl of her hand.

"Who?"

"Elliot," repeated his mother. "His boyfriend or partner or whatever they were. I'm sure I told you about Elliot."

"You didn't...are you saying...?" said Henry, but his mother didn't notice.

"Can't say I didn't see that coming. I have a very good sense about that sort of thing. Always was something a little faggoty about him."

Henry had no ability to speak or to think. He put his wine glass down a little too quickly and watched it wobble, wondering if it would tip over. The wobbling seemed to go on forever, even though it couldn't have been more than a half a second, and all that time he held his breath and felt his stomach transform into a ball of lead. "Excuse me?"

"Oh don't be so sensitive about it," his mother said. "It's not like he was your father. Your father never would've been like that. He was a real man. I wish you could have met him."

Henry's stomach remained heavy and cold as his mother, oblivious once again to the harm she had done, poured another glass of wine. He watched her fall, as she often did, into deep reminiscence and longing for the deceased father he'd never known. Henry seethed in silence. All he could do was listen as she rattled off his father's many manly traits, things he had heard so many times before, how handsome and funny his father was, how she wished he could have raised Henry instead of Stephen, how, tragically, Henry wasn't even born yet when his father was killed in that train crash in West Virginia.

• • •

Seeking Akande meant seeking the ocean, and so the four wayward time travellers were forced to "commandeer" an automobile to drive them across Twenty-First Century America to the nearest coast. They chose a truck large enough to carry the Machine, Bindra and Zelda in the bed while Marc sat in the passenger seat and Lumen, being the only one among them who had ever operated a motor vehicle, drove.

Bindra stared out over the empty plains as the stolen truck cruised over the open highway. Morning was coming and the sun was conquering the navy blue of night with streaks of pink and purple and orange. She watched Zelda wrap bandages around the wounds on her leg and hand. She wondered if Akande would greet them as friends or as enemies. She worried about Sol and whether he had escaped Lupita's conquest of Twenty. She agonized about Thurmond and whether he could be beaten, or whether she should disappear back to Twenty-Two, back to India, back to the mountains and her family.

All the while, Zelda tried to explain everything she'd seen in 1866 and everything she'd learned about Thurmond.

"He's normal," said Zelda.

"Normal?" said Bindra. "What does that even mean?"

Zelda shrugged as she pulled another strip of cotton around her leg. "I don't know. He's normal. He's normal, charismatic, charming, funny, modest, and he's completely insane."

"I thought we already knew that. How can he think he can time travel onto a moving train? It's impossible without an anchor point."

"That's what I thought," said Zelda. "But how does Akande do it? With his boat?"

"You heard Sean. He has some sort of artificial anchor point on board."

"Supposedly…"

"Fine, supposedly," said Bindra. "But if Thurmond has that sort of technology, how does he get it on a train?"

"I don't know," snapped Zelda. "Maybe he shrank it. Maybe he stole some sort of technology from the future. Maybe your boyfriend built it for him."

"He's not my boyfriend." She glanced quickly at Lumen through the window of the truck to make sure he hadn't heard anything. "He just…" continued Bindra. "We kept a lot of things secret from each other, you know? I mean I don't even know his last name. But I thought there was something between us, at least. And this whole…legend business, I mean, it's really overwhelming, you know—"

"Oh, Bindra, listen." Zelda lifted her bloody, bandaged palm in front of Bindra's face. "It seems like we're starting to have a moment here, and it's probably best if we just put an end to that now."

"What is wrong with you?"

"It's nothing personal," said Zelda. "I just don't want you getting the impression that we're friends. So I suppose in that sense, it is a little personal."

Bindra glared at her.

Zelda held her stare for a moment before relenting, rolling her eyes and nodding. "Fine, yes, I see how that must strike you as rude. You have to understand, I am an ancient. I come from a time when death is always present, and we try not to get attached to people. We don't make friends when I come from. The closest thing to friendship I can ever offer a person is to say I trust them not to kill me. It's just a cultural difference."

Bindra shook her head and stared out at the empty fields passing as they sped down the highway. "Fine. How long were you in 1866?"

"It felt like a day and a half."

"And in that time you didn't learn anything useful about Thurmond, did you?"

"It depends on your definition of 'useful,'" said Zelda. "I did, for example, learn he is apparently a native of Twenty and a resident of Nineteen. And I learned a great deal about his character."

"Such as?"

"He believes," said Zelda. "He believes he can do what he says. He believes he can beat fate. He believes he's a ripple. He believes he exists because of interference. He believes he can raise the dead and change the past. And he believes that he should, for the good of the traveller community. He says he's going to save everyone—all the laymen, all the time travellers. And he means it."

"Sure. Did he mean it when he murdered Sean? Who was that supposed to save?"

"That's another interesting thing. He doesn't think he's murdered Sean. He thinks he's murdered you."

"Really?"

"Yes," said Zelda. "And he's quite worked up about it. Said it was the hardest thing he's ever had to do."

"How thoughtful. Did he explain why he hates me so much?"

"It wasn't hate." Zelda shook her head. "It was like…resignation. It was as if it was necessary to kill you. He said you were the only one who could stop him."

"Did he happen to say how?" said Bindra.

"We didn't get that far; things came up. Maybe it's because of *the legend*." She said the last two words with mock seriousness.

"What are you talking about?" said Bindra.

"What the two idiots were saying," said Zelda, nodding toward Lumen and Marc. "The legend about how you defeated Thurmond by shouting his real name."

"I don't know his real name. For all I know it could be 'Thurmond.'"

"True. And he never told me either. What if we asked Mr. Disaster?"

"We can't," said Bindra, closing her eyes. "He's dead."

"We're time travellers," said Zelda. "We can find him before he's dead."

"It doesn't matter. I don't think he knew Thurmond's real name either." She felt herself falling asleep as the car bumped along.

"That's not what I meant," said Zelda.

"What did you mean?"

"I meant he might know why Thurmond wanted to kill you. Since he set it all up."

"Set what up?"

"He lured you and Sean to 2003, didn't he? Then he told Thurmond when and where you'd be so he could kill you."

"No, that doesn't make sense," said Bindra. "Mr. Disaster was surprised when he saw me. Sean didn't tell him I'd be there."

"Well, someone knew. Thurmond knew you'd be there. Who else knew where you'd be on June 17, 2003?"

"No one," said Bindra as she drifted to sleep. "Just me and Sean and Mr. Disaster…"

And Henry Zoller, she thought. In her mind, his face flashed before her eyes. That entire evening came back to her in flashes. Him carrying her to safety, giving her disgusting, but lovingly made tea. His laugh, his smile, and how, when she told him she owed him a favor, he didn't ask her to change the past for him. All he wanted to do was to learn. All he wanted was to be a time traveller like her. And he knew. He knew she was there. He knew she was then. Henry Zoller knew. Bindra's eyes shot open.

"No," she said quietly.

"What?" said Zelda.

Bindra shook her head and searched the pink morning sky for a different answer.

"No," she said again. "No, no, no."

"What in Mórrígan's name are you on about?"

"NO!" Bindra shouted as she started beating on the window of the truck. "Stop the car. Stop the car!"

Lumen brought the truck to a sliding halt. Bindra leapt from the bed and stumbled into a field at the side of the road. Lumen followed her.

"Bindra, what's wrong?" he said. "Are you okay?"

"NO!" she screamed at the ground.

She lifted her hands to her head and started tugging at her hair. She saw her tears pock the dirt below with tiny craters. Her knees bent and she crumbled to the ground and cried.

"Henry!" she shouted. "Henry!"

• • •

Disaster always follows the same pattern. Every catastrophe has a point of no return. It's like anything else—bound to the laws of physics and chemistry and, yes, a little bit of unpredictable human nature. But even that follows a pattern. In every instance where a human being realizes that he or she has been impacted by a disaster, there is also a point of no return. And it's usually a point no one notices.

Henry Zoller did not notice at first when Will was late visiting him at his home in Jackson Park over the winter break of their senior year. The trip was to be brief, and they were to pretend at being nothing more than friends in order to avoid tipping off Henry's mother about their relationship. But Henry was distracted, by what exactly he could never remember, from noticing that Will did not arrive at the designated time. He didn't even really notice that Will wasn't replying to his text messages as the night grew darker. The point of no return for Henry Zoller and for Will had long since passed when Henry saw the local news reporting what happened on Interstate 66. The first car slid. The second car stopped in time, but the truck behind him couldn't and it slipped over. The next few cars slid, another car flipped. Seven people died. Seven people had to die. It's an event that had to happen. But there was no way for Henry Zoller or the family of William Thurmond to understand that.

When the funeral was over and all tears had been shed, there was to be no more hiding for Henry Zoller. He told his mother the truth—not only about who he was but about who she was. He refused to live in the meticulously crafted, carefully contained personality he had cultivated since his youth. He refused to live an untruthful life, and because his life as Henry Zoller had, for the most part, been untruthful, he shed the name itself and adopted the name of the only man he'd ever loved. And because there was no place in the world for Henry Zoller to live, he had to find a world in which he could live as Thurmond.

And so the red book came roaring back into his consciousness. Bindra Dhar once again dominated his thoughts. The world of the time travellers felt tantalizingly close, and the determination to cross into that world consumed him with invisible and horrible fire. Searching for a doorway into that realm became the driving force of his life. He found clues to that doorway in dusty library bookshelves and in the whispers of wary strangers who hesitated to tell him too much.

He disappeared completely from his former life, and the friends of Henry Zoller wondered and worried about what had happened to him. Having no other explanation on hand, many came to terms with the idea that in the despair of having lost Will, he took his own life in some quiet, anonymous way. And in one sense, he had done just that. For years, the man who had become Thurmond thought of nothing else but time travel. He gave no time to human interaction, or to a job, or to chronological life. He allowed his health to deteriorate. He slept beneath bridges or in open fields or in homeless shelters. The red book became the only possession he still carried from his previous life. He suffered greatly, enduring bouts of depression and anger that sometimes evolved into violent rage. He saw nothing, heard nothing, read nothing, and absorbed nothing that would not bring him closer to learning how to time travel. And so after years of despair and obsession, the man who had become Thurmond did what few time travellers had ever accomplished.

He taught himself the Knowledge.

29

THE GALLANT

THE *ALARINKIRI* was as Bindra remembered it, with its opulence and stateliness, the impressive paintings of the century's most important moments and the imposing statues of Akande the Gallant lining the throne room. Akande sat on his throne staring ponderously at the floor, his gleaming white suit replaced by a simple, mournful, cream-colored dashiki. All around the centurion, his remaining troopers buzzed about, passing dispatches to each other and keeping track of Lupita's progress as she marched across the Twentieth Century. The troopers of the Twenty-First, Bindra could see, were in battle-mode while their centurion still grieved for their lost colleague and his lost friend.

The tense discussions and battle planning ceased as Bindra, Zelda, Marc and Lumen made their way to the end of the throne room's red carpet. The four of them bowed to the weary centurion, and Akande the Gallant was pulled briefly from his despair and spoke to them with a heavy sigh. "What do you want?"

"It is good to meet a fellow traveller, Your Honor," Bindra said.

"To make the road less lonely," said Akande. "What do you want?"

"Your Honor," said Bindra. "We are members of the Independent

Intercentury Interference Task Force, and we're seeking asylum in the Twenty-First Century."

Akande rolled his eyes slightly and briefly smiled through his sorrow.

"You and a thousand other people," he muttered.

"We have come a long way, Your Honor," said Bindra. "We ask for refuge and for your allyship in the fight against the criminal called Thurmond."

"Trooper Dhar," interrupted one of Akande's troopers. It was a dark, lanky, bearded man holding a large map of the Twenty-First Century. "My name is Hector Romero, captain of the troopers of the Twenty-First. Let me be very clear about our situation. Lupita Calderon and the troopers of the Nineteenth have invaded a bordering century. The Twentieth has fallen. Its centurion—your centurion—has disappeared. We do not yet know if Lupita intends to invade our territory. This is an unprecedented crisis."

"I am already aware of that, Trooper Romero," said Bindra.

"Then perhaps you'll understand that we have more important things to worry about. Thurmond is the least of our concerns."

"Thurmond is the source of this crisis," Bindra insisted. "Thurmond is the crisis."

She ignored the indignant trooper and turned her appeal directly to Akande the Gallant.

"Your Honor, I was with Sean Logan when he died," she said bluntly. "I know how much he meant to you, and I want you to know how much he meant to me."

Akande looked into her eyes for a moment, but soon he appeared too pained to keep her stare and he looked away.

"Lupita Calderon was not responsible for Sean Logan's murder," Bindra continued. "Neither was Sol Christie. Your troopers are right, Your Honor. This is an unprecedented crisis. Three centuries are at war with each other; three hundred years have been plunged into chaos—chaos that Thurmond has created and exploited. Thurmond does not care who governs, invades, or conquers Nineteen or Twenty or Twenty-One. His goal is to tear at the fabric of spacetime. Forgive me, but Trooper Romero is wrong. Thurmond is the greatest of your concerns."

Again Akande struggled to pull himself from his own depression. He leaned back in his throne, and in doing so he appeared to straighten himself a bit taller than when Bindra had first approached him.

"The last time I sent people to stop Thurmond," he said quietly, "one of them did not return. What advantage do we have now that we did not have before?"

"We will show you." Bindra motioned to Marc and Lumen, unwilling to take her eyes from Akande's for fear that she would lose him again.

Marc and Lumen rushed to the rear of the throne room and rolled the Machine through the grand entrance. The troopers of the Twenty-First craned their necks to see what the travellers had brought. As they rolled the Machine, however, the wheels became caught up in Akande's red carpet. The giant black box came to a sudden halt. Lumen threw his weight behind it as Marc tried to maneuver it in the right direction. Zelda shook her head with embarrassment. Bindra bit her lower lip to contain her composure. Akande watched the sad spectacle for a few moments before shaking his head and rising from the throne.

"Okay, okay, enough of that," he said as he walked past Bindra toward the Machine. "You're ruining my carpet. What is this thing?"

"Your Honor," said Bindra, "this is a—"

"It's the Machine," said Trooper Romero, brushing past Bindra. "The one Lupita told us about."

So, thought Bindra, Lupita had already made her offer.

"Lupita Calderon wants to give me the entire Twentieth Century," said Akande loudly as he examined the black box. "In exchange for this?"

"Your Honor, this Machine is incredibly powerful," said Bindra. "It can, in theory, find anyone at any time in any location. In the hands of someone like Lupita Calderon it's a dangerous weapon, but in our hands it could be the key to defeating Thurmond."

"Who would build such a thing?" said Akande.

Lumen nervously cleared his throat. "We did, Your Honor. We built it for Walter Franklin Brooks, for the Society of Black Time Travellers. It was meant to be a tool for knowledge."

Bindra watched as Akande gingerly touched the top of the Machine.

"Knowledge is power," he said. "What is stopping me from refusing Lupita's offer and keeping this for myself, for my own uses?"

"Nothing, Your Honor," said Bindra.

Marc shifted uncomfortably, prepared to interject. Lumen raised his hand to stop his companion.

"Your Honor, please," said Trooper Romero. "You must hand this over to Lupita immediately."

"You would have me acquire a new century?" said Akande without taking his eyes from the Machine.

"Who cares about the Twentieth Century?" said Trooper Romero. "You don't need the trouble. But possessing Twenty would put a hundred years between us and Lupita. She has far more troopers than we do, and she is gathering more. If you do not give this device to her she may well come and take it."

"She would not dare," said Bindra. "It would mean war."

"Keeping this Machine means war," said Romero. "Giving it to Lupita would keep the peace, Your Honor. You can bring peace to these centuries."

"The only way to bring peace to the centuries is to defeat Thurmond, Your Honor," said Bindra. "This Machine can help us do that. If you give it to Lupita, you'll be giving a dictator unlimited power."

Bindra came closer to Akande so he could still hear her whisper. Trooper Romero nervously moved to block her but Zelda stared him down.

"Your Honor, we came here because we believed you would use this power responsibly," she said. "I came here because I believe you will never touch this Machine. I believe you will allow it to remain, safe from Lupita, in your realm, and you will allow us to use it against Thurmond. I believe you will do these things because you know that Thurmond is the real enemy here, the only enemy. He is the one who took Sean from us, the one who is taking so much from us, even now. I believe you are who you say you are. I believe you are Akande the Gallant. I hope I am right."

Bindra watched as Akande gently nodded to himself. He let his fingertips bounce against the top of the Machine, as if he could feel the power that was so close to being his and his alone. She watched as those same fingertips left the Machine and he turned back toward his throne.

"This Machine does not belong to Lupita Calderon," he said.

Trooper Romero started after him. "Your Honor, please—"

"Nor does it belong to me," continued Akande. "It belongs, as the boy said, to the Society of Black Time Travellers. I am compelled to keep it safe until such time as it can be reclaimed."

Akande the Gallant once again sat on the throne of the Twenty-First Century with royal straightness and stature.

"As for the Independent Intercentury Interference Task Force," he said. "Your request for asylum is granted. My century is your century. You shall have sole authority over the operation of this Machine—so long as it remains under the supervision of its makers." He pointed stringently at Lumen and Marc. "Trooper Romero."

"Yes, Your Honor?"

"We are as safe from Lupita Calderon as we will ever be," said Akande.

The centurion allowed a moment for this declaration to hang in the air of the throne room. He leaned to his side and pointed a finger at Trooper Romero.

"You and the rest of the troopers of the Twenty-First will direct your efforts to stopping and apprehending the criminal time traveller known as Thurmond. I want it spoken across spacetime that when other centuries descended into chaos, Twenty-One did what was right."

Akande the Gallant looked again to Bindra and gave her an approving nod. "Now, Trooper Dhar. What does the Independent Intercentury Interference Task Force need to complete its mission?"

"We need a library. The bigger the better."

Akande grinned. "You are in luck. I never leave home without one."

30

GHOSTS IN THE MACHINE

THE CAPTAIN of the *Alarinkiri* was an enormous, muscular woman with a shaved head. She escorted Bindra and Zelda through the narrow passageways of the ship, while somewhere behind them they could hear the frustrated sounds of Marc and Lumen trying to maneuver the giant Machine. The captain came to twin doors at the end of a corridor and searched through her ring of keys for the right one. Finding it, she unlocked the doors and slid them open. Bindra and Zelda followed her onto a balcony overlooking an open room lined with books, paintings, and globes. In one corner sat a lonely computer station.

The centerpiece of the library was a section of wall that held no books but instead displayed two giant maps: one of the world and one of the Twenty-First Century. Both maps appeared to be paper but were also constantly updated with information—written, erased, and written again by invisible hands from the past. The world map showed the *Alarinkiri's* current location, sliding south along the coast of Nova Scotia.

"The geographic map is synced with the ship's navigation and with the century map," said the captain. "His Honor needs to know when and where the ship is located at any point in Twenty-One so as to allow for easy travel. As you can see, Akande likes to keep us along the coasts so he can easily make landfall as needed. Now as for the library, you'll find it is small but fairly diverse. Books from all over Eighteen, Nineteen, Twenty, Twenty-One and Twenty-Two."

"I see," said Bindra. "And the computer, can it access the internet while we're at sea?"

"Certainly," said the captain. "We're hacked into several American military satellites. It's not that hard, really—their current codes are all public records in the future. Do you have any other questions for me?"

"Can you tell us how Akande turned this ship into an anchor point?" said Zelda.

"Wouldn't tell you if I knew," said the captain. "I'll leave you to it. Don't steal anything."

She pushed past Lumen and Marc as they hauled the Machine onto the balcony. With Bindra and Zelda keeping the Machine steady, the four time travellers slowly rolled the Machine down the stairs, bouncing the wheels step by step. With every bounce, the electric innards of the device would rattle and Lumen and Marc would moan and fuss as if they were absorbing the Machine's pain. Eventually they brought it to the bottom of the steps and wheeled it into the library.

"This might not work the way you want it to," said Marc.

"Why not?" said Bindra. "It worked before."

"It worked in a real library. This is tiny by comparison. Instead of asking a library a question, you'll be asking a little ship, and they probably don't have any documentation about Thurmond on this boat that it can read."

"Not yet," said Bindra.

"What does that mean?"

Bindra turned to Lumen and nodded at the computer station in the corner. "Can you find him?"

Lumen paused, staring at her before closing his eyes and nodding. "Yes, I see. I can try."

CHAPTER 30: GHOSTS IN THE MACHINE

He walked to the computer and Marc set about readying the Time Machine, fumbling with the mess of wires inside the contraption and struggling to turn it on. Zelda watched the endeavor while Bindra quietly sequestered herself in a corner of the library, absently looking through the stacks of books.

"What're you doing?" said Zelda's voice behind her.

"I was thinking," said Bindra. "I knew Lupita was coming. When we were still in 1980, in the library, before you returned. I could feel that her troopers were coming before they arrived."

"Really?"

"And it happened before," said Bindra. "The night Sean was killed, I could feel Thurmond coming before he arrived."

Bindra felt a sharp pain in her right shoulder. She yelped and reeled and caught a glimpse of Zelda holding a clenched fist.

"Ow!" she shouted. "What was that for?"

"Just checking," said Zelda, and she went back in for another punch. Bindra blocked it with the palm of her hand.

"Stop it!"

"Relax. I know what's going on. I think."

"What is it?" said Bindra. "I can tell the future now?"

"A little bit," said Zelda. "It's because of what you've been doing with that one." She nodded at Lumen typing away at the computer.

"Tug-of-war?" said Bindra.

Zelda nodded. "You've been spending a lot of time in the moment. Weird things happen when you live in the moment. We're always time travelling, even the laymen. Just moving from one moment to the next. But you keep stopping. Since you're existing neither in the past nor the future, your brain has time to perceive things that haven't happened yet, or at least get an idea of what's likely to come next."

"How is that possible?"

"It's not that strange. All your brain does, all the time, is react to things, and sometimes it reacts even before things happen. Like this."

She clenched her fist and sent it toward Bindra's shoulder again. Bindra flinched and dodged before Zelda stopped her fist.

"See?" said Zelda. "You're not special."

Bindra thought over this new information carefully as Zelda started away from her. "Can you feel things now?"

"What?" said Zelda.

"You were with me in the basement. You were with me in the moment, not going upstream or downstream. So I was wondering if, since that happened, can you feel—"

"I'll stop you there," said Zelda. "What happened to me in the basement..."

She stumbled over her words and seemed not to know what to say next. Bindra found this surprising since Zelda rarely seemed to be caught off guard. Zelda's eyes darted up and down as she prepared what she had to say.

"I have been through a lot of things," she said carefully. "I have been through a lot of pain. What happened in that moment was the worst thing I have ever felt."

"Whoa, um...I'm sorry," stammered Bindra. "I'm really sorry, Zelda. That's never happened before. I didn't know what else to do, I had to pull you back to us—"

Zelda held up her hand. "It's okay. You did what you had to do. What you're doing, with your boy, with your tug-of-war games, it hasn't hurt you yet. It's making you a stronger traveller, and it may even make you see a little bit of the future. But that's only when you're in control. What happened to me is what it looks like when you're not in control. Do you understand?"

Zelda came closer to Bindra and spoke to her quietly and sternly. "I told you I was not your instructor. So I'm only going to tell you what you should already know. Time is a powerful thing. You can sail across it, you can dive into it, but it is always moving you and no one can resist it forever. If you try to stay still for longer than time wants, time will crush you."

Their private talk was interrupted by the sudden electric whir of the Time Machine coming to life behind them. Zelda kept a suspicious eye on Bindra as they joined Marc, watching the green letters materialize on the black screen. Bindra heard the printer at the computer station working its heart out. Lumen had found what she needed.

Question.

"I'll remind you both that this probably won't work," said Marc.

"Thank you, Marc," said Bindra. "But that more or less applies to this entire mission. Lumen?"

"Coming," he said from across the room.

Lumen handed over a white piece of paper, wet with thick, fresh printer ink. Zelda looked over Bindra's shoulder. The young man in the photograph was smiling, clean-shaven and less chiseled than the man she'd met in 1866. But it was definitely him.

"It looks like he hasn't posted anything in the last few years," said Lumen. "This is his most recent profile picture, from November 24, 2007."

"It'll do," said Bindra. "Can I borrow a pen?"

Marc reached into his pocket and passed a pen to her. "What is the point of this?"

Bindra took the pen and started writing below the photograph. "It can scan writing and photographs, right? Anything a human being consciously preserved for posterity?"

"That's right," said Marc.

"I think it's time to make the Machine play by our rules," she said. She placed the photograph, now with the words *Henry Zoller, November 24, 2007* written beneath it, atop the Machine. Bindra leaned over the Machine's keyboard and began typing.

What can you tell me about Thurmond the time traveller?

The Machine paused for several moments, leaving the monitor black except for Bindra's question. Finally it replied with three consecutive lines.

Thurmond the time traveller is dangerous.

Thurmond the time traveller is deadly.

One should not seek Thurmond the time traveller.

"Why is it saying the same thing as before?" asked Bindra.

"Sometimes it repeats information it thinks is important," said Lumen. "It remembers."

Bindra sighed and returned her hands to the keyboard.

When is Thurmond the time traveller?

The screen remained black as the fans and gears inside the Machine sped up and slowed down. Then the screen lit up with green letters.

This is unknown.

"You have to ask it," said Zelda quietly. "You have to say his real name."

Reluctantly, Bindra stared back into the blackness of the Machine's monitor. She lifted trembling fingers over the keyboard and began typing.

What do you know about Henry Zoller?

Again the Machine took its time mulling over an answer.

See Henry Zoller in 2007.

Did Henry Zoller become a time traveller?

See Henry Zoller was not admitted into the Time Travellers' Guild.

Did Henry Zoller become a time traveller without admission to the Time Travellers' Guild?

Yes.

How?

See Henry Zoller in 2007.

See the face of Henry Zoller in 2006.

See the face is older, but see it is Henry Zoller.

CHAPTER 30: GHOSTS IN THE MACHINE

See the conclusion. See Henry Zoller became a time traveller.
This is all that is known.

Bindra pushed away from the keyboard. There was no way it was a coincidence. Henry Zoller learned how to time travel. Henry Zoller became Thurmond. And, she remembered, Henry Zoller only knew about time travel in the first place because she had told him. She introduced him to time travel and promised to instruct him. If she had kept that promise, perhaps she could have taught him how to use the Knowledge. She could have taught him right from wrong the way Mr. Brooks had taught her. But she wasn't there for him. She'd shown Henry the Knowledge and never followed through. She had half-baked a time traveller.

"Bindra?" said Zelda, disturbing her thoughts.

Bindra looked sadly into her eyes. "It's my fault," she said quietly.

Zelda nodded. "That is why you can stop it. Ask it the question."

Bindra turned again to the Machine and bit her lip, feeling a tear roll down her cheek. She started typing.

Where is Henry Zoller in 2006?

31

ERROR CORRECTION

JULY 24, 2006, was a bad day for Nathan Hocking. Once the powerful president of Continental Railways, Hocking was now eighty-seven, living out his final days in lower Manhattan, constantly forgetting things and losing items around his penthouse apartment. His usual nurses neglected to pay a visit that day, or perhaps they had come to check on him and he forgot. He didn't like the nurses. Though he'd never witnessed them doing so, he was certain they were stealing things from his apartment.

As Hocking shuffled through his office, supported by his cane, trying to find the important legal documents he needed to sign, he started to hear a strange noise coming from his parlor. It sounded like someone was playing a simple piano melody, which surprised Hocking because he was not expecting visitors and he did not own a piano.

Hocking came into his parlor to see that there was, indeed, a piano in his home, which he could not remember buying or receiving. And sitting at the piano was a man wearing a black suit and tie. Hocking was certain he had never seen the man before.

"Who the hell are you?" growled Hocking. "And how did you get in here?"

The man stopped playing and turned to him. "You may not remember. That's to be expected," said the stranger. "But I just wanted to have one last talk with an old business partner."

"Business partner? This is nonsense. Nurse! Where in the hell are those nurses?"

"I'm afraid they're gone, Nathan," said the man at the piano. "Taking care of other people. But I don't think we need them."

"Who are you?" Hocking demanded again. He had the creeping suspicion that maybe this really was a business partner, or maybe even a family member, and his memory was just so far gone that he couldn't tell. The stranger stood up and approached Hocking, trying to cool his anger and guide him into a comfortable chair. Hocking simply could not remember who this alleged business partner was. He also couldn't remember where this chair had come from.

"It's all okay, Nathan," said the stranger. "It's okay that you don't remember me. We've never met."

"We haven't?" barked Hocking. "Well then, what is this? You coming in here and calling me your business partner—"

"We had a slightly different relationship than most of your other partners. You worked with my associate, Francisco DuPree. You agreed to build something for us, and in exchange, he gave you this."

The stranger pulled something from his jacket pocket and showed it to Hocking. It was an enormous, pinkish diamond—a gem the old man hadn't looked upon in sixty years, having stored it away to avoid having to explain its provenance.

"The Sanguine Diamond," whispered Hocking. "Where did you get that? You stole that from me!"

"I didn't steal it," said the stranger gently. "Your family didn't know what to do with it and I offered to take it off their hands to avoid awkward questions."

"What in God's name are you talking about?"

"Did you build it, Nathan?"

Hocking glared at the stranger. "Build it?"

"Come on." The stranger gestured with the diamond. "This wasn't the only thing we gave you. I passed you information, I directed your investments, I guided your company to the top, and in exchange, did you build what I asked you to build?"

"Yes, I built it. I built it and it didn't do any good. We nearly lost the company after the disaster and the board forced me to step down to cover their asses. It didn't make one bit of goddamn difference that I built that thing for you. The train still crashed!"

At this news, the stranger simply stared at the floor, nodding slowly to himself. "As long as you built it, Nathan, to my specifications, the train will not crash. I just haven't yet stopped it from crashing."

The stranger stood up and straightened his jacket. Hocking tried to follow him but found he was too weak to leave the chair.

"Where the hell do you think you're going?" he demanded. "Coming in here, uninvited, stealing from a dying man's own home."

"It's not your home, Nathan."

"The hell it isn't! I'm here, my things are here."

"Not for long," said the stranger. "I only came to confirm you did your part, to say goodbye, and to make sure you're gone before the authorities arrive."

"You're a crazy person," rasped the old man.

Hocking suddenly found it was very hard to breathe. Not only did it feel like his windpipe was closing in on itself, his lungs felt like they were being pricked by a dozen needles every time he took a breath. He issued a couple of dry coughs to clear whatever was blocking his air, but he only felt more pain. As his wheezes became terribly audible, he looked up at the stranger.

"You're not going to get me some help?" gasped Hocking. "Find the nurses? Call 911?"

"No, I don't think I will," said the stranger. "There's no way for you to know this, so don't feel too bad about it. But you killed my father."

"Excuse me?"

"You allowed a known drunk to drive that train. Because of you, seventy-two people died, including my father. Luckily, you can know you died and met your creator having helped me stop it from ever happening. But that doesn't make me any more sympathetic to your demise."

"So you're just going to stand there?" coughed Hocking. "You're going to let an old man suffer and die right in front of you?"

"Nathan, please. I thought by now you would've realized what's happening here."

Hocking again struggled to get out of the chair but instead fell on his hands and knees, hacking and coughing at the floor.

"You don't remember the last time you saw your nurses or your family," said the stranger as he strolled around the room. "Some of your things are here, yes, but there's so much here that isn't yours. You must've had the feeling in the last few days that this isn't your house. There's a simple reason for that. It's not your house. Someone else lives here, not you. Because you're dead. I killed you three years ago."

Hocking vomited and fell into dizziness as he tried to follow the stranger around the room with his eyes.

"I know, it probably doesn't make a lot of sense," said the stranger. "How can you be dead and yet still be here? You see, the way time travellers keep it straight is that we say time is like a river. If I change something—like killing you, for example—well, that's like tossing a rock into the river. It makes a splash and sends ripples out everywhere. It's just a question of how long it takes for the ripples to arrive on the shore."

The stranger crouched down next to Hocking and looked into his eyes.

CHAPTER 31: ERROR CORRECTION

"It's funny, actually," he chuckled. "You can be reading a book and if another time traveller in the past writes a note in the same book, the words just sort of appear."

The stranger opened his palms in front of Hocking's heaving face to illustrate the effect and smiled.

"It can be spooky the first time, but you learn to enjoy it. Anyway, it's the same principle here, just a lot worse for you. You see, you're being corrected by time. Your family knows you died three years ago. Everyone on Earth knows you died three years ago. The last thing that time needs to fix is you."

By this time, of course, Nathan Hocking couldn't really hear the stranger. His brain was no longer processing information. His body, his matter, all the atoms that made his physical being, were becoming aware that they were not supposed to occupy this location in spacetime. They were, in fact, supposed to be busy decomposing in a marble mausoleum, and so they began to disappear. In a final culmination of a weeks-long corrective process on the part of the physical universe, Nathan Hocking tumbled over and vanished before his head hit the floor.

32

TIME LAPSE

AT AROUND THE SAME TIME Nathan Hocking
was demanding to know why there was a stranger in his apartment,
a squad of time travellers, led by Bindra Dhar and Zelda Clairing,
converged on lower Manhattan. The two troopers of the Independent
Intercentury Interference Task Force (which Zelda now referred to as
the "Triple-ITF") had caught a lucky break, and that break was due
in part to Akande's captain of troopers, Hector Romero, and his first
love: photography.

It happened that on July 24, 2006, a time-lapse camera was sitting
atop a building near Battery Park capturing images of people bustling
through the city streets. Some years later, a single frame captured by that
camera was included in a book of photographs of New York City. Some
years after that, a copy of that book found its way aboard the *Alarinkiri*
in the collection of professional time traveller and amateur photogra-
pher Hector Romero. There it was scanned by the Time Machine, which
noticed a face in the crowd in the lower corner of the frame. The face was
tiny and blurry, but the Machine was able to recognize it as the aged face
of Henry Zoller entering an apartment building on Pearl Street.

Bindra, Zelda and Romero stopped across the street from that same building. Lumen and Marc hid behind a taxi not too far behind. Romero watched as his fellow troopers of the Twenty-First—all of them wearing the tailor-made suits and ties that Akande preferred for his troopers—surrounded the building in pairs and started directing the laymen away. One such layman approached Bindra, Zelda and Romero.

"Hey, what's going on around here?" said the layman. "Is something up with the building?"

"Gas leak," said Romero immediately. "Bad one, I'm afraid. We need to keep everyone away from here until we can investigate."

The layman simply shrugged and walked on, but Romero stopped him with a wave. "Hey, before you go. What's the time?"

"Uh," said the layman, checking his watch. "It's 11:57."

Romero turned to Zelda and Bindra.

"If the Machine is right, Thurmond is already in the building," said Bindra.

"Excellent. The cover story should keep the laymen away," said Romero. "At least for a while."

"Good thinking," said Bindra.

"Okay, here's what I'm thinking," said Romero. "My troopers have the place surrounded. No one goes in and no one comes out. So I think the three of us go up, floor by floor, until we corner him."

As he said this, Romero reached into his jacket pocket and retrieved a small snub-nosed revolver of the sort time troopers prefer to carry, as they do not eject spent casings and therefore do not leave artifacts in the past, in accordance with the *Time Travellers' Revised Code.* Romero opened the chamber and began loading rounds into the gun, at which point Bindra vigorously shook her head. "No, no. Absolutely not."

"What's wrong?" said Romero.

"We are not here to kill Thurmond," said Bindra. "We'll confront him, we'll arrest him and we'll put a stop to his plans once and for all."

"Excuse me," said Romero. "Isn't this the same man who had no trouble killing Sean Logan?"

"Yes, but he meant to kill me," said Bindra. "And only because he had to, because he knew I would figure out his true identity. And he feels guilty about it, didn't you say that, Zelda?"

"So we're supposed to use his guilt against him?" said Zelda.

"Exactly. I am going to go in there, and I am going to talk to my friend Henry. I'm going to tell him he's made a mistake and that it's not too late to surrender before anyone else gets hurt."

"This is ridiculous," said Romero, tossing his arms in the air.

"I agree," said Zelda. "Which is why I'm going too."

"May I remind you, this is the Twenty-First Century?" said Romero. "Don't you think the troopers of the Twenty-First should handle this?"

"I think the troopers of the Twenty-First will do a fantastic job of keeping the building surrounded," said Zelda, "while the Triple-ITF does its work."

Zelda drew her lightning gun and started walking toward the building. Bindra started to follow, but she stopped when Romero grabbed her shoulder and pulled her around. He leaned in close and whispered in her ear with a deep voice. "Sean Logan was a friend. You have ten minutes, and then I'm coming in there." He released Bindra's shoulder. She nodded at him and then walked across the street, into the building.

The lobby of the apartment building was painted stark white with a pair of glass and wrought iron double doors guarded by two plastic ferns. Bindra found Zelda inside the lobby staring at a gold-rimmed plaque bearing a list of tenants in the floors above.

"He's on the top floor," whispered Zelda.

"How do you know that?" said Bindra.

"Look at the top."

Zelda stepped away from the plaque and Bindra looked at the top of the plaque. The tenant of the top floor penthouse was listed as "I.F. Khofi." "Hey," whispered Bindra. "What does this mean?"

Zelda replied by lifting a finger to her mouth and ordering Zelda to "Shhh." Then she opened the double doors and lifted her lightning gun. Bindra followed Zelda through the doors and into a long, empty, marble concourse lined with half a dozen elevator doors. The concourse was silent except for the sounds of car horns outside, the soft footfalls of the two women creeping along the corridor, and their rapidly accelerating breaths.

The two of them jumped when one of the elevators rang its electric bell and opened its doors. Zelda came dangerously close to pulling the trigger on her lightning gun before an elderly woman in a black dress and pearls stepped out of the elevator and into the concourse.

"Goodness me!" said the woman, clutching her white handbag.

"Sorry, ma'am," said Zelda. "There's a, um…a gas leak."

Zelda lowered her weapon and the old woman shuffled around her and Bindra, making quickly for the door, muttering to herself. "Dear Lord in Heaven, New York just isn't safe anymore…"

Zelda and Bindra watched her go through the lobby's double doors and then looked at each other for a brief laugh. That's when they heard his voice.

"Zelda?" said Thurmond.

Zelda wheeled around and pointed the lightning gun down the corridor of elevators, but she was too late. He was standing next to a closing elevator door with his own gun drawn and trained on her.

"I wondered if I would see you again," said Thurmond. "I must say, I'm quite happy you're still alive."

"And what about me?" said Bindra.

Zelda tried to stop her as she passed, but Bindra could not be deterred from placing herself between Zelda and Thurmond. Bindra was hypnotized by Thurmond's face. To her, it seemed she had seen Henry Zoller only a few weeks before, but here he was in front of her—older, harder and shocked at seeing her alive. In the time that she had known Thurmond's real identity, she had held onto some hope that perhaps he could be reasoned with, that perhaps she—and maybe only she—could convince him of his errors and bring him back from the edge. She had, in some sense, created Thurmond, and so maybe she could destroy him and retrieve Henry Zoller.

"Bindra Dhar," he said in a broken voice.

"I really hope this isn't you, Henry," said Bindra, shaking her head. "I know this isn't you."

"I saw you die," said Thurmond. "I killed you and I saw you die."

"Maybe you did at one time. But that's not what happened. And I'm glad that's not what happened, because I know that's not who you are, Henry. That's not the boy who saved my life. I'm glad that's not who you are."

Thurmond's fingers drummed along the side of his gun, but he never lowered it, nor did he show any signs of relenting where he stood.

"I'm glad you're still here, Bindra. I am glad to learn that time travel can still surprise me."

"Henry," she said. "Please, let's figure this out together. Just put your gun down. There are still laymen in this building and outside, and we don't want to put them in danger, do we?"

"Do you really think anyone will be in less danger if I put this gun down?" said Thurmond. "None of us are ever safe from danger, Bindra. I have learned that lesson enough times. So have you, and so have my followers. That is why we are going to save everyone."

"You cannot pretend your cause is noble when it all hinges on murder, Henry."

Thurmond let out a dry laugh and looked to the ceiling, biting his lip before looking back to Bindra.

"Listen to me, Bindra. You once introduced me to time travel. When you did that you introduced me to a completely new way of seeing life. Now, the Guild, the law, the customs of time travel all tell us interference is dangerous, but what if we're wrong? What if we're not supposed to shun interference, but instead embrace it as a service to humanity that only we can accomplish? Just consider that, Bindra. Consider the possibility that we all have to be introduced to a new way of seeing life."

Behind her, Bindra heard Zelda clearing her throat.

"Allow me to introduce you to a new way of seeing life," said Zelda. "This building is surrounded by troopers of the Twenty-First. You have nowhere to go."

"There should never be violence between time travellers," said Thurmond. "If we have to fight it out in this hallway, Zelda, that would be a real tragedy, and I assure you my only aim is to prevent tragedy, not create it."

"If you don't surrender, I promise I'll create some tragedy right now," replied Zelda.

Bindra watched the two of them lock their stances, aiming weapons at each other, and after frantically considering her options for how to defuse the situation, she stepped directly in the line of fire between them and held out her hands in both directions. "Okay, Henry. I want you to convince me."

"What?" said Zelda in a disgusted voice.

"I'll go with you," she said to Thurmond. "I want to see your side of this. I want you to convince me, if you and I can leave here peacefully."

"Bindra!" she heard Zelda shout behind her, but she kept her eyes on Thurmond. He turned his head, scrutinizing her with narrowing eyes.

"Let me go with you, Henry," she said again. "I know you're afraid of me. I don't know why, exactly, but I know that there's something about me that threatens your plan. But I don't want to be a danger to you. I don't want anyone to hurt you, and I don't want you to hurt anyone else. If I go with you, if I'm by your side, and if you convince me that you're right and everyone else is wrong, then I can't be dangerous to you, can I? And if I still am, well, you can just shoot me, right?"

"You're being serious?" said Thurmond. "This isn't a trick?"

"No tricks. Not at all. I introduced you to time travel. I should have instructed you, and I didn't. Now show me what you've learned. Show me why I'm wrong. I'll go with you, Henry, right now."

"No!"

The shout came from behind Bindra, but it wasn't Zelda's voice. It sounded lower and more frightened. Bindra turned and saw Lumen standing there with the wrought iron double doors shutting behind him looking at her with wide and horrified eyes. She was watching him when the gun fired and the bullet whipped past her ear. She was watching him when the dark hole opened up in his shirt, just above the hip, and he started to wobble. The crack of Thurmond's pistol and the accompanying smell of sulfur conjured up the buried memory of the last time she'd encountered him in the tunnels, the night Sean died for her. The memory came flashing back through her mind while she watched Lumen slump against the corridor wall. She glanced back only briefly to see smoke swirling around Thurmond's face, and for an instant, in her mind at least, he was soft, innocent Henry, staring at the pistol in his hand, horrified at what it had done.

Bindra turned in Lumen's direction. She ran and dove and slid along the marble floors until she reached his collapsed and bleeding body. She draped herself over him, offering what little protection her own body could provide. She listened to the repeated crack of Thurmond's pistol and saw the flashes of Zelda's lightning gun against the wall. Their duel in the corridor couldn't have lasted more than a few seconds, but in Bindra's imagination, it might as well have been hours.

When the battle of light and noise finally ended, Bindra summoned the courage to look behind her, worried she would find the dead bodies of two friends. Instead she found an empty, smoking corridor.

33

SNAPBACK

ONLY ZELDA'S EGO had been harmed during the duel with Thurmond. She was frustrated that none of her lightning bolts had brought him down, and now she was forced to chase him, first down the elevator concourse and then through an empty stairwell. The saber injury to her leg kept her limping behind, and Thurmond easily outran her, to the point that he was no longer in sight when she descended a short staircase into a concrete semi-basement. When she arrived, she found an emergency exit door that was slowly closing.

When Zelda burst through the emergency exit, she found herself in an alley littered with rubbish, and she was overwhelmed by sunlight and smells and city noises. But Thurmond had disappeared. She heard the slapping sounds of feet running on concrete and looked to her left, seeing two troopers of the Twenty-First rushing her way.

"Which way did he go?" she shouted to them.

"We didn't see anyone," yelled one of the advancing troopers.

"Damnit," muttered Zelda before turning around to look down the other end of the alley.

There she saw a pile of full garbage bags lying on the concrete, spilling their contents as if they'd been shoved aside. When she walked around the garbage pile she saw a metal storm drain cover lying askew, revealing a dark, gaping hole into the ground. Without thinking or consulting the troopers behind her, Zelda dropped into the hole, climbing step by step down the rusted iron ladder into darkness.

One of the many reasons Zelda was proud of having grown up in the ancient B.C.s was that her eyes easily adapted to darkness. The ability to see in the dark is essential to surviving in a time before electricity, and it helped her to easily navigate the tunnel. To her disappointment, she exited the smaller tunnel only to enter a much larger tunnel, and still Thurmond was nowhere in sight. Zelda walked into the larger tunnel and stepped onto gravel. With her ancient, attuned eyes, she was able to make out the contours of iron rails and wooden ties running the length of the tunnel.

Of course, thought Zelda. She'd heard about this. Downstream of Nineteen, the laymen started putting railroads underground. A silly idea, in her opinion, but that was none of her concern. She looked from left to right, wondering which way down the tunnel Thurmond might have escaped, when he interrupted her thoughts by leaping out of the darkness and jumping on top of her.

With his weight on her back, Thurmond tackled Zelda to the ground, grabbed her hair and started forcing her head down over the iron rails. As he pushed her, he struggled to utter threats into her ear.

"Let me do my work!" grunted Thurmond.

Zelda wrestled an arm free enough to elbow him in the face. Thurmond leapt off her back with a bleeding nose and fell against the tunnel wall. While she lifted herself up, Zelda saw Thurmond run down the tracks. She chased after him and leapt on his back, forcing him against the rails. But her victory was interrupted by a sudden, blinding emergence of light in the tunnel.

CHAPTER 33: SNAPBACK

The two time travellers looked down the tunnel and saw the head of New York City subway train speeding in their direction. Zelda and Thurmond looked at each other, matching their fearful eyes with one another.

"We should run for it," said Thurmond.

"No," said Zelda.

She forced him even harder against the tracks, holding tight to his shoulders.

"What are you doing?" he yelled.

"This is the end of it, Thurmond," she growled over the noise of the approaching train. "We die here, together. That's one thing you learn growing up in the B.C.s. How to take one for the tribe."

Thurmond's eyes flashed to the oncoming train and then quickly closed. After a moment, he opened them again and started nodding at Zelda. "You feel that?"

"Feel what?"

Thurmond laughed. "Battery Park. The Battery Park anchor point."

Zelda had been so prepared to die and kill Thurmond in the process that she forgot she could feel the pull of the Battery Park anchor point. Close enough for a snapback, she thought, if he was as good a time traveller as people claimed. She looked down at him and shook her head.

"I'm ready to die, Thurmond," yelled Zelda over the noise of the train. "Let's see what you've got."

Thurmond stared coldly into her eyes before shutting his own.

Darkness and icy water enveloped them both. The coldness shocked Zelda into gasping one last time before her head plunged under the surface. In her sudden, drowning state, she was forced to release her grip on Thurmond. Saltwater blurred and burned her eyes as she searched for the escaping traveller, but all she could see were white bubbles against blackness. She righted herself and swam as quickly as she could to the moonlit surface, knocking into a floating chunk of ice as she made it to the top.

Zelda surfaced with a scream and a gasp and tried to focus on keeping her body from shutting down from shock while also searching her periphery for Thurmond. Blindly treading water, she floated against something solid and wooden—the leg of a small pier. Wrapping her arms around it, she looked up to the sky. Clouds were partially blocking the constellations, but she could still make out the placement of Venus and Jupiter. If she remembered her astronomy, the planets told her Thurmond had brought both of them to the late Eighteenth Century when the very edge of Manhattan was still water.

That was almost impossible. It would mean he took the two of them more than two centuries upstream. Zelda looked out over the harbor, searching for Thurmond while she shivered uncontrollably, but she saw nothing. He had disappeared among the ice blocks.

34

THE PARALLEL KING

ZELDA CONSIDERED HERSELF a well-travelled time traveller, but she rarely made any journeys to Eighteen. She knew enough to know that it was an age when the laymen still believed many superstitions that could put a time traveller in a precarious position. She knew that the local centurion, Percy Hollingsworth, was considered a strong but reclusive leader, and there were rumors that questioned his mental state. She also knew that she was stuck. The battle with Thurmond had left her exhausted and definitely unable to travel more than a few minutes. She needed rest, perhaps more than a day's worth, and for that she needed somewhere to stay, somewhere that would have clothes appropriate for the century so she wouldn't be caught in Twenty-First Century jeans and a sweatshirt, and most importantly, somewhere with a warm fire so that she didn't die.

Zelda stayed in the shadows as she crept along the cobblestone streets of lower Manhattan, peeking around corners to avoid the red-coated laymen stalking the alleyways with muskets. Her nerves felt heightened and numbed at the same time, a sensation she attributed to hypothermia. She attempted absolute silence as she snuck through the streets, but with water dripping from her clothes and wheezing out of her shoes she couldn't avoid making noise as she searched for the closest safe house.

The century-spanning network of safe houses and inns is a vital unregulated amenity for time travellers who are on the road. Establishing a time traveller inn is much the same as establishing any sort of business as a layman, except that if your inn stays in business just for a few years, it provides only a small window of safety for any travellers passing through. For this reason, it behooves a time traveller to be aware of the available safe houses in any given decade and their general location. It was a skill that Zelda, who favored a more spontaneous method of time travel, had never fully developed. The only safe house she knew of in the city of New York was the one everyone knew of—the Blind Watchmaker, north of the city atop the Church Street anchor point.

This far north and this late at night, Zelda had little fear of encountering any of the laymen soldiers occupying the city, but she knew she had to get to the warmth of the Blind Watchmaker while she could still walk. Peering through the woods on the edge of town, she saw its stone walls and wooden beams, and the sign that hung over the doorway, bearing the name of the inn and the universal symbol of time travel. She wrapped her arms around herself and shuffled toward the door as a few soft, thick snowflakes started to fall around her. She threw open the heavy tavern door, releasing a welcome wave of warmth.

In the orange light of the fireplace and candelabras she saw an elderly woman tending to the bar and two patrons hunched over warm beer. The trio was dressed appropriately for the 1770s and regarded Zelda's attire with suspicion.

"It's good to meet a fellow traveller," Zelda stammered through chattering teeth.

The elderly barkeep narrowed her eyes as she studied Zelda.

"To make the road less lonely," she replied sternly. "I suppose you need a place to stay."

Zelda nodded.

"Come along, deary," said the old woman, nodding to a door.

Zelda lined up behind the barkeep, and the old woman pulled the door open with a long creak. Then she walked Zelda into the Blind Watchmaker's expansive backroom parlor where dozens of time travellers lazed about on couches and chairs, resting and chatting and drinking and playing chess. There were only a few windows on the walls, and beyond the frosted panes, Zelda could see the snow was now falling hard and fast. Multiple hearths and candelabras kept the otherwise dark room draped in dancing firelight. Almost immediately after Zelda entered the room, two men and a woman surrounded her.

"A newcomer to Eighteen, I see," said the first man. "You shall need clothes. I have some very fine outfits for the out-of-century traveller, very fine indeed, for twenty pounds, just twenty pounds for a fellow traveller."

"Twenty pounds?" scoffed the woman, pushing her competitor aside. "For your rags? This scoundrel means to rob a fellow traveller, he does! Twenty pounds shall go much further with my outfits, m'lady, all the proper research done right-wise so as not to arouse the suspicions of the laymen—they burn witches here, you know!"

"Come off it, come off it now," said a new man, pushing into the fray. "My outfits are all in order and far cheaper than twenty pounds, I should say. Why, for twenty pounds, I'd be obliged to toss in an extra corset."

"Two corsets!" said the woman.

"One corset and a Sony Walkman from Twenty!" exclaimed the first man. "You'll find we're not much in the way of music here in Eighteen, so what do you say?"

"All of you be quiet," bellowed a voice from behind Zelda. She turned and saw a stocky, bearded man approaching, frowning and flaring his eyebrows.

"Stop harassing this traveller," he ordered. "She's clearly cold and in need, so she shall dress on the house."

"Excuse me?" said the elderly barkeep.

The old woman's suspicion was satisfied when the man produced several coins and handed them over.

"I'll get her something dry," said the old woman as she left.

"Now you three can go peddle your wares elsewhere," said the bearded man.

"Yes, Trooper," mumbled the trio in near unison.

• • •

Less than an hour later, Zelda emerged from one of the rooms above the inn with a set of dry clothes provided by the barkeep. She found the stocky time trooper who had helped her waiting in the corridor.

"Let me thank you again, Trooper," she said to him.

"Not at all, madam. It's the least one can do for a fellow traveller. But will you permit me to ask about the nature of your visit to Eighteen?"

Zelda hesitated as she followed him through the hallway. She couldn't tell him she was a trespassing trooper, and she wasn't about to try and explain the Independent Intercentury Interference Task Force. So she lied as best she could.

"I'm just passing through. Trying to get to the Salem witch trials. It's a long journey from Twenty-One to Seventeen."

"I can imagine. But I should warn you, the witch trials are a protected zone, and from what I hear, His Honor Nikolai Rovniak keeps the events under strict supervision."

"Well," said Zelda. "Perhaps a kind trooper such as yourself could ask for a reference of good character from His Honor the Eighteenth Centurion."

Now it was the trooper's turn to hesitate as they arrived at a balcony overlooking the inn patrons milling about below. "I'm afraid I'm not that kind of trooper."

"What do you mean?"

"My name is Elijah Frost. And I am a trooper of the Eighteenth. But I do not answer to His Honor Percy Hollingsworth. I am a trooper of the Parallel King."

A woman seated directly below them apparently heard his words, because she immediately stood with her pint of beer aloft and shouted, "God save the Parallel King!"

The patrons of the Blind Watchmaker replied with resounding conviction.

"God save the Parallel King!"

"And God damn you, Elijah Frost!"

The woman with the pint of beer turned back to the balcony and scolded the trooper.

"Why must you pester every woman you meet with talk of politics?" she said to the laughter of the other patrons.

"Who is the Parallel King?" said Zelda.

"No one knows," said Elijah. "No one's ever met him. There are only rumors."

"But what about Percy Hollingsworth?"

"Old Percy," announced the woman below them, "is a nutjob! Everyone knows it!"

"Centurions are not supposed to rule over their native centuries," said Elijah. "Knowing what happens to everything and everyone important to your former life can drive a centurion mad, so usually the commissioners don't allow it. But Percy asked for a special exception and the commissioners gave it to him. Now he's completely lost it."

"He's a madman!" said the woman below them.

"A lunatic!" shouted another patron.

"He's a fiend and a dictator!" bellowed another. "Down with Percy!"

"Down with Percy!" joined the crowd. "Down with Percy! Down with Percy!"

Elijah smiled as the chanting petered out.

"In the event that a centurion can no longer effectively govern his or her century," he said to Zelda, "the commissioners will have them removed and replaced. But that means there are two centurions governing the same century, the one who is doomed, and the replacement."

"The Parallel King," said Zelda. "And you think that's happening now in Eighteen?"

"According to rumor," said Elijah. "A Parallel King has been appointed by the commissioners—the rightful king of Eighteen. But many residents of Eighteen are still loyal to Percy, and many more still fear him. The Parallel King remains in hiding, gathering troopers and support. When Percy is gone and the Parallel King comes to take what is his, he will find loyal followers waiting to serve him."

Elijah looked over the balcony and shouted above the crowd. "God save the Parallel King!"

"God save the Parallel King!" the inn replied.

Zelda nodded in agreement and hoped the Parallel King wasn't named Thurmond.

Amid the cheering came a commotion from one end of the room. Zelda saw several men crowded around the door to the tavern and another, younger, disheveled-looking man pushing his way through. Zelda could see he was yelling something over the crowd, but with the chanting and cheering she couldn't make out what it was. Soon the patrons settled down and his words became clearer.

"They're coming!" he shouted. "Troopers of the Eighteenth, and Percy himself!"

As he finished, Zelda heard a rolling, rumbling sound in the distance, followed by the shattering of every window on one side of the room. Glass and snow blew over the inn patrons as they dove for cover from the musket fire. Elijah Frost bellowed over the panicked crowd, "Lights out!" Several of the people below set about blowing out the candles and smothering the fires. Zelda saw other patrons pulling large bundles out from behind bookshelves and unraveling them on the tables. Muskets were then passed out among the group, and the revolutionaries took to their positions as more musket balls struck the side of the inn.

As Trooper Frost rushed to direct the defense, Zelda crouched and crawled along the balcony to the room where she'd left her clothes. Once inside, she closed the door behind her and the sounds of the musket battle fell away. Inside the room there was only darkness and the blue glow of moonlight piercing the blizzard clouds outside. In the darkness, she rifled through her soaked clothes for the lightning gun. She found it and tried to check the ammunition when the window above her shattered as a musket ball flew into the room.

Zelda stood and looked through the broken window. She counted nine troopers of the Eighteenth on horseback, recognizable for their distinct black-and-red uniforms. They rode through the snow directing the attack, but they were not the ones doing the shooting. Zelda was shocked to see the troopers were joined by at least two dozen laymen soldiers in scarlet coats, marching slowly on the house and pausing to fire volleys of musket balls when ordered.

The revolutionaries were streaming out of the building with their weapons raised, but they were quickly dispatched by musket fire. Those who survived attacked the soldiers ferociously, sparking a bayonet-to-bayonet melee that Zelda could barely discern from her position.

Zelda saw one of the troopers dismount and give a signal to the others. The eight remaining troopers rode slowly around the battlefield and revealed their own guns. From horseback they began firing into the melee without regard for whether they were killing their foes or their hired laymen. They did not carry single-shot flintlocks appropriate for the time, Zelda saw, but high-capacity automatics from another century, allowing them to slaughter at a faster rate than any of the revolutionaries or laymen mercenaries could defend against.

Into this massacre strolled the lone commanding trooper, pulling from a back-mounted sheath an enormous broadsword. Sparkling in the moonlight, the huge blade sliced through the survivors. One by one, revolutionaries would face the trooper head-on, but the trooper struck each of them down with a few swipes of the broadsword.

Then Zelda saw the trooper confronted by a much larger traveller with his own sword, and she realized it was Elijah Frost, trooper of the Parallel King. The trooper's broadsword neatly cut him in half, spilling hot blood onto the snow and shocking Zelda into an action she immediately regretted. She stood in full view of the shattered window, aimed the lightning gun down at the commanding trooper and fired.

The trooper noticed Zelda's appearance in the window and lifted the broadsword in the air. The lightning from Zelda's gun struck the sword at the very tip of the glinting blade, and the lightning bolt froze in a vibrating, unstable, blindingly bright but otherwise straight line. In the white, electric light, Zelda saw for the first time that the commanding trooper was in fact a woman, younger than herself, with black wavy hair, who glared up at her with wild dog eyes. The trooper seemed to sneer at her just before tipping her sword slightly forward.

As if by the trooper's command, the lightning bolt doubled back and smacked the gun from Zelda's hand. As the weapon fell to the hardwood floor, Zelda's arm fell limp at her side in a mixture of pain and numbness. She looked again through the window and saw the trooper vanish into the blizzard. Zelda had just enough time to realize the trooper had time travelled, using the Church Street anchor point. She grabbed a pillow from the simple guest bed and held it out in front of her face.

Instantly, the broadsword cut down through the pillow, sending Zelda tumbling backward in a snowstorm of down feathers. Amid the swirling feathers, Zelda couldn't quite see the attacker as she tried to push herself back up, but she did feel the trooper's boot pushing her back onto the floor. Then the edge of the sword rested gently on her neck and she saw the wild eyes of the trooper staring down at her.

"Where did you get that?" said the trooper, nodding to the lightning gun lying against the wall. "It's a neat little device. But I'm afraid mine has the same maker." The trooper twisted her sword so Zelda could see— along the flat edge of the blade was engraved, "*The Family Listratta.*"

Zelda flicked her eyes to the lightning gun on the floor. She could just barely make out the inscription.

A gift from the Family Listratta to the Family Christie

The trooper kept a firm grip on Zelda's neck as she pushed her out of the room, down the stairs, through the tavern door and into the snowy darkness.

"If you try to travel anywhen," the trooper warned her, "I'm coming too."

Not that it would have mattered. Zelda was still exhausted. The trooper shoved her forward, past the remains of the battle between the revolutionaries and the mercenaries. The other troopers had by this time dismounted and tipped their tricorn hats as the commanding trooper passed. From the darkness of the road, Zelda heard the growing rumble of oncoming horses.

Three horsemen arrived first, followed by an ornate carriage. Leading the horsemen was a stoic and sharp-figured young man in a red-and-black trooper's uniform. The horseman surveyed the battlefield with a pronounced look of nonchalance, but Zelda noted the same wild quality in his eyes as the trooper who held her prisoner.

That same trooper kicked Zelda's knees out from under her, forcing her to kneel before the horseman and the carriage. From this position, she watched as the newly arrived trooper scrutinized the scene. "Is it wise to use laymen like this?" he said finally.

"We told them they'd be paid ten pounds each," said the trooper holding Zelda's neck. "They were all supposed to die at Princeton anyway. We gave them an extra day."

"I suppose I can't argue with that logic. And is this her?"

"Yes, sir. This appears to be Zelda Clairing, trooper of the Nineteenth."

"Trooper Clairing," said the horseman. "I don't think I need to tell you you're under arrest for trespassing?"

Zelda prepared to reply, but she and the troopers were distracted by a commotion from the carriage. The carriage door swung open and a short, pale, spindly man emerged wearing flowing gold robes and an embroidered tricorn. He flew past Zelda and ran to the bodies piled up in the snow and proceeded to furiously kick them.

"Traitors!" grunted the little man. "Traitors, all of you! That should teach you!"

The little man seemed to tire himself out, and he started fumbling with his pants. As Zelda and the troopers watched with stunned faces, the little man urinated, with some difficulty, on one of the bodies.

"Um," interrupted the horseman. "Your Honor—"

"And you!" shouted the little man, who turned and pointed at Zelda. "You're here because of him, aren't you? The usurper! The Parallel King! I know he's out there, plotting against me, always plotting…"

Percy Hollingsworth, the Eighteenth Centurion, paced back and forth in front of Zelda, his head hung down staring at the snowy ground, muttering to himself. Zelda noted the horseman watching his king with frustration and concern.

"And the commissioners!" shouted the centurion, lunging again at Zelda. His face became red and she felt flecks of his saliva hit her face as he raged. "Cowards! Little shits and cowards! Plotting against me, all of them! Did they send you! DID THEY? Told you I was crazy, did they? Said I was unstable? DO I SEEM UNSTABLE TO YOU?"

"Your Honor," said the horseman. "Perhaps it would be best for you to return to the Century Seat, so as to avoid danger. There may be more traitors in the vicinity. I think we can handle things from here."

The centurion seemed to calm down and the red in his face dissipated. He nodded absently and stumbled back toward the carriage, staring again at the ground. "Yes, yes," he muttered. "Quite right, quite right..." The centurion climbed back into his carriage and nodded to his captain.

"Praise Thurmond," said Percy.

"Praise Thurmond," answered the young captain.

"Praise Thurmond," said the surrounding troopers.

The trooper gripping Zelda's neck mumbled something that was not "Praise Thurmond."

Percy disappeared into his carriage and slammed the door. The carriage sped away back into the night, leaving Zelda and the troopers of the Eighteenth speechless.

"He seems to be getting worse," said the trooper holding Zelda's neck.

"We shall not speak of it," said the horseman sharply.

"What are we going to do with her?" said the trooper as she jerked Zelda's head.

The horseman looked at Zelda and frowned as he considered her. "Thurmond wants us to kill her. But His Honor thinks she could have information about the commissioners' plans."

The trooper sighed and shrugged. "Do you want me to torture her?"

The horseman rolled his eyes and shook his head. "That would just be inconvenient."

"Agreed," said Zelda.

The horseman smiled gently and nodded at her. "We'll stash her away somewhere, so if we do need information, we'll know exactly where to find her."

"Fine," said the trooper. "Crokessee?"

The horseman nodded. "Crokessee," he agreed.

Zelda was intrigued, but she was unable to finish asking, "What is Crokessee?" before the hilt of the trooper's broadsword came down on her head and everything went dark.

35

RETCON

BINDRA WALKED WITH A TRIO of troopers as they carried Lumen. He was pale and slipping in and out of consciousness, but miraculously he was still alive. They brought him through the lobby of the building and out the front door, and there Bindra was met by Hector Romero who stopped her from leaving.

"I need to go with him," pretested Bindra.

"He'll be fine," said Romero. "They'll get him to the *Alarinkiri*. Akande has excellent doctors. You and I need to stay and figure out what happened here."

"What happened here," said Bindra, "is I was seconds from a peaceful resolution, and now Thurmond is missing, Zelda is missing and Lumen could be dying. Why on Earth did you let Lumen in here?"

"He panicked. Said he was worried about you and just rushed into the building before I could do anything. What, did you want me to shoot him instead?"

Bindra put her hands on her hips, took several deep breaths and looked from left to right. Through the lobby doors she could see the troopers, now joined by Marc Kurtzman, carrying Lumen away. The other way, in the elevator concourse, she saw more and more laymen tenants milling around. The air still smelled sulfuric from Thurmond's gun, and there was a lingering static electricity from Zelda's. Bindra turned to Romero. "We should check the top floor."

"Why?"

"I don't know. Zelda said he would be on the top floor, but she didn't explain why."

Bindra looked again to the gold-rimmed plaque on the wall of the lobby, and at the name listed for the penthouse level of the building. What was it about the name "I.F. Khofi" that convinced Zelda that's where they would find Thurmond?

"We'll go up there and check it out," said Romero. "But we have to evacuate the laymen first."

"How do you plan to do that?"

As an answer, Trooper Romero revealed a badge that identified him as an agent of the Federal Homeland Investigative Service.

"What does the Federal Homeland Investigative Service do?" said Bindra.

Romero shrugged. "I don't know. We made it up. But it sounds official."

"And that works?"

"Almost every time."

So for half an hour, troopers of the Twenty-First went door to door, posing as members of an agency that does not exist, evacuating residents from the building. Other troopers stationed themselves at the lobby doors, showing forged badges to residents, police and passersby, explaining that the government was investigating a very serious matter inside that they couldn't openly discuss. The entire incident would remain a popular urban legend on conspiracy websites for years to come.

Bindra and Romero rode the elevator up to the top floor and knocked on the door of the penthouse apartment. Whoever I.F. Khofi was, neither he nor anyone else came to the door, so the time travellers simply broke in and began searching the abandoned apartment. Bindra saw nothing out of the ordinary in the living room. There was an L-shaped couch, a clean coffee table and a glorious view of the New York waterfront. She walked over to the grand piano sitting in the corner of the room. "I don't see anything."

"Me neither," said Romero. "Any chance Zelda was wrong? Maybe he was on another floor."

"I don't know. I don't even know why she thought he would be on this floor."

Bindra lightly touched her fingers to the piano keys and pressed a couple of the high notes.

"Did you hear something?" said Romero.

Bindra took her hand away from the piano and looked at him. "What's that?"

"Sorry," said Romero. "I just thought I heard a piano for some reason."

Bindra frowned and looked from Romero to the piano and back to Romero again. He was walking to another corner of the living room, examining the pictures on the wall. "Maybe we should contact the Clerk and the commissioners about what's happened here."

"I disagree."

"This is a very public place, Trooper Dhar," said Romero. "The lay-men authorities will eventually need a more detailed explanation for what happened here, one that we cannot give them. The commissioners should be alerted about what we're dealing with."

"I assure you, Trooper Romero, the commissioners know what we're dealing with. And their response to the Thurmond crisis has so far been to sit and hide and hope it all goes away."

"I can't say I blame them."

With that, Trooper Romero made a motion that confused Bindra. He looked quickly over his shoulder and then seemed to absently fall straight down to the floor. The trooper looked angrily around him and quickly stood back up, spinning around and staring at the corner.

"What just happened?" said Bindra.

"I…" stammered Trooper Romero. "I don't know. I was sitting in that chair and now it's just gone."

"There was never a chair there."

"Yes there is," he said. "Was. It was right there."

Bindra joined him in staring at the corner where the phantom chair had allegedly been. Then she looked down at the floor, gently toeing the fine, soft, ivory carpet. She reached into her pocket and found the pen Marc had given her in Akande's library. Then she held it high above the ground and dropped it.

The pen landed softly on the carpet, yet still she heard a loud clatter, as if the pen had instead landed upon hard floor. She lifted her foot and brought it down as hard as she could. Again she heard a sharp noise inconsistent with the softness of the carpet.

She looked back up at Romero and pointed to a corner of the room. "What color is that wall?"

"What?"

"What color is the wall?"

"I don't know, it's…" he began. "It's like a lavender, light purple color."

"No," said Bindra. "No, it's beige."

"Are we looking at the same thing here?"

"No," said Bindra. "I don't think we are."

They continued staring at the wall in silence.

"I've heard of this before," whispered Trooper Romero. "It's a retcon."

"A what?"

"Retroactive continuity. It happens when the past is changed permanently. Everything has to be corrected, but not everyone sees the changes at the same time."

CHAPTER 35: RETCON

"He must have changed something big," said Bindra. "So the question is, what was here that was so important that he had to change the past?"

Bindra searched back into the collection of hints and clues she'd gathered in her mind. Thurmond's aim, to stop the train crash in 1984, had always seemed simple. It was his methods that remained a mystery. How could a time traveller jump onto a moving vehicle with no anchor point? What did this apartment have to do with that ill-fated train? And how, she asked herself, had Zelda known exactly which apartment to go to?

"Come with me," she finally said.

Trooper Romero followed Bindra to the elevator and they silently rode back down to the lobby. There, Bindra returned to the plaque displaying the names of all the building's tenants. I.F. Khofi was still at the top.

"Look at this sign," said Bindra. "What is the name at the very top?"

Romero narrowed his vision and looked carefully at the sign. "Um. It says 'Nathan Hocking.' Is that important?"

"All right," said Bindra. "We should contact the commissioners."

36

THE UNACCEPTABLE ALTERNATE

FOR THREE DAYS, the *Alarinkiri* sailed hundreds of miles south along the East Coast of the United States. For three days, dispatches flew between continents and centuries, apprising the commissioners and the Clerk of Admission and Expulsion on what had come to be known as the "Thurmond crisis." For three days Bindra Dhar barely slept. Instead, she locked herself in the ship's library and asked the Time Machine every question she could think of. She wrote and rewrote every scrap of information she had about Thurmond and his plan, trying to shake loose the answers. She read and studied the papers confiscated from Mr. Disaster's tunnel headquarters, especially the report on the *Appalachia Arrow* disaster, written by the investigators Shaw and Kim. When she was ready to add new pieces to her theory, she would present them to Lumen who was still recovering in the *Alarinkiri's* infirmary.

"We know that he wants to stop the Continental Railways crash of 1984," she told Lumen late one night. "From what Zelda saw in 1866, it seems that this attempt at intervention is supposed to be a demonstration for his followers; the first step in a crusade to prevent every major tragedy in history.

"The question, then, is how he plans to accomplish this," continued Bindra. "Thurmond is telling his followers that they have to get 'as close as possible' to stop the disaster. That seems to suggest that Thurmond plans to get his followers on that train somehow, and that somehow, he succeeds."

"That's impossible," said Lumen. "You need an anchor point to time travel; it's impossible to travel onto a moving object."

"Except for this boat," Bindra pointed out.

"Okay, so ask Akande how it works."

Bindra shook her head. "He won't say. But Sean said once there's a machine on board that replicates the effects of an anchor point. How could he get one of those on a train?"

"He can't. There has to be another way he gets on the train."

"Exactly," said Bindra. "But then there's this person in New York, Nathan Hocking. He was the man Zelda and Solomon chased in 1946, the president of the railway company. Thurmond paid him for something, but we don't know what. And then he retconned him. He must've killed Hocking in the past and completely erased him before we could talk to him. It has to have something to do with how he gets on that train."

Bindra sat down at the foot of the bed and stared at the tile floor.

"When Sean and I talked to Mr. Disaster, he told us that some of the survivors from the crash said they were saved by people who were not passengers and who were never identified. I think that means Thurmond and his followers can successfully time travel onto that train, and if they can, so can we. That's how I stop him. If I can figure out how he does it, I can stop him."

She looked up at Lumen. His eyes were closed, his head peacefully tilted to the side. He was asleep, as he had been the whole time, as he had been for most of the last three days. He'd lost a lot of blood, the doctors said. He would live, but he needed lots of rest. So Bindra had to settle for imagining what he would think of her theories. It was still better than nothing.

Bindra stood up and walked around to Lumen's bedside. Carefully she sat on the bed next to him, took up his hand, and looked down at his sleeping face.

"I think I know what you would say to this. But I can't help feeling like this is mostly my fault."

Lumen did not contradict her.

"Fine," she said. "I'll be honest. I think this is completely my fault. A long time ago, I told a boy named Henry Zoller about time travel, and somehow he turned into Thurmond. And when Thurmond decided he needed to kill me, I should've just taken care of it. But instead, you and Sol and Zelda and Sean, you all tried to help me. And you're here and Zelda and Sol are missing and Sean is dead. Because of me."

"I disagree," said a voice behind her.

Bindra turned and saw the Clerk of Admission and Expulsion leaning against the doorway with his bow tie, his boyish hair and his leather satchel.

"But I don't think you really want my opinion," he said.

"Are the commissioners here?" said Bindra.

"Yes."

Bindra stood up from Lumen's bed and quickly wiped her eyes. "I need to talk to them."

"There will be time for that," said the Clerk. "But there are other matters we must attend to. When is Trooper Clairing?"

Bindra shook her head. "I don't know."

"When is Solomon Christie?" said the Clerk.

"I don't know that either."

The Clerk nodded and looked away. "Okay," he said. "Okay."

"I need to speak to the commissioners," said Bindra. "There's something I have to do—"

The Clerk reacted with uncharacteristic annoyance. "The commissioners..." he started with his hand raised. He seemed to catch himself and regain composure before continuing. "The commissioners don't really want to hear from you right now, Bindra. You were explicitly told to do nothing, and the commissioners don't like to be disobeyed. I think it is in your best interest to tell me whatever you plan to tell them."

"I want to go back," said Bindra. "I want to go back in time, to when I first met Henry Zoller. I'll go back, I'll teach him time travel—the proper way. I can guide him away from becoming Thurmond, I know I can. I can fix this from the beginning."

For a long time after she spoke, the Clerk said nothing. He just stood there with his arms folded across his chest, staring at the ground in front of her feet. When he did speak, his voice was soft and curious, as if he hadn't heard anything she'd said.

"Do you have any hobbies, Bindra?"

"What?"

"Time travel can be a stressful profession," said the Clerk. "All of us could use a hobby. For example, I'm rather fond of fly fishing. Though I confess, I'm not very good at it. I'm terrible about getting my line tangled, you see. And do you know the thing about trying to untangle a fishing line?"

Bindra shook her head.

"It is very easy to make things worse. Usually it's best just to cut bait." The Clerk took a half step toward her and stared into her eyes. "Do you really think the commissioners would let you attempt something like that? The ripples such a change would create are unimaginable. Thurmond has simply done too much already, you can't just put him back into a bottle."

"Is that your opinion?" said Bindra. "Or the commissioners'?"

"The commissioners have other things to worry about right now."

"Like what?"

CHAPTER 36: THE UNACCEPTABLE ALTERNATE

"Lupita Calderon," said the Clerk. "Bindra, there cannot be a war between centuries. They want Lupita out of Twenty as soon as possible. Your message said Thurmond is a resident of Nineteen, yes?"

"That's what he told Zelda."

"And that is Lupita's territory. The commissioners want to deal with her. Nineteen retreats from Twenty, we find Solomon and put him back in power, and Lupita gives us access to her century to find Thurmond."

"How are they going to get her to agree?" said Bindra.

"What?"

"How are the commissioners going to get Lupita to agree to this deal?"

The Clerk breathed deep and averted his gaze. "By giving her something she wants."

Bindra shook her head and brushed past him, flying down the corridors of the *Alarinkiri* to the library. She could see from the balcony that the Machine had disappeared, but still she ran down the stairs looking for it. When she heard the Clerk walking down the stairs behind her, she twirled around to face him.

"That Machine doesn't belong to you," she yelled.

"Nor does it belong to you," he countered.

"It doesn't belong to you, or to Lupita, or to the commissioners!" yelled Bindra as tears streamed down her face. "That Machine was built by two of the smartest people I've ever known for one of the greatest time travellers who ever lived, and it doesn't belong to you!"

"You are crossing several lines and it's time to step back, Trooper."

"Don't call me Trooper. I didn't do any of this as a trooper. I did it because even though you and your idiot commissioners told me not to, I believed stopping Thurmond was the right thing to do. I believed in that even when I didn't believe in you, because that's what my instructor taught me, the very instructor you've disrespected by stealing his Machine."

Walter Franklin Brooks told me nobody gets to change the past, nobody gets to have that much power, and I still believe in that. That is why I am begging you—let me go back and instruct Henry. Let me stop Thurmond from even beginning."

"You believe nobody gets to change the past, yet you'd make an exception for yourself?" challenged the Clerk. "Thurmond is a disaster. You don't get to prevent him any more than he gets to prevent a train wreck."

"Oh, yes, of course," exclaimed Bindra, tossing her hands over her head. "How could I possibly forget my real purpose in all of this? My only job is to make sure seventy-two people die, isn't it?"

Bindra stared down the Clerk and gathered together the strength to make her next words as icy as possible. "I hope Thurmond wins."

"Leave us," said a quiet voice.

Bindra looked up at the balcony to the map room and saw a thin young woman with soft brown skin standing at the top of the stairs. Her gaze was gentle and vaguely detached, and her chin stayed upright even as she stared down at them. She wore a white lace dress and she held a weathered book.

"Leave us, Clerk," she said gently. "I'd like to have a moment alone."

The Clerk turned and climbed the stairs, nodding to the woman as he left and closed the doors behind him.

"I know you," said Bindra. "You carried Sean's ashes. You were the one who sang at his funeral."

The woman nodded. "It's one of my many responsibilities."

"Who are you?" said Bindra.

The woman smiled as she slowly started walking down the stairs. "I am just an idiot commissioner. Actually, I'm the idiot commissioner who recommended that you were ready for a trooper appointment and that your application should be approved. For what it's worth, I'm also the idiot commissioner who voted not to deal with Lupita Calderon. But as usual, the vote was two-to-one."

The woman came to the end of the staircase and smiled at Bindra. "I'm Emily Sutton. A commissioner of time travel."

Bindra, unsure of how to behave around a commissioner of time travel, stood rigid and slowly bowed. "I'm sorry if I have offended you, Commissioner Sutton."

The commissioner gestured for her to stand straight. "That's not necessary, Trooper Dhar. Commissioners do not require the same vapid formalities as centurions."

Commissioner Sutton retrieved a pair of glasses from her pocket, flipped open her book and began circling Bindra. "I am troubled, Trooper Dhar, by your newfound appreciation for Thurmond and for interference."

"I have no appreciation for interference, Commissioner," she said quickly. "But Thurmond is a human being, like all of us. He deserves mercy and an opportunity for reform."

Commissioner Sutton looked up from her book with her glasses so close to the end of her nose Bindra thought they might fall off at any moment. "Very good, Trooper Dhar. I've always admired your capacity for mercy."

The commissioner looked back down at her book and flipped again through the pages. Bindra watched as each thick, starched page swung and flopped and crashed like angry ocean waves, and she wondered what the commissioner saw in them.

• • •

In 1947, few buildings in America were as spectacular as the Grand Republic Hotel in Baltimore, Maryland. And few could argue there was any hotel more splendid than the Grand Republic on New Year's Eve.

As the clock approached midnight on December 31, 1947, the swing band in the grand ballroom paused and let the partiers take over.

They counted down the seconds left in the year as a slender, close-bearded man in a wide-lapel tuxedo strolled across the room between the white and silver Christmas trees and arrived at the hotel bar in the year 1948.

The man walked past the bar and down the line of dark and lonely booths to the only person sitting in the whole place. It was a man he'd never met and never seen, and yet he knew it was him, right where he said he would be. Thurmond sat in the booth with his back to the door and looked across the table at His Honor, Solomon Christie, the Twentieth Centurion.

"It's good to meet a fellow traveller," said Solomon.

"To make the road less lonely," said Thurmond.

The partiers in the grand ballroom sang longer and longer. *We've wandered many a weary foot since the days of auld lang syne...* A passing barkeep paused at their table.

"Can I get you two gentlemen a drink?"

Solomon looked to Thurmond. "Champagne?" said the centurion.

"It's tradition," replied Thurmond.

• • •

Commissioner Sutton spoke more to her stiff pages than she did to Bindra. "I am still troubled by what you have said to the Clerk, that your only job is to make sure seventy-two people die. I suppose your heart is in the right place, but that is rather cynical thinking."

"Thurmond's heart is also in the right place," said Bindra.

Sutton adjusted her glasses and looked at Bindra. "You're certain of that?"

Bindra closed her eyes and raised her hands as if to fend off an invisible enemy. "I know he's a criminal. I know that. But in the end, all he wants to do is save lives."

"Without regard for any repercussions."

CHAPTER 36: THE UNACCEPTABLE ALTERNATE

"And that makes him evil?" said Bindra.

"It makes him dangerous."

• • •

Thurmond reached into his jacket and pulled out a small red book. He flipped through its pages and tore one out, slipping it onto the table. Solomon took it up and read a message in his own handwriting.

We should talk. Grand Republic Hotel, Baltimore, Maryland, USA. January 1, 1948. I shall see you at Midnight. Solomon Christie III.

"Oh thank you," said Sol, taking a red book from his own pocket. "Now I know exactly what to write."

Sol started copying his own message, and Thurmond was amused that without trying, the placement of Sol's letters somehow remained exactly the same. The barkeep set down two glasses of champagne.

"I still don't quite understand that," said Thurmond, taking up his glass.

"This book is new," said Sol without looking up. "Yours is old."

"But then your message should've always been there. I only saw it today."

"'Tisn't about what is there and what is not," said Sol, closing his red book and putting it in his pocket. "'Tis about what you can see and what you cannot."

Thurmond smiled, took back his red book and sipped. "Sean Logan?"

"Yes," said Sol. "It was found amongst his possessions upon his death. When Bindra deduced your identity I thought, perchance, it might allow us to communicate directly and see if we might settle this like gentlemen."

"It's funny," said Thurmond. "For a long time I only remembered killing Bindra. It's only in the last two years or so I remember killing Sean instead."

"Do you expect that to unsettle me?" said Sol. "Speaking so openly about murdering your fellow travellers?"

315

"I wonder, though. How does the writing in your book stay preserved in mine?"

Sol sipped. "There is a vault," he said. "When the pages are full, you give the book to the Clerk of Messages, she catalogues it, stores it in the vault, distributes as necessary."

"Really?" said Thurmond with a laugh. "Fascinating. Intricate."

"Yes. Yes. You should have had a proper instructor. To explain all of this."

"Do you think maybe that's why I am the way I am?"

"I am not in a position to say what way you are and what way you are not, Henry."

"Must be a big vault."

"'Tis," said Sol. "'Tis."

"And that ends up in there somehow?"

"Yes. 'Tis my next stop after I leave here."

"And what if you don't leave here?"

"If I don't leave here," said Sol, "I don't deliver the book to the Clerk of Messages, it never goes to the vault, you never receive my message, you never come here and I drink my champagne in peace."

Thurmond nodded. "I love a good paradox."

They both sipped. Auld Lang Syne faded.

"What do you want?" said Thurmond.

"What do you want?" said Sol.

Thurmond shrugged. "A dramatic paradigm shift in the time travel community. A reorganization of our priorities, oriented toward the alleviation of human suffering as opposed to...whatever it is we do now. Adventurism? I think I've made it clear what I want, Solomon, but what do you want?"

"Largely the same thing," said Sol.

"Then why are we here?"

"Because you do not know what you are doing."

"And whose fault is that?"

• • •

Bindra walked around one of Akande's library tables, not so much to run away as to separate herself from the commissioner. "I have spent more time than most travellers trying to stop Thurmond. I'm sure you know that."

"I do," said Emily Sutton.

"I am perfectly aware of how dangerous he is," said Bindra. "But I am also very aware that the law he is trying to break is a law that says seventy-two people must die."

"Our laws are not perfect. But they are not arbitrary."

"He doesn't know that. He should have been taught better. He should have been instructed…no, that's wrong. Wrong phrasing. I'm erasing responsibility. I should have instructed him. I should have been there for him, and I should not have introduced him to time travel and then just left him—"

As Bindra spoke, Commissioner Sutton stopped listening and held up a finger. "Are you blaming yourself for Thurmond's actions? For his violence? For the violence he committed against you?"

"Thurmond never hurt me," said Bindra.

"Yes he did." The commissioner's eyes became glassy, and she stared off as if she was fixated on the bookshelf over Bindra's shoulder. She closed her book and hugged it close to her chest. "Yes he did," she said again. "Maybe you don't remember it, but I do. I read all about it. He shot you four times and the fourth one pierced your lung and you drowned in your own blood. Now, they said you probably lost consciousness before that happened, and that made everyone feel a little better, but the troopers who pulled you out of that tunnel said blood was spilling out of your mouth the whole time. One of them had the same nightmare for years. We all came to your hometown and apparently I sang a song in Hindi just before we put your ashes into this nice little stream in the Valley of Flowers. It sounds beautiful, doesn't it?"

The commissioner's glassy eyes swung to meet Bindra's and she smiled.

"There's a whole reality where that happened, Bindra," said Sutton. "As wispy and real as the smoke over a fire. It's all written in a book somewhere, fortunately not the book we're in right now. And it is what we call an acceptable alternate."

Then she took the book from her chest and opened it again.

"Would you like to know what an unacceptable alternate looks like?"

• • •

"You have no idea what will happen if you stop that train from crashing," said Sol.

"I know that seventy-two innocent people will get to live out their lives," said Thurmond.

"Yes, but after that—"

"Unintended consequences," said Thurmond.

"Yes."

"Can be taken care of at a later date. All wrinkles can be smoothed out—"

"If that were possible—"

"We have nothing but time—"

"You think others haven't tried?"

"What we lack is compassion."

Sol was tired of the game. "Who is on the train, Henry?"

Thurmond shifted his jaw and stared Sol down for another sip of champagne.

"A lot of people who don't have to die," he said.

• • •

"We get together sometimes," said Sutton into her book. "Commissioners, I mean. There aren't as many of us as there are of you, but we gather at times. And we joke about how time travellers would react if they understood the full consequences of their actions."

Again she looked up from her book and stared at Bindra above the top of her glasses. "Would you like to know what I know?"

A memory flashed into Bindra's mind of something the Clerk had told her so long ago. *It's a horrific burden, knowing everything.*

"Yes," said Bindra.

Commissioner Sutton looked back into her book and ran her finger down its pages. "Let us see. Ah, here's a good one. There's a certain young man, just got his first job as an elementary school teacher. He's supposed to die on the *Appalachia Arrow*, but instead it says here he continues teaching, rapes eleven of his students over a period of nine years—oh, and he also murders two of them before being caught.

"There's also the matter of the engineer," continued the commissioner. "I'm afraid he continues his habit of drinking and driving after an uneventful career with Continental Railways and instead of dying in the West Virginia wreck, he is killed in 1989 when he slams into a van on a California highway. A family of five dies with him.

"But this is the one I find most troubling," said Commissioner Sutton, pointing at a page. "In 1995, the Continental Railways *Omaha Limited* derails in eastern Iowa, killing 134 people. Now, the reason you're not aware of this disaster is because after the *Appalachia Arrow* derailment, Continental Railways enacted stricter safety policies, which saved the *Omaha Limited* and its passengers. But since the *Appalachia Arrow* disaster never happened, Continental Railways didn't see the need to make any changes."

"You're saying all of these things happen because Thurmond stops the train from crashing?" said Bindra.

Commissioner Sutton removed her glasses and looked up at her. "You tell me," she said, turning the book around so that Bindra could see its pages.

She stared at the book for a moment, confused. "It's blank."

"Good."

● ● ●

"Lots of trains crash," said Sol. "Lots of planes, too, and cars. People go to a myriad of untimely deaths, but you've made this one disaster your life's work. Is someone on that train, Henry, someone who matters to you? Are you putting untold lives, not to mention the very fabric of spacetime, in danger for one person?"

He leaned over the table so that the light above them fell harsh on his features.

"And is that not travelling out of selfishness, Henry?"

Thurmond leaned in as well. "I will tell you who is on the train, Solomon. People who don't know they live under your power. People who don't know you have authority over their happiness and their daily lives. People who don't know you can decide whether they live or die. People who don't know you've already decided."

"Centurions only rule time travellers," said Sol.

"Exactly," said Thurmond, with an outstretched finger. "And now you get to decide how to rule."

● ● ●

Commissioner Sutton closed her book and placed it back under her arm. "I'm not going to go through the rest of them. Mostly because I think you understand my point, but also because—and this is the truly frightening part—I don't know all of them. The only alternates I know of are the ones I see in the book, just as the only alternates Commissioner Lee and Commissioner Long know of are the ones they see in the book. And even then, we might not see everything."

CHAPTER 36: THE UNACCEPTABLE ALTERNATE

The commissioner stared deep into Bindra's eyes and spoke with a tone that was equal parts sweet and ominous. "Whenever you time travel you create alternate realities, quite by accident, the full extent of which are infinite and terrifying. Imagine the sort of realities someone like Thurmond might create on purpose."

• • •

"You say you only have control over the time travellers," said Thurmond. "That's fine. I am a time traveller, and I intend to save everyone on that train. Command me not to, constrain me, and they will die. It's as simple as that."

• • •

"So, yes," said Commissioner Sutton. "I want you to make sure that train crashes. I want you to make sure that seventy-two people die on a hillside in West Virginia. Our responsibility—yours and mine—is to preserve this reality as best we can. This reality is messy, tragic and unfair. The alternates, however, are worse. I read them every day in this book. And if the time comes when you can read them, then they might as well be set in stone."

• • •

"Can you honestly say, Solomon, that you've done your duty as the Twentieth Centurion?"

"No," said Sol. "I cannot." Sol pushed back from the table and crossed his arms, averting Thurmond's gaze.

"Exactly, Solomon," said Thurmond. "We both know that's why you haven't arrested me tonight. Why you won't even try to arrest me tonight. Because you know, in your heart of hearts, that you don't deserve to."

Sol clenched his teeth and still refused to look Thurmond in the eye.

"You know you have no right to command me now," said Thurmond. "You shirk responsibility for your entire life, and now, when fulfilling your duties means killing people, now you decide to fulfill them? My, my, Solomon, what unfortunate timing."

He swallowed the rest of his champagne and stood over Sol, buttoning his jacket and bowing dramatically. "Come rise to your station, Your Honor. You know when and where to find me. But I think we both know, whether I am right or wrong, you don't deserve a say in how this turns out."

With that, he left.

●●●

The commissioner smiled at Bindra and turned to leave. She was halfway up the staircase when Bindra thought of a final challenge to throw at her. "Why don't you stop him?"

Commissioner Sutton turned and looked down at her. "I'm sorry?"

"If stopping Thurmond is so important, why don't you go stop him?" said Bindra. "Why do you need me to do it?"

Commissioner Sutton laughed and looked at Bindra with a curious stare.

"I don't know how to time travel," she said, and with that she left the library.

37

CROKESSEE

WHEN SHE WOKE UP, half of Zelda's face was submerged in putrid saltwater. She spat it out and struggled to roll over. The sun was high and hot and lurching one way and then another, and then Zelda realized it was actually she who was lurching. She was in a small wooden boat floating in the ocean. Her arms were out in front of her and her wrists tied. She was accompanied in the small vessel by the two black-uniformed troopers of the Eighteenth—the young captain who had ridden upon a horse and the wild-eyed woman with the silver broadsword.

"Listratta," Zelda said weakly. "Ginnifer Listratta."

The wild-eyed girl briefly stopped her rowing and looked down at Zelda. "So you've figured it out? She's figured it out."

"Great," said the young captain, rowing at the front of the boat.

Zelda rolled again, struggling to speak through a severe headache. "That would make you Llewellyn," she said to the young captain.

"Very good," said Llewellyn Listratta.

What exactly constitutes a so-called "Great Time Travelling Family" is notoriously hard to discern, but the Family Listratta certainly ranks among the more powerful clans and none of the others can match the Listrattas for numbers. No one really knows how many Listrattas there are. Zelda, like most travellers, was well aware of the prestige and mystery of the Family Listratta. In particular Zelda knew of Llewellyn and Ginnifer. Llewellyn was supposed to be the favorite son, the heir apparent, the strategic mind of the family. Ginnifer was supposedly the bulldog, the doer of dirty deeds, but still the beloved Listratta princess. And here they both were, slumming it as troopers of the Eighteenth. Zelda stared at the ever-nearing shore and laughed at their irony as much as she did at her predicament.

"Two Listratta kids, given everything they could ever want," she said aloud. "What could you possibly want from Thurmond?"

"The same thing everyone wants from Thurmond," said Llewellyn. "We would very much like him to change the past."

"Why would you want that?" said Zelda. "The past has been so kind to the Listrattas."

"It's family business," said Llewellyn.

This was the typical response when anyone asked what exactly the Listrattas were up to.

"Aside from that," said Ginnifer. "Thurmond is a daft bloody freak."

The three of them, prisoner and captors alike, laughed at this declaration.

"Well I suppose if that's how you really feel," said Zelda, "you'll let me go?"

"Apologies, Trooper," said Llewellyn. "Thurmond might be deranged, but he is the power now."

"And the Listrattas go when the power is?" said Zelda.

"So you've figured it out," repeated Llewellyn.

Zelda glanced again at the shore ahead of them. The beach looked lonely and deserted, but as she studied it she realized it did not stretch to the horizon but instead wrapped around itself. They were taking her to an island.

CHAPTER 37: CROKESSEE

"Crokessee?" she said.

"That's right," said Ginnifer. "Crokessee Island."

"Never heard of it," said Zelda.

"That's because it's destroyed," said Llewellyn. "In 1800. A hurricane strikes the Carolina coast and wipes it off the map. Which makes it a very nice, very discreet prison for the dissidents of Eighteen."

"Prison?" said Zelda. "You know I'm a time traveller, don't you?"

"Exactly, Trooper," said Llewellyn. "Which is why you've probably felt by now where the nearest anchor point is. Three miles off the coast, and a hundred feet below the water. The only anchor point from here to the Chesapeake Bay. So if you want to escape by time travel and try to snapback your way off the island, by all means go ahead. But I do hope you can tread water."

The tiny boat slushed against the beach. With unnatural speed, Ginnifer Listratta grabbed Zelda by the arm and shoved her out of the boat and into the surf. With Llewellyn following, Ginnifer pushed Zelda up a soft, shifting dune, the sand burning her feet more and more as she neared the top. There, amid the waving dune grass, was an elderly woman dressed in black lace, sitting at a simple wooden table. Before her lay a wide, yellowed ledger. As Llewellyn grabbed Zelda's other arm, the elderly woman gazed at her.

"Welcome to Crokessee Island," said the woman, putting a quill to the ledger pages. "Who, may I ask, is our newest guest?"

Zelda opened her mouth to speak, but Ginnifer Listratta punched her in the side.

"Make something up," said Ginnifer over Zelda's wheezes.

"Very well," said the old woman. "And what crime has this person committed?"

Again, Zelda tried to speak, but Llewellyn shoved her. "Make something up," he said.

"Very well," said the old woman as she began writing. "An enemy of Thurmond."

Zelda could practically feel the Listrattas' eyes rolling.

"Fine," grunted Llewellyn.

"Would you like me to escort the new guest into camp?" asked the old woman.

"No," said Llewellyn swiftly. "I think it's best if we show her around, thank you."

Ginnifer Listratta shoved Zelda forward, past the old woman's desk, and down a sand path bordered by tall patches of marram grass.

"Crazy old bat," muttered Ginnifer. "Creeps me out every time."

"See, this is what you have to understand, Trooper," said Llewellyn behind her. "We hate these people. These Thurmond fanatics, these interferers. Truly, what is the point of interference? All that work, for what?"

"Make life better for the laymen, brother," snarked Ginnifer. "Haven't you been listening?"

"Who cares about the bloody laymen?" said Llewellyn. "Let them learn the Knowledge like the rest of us, or let them suffer. No need to complicate things."

Ginnifer shoved Zelda again to keep up the pace along the sand path. They were descending rapidly into the dunes of the island, and Zelda had trouble keeping her balance in the shifting sand.

"For that matter," continued Llewellyn, "this whole grudge against the Guild—no more troopers, no more centurions, no more commissioners, all that madness—who would want that?"

"I suppose," offered Zelda, "it's a message of rebellion?"

"So I've gathered," said Llewellyn.

"Anarchical utopia," said Ginnifer, pushing Zelda forward once more. "The disassembling of traditional power structures in order to establish a more amicable, peaceful and liberated situation for all time travellers."

CHAPTER 37: CROKESSEE

"You really have been paying attention, sister," said Llewellyn. "I don't even know what you just said."

"The short version is this," said Ginnifer. "The Guild doesn't allow interference, the Thurmondites want to interfere, therefore the Guild is a tyranny and must go."

"Fair enough," said Llewellyn. "But that brings us back to my original point, which is who gives a rat's anus about interference? Forgive my callousness, but saving the lives of a few laymen doesn't seem important enough to go dismantling the Time Travellers' Guild over."

They came to the bottom of the dunes where the pathway was overwhelmed by grass and palm trees. Llewellyn stopped and turned to Zelda, continuing his lecture.

"You see, that is where this so-called gospel of Thurmond falls apart for me. Power structures are not that bad. Power structures are good, especially for the people who aren't actually in power. If the structure doesn't work for you, grab onto it, but don't destroy it. If you destroy it then you've got to build one from scratch, and who has the time for that?"

"I have a question," said Zelda. "When Listrattas are young, do they teach you mathematics and reading and all that or is it just lessons in seeking and obtaining power?"

Llewellyn laughed. "Family business," he said, as if these words explained everything. "Time is a river. The only reason our family hasn't drowned is because we grab onto whatever's available."

"And Thurmond?" said Zelda.

Llewellyn Listratta shrugged. "He's a power structure."

With that, Ginnifer grabbed hold of Zelda's shoulders and pushed her through the tall grass.

She emerged from the foliage into the interior of the island, a sand clearing surrounded on three sides by high dunes like the one she had descended. A rolling black rock face bordered the far side of

327

the interior. Between her and the rocks, Zelda saw hundreds of people dressed in muted rags and milling around aimlessly beneath the oppressive sun. The prisoners of Crokessee looked to Zelda to be from all different time periods, but they were united by leathery suntans and emaciated bodies.

"What is this?" she whispered in horror.

"This is your new home," said Ginnifer as she squeezed her prisoner's arm and dragged her forward.

"There are no guards at Crokessee," said Llewellyn, "because there is nowhere to go. If you try to time travel anywhen, you'll drown. You can try to swim to the mainland, if you like, but there's only wilderness for weeks in every direction."

"This is inhuman," Zelda sneered at him. "The commissioners would never allow you to do this."

"The commissioners made Percy king of this century," said Llewellyn. "And then, it seems, they changed their minds and gave us a Parallel King. So now poor, paranoid, demented Percy sees enemies everywhere he turns, and those enemies end up here. So really the commissioners are very much allowing us to do this. See what I'm talking about? If they had just kept the existing power structure..." He tossed his hands in the air and sighed. "Ah well. You're up, Ginny." He walked back up the dune.

Ginnifer Listratta pulled Zelda's arm and hair and started dragging her into the middle of the clearing. Zelda protested and dug her heels into the ground, but the trooper of the Eighteenth simply pulled her through the sand.

"Listen up, all of you!" Ginnifer announced to the prisoners of Crokessee. "I want you to meet someone."

Ginnifer tossed Zelda into a knob of marram grass. Zelda rolled over on a sore shoulder and breathed sand into her nose. She felt herself tapping into the ancient rage.

CHAPTER 37: CROKESSEE

"This—strange as it may seem—is a trooper," said Ginnifer to the prisoners. "Or at least she was, once, putting criminals like you into places like this."

Ginnifer Listratta drew her broadsword from its sheath and let it sparkle in the sun. Then she kicked Zelda in the stomach with the tip of her boot. Zelda shouted and growled in pain. Her natural inclination, of course, was to fight. But her wrists were still tied, and fighting, at least the way she was used to fighting, involved time travel, and she could feel the pull of the distant anchor point, beckoning her to a watery end.

"But now, my friends, is the time of Thurmond," said Ginnifer to the prisoners. "And look here how far the mighty have fallen."

Ginnifer flipped her sword so that she held the blade with gloved hands and brought the edge of the hilt down hard on Zelda's back.

"This trooper has made herself an enemy of Thurmond! And so she has made herself an enemy of His Honor, Percy Hollingsworth, the Eighteenth Centurion."

Ginnifer stood over Zelda's body and thwacked her across the face as if it was a golf ball and her sword was the club. Zelda cried out. Many of the prisoners winced.

"Let this be a lesson to each of you," commanded Ginnifer. "Percy is the law. And Thurmond is the truth."

At the word "truth," Ginnifer stomped her boot down on Zelda's knee. The gathered prisoners started to grow restless. At every blow Ginnifer delivered, more of them seemed ready to intervene.

"Thurmond loves you!" said Ginnifer. "Thurmond will lead you out of the darkness! And I am afraid the penalty for betraying Thurmond's love is high."

As Ginnifer spoke, she took her eyes briefly off of Zelda who was able to push herself weakly off the ground. Tripping and sliding in the sand, Zelda launched herself at Ginnifer Listratta. She was no longer governed by her logical, cultured, Victorian mind. Now the ancient side of her was in charge.

Ginnifer easily avoided Zelda's animalistic charge. She tossed her broadsword into the air and caught it by the handle, dodging Zelda while slicing her across the thigh. Zelda collapsed and shouted angrily into the sand. Ginnifer looked at her audience of prisoners and gestured to them.

"Praise Thurmond," she said, almost inquisitively.

None of the prisoners reacted except with angry downward stares.

"I'll hear one of you say it," she said. "Praise Thurmond."

Experienced as she was with her favorite weapon, Ginnifer swept the blade over Zelda again, slicing across her shoulder so as to draw minimum blood and maximum pain. "Praise Thurmond."

She cut across Zelda's right ankle next. Zelda yelped and rolled over, looking for her attacker but seeing only the blinding sun. Then came the silver blade again, cutting quickly across her cheek. "Praise Thurmond."

"Praise Thurmond," said another voice.

Ginnifer looked up. A skinny older man had walked out ahead of the prisoners. He seemed to be clenching his jaw as he looked at Ginnifer with conviction.

"Praise Thurmond," he said again. "I think that's enough."

Ginnifer smiled at him. "Very good. I think you're right."

Ginnifer placed the end of her blade on Zelda's chest and Zelda prepared for it to drive through her. Instead, Ginnifer flicked the sword upward and sliced through the rope binding her wrists. Then she hunched over, winked and whispered to her new prisoner, "To hell with Thurmond."

38

SACRIFICE TO THE SAND

ZELDA WOKE UP IN DARKNESS. Her injuries still burned and her joints were still sore. Around her she heard the sound of dripping water, echoing off rock walls. She opened her eyes and saw only rock above, lit by flickering candlelight. She was startled, and therefore pained, when she heard a voice near her.

"It's good to meet a fellow traveller," said the voice.

Slowly, Zelda turned to her right and discovered she was sharing this tiny space with about half a dozen other people. The Crokessee prisoners, men and women alike, all looked far older than she, but she suspected this appearance was compounded by the circumstances of their incarceration. The foremost of the prisoners who gathered around her was the old man who had saved her from Ginnifer Listratta. It was he who spoke once more. "It's good to meet a fellow traveller."

"To make the road less lonely," she replied before coughing painfully.

The old prisoner knelt by her and put a metal cup to her lips. She sipped cool, dank water that tasted only a little salty. "Do you know how to escape from this place?" he said.

She looked at him with confusion and then looked to the other prisoners. Each one looked eager for an answer and hung their heads when she shook hers.

"No," she said. "Why would I?"

"You're one of them," said a grizzled woman, nodding vaguely upwards. "One of the troopers."

"You put people in places like this," said another prisoner.

Zelda shook her head again. "I'm a trooper of the Nineteenth. We don't put people in places like this. No one does."

Zelda started pushing and pulling herself into a seated position. The old prisoner tried to help her but she shook him off. She winced and cried but was determined not to let pain keep her on her back. When she finally did sit up, she took a moment to catch her breath and looked around the cramped space. "Where are we?"

"The caves," said the old prisoner. "On the western side of the island."

"The guards force us into these tunnels every night," said another prisoner.

"There are no guards at Crokessee," said Zelda, repeating the Listrattas.

"There are," said the old prisoner. "When they're needed."

"When are we?" said Zelda.

"No one knows," said the old man. "We spend our days in the sun and our nights in here. No one sees the stars so no one can be certain what year it is."

Naturally, thought Zelda. They'd thought of every angle.

When she thought of the word "they," she couldn't be sure of what she meant. Thurmond and his followers. Percy and his troopers. The Listrattas and their power structures. Even Lupita, who, to protect her people, would break laws, conquer centuries and do evil, but would not do what was right. All of these people, and their selfishness, had led her to this place where there was no escape. For the first time in her life, Zelda felt helpless. It might very well end here, she thought, in a cave, staring at a rock wall. One by one, the Crokessee inmates gave up on her, leaving her alone with her thoughts. When the last prisoner had shuffled off into the tunnels of Crokessee, Zelda was still there, trying to come to terms with a sudden and yet excruciatingly slow demise.

Through the night Zelda remained that way—sitting in a prison of stone, existing in a daze, running through her options. There was nowhere for her to go, no guards for her to fight, and no way to safely time travel. Everything she knew how to do, everything that made her who she was, it was all useless to her in Crokessee. So she spent the night not wallowing in despair or raging against her predicament, but paralyzed, overwhelmed by thoughts of all the actions she could not take.

She felt out of her own body the next morning as she limped slowly from the cave. White light streamed through the tunnels and Zelda sensed the other prisoners were stirring. Her injuries had healed only marginally, but the pain, severe as it was, was watered down by the foreign sensation of helplessness that Crokessee seemed to exude from the rocks and sand.

As she left the cave, the other prisoners paused their conversations and stared at her. She looked at each of them with the same dazed expression and shook her head. She must have conducted the same brief interaction with a hundred different people as she shuffled through the sand clearing and up the dunes.

Zelda spent the day atop the dune, staring out at the green ocean from whence the Listrattas had brought her. She closed her eyes and imagined she was home. Not her home in Nineteen. For the first time in her adult life, she imagined she was home in One, in the B.C.s, on the coastal hills of her little island the people in these years called Ireland. She reflected, and briefly even smiled, at how even a thousand years removed, the smell of salty ocean was the same. But most everything else was different. Here the ground was sand instead of rock. The climate was far warmer. She must still be in North America, she surmised, for the Listrattas could not have taken her too far from New York. Somewhere on the eastern coast of North America. "The Carolina coast," Llewellyn had said. Bitterly she fought back against these thoughts. Knowing where she was would not help her, and she didn't have time for thoughts that wouldn't help her. Or comfort her. She was happy to allow thoughts of home comfort her at this, the ignominious end of her life.

So she allowed herself to fall into a fantasy. Perhaps she fell asleep or perhaps she did not. But in any event, she convinced herself, however briefly, that she was sitting not on sand but hard, cold rock. She faced not the mighty Atlantic but the wild and windy Irish Sea. She was accompanied not by gaunt prisoners of a mad tyrant, but by the friendly faces of her village, of her brothers and her mother, and even her father. It was a warm fantasy, and one she happily stayed in for nearly the whole day. But all the while something called to her. She knew what it was. It was the part of her she tried to repress. The part of her that called upon her to fight even when it might be smarter to run. The part of her that provoked ancient emotion at inopportune times. The part of her that told her Lupita was wrong just as it had told her that her father was wrong, when in both instances the proper thing to do would have been to follow the rules. Now the ancient part of Zelda was calling her back to the modern world, out of the fantasy and into reality, where something she had seen before she closed her eyes was nagging at her. When she finally acquiesced to her ancient soul and opened her eyes, she saw the sun hanging low above the water. She looked down on the weathered beach below her and saw what had been nagging at her mind. In a flat space of beach, at the foot of a ridge of dunes, was a dark spot in the sand. She watched it carefully, trying to convince herself it was just an inconsequential discoloration, but soon she had to accept the fact that it was most definitely a hole—a pit with a pool of brown water at the bottom.

CHAPTER 38: SACRIFICE TO THE SAND

Zelda stood up in spite of herself. She knew there was no point in examining the hole, for there was no way a hole in the sand could be her deliverance. But then, on the other hand, there was nothing else to do on Crokessee.

Stumbling and trudging all the while, she made her way across the dune and onto the beach, walking to the edge of the hole. The sides of the pit sloped gently inward and the hole spread out about the width of a house until it reached the lapping edge of the surf. Zelda slid to the bottom of the pit where she sank to her ankles in brackish water. Small fish and crabs swam around in the pool, trapped in the pit by the last high tide. For a second, Zelda thought the fish were swimming in a certain pattern, the crabs dancing to a peculiar beat she could not hear. Once again she scolded herself.

"This is pointless."

But still, she could not escape it. The fish were behaving oddly. The more she looked into the pool of water, the more inescapable the pattern became. The fish were swimming rapidly in a circle, and the crabs, moving slower but with the same determination, were performing their underwater sideways walk along the same curve. Zelda crouched over the water and reached down into the center of the circle of sea creatures, plunging her hand into the soft, cool sand until she touched upon something sharp and hard. She pulled from the water a small, unassuming rock. She opened her hand wide and allowed it to rest in the center of her palm. Certainly, she told herself, she must be imagining what she was feeling. But the tingling on her palm was too real to deny.

The small rock was an anchor point, or at least a piece of one, a tiny fraction of what was once a great concretion of minerals radiating invisible, but powerful, psychic energy. It was too small to actually use for the purposes of time travel; its psychological magnetism was too weak compared to the one she could feel out there in the ocean.

"It was my idea," said a voice behind her.

Zelda reeled around and looked above her. At the edge of the pit stood the old woman who had met her upon her arrival to Crokessee. Her black lace dress fluttered in the beach wind.

"What idea?" said Zelda.

"To dig up the only anchor point on this island," replied the old woman pleasantly, "and scatter the pieces at sea."

The old woman looked away from Zelda to survey the dunes and the ocean waves.

"Now it beckons us all to our doom," said the old woman. "Now, time travelling off Crokessee Island would only take us out to sea. It is only fear of death that keeps us from escaping. It is only fear that makes Crokessee a prison. In that way, you might say this entire island is my creation."

"You must be very proud," said Zelda.

"Oh yes. I am proud of all my years in the service of Thurmond." The old woman turned again. "Come, Zelda. There is something I want to show you."

The woman in black drifted away across the sand. Zelda climbed up the side of the pit and followed after her. The black lace figure walked with purpose along the beach dunes, off to a sloping and uncertain horizon.

"The Listrattas didn't tell you my name," said Zelda.

"And yet, I know," said the woman.

"How?"

"Because we have met. For you, perhaps, it was only yesterday. But for me it was a lifetime ago. When I was a little girl, he came to me in the night. He said he would show me my sister when she was all grown up. And he did. That was the night I met you."

Zelda stopped and stared at the old woman as she walked on. Eventually the woman paused and turned around to face her.

CHAPTER 38: SACRIFICE TO THE SAND

"Sarah Caldwell?" said Zelda.

The woman gave no expression. "Come along," was all she said. "The sun will leave us soon."

Cautiously, Zelda kept pace with Sarah Caldwell but kept scanning the horizon in all directions. She had the unsettling feeling they were being watched. The sunlight was rapidly disappearing as they approached the edge of the dunes.

"You served Thurmond," said Zelda. "How did you become his prisoner?"

"I displeased him," said Sarah. "We all may displease Thurmond from time to time, though we may not know why. I am happy to pay my debt to him."

The wind started to blow swiftly from the surf. Darkness grew around them, but though she searched, Zelda could not yet see the stars.

"Won't the guards come?" said Zelda. "And force us into the tunnels?"

"I suspect they shall. But that is fate. Fate calls us all eventually. Tonight it calls you, Zelda."

Her words took Zelda's gaze from the sky. She looked forward and saw they'd reached the edge of the dune. Down the sloping sand, at the edge of the water, she saw a long pole standing straight up in the ground. Surrounding the pole stood several figures, prisoners like her, but wearing horrific masks made of palm bark.

"What is this?" Zelda said over her shoulder.

Sarah Caldwell grabbed her shoulder and shoved her over the edge of the dune. She tumbled through the sand until she hit the hard bottom. There the masked prisoners seized her, and as she struggled against them, they dragged her toward the pole, preparing a length of rope. She swung her head around and saw Sarah hike up her black dress and flow gently down the sand dune.

"What are you doing?" she screamed at Sarah.

"Thurmond does not want you alive," said Sarah. "The Listrattas disobeyed Thurmond's command. They, too, shall be punished when fate allows. But tonight, it is Thurmond's will that you die, Zelda. Thurmond's will must be done."

The masked prisoners pushed Zelda forward, marching her to the pole, and began to chant calmly in dull tones; "Praise Thurmond…Praise Thurmond…"

"You must understand, Zelda," said Sarah, following behind. "Thurmond is building a new world. A new theory of time travel. Thurmond is going to save everyone. Any sacrifice in the pursuit of his vision is well worth it. Don't you see this is the truth?"

Zelda did not hear much of what she said. Instead, she devoted all of her energy, all of her rage and all of her pain, to swinging the man holding her right arm forward against the pole. He smacked his head against the solid wood beam and fell into the sand. Zelda gripped the wrist of the woman who held her other arm and swung her over her shoulder.

With a hideous, haunted shriek, Sarah Caldwell wrapped her arms around Zelda from behind and pushed her to the ground. Then Zelda was facing upwards, watching the crazed features of Sarah's ancient face as the old woman choked her. Zelda bashed her fists uselessly against Sarah's head before finally gripping the sides of the old woman's face. She strained to place her thumbs right over Sarah's eyes, and when they were in proper position, she proceeded to push. Blood squirted down onto Zelda's face and the old woman screeched. Zelda freed herself as Sarah reeled away. The sun had finally set.

Zelda scurried away from the masked prisoners and up the sandy dune, hearing Sarah's whimpers behind her. The sand was starting to swirl in the wind, stinging her face and arms. But soon she realized that although the sand was moving, it was not caught in the wind. There was no wind at all. Still it stung, and she looked down at her forearm. Sores were burning along her skin, and the sand particles flying through the air had a distinct metallic sparkle.

All around her the prisoners were also scrambling up the dune, ignoring her completely. She turned around and looked down into the pit. There, around the pole, the metallic sand was swirling in a heavy cloud. Just outside the cloud knelt Sarah Caldwell, looking up into the sky with bloody holes instead of eyes.

"Brothers! Sisters!" she shouted, stretching her arms wide. "I see him! I can see his face! Thurmond calls upon me! I shall be his sacrifice!"

The cloud of sand exploded and the metallic particles washed over Sarah. Her screaming flesh dissolved quickly, leaving an ashy skeleton to collapse to the ground before it, too, disintegrated.

Zelda turned and pushed even faster up the hill. Once she came upon the plateau of the island dunes, she broke into a sprint, hindered by her limp and the shifting sand beneath her feet, but still fast enough to keep ahead of the deadly cloud. The masked prisoners also kept ahead of it, for the most part. She heard the screams of those who did not.

In the darkness, she found the head of the path that led down into the island valley. She brushed past the foliage on either side of her, glancing back at the approaching cloud. The metallic sand was gaining on her, and she felt particles touch and burn her skin as she tumbled into the clearing. She rolled over in the sand and stood up as the metallic cloud crashed into the valley. Running across the open, dark valley, she saw the rocky cliffs to the west and hoped she would be able to find an entrance to the caves before the cloud overtook her. The cloud itself made no noise, but in the distance, coming from all across the island, she heard screams and painful howls.

As she approached the cliffs and started scrambling up the rocks, Zelda saw a shadowy figure among the boulders, waving to her. With the metallic cloud close at her heels, she climbed and pulled herself ever closer to the shadow, and when she reached him she could tell it was the elderly prisoner who had taken care of her the night before.

"In here!" he shouted, and he grabbed her by the shoulder and pulled her into a dark opening in the rock.

Zelda collapsed on the floor of the tunnel and stared outside. The cloud rushed over the opening of the cave but did not enter. Instead it hung there at the mouth of the tunnel, millions of glimmering, metallic particles floating in the air, blocking any view of the outside and the stars above.

Zelda and the prisoner panted and regained their breath. Zelda nodded at the cloud. "The guards?"

The prisoner nodded. "The Listrattas brought them here from Twenty-Three. They hide in the sand and activate when the sun goes down."

"Who are the people in masks?" said Zelda.

"Ah, yes," said the prisoner. "The Thurmondites. They followed Thurmond on the outside, and now they worship him like a god. Doesn't matter to them that he put them here."

"Why would Thurmond put his own followers in this place?"

"They failed him. They failed to stop that damned train crash. Every time he and his people fail, he puts them here. He can't let them tell the Troopers what they know. But he can't bring himself to kill any of them either. At least that's what he told me."

Zelda looked at the old man. "You were one of them?"

The old man nodded. "I remember you, too. You shot me, I recall. With your lightning gun."

"I'm sorry about that," she said quietly. "Thurmond put you here?"

"I failed him. And I was expendable. Like most of us are. Even Sarah Caldwell, and she's a true fanatic."

"Not anymore," said Zelda.

"She's dead?"

CHAPTER 38: SACRIFICE TO THE SAND

"Yes. But she still proved herself useful before the end."

"How's that?"

"I know how to escape from this place."

39

OCCAM'S RAZOR

ZELDA KNEW that before she could even consider escaping from Crokessee Island, she needed to know the year. And so before she could put together any other piece of her plan, she first needed to see the night sky, an act that required significant planning of its own. The first step, naturally, was to find a piece of metal. But, as is usually the case, as soon as she needed a common piece of metal, Zelda could not seem to find one.

"I still don't understand," declared the old prisoner during one of their planning sessions. Zelda had been holding such meetings every night in the darkness of the island cave. "What is the purpose of the metal?"

Zelda sighed. "No one here knows what year it is, correct?"

The gathered prisoners shook their heads.

"Exactly," she said. "Time travel is travel, and travel is navigation. If I don't know what year I'm starting from, I can't very well navigate, can I?"

"But even if you did know the year," said one of the prisoners, "how would that help us? If we try to time travel, we'll just end up in the ocean."

"One thing at a time, please," said Zelda. "First the year, then the travel plans."

"Very well," said the old prisoner. "But how does a piece of metal help you learn the year?"

"Isn't it obvious? They keep us in these caves so we don't see the sky. They know that's the only way we can find out when we are. We need to see the stars, but we can't do that with the guards keeping us in here. So what we need to do is dig a hole, right through the rock. We'll put a mirror through the hole and get a look at the night sky. But to do that, I need a mirror, and to fashion a mirror, I need a piece of metal."

"Oh well, then it's obvious," said the old prisoner. "You need Ephraim and his razor."

So the old man and his fellow prisoners escorted Zelda through the dunes to find Ephraim. She had begun to notice that the prisoners of Crokessee Island liked to organize themselves into tribes. There were the Thurmondites, of course, who now seemed scattered and leaderless ever since Sarah Caldwell had been consumed by the guards. But there were other pockets as well, including the one that comprised the old man and those who followed him. Now, however, it seemed these prisoners did not necessarily follow the old man. Zelda got the distinct impression they were following her instead. She noticed their behavior around her. They watched her movements carefully, became silent whenever she spoke and hung upon her every word.

"Why are they so fascinated by me?" she whispered to the old man as they sought out Ephraim.

"You are part of the legend. You have to understand, Zelda, you're a young time traveller. We are old. We've spent most of our lives trying to help Thurmond get aboard that train. You stopped us every time. You and Bindra Dhar."

"I haven't stopped anything yet."

"You will," said the old man. "Or maybe you will not. The river of time is scattered with realities in which Thurmond failed. That is why

344

we have hope you can get us off of this island. Because we have seen you defeat him. Perhaps we are in the reality where he succeeds. But in the meantime, Thurmond put us here. Thurmond is our enemy. And the enemy of our enemy is our friend."

"Well, that's very nice," said Zelda. "But if you could tell them to stop staring, the living legend would appreciate it."

Soon they came to a high, rocky dune and struggled up to the cave where Ephraim dwelt. Ephraim, Zelda found, was even older than the old man who was the enemy of her enemy. He sat cross-legged against the rock wall, draped in many layers of rags, attended by allies who whispered suspiciously in his ear as Zelda and the old man appeared. Ephraim eyed Zelda carefully, stroking the tangled beard that stretched down in between his legs, as she sat across from him.

"Are you Ephraim?" she said.

"Please," he wheezed with a dry, accented voice. "Traditions keep us civilized in uncivilized times."

Zelda nodded. "It's good to meet a fellow traveller."

"To make the road less lonely," he replied. "I am Ephraim. And you are the trooper the Listrattas brought to Crokessee."

"I am."

"Tell me," said Ephraim. "Whom do you serve?"

Zelda deflated. Even in these most dire of circumstances, memories of her renunciation remained sore and she tried not to think of them. "I once served Her Honor, Lupita Calderon, the Nineteenth Centurion. Now I serve no one."

"I disagree," said Ephraim. "I know of Lupita Calderon. She will surely be enraged when she learns one of her troopers has been taken captive by Percy and his minions."

"I don't think she will care much at all. She and I have had a falling-out. As I said, I no longer serve her."

Ephraim's eyes narrowed as he stared into hers.

"Ephraim," said the old man behind Zelda. "We have come to ask a favor. We need the razor—"

"Quiet, Thurmondite," hissed Ephraim. "You and your tribe are a shame upon the profession, a disgrace to time travellers everywhen. I would never have allowed you to set foot on my end of the island were it not for your guest. It would be wise for you to let her speak."

"I have an idea," said Zelda. "An idea of how to escape. I do not know if it will work. But I know I can't do it without your razor."

Ephraim smiled vaguely. "The razor... I came to this century years ago, hoping to serve the Parallel King. I volunteered to do my part to defeat Thurmond, while others came to serve him."

"We were betrayed," muttered the old man behind Zelda.

"Betrayal first requires collaboration," said Ephraim. "In any case, when I was taken, the razor was the only thing I managed to smuggle into Crokessee. I have never used it once. I waited for a person who could be trusted."

"How can I prove to you that I can be trusted?" said Zelda.

"By telling me whom you serve," said Ephraim.

"I've already told you."

"You lied. Service is a complicated thing. We here have all served others, and that service brought us to this place. To serve is to be betrayed, eventually. I must know who my razor will serve, and so I must know who you serve, Zelda, so that I may know who might betray me now."

Zelda looked away from Ephraim and stared at the sand. Then, after a few moments' pause, she began to laugh.

Ephraim's eyelashes fluttered. "Have I said something amusing?"

"Oh, it's nothing," laughed Zelda. "It's just that I've just told you I can get us out of this place and you think we have time for your stupid riddles?"

Ephraim cocked his head to the side. "Pardon me?"

"Oh, you heard me," laughed Zelda. "You want to know whom I serve, old man? I serve myself, and myself alone. I want to get the hell out of here. You can come with me if you want, but I am leaving. Me. Because every moment I spend wasting away here, Thurmond is out there getting stronger."

"So you wish to fight Thurmond?" said Ephraim.

"No," said Zelda. "No, you doddering old geezer, I don't wish to fight Thurmond—I've *been* fighting Thurmond. That's why I'm here, and that's why I have to get out of here. Thurmond is out there, collecting followers, killing people, destroying time itself, and I'm here, with you, doing puzzles."

Zelda lunged forward and bent over with her hands on her knees, putting her face inches from Ephraim's own. Ephraim's attendants stirred, but the old man put up his hand and they did not intervene.

"There was one time, old man," said Zelda with a vicious smile. "One time when I refused to fight Thurmond. I didn't believe he was real, or I didn't want to, but mostly I didn't care. And then I had to watch a fellow trooper, a fellow traveller, scattered in the river because I wasn't there to help."

Zelda felt her face getting tighter as she strained to hold back the same tears that tormented her at Sean's funeral. She kept up her sarcastic smile and opened her eyes ever wider.

"I will not die on this island," she wheezed to Ephraim. "I will die fighting Thurmond and anyone who keeps me from getting to him."

Ephraim breathed deep and nodded. He would not look her in the eye. "One might say, Zelda," he finally said, "that you serve a memory? A memory of this person you failed to help?"

Zelda exhaled and stood up straight. It was not a perfect explanation. She had not known Sean very well. His memory did not consume her thoughts. But the image of his funeral—certain as she was of her own skills that she could have prevented it—haunted her still. Zelda had only ever served her own rage, and her rage never had a face. But now it had an image—white ash disappearing in a muddy river.

She shrugged at Ephraim. "Whatever makes you feel better, old man."

Ephraim nodded again and motioned to his attendants. The one who sat at his left stood and began digging at the sand where he had been. He pulled out a flat item wrapped in rags and handed it over to Ephraim who slowly presented it to Zelda.

"I do not know if it will work," said Ephraim. "I have never used it. I have never even turned it on."

"Turned it on? What are you talking about?" Incredulously, she unwrapped the layers of rags and pulled out the object inside. "Ephraim?"

"Yes, Zelda?"

"What in Mórrígan's name is this?"

"That," said the old man, "is a Motorola Razr. The finest mobile device ever made. Let no one tell you different."

"What is this, a joke? Are we going to call for help?"

"Of course not. That would be silly. There are no cellular towers in this century."

"I came here for a razor!" shouted Zelda. "If I'm going to get out of here I need to know what year it is, and for that I need to see the sky, and for that I need a mirror! Just a hunk of metal I can sand down, anything! Not a goddamn telephone!"

"What about a camera?" said Ephraim.

Zelda rolled her eyes. "Yes, a camera would be great. So would a boat, or an aeroplane, or maybe the Listrattas could show up and say, 'Hey, guess what? We're not crazy anymore and you can all go free, hooray!' But this..." she shook the phone for effect, "...is not a camera!"

CHAPTER 39: OCCAM'S RAZOR

Ephraim smiled with twinkling eyes. "Zelda, my dear trooper of the Nineteenth. The Twenty-First Century is full of all sorts of wonders."

Neither Ephraim, nor any of the prisoners, knew exactly how much battery power was left in the mobile phone, so none of them turned the device on until the plan was completely in place. The prisoners spent several days and nights digging through the cave wall, which extended only a few inches before it gave way to soft but tightly packed sand. During the day they estimated the location of the end of their tunnel and dug straight down until they had an L-shaped shaft several inches wide. When night fell, Zelda would reach through the tunnel with the camera's eye facing upward, and when she felt the end of the shaft she would begin snapping as many photographs of the night sky as possible.

Zelda reminded the prisoners over and over again that it was almost certainly not going to work.

The shaft could collapse and bury the phone, vision of the night sky could be blocked by sand, or it could simply be a cloudy night. Hanging over everything was the question of whether the phone still had any battery charge in the years since Ephraim had smuggled it onto Crokessee, and if so, how much. They may have only moments, Zelda knew. They may not even have that.

Still, the Crokessee prisoners followed her directions without complaint and without even asking her how she planned on escaping after they knew what year it was. When everything was prepared and night fell, the prisoners gathered around Zelda in the darkness of the cave and waited for her to switch on the Motorola Razr. She pressed and held the green power button, and for several moments the phone's tiny screen remained black. No one spoke or breathed.

Then they saw Zelda's sweating face illuminated in unnatural blue and white. The prisoners allowed themselves a light clamor over their good fortune, and some, who had not travelled past Twenty, were shocked by the magical device which Ephraim swore was capable not only of wireless telegraphy but photography as well.

Zelda tried to calm the group and also push back the huddle as she waited for the phone to load and reveal how much battery life it had left. She glanced up at Ephraim as they waited. He noticed and nodded. "Just give it a moment."

Finally the phone's home screen came online, and in the upper right hand corner of the tiny, blindingly bright rectangle, they could see a small battery symbol with two white bars. Ephraim sighed in relief. "Good. It's half full."

"I guess we can take our time then," said Zelda.

As she spoke, one of the white bars disappeared and Zelda began shoving. "Move!" she shouted. "Move out of the way!" She rushed to the wall and pushed the cell phone through the shaft in the rock and sand.

With her fingers outstretched, she felt the end of the shaft and turned the cell phone upward so the camera's lens was facing (she believed) the night sky. Then with her index finger she started pressing the photo button.

"We still have to see the pictures before the battery dies," advised Ephraim a few moments later. "Don't get greedy."

Zelda nodded breathlessly. Her heart was pounding. "Okay. Let's find out."

She started pulling the phone back through the shaft, but as she did, she felt a shift. It was not the sand, as she had expected, but the cave wall. The porous rock crumbled, swallowing her arm from shoulder to elbow. Reflexively Zelda pulled sharply, trying to free her arm from the rock, but in doing so, she not only found that she was stuck, but she also lost her grip on the cell phone.

The other prisoners, seeing her dilemma, rushed to help free her, but Zelda waved them off. "I dropped it. Hold on."

CHAPTER 39: OCCAM'S RAZOR

Zelda felt around the sand shaft for the lost phone. The sand, too, felt as if it might be crumbling.

So, counter to logic, Zelda pushed her arm forward into the shaft, effectively getting herself more stuck. But as she did, she felt the cold metal of the cell phone against her fingertips and grabbed it and gripped it tight.

"Okay. Got it."

With her free arm she pushed against the side of the cave wall, straining to free herself. The other prisoners came forward and wrapped their arms around her waist. She placed her feet against the wall and pushed. The rock started to give way, slowly and painfully. The jagged, porous stone left gashes along her arm and she screamed. Still she pushed and the others pulled until finally her hand popped out of the shaft, still gripping the phone.

Zelda fell on top of her rescuers and quickly looked at the screen, which, mercifully, was still illuminated. She righted herself and, ignoring her wounded and bloody arm, went to work laying the phone next to a flat plain of sand the prisoners had prepared. Together, the prisoners scrutinized the photos of the sky and placed pebbles and stones of varying sizes onto the flat spot of sand to reflect the stars and planets captured by the phone's camera. They did this silently and rapidly, settling disputes and disagreements as quickly as possible, fully aware that the Motorola Razr's precious life was—

Gone.

With no warning, the dizzying blue light disappeared. With hot tension the prisoners looked at the star map they'd created from their pebbles, and hoped it was enough.

Then the shouting began.

Time travellers can be argumentative about any number of things, but astronomy is one of the more passionate topics. Because astronomy is usually the first thing a time traveller's instructor will drill into their apprentice, every time traveller who ever lived is convinced they have the most adept grasp of the subject.

The prisoners of Crokessee Island were no different. Though they were careful not to disturb the star map, arguments raged into the night about the positions of different constellations and whether one pebble was Mars or Venus. Zelda tried to bandage her arm but never quite finished, for she too was drawn into a shouting match over the brightness of Vega.

Some hours later, most of the disputes had been settled. Zelda, now with a fully bandaged arm, had taken command of the group to try and preserve some semblance of democratic civility.

"So we agree," she announced, pointing to a corner of the star map, "that this is the lower half of Orion?"

The tired prisoners nodded, some begrudgingly.

"Okay," said Zelda. "So it all comes down to this. I'm going to make a declaration, and please keep in mind, I was on the other side of this an hour ago. But I've been convinced and I think it's correct."

She pointed at one of the pebbles. "This is Jupiter."

Half of the prisoners nodded in victory. The other half grumbled, but Ephraim, who led this faction, spoke with conciliation. "If you really think so, we'll go with it."

Zelda nodded and stared down at the map. "All right then. We're in 1715. Three hundred years, people. We have to travel three hundred years."

40

THE DEATH CULT OF ZELDA

SO ZELDA BEGAN HER CALCULATIONS.
They started simply enough. The average time traveller can only go thirty years before needing a rest. Some, with experience, can travel farther. The prisoners of Crokessee were all experienced travellers, but they were also weak and emaciated, so Zelda erred on the side of caution and assumed none of her escape partners would be able to go beyond thirty years before needing a break. She started with the assumption that she would need at least ten co-conspirators, working as a team, to go three hundred years into the future.

But then it was also a matter of weight. If they worked together, every escapee would have to transport nine other people thirty years. Going downstream in time is always easier than going upstream, and Zelda accounted for that. But still, it would be a hard slog. The problem could be solved one of two ways. She could reduce the number of escapees, thereby reducing the weight each traveller had to carry. But that would also mean each traveller had to go farther. It would also limit the number of opportunities for someone to survive and send rescue for the others on the island. So Zelda went with the second option. She needed more, not fewer, co-conspirators. She set the ideal number at fifteen.

Zelda and her tribe spent several days trying to recruit more escapees to their effort but found surprisingly few takers. The Thurmondites were out of the question. Not only were they inherently untrustworthy for obvious reasons, they also relished in their incarceration as a sacrifice to Thurmond. Others were reluctant because they believed any movement toward escape would be noticed by the Listrattas and harshly punished. But most believed Zelda's plan was crazy and would result in certain death. Even if she and her co-conspirators could travel three hundred years, working in shifts, treading water the whole way—itself a probably deadly proposition—what would be the point? Once they reached the end, wouldn't they still be floating in the middle of the ocean?

Zelda had a very tenuous theory that made her think otherwise. She didn't want to get too specific with any details of the plan for fear that the Listrattas could have placed informants among the Crokessee inmates. But something Sarah Caldwell had said gave her an idea, and if she was right, not only could they survive the escape, but she also believed she knew how to stop Thurmond. If she was wrong, she, as well as fourteen other people, would surely drown in one century or another.

So it was a mixed bag.

Given those odds it made sense to Zelda that few of the prisoners wanted to join the escape. But she needed at least fifteen. So she left it to her followers, who had spent years on Crokessee and knew the other inmates well, to pick up the extra conspirators. The men and women who completed the final fifteen were experienced travellers, longtime Crokessee inmates with nothing to lose. Zelda silently referred to them as the Committee of Escape, a Division of the Independent Intercentury Interference Task Force. They referred to themselves as the Death Cult of Zelda.

She appreciated the dedication and the open honesty.

The day came when there was nothing left to do but jump. Zelda's calculations were complete. Each member of the Death Cult was aware of his or her responsibilities. Everyone knew, more or less, what they were in for.

So the members of the Death Cult of Zelda lined up at the edge of Crokessee as the sun started to fall on the horizon. They were alone on the beach, for although the other prisoners hoped they would make it and send for help, none would risk being consumed by the guards at sunset just to bid them farewell. Zelda wondered if, on their end of the island, the Thurmondites were blissfully preparing another sacrifice to their own death god. Zelda turned her head one last time and scanned the dunes and scrub grass. The old man, her first friend on Crokessee, caught her eye.

"Miss it already?" he said.

They smiled at each other and grabbed each other's hand. One by one, each of the Death Cultists held hands. The wind picked up. Zelda glanced and saw the sand whirlwind developing on the far side of the island. The guards of Crokessee were awake and advancing.

"All right," she declared to her Death Cult. "I'm taking the first thirty. Everybody hold on."

Wind swept off the surf. Stringy, salty hair blew in front of her eyes. She felt brief, burning pecks on her skin as the guards started to arrive, hungry for human flesh.

"We'll all get through together," she declared.

Zelda closed her eyes.

Water enveloped her instantly, and she lost the hands of the escapees on either side of her. She twisted aimlessly, not knowing how deep she was, struggling to hold her breath until she could reach the surface. She kicked and shoved through the darkness in the general direction of up, or what she thought was up. Her eyes were blinded by swirling bubbles and green water. She regained sight only as she breached the surface of the waves.

The world was bright. Zelda swept her head around, seeing only water and some of the other escapees swimming toward her. She leaned back and floated with her head facing the sunlit sky. She meant to yell something helpful, like "Everybody get together," but didn't.

Instead she roared like a dying animal.

Everything hurt. More than it usually did. She knew that carrying fourteen other people thirty years was going to be hard, but she wasn't prepared for the experience of carrying that much weight that far only to end up in an angry, convulsing ocean.

She became aware of the other prisoners gathering around her, holding onto her and forming a single, floating mass of time travellers. But she was too exhausted and delirious to even open her eyes, let alone acknowledge and count all of them.

"Is everyone here?" she said breathlessly. "Is everyone here?"

"Yes." She recognized the old man's voice. "We're all here, Zelda. You did great, you got us all here."

"Who's next?" she said.

"It's me," she heard Ephraim say. "Are we all together?"

She heard tired murmurs of affirmation. Then, underwater again.

Then, underwater again.

Then, underwater again.

Then, underwater again.

Eventually she passed out. She wasn't sure when. It was all water to her. The whole world was water. Sometimes it gently lifted her up and down. Sometimes it came crashing over her. Sometimes it was absolutely still and she almost forgot it was there. But it was always there. They were moving downstream in time, she knew that. But falling downstream, more like. Perhaps the plan was falling apart and perhaps they were limping along. When she regained a usable bit of lucidity, it was night. She knew it was night even though her eyes were closed. The sunlight didn't force its way in the way it would if it were day. She was being held up by someone—not floating of her own accord, nor floating on a piece of driftwood, but being held by a strong arm. The water was calmer than she had so far experienced. She felt only the fish nibbling at her toes.

Zelda opened her eyes. The old man was right in front of her, tired but still treading water. Another Crokessee prisoner was holding her afloat. He must have been slowly kicking his legs to tread water because she briefly felt his rough skin brush against her ankle. Zelda heard the other escapees floating nearby. They were all staying together as she had instructed.

"How are we doing?" she asked the old man weakly.

He looked up at her slowly and smiled a bit. "Making progress," he said, nodding at the sky.

She looked up. In the middle of the ocean the stars are brighter than one can properly put into words, and for a time traveller, to see such a sky is like seeing a favorite book come to life. Zelda had forgotten what a privilege it was to see the night sky and let it flood through her eyes and fill her with joy until she giggled into the surface of the Atlantic Ocean.

"It's 1903," she said.

"Very good," said the old man. "They can't take that away."

"How is everyone?"

The old man's smile disappeared. "We lost someone. A few years back."

"How?" said Zelda.

"Don't know. She was there on the surface. Then she just disappeared under the waves. Like she was pulled under."

Zelda had expected, of course, that some members of the party might die from exhaustion, or dehydration, or exposure, and would simply float away or sink. But in her semiconscious state, something felt wrong. Again the leg of the man holding her brushed against her ankle, but for some reason his skin felt sharp, like sandpaper. Then she felt the same skin again, on her other leg, and this time the thing nudged her enough that she felt its full weight. It was not a leg.

Her head fell forward and she saw one or two blood drops fall into the ocean. She looked up at the old man. He, too, had blood trickling from his nose. Each of the time travellers had made several jumps by that time, and so each of them had experienced sudden and severe pressure changes. Each of them left a faint trail of blood in the ocean, and Zelda was beginning to realize why people were disappearing from their party.

"I think..." mumbled Zelda.

"What's that?" said the old man.

"I think we have to go."

He nodded. "Okay. How far?"

She shook her head. "Doesn't matter. Just need—"

The arm that held her above the water jerked suddenly, and in its owner's panic, the hand of the arm locked around her neck and dragged her under the water. The shock of being submerged cleared Zelda's vision, and in the blue, three-dimensional darkness of the ocean, she saw the prisoner who had been holding her afloat was now several feet below her, twisting about as a red cloud expanded from his body. The reason for his distress did not quite register in her mind until a sharp black figure darted again at the time traveller, snapping him in its jaws and pulling him into the cloud of blood where they both vanished. With arms and legs spinning, Zelda pushed herself to the surface.

"Everyone together," she screamed.

The spectacle beneath the waves had shocked her from her stupor.

"What is it?" said the old man.

"Sharks," she replied breathlessly. "Everyone together!"

The survivors struggled together and joined hands.

"I'll take us," said Ephraim. "How far?"

"Doesn't matter," said Zelda. "Five years."

"Okay."

At some point in her training to become a time traveller, Zelda was probably taught that most animals—including sharks—are naturally drawn to anchor points, but she had long since forgotten this. What's more, generations of sharks in that region had long been aware that from time to time, helpless, meaty creatures sometimes appeared for no reason in their waters—scores of Crokessee prisoners attempting to escape were transported there by the underwater anchor point. Sharks are not especially clever creatures, but they retain plenty of instinctual memory when an easy meal is involved.

So when Zelda opened her eyes again after being plunged into the ocean five years in the future, she found the sea was churning with sharks. She came to the surface at the same time as one of the other prisoners, and a black fin passed between them. The fellow prisoner looked to Zelda. "What do we do?" she said, just before her body was rocked sideways and she was dragged away beneath the waves.

Zelda spun around looking for survivors. She heard Ephraim shouting. "To me! To me, again!"

The survivors swam to Ephraim as fins whirled around them. Zelda could see his face was white. Blood gushed from his nose.

"You need to rest," she said to him.

"No. You do."

The waves lifted them violently, and Ephraim took them downstream.

Over and over Ephraim took them downstream. Zelda and the others repeatedly tried to convince him, but he refused every time, until finally, he could go no farther. The sea was not violent, but the waves lifted and lowered at great lengths. Two more of the escape party had disappeared, either from exhaustion or the sharks. Ephraim was pale and ragged, but the others were in much better shape. Still, Zelda knew the sharks would soon be near. Ephraim was still bleeding into the sea.

She bobbed up to him. "We can't stay here."

He nodded and weakly patted her shoulder. "You can't stay here," he said with sad eyes. He looked up at the sky. It was not yet dark, and clouds were over them anyway. "Service is a complicated thing."

He turned from the clouds and looked back at her. "I will die fighting Thurmond." Then he used his remaining strength to push away from her. He floated up along the waves, dragging blood behind him. She wanted to reach out and pull him back, but she knew it wasn't his plan, and she knew she didn't have the time.

She swam back to the escapees. "On me. One more time."

"How far?" panted the old man.

"Thirty years."

He looked at her incredulously. "Are you sure you can handle that? We should break it up."

"No," she said, shaking her head. "We can't stay in the water. It's the last stretch. I can take it."

The old man didn't believe her, but he nodded anyway. One by one, the surviving members of the Death Cult of Zelda gathered around her and put their hands on her shoulders. Privately—and publicly—Zelda had always mocked those time travellers who always seem to need to count themselves down before they make a jump. It's the sort of thing apprentices do, not experienced travellers. But now, at the end of the long escape, unsure if her gambit would work, equally unsure she would survive the jump to find out if it did, she relented.

"One..." she started. "Two..."

"Three."

41

EXPULSION

THE OFFICE OF THE CLERK does not exist merely to speak for and cater to the Commissioners of Time Travel. The Clerk does the bidding of the commissioners, and since the commissioners are the ultimate authority, the Clerk and his officers wield incredible power over their fellow travellers. For instance, officers of the Clerk of Admission and Expulsion have the unfettered power to go back in time, seize the ruler of a century, and drag him, screaming, into the future.

The Clerk waited pleasantly in Hearing Room 104 as his officers hauled Percy Hollingsworth through the empty halls of the Headquarters of the Time Travellers Guild. The indignant wails of the Eighteenth Centurion echoed harshly off the marble floors and walls of the great hall before the officers finally forced the deposed ruler through the doorway into Hearing Room 104. The Clerk watched as the struggling king was dragged to the lone wooden chair in the corner of the room and made to sit, at which point the chair deployed hidden restraints around the prisoner's arms and legs.

The raid on Crokessee Island had yielded to the Clerk a mountain of evidence for Percy Hollingsworth's rampant crimes against his fellow travellers. Though the Listrattas had unfortunately fled—tipped off, it would seem, about the imminent raid—the surviving Crokessee prisoners had been freed and were being thoroughly interviewed about the atrocities committed against them. Now the only thing left for the Clerk to do was to issue notice of the commencement of trial.

The Clerk stood before the chair and addressed the deposed king from a yellowed piece of paper retrieved from his ever-present leather pouch.

"Percy Hollingsworth," he began, "His Honor, the Eighteenth Centurion—"

"You've no right to address me in this manner!" screamed Percy. "You've no right to do any of this!"

"You are hereby accused of grave crimes against your fellow travellers," continued the Clerk.

"I'll see you hanged! I'll see you drawn and quartered!"

"Among these crimes are murder, torture, and false imprisonment—"

"You will lose everything! Everything!"

"Infringement upon the rights of time travellers," read the Clerk. "Blatant and malicious disregard for the *Time Travellers' Revised Code*—"

"You've already lost! The commissioners have no power anymore! The new age of time travel is upon us!

"And finally, you are accused of colluding with the criminal time traveller known as Thurmond," said the Clerk, retrieving a fountain pen. "By the power vested in me by the Time Travellers' Guild I hereby affix my signature upon this official accusation and issue it henceforth to the commissioners."

The Clerk signed the yellowed paper and carefully folded it. Then he passed it off to one of his officers who promptly left Hearing Room 104.

"Percy Hollingsworth, your trial has officially commenced," said the Clerk.

Another officer entered Hearing Room 104 and passed to the Clerk another folded piece of paper.

CHAPTER 41: EXPULSION

"Percy Hollingsworth, your trial has officially concluded." As the Clerk unfolded the paper, the Eighteenth Centurion struggled violently and impotently against his restraints.

"This is impossible!" shouted the king. "No one has the power to try me!"

The Clerk ignored the raging monarch and read the commissioners' order aloud.

To THE CLERK OF ADMISSION AND EXPULSION—

IN REFERENCE TO your accusation of high crimes against His Hon. PERCY HOLLINGSWORTH, the EIGHTEENTH CENTURION—

WHEREAS, these accusations have now been investigated and deliberated for a period of fourteen years—

WHEREAS, these accusations are found to be factual—

WHEREAS, these crimes are of an utmost hideous nature—

THEREFORE, His Hon. PERCY HOLLINGSWORTH, the EIGHTEENTH CENTURION is found guilty—

AND, Due to these high crimes, our sentence against His Hon. PERCY HOLLINGSWORTH, the EIGHTEENTH CENTURION is located herein—

Expulsion.

SO ORDERED.

Commissioners MAIER, ABDULLAH, and CURTLAND.

The Clerk, who could no longer even be bothered to register the incoherent screams of the deposed centurion, took his brown leather pouch from his shoulder and carefully opened it. The pouch did not open so much as it unfolded and revealed a series of sinister silver instruments, each with its own purpose in the expulsion process.

The first was a simple electric razor. He flicked it on and approached Percy Hollingsworth. As his officers held the centurion's head still, the Clerk shaved a small square of hair from a spot on the man's head just a bit above his left ear.

Then he removed the second instrument, a heavy metal cylinder about the width and length of a permanent marker. This was known as an electric lobotomizer, though that was not an entirely accurate descriptor of what it did. The front of the instrument came to a dull point, and at the rear was a flat, thick circle. The Clerk gently held the electric lobotomizer in his left hand while retrieving the third instrument from the pouch—a small, silver hammer.

With his officer still keeping the screaming centurion's head immobile, the Clerk placed the point of the lobotomizer in the middle of the shaved square.

"Percy Hollingsworth," he said. "The commissioners have sentenced you to expulsion from the community of time travellers. As the Clerk of Admission and Expulsion, I am hereby bound to carry out this sentence by neutralizing your brain's ability to transport your matter through time. You will survive this process. But you will live the rest of your days chronologically. Do you have anything to say?"

Percy Hollingsworth had a lot to say, but most of it seemed to be unintelligible shouting, so the Clerk ignored it, held up the tiny hammer and slammed it against the flat circle at the back of the electric lobotomizer. There was a sharp crack and a brief flash of light. The former centurion's head snapped backwards. His arms and legs seized up and his hands balled into fists. His eyes were glassy and fixated on the ceiling. Finally, all the muscles in his body relaxed and he passed out. He would wake up several hours later, and he would never time travel again.

42

SOMETHING RESEMBLING A PLAN

ZELDA ROLLED HER HEAD to the side, not wanting to wake from her comfortable daze. She opened her eyes and saw a young man sitting on the bed next to hers.

"You're alive," said Lumen cheerfully.

"So are you," she said, and rolled her head again to look at the ceiling. "Life isn't fair."

Zelda's plan had been too ridiculous to work, but at this point in her life she was learning to cope with impossible things happening at an alarming rate. In the cave on Crokessee Island, she had spent long nights trying to visualize every detail of the maps on the wall of Akande's maritime library. She assigned her traveller skills of memorizing the night sky to the effort, and she pinpointed when the *Alarinkiri*—a floating anchor point—would next appear off the Carolina coast. Her final jump carried her and her surviving compatriots onto the deck of Akande's yacht.

Though emaciated and delirious, the escapees delivered enough details to the Clerk and his officers to locate and raid Crokessee Island, leading to the capture, trial and expulsion of Percy Hollingsworth. As all of this unfolded, far away and long before, Zelda recovered in the *Alarinkiri*'s infirmary.

On some occasions Bindra would join her and they would soberly confer for hours. Marc and Lumen, who had already recovered enough to leave the infirmary, noticed these meetings and inquired about what was discussed, but neither trooper revealed anything. Even Akande the Gallant was uncertain about what schemes passed between the two. Akande's troopers of the Twenty-First took to loitering outside the infirmary, waiting for a plan that now looked like it would come from these women rather than from their leaders. So when the day came that Zelda had completely recovered, Bindra opened the door to find Hector Romero leaning against the wall with half a dozen troopers of the Twenty-First behind him, all looking expectantly to her.

"Call everyone together," she said simply. "We're meeting in the library."

Two dozen time travellers can make any room a little stuffy, especially when that room is a tiny shipboard library. Akande issued orders for an emergency meeting of the Court of the Twenty-First Century, calling back those three who happened to be in other years. The sailors, cooks, engineers and others who made up the *Alarinkiri*'s crew attended as well. Akande was there.

All of them surrounded Zelda and Bindra who stood beneath the maps of the world and the century and prepared to deliver their theory.

"Is the Clerk coming?" asked Bindra.

"I didn't tell him about this," said Akande.

"Why not?"

Akande shrugged. "Because I thought he might say no."

Bindra smiled and nodded. She paused to collect herself. "Thurmond's real name is Henry Zoller," she told the group. "We know he intends to stop the *Appalachia Arrow* crash of 1984. We know he plans to do this by time travelling onto the train, subduing the engineer and guiding it around the bend at Rosbys Rock, West Virginia. The only question has been how can he and his followers get onto that train?"

"We know he needs an anchor point, obviously. A mobile anchor point, like the one we're all standing on right now," said Zelda, before looking straight to Akande. "That's part of the mystery of this ship, isn't it, Your Honor? You created that mystery, and you allowed others to create an explanation—that you had access to technology that can recreate the effects of an anchor point. But that's not true, is it?"

Akande looked away and soberly shook his head.

"It's impossible to simulate the effects of a natural anchor point," said Bindra. "Only the real thing will do."

Bindra gazed at Akande for a moment with her arms crossed. Then she turned to Zelda and nodded.

"On Crokessee Island," said Zelda, "I encountered a follower of Thurmond who was proud to reveal the means of our imprisonment. She told me it was her idea to dig up the island's only anchor point and sink it offshore, dooming us all to snapback into the ocean if we tried to time travel away. Obviously she can't be blamed for failing to anticipate an escape artist like myself. But in any case, prison gives you plenty of time to contemplate new theories of time travel, and I started to wonder, if you could relocate an anchor point, could you use an anchor point as raw material?"

"You don't have an anchor point on this ship, do you Akande?" said Bindra. "This ship is an anchor point, isn't it? You dug one up, crushed it, melted it, or whatever you needed to, and used it to build the *Alarinkiri*."

"It was not well-travelled," said Akande. He was firm, but defensive. "All environmental factors were considered."

"Regardless, Your Honor," said Zelda. "Someone else had your idea."

"The man Thurmond retconned in New York was Nathan Hocking," said Bindra. "He was the president of Continental Railways at the time of the crash, and it seems like Thurmond has been courting him since at least 1947. A great friend to have if you wanted to build your own train out of unusual material."

"If Thurmond had the president of the company in his pocket, why couldn't he just stop the train from leaving the station?" said Trooper Romero.

"'Interference must be done with a scalpel,'" said Zelda. "Thurmond's words. According to his theory, everything else about the day's events must remain the same. The train has to leave the station, driven by the same person, occupied by the same passengers."

"The only thing he'll try to change is the only thing he needs to change," said Bindra. "The reason for the disaster."

"That's also why he can't just buy himself a ticket," said Zelda. "He has to jump on and jump off, and to do that he needs to build a train out of an anchor point. That's his way on board, and it's also our way on board."

The troopers of the Twenty-First perked up a bit. Finally, something resembling a plan.

"If we want to stop Thurmond without causing more damage on top of his own interference, we have to follow him onto the train using his own method," said Bindra.

Akande the Gallant stepped forward with an outstretched finger next to his ear, clearing his throat. "What you are saying is that we will have to find the same anchor point he's repurposed, travel to 1984, and that will, you believe, place us aboard a train careening to certain doom?"

"I understand your skepticism, but I assure you, more ludicrous plans have worked out," said Zelda. "Otherwise I wouldn't be here."

"We also appreciate that you've included yourself in that 'we', Your Honor," said Bindra.

"Yes, very gallant of you," added Zelda.

CHAPTER 42: SOMETHING RESEMBLING A PLAN

Akande ignored the compliment. "Even if the jump didn't kill us all, there are millions of anchor points in the world. How can we expect to find the one Thurmond has recycled for his train?"

Zelda glanced at Bindra, who avoided everyone's eyes, scrutinizing the floor while scratching her head.

"I, uh..." said Bindra. "I know which one it is."

"How?"

"Because I was there. When Henry Zoller learned about time travel."

43 THE APPALACHIA ARROW

ONE EARLY MORNING IN 2003, Bindra Dhar hunched over the railing of a small ravine bridge in the neighborhood of Jackson Park, staring at the rocks below and listening to the soft footsteps of time travellers behind her. She gazed around at the ravine, the abandoned swimming pool, the decrepit tennis court, all of it sitting atop a forgotten anchor point. Soon she became aware of Zelda's presence at her side. She looked over to see her partner gazing stoically, and somewhat serenely, out over the ravine. Then Zelda noticed that Bindra was watching and frowned while she pulled a canvas backpack over one shoulder.

"What?" demanded Zelda.

"Nothing. I just hope we're being smart about this."

"Oh, Bindra," said Zelda, putting her hand on Bindra's shoulder. "We are definitely not being smart about this. This is all a terrible idea."

Bindra flexed her eyebrows. "Thank you for the encouragement."

They both turned their attention back to the ravine. Bindra knew better, of course, but she could not bring herself to go on without saying something at least mildly meaningful to Zelda. "There were a lot of times when you could have left," she blurted.

"Please stop," said Zelda.

"I just mean you don't have to be here."

"Shut it."

"You stuck with me. You went through horrific things to help me. I won't ever forget it."

Bindra stared once again at the side of Zelda's face. She thought she heard a faint sigh from her friend, whose eyes kept darting leftward to see if she was still staring. Finally those same eyes rolled over and Zelda turned to face her, though she would not look her in the eye. "I suppose I should say something before we do this."

"Yes?"

"I trust you not to kill me. Don't let it go to your head."

"I won't," said Bindra, and she let it go to her head.

They stepped out onto the rocks of the creek where their task force stood waiting. Akande was there with his nine surviving troopers of the Twenty-First. There was Marc and Lumen, and Bindra and Zelda brought the number to fourteen. Fourteen might be enough, thought Bindra. Twenty would be better. A hundred would be better. Fifteen would be infinitely better because it would mean Sean was still alive to take his place among Akande's troopers. But fourteen would do because it would have to do.

The time travellers gathered, almost by instinct, in a circle around Zelda and Bindra. Zelda opened her backpack and let Bindra pull out seven identical watches. Zelda pulled out the remaining seven, and the two of them handed the watches to the encircled time travellers. They were nothing but cheap digital watches that would do what the task force needed them to do but would not be anachronistic if left behind in 1984.

"Do not set them now," advised Bindra. "It'll be the first thing we do once we get on board. Remember, if we do this right, we'll all be on a train headed for certain destruction. So please, mind the time."

CHAPTER 43: THE APPALACHIA ARROW

The time travellers secured their watches and kept their eyes on Bindra. She sensed the expectation of a speech.

"No one gets to change history to make themselves feel better," she said finally. "Moments are our landmarks, our mountains and forests, our rivers and lakes, moments are our sacred lands, and a person cannot simply bulldoze through them when they become inconvenient. That's how Thurmond made an enemy out of me. And I am not afraid of Thurmond. He's already killed me once."

She looked over to Zelda who kept her hands pocketed while she listened. "Well said."

"One moment," said Akande.

The Twenty-First Centurion broke from the circle and pulled off his red sash. He walked to a small tree at the side of the creek and gently hooked the sash around one of the branches. He rejoined the circle.

"We are invading a foreign century," said Akande. "It is not the place of a centurion, so you must consider me an equal. Just another member of the Independent Intercentury Interference Task Force."

"Is it too late to rework that name?" whispered Zelda.

"Yes," said Bindra. "Is everyone ready?"

So fourteen time travellers stood in the creek bed of Jackson Park in 2003 and joined hands. Seven of them had been designated to do the transporting and mentally tethered themselves to the anchor point. Bindra was one of those seven. She closed her eyes and focused on a moment— the moment on February 23, 1984, when the *Appalachia Arrow* still might not have crashed.

The ground under Bindra's feet went from solid to shifting and rocking, and she almost lost her balance. The fresh, breezy air was instantly replaced by the still, stale atmosphere of public transportation. The effect was horribly disorienting, and she bent her knees and shook her head to regain control of herself. When she opened her eyes, she found herself and her team of time travellers in the deserted trailing dining car of the *Appalachia Arrow*. She remembered these surroundings from the photographs in the disaster report. But in those photographs, of course, her surroundings were mangled and battered.

Bindra looked around the train car and saw the rest of her task force had arrived, and most of them were likewise trying to regain their balance after a most unusual time jump. Trooper Romero shook off his dizziness and looked up at a clock on the wall.

"3:37!" he called out.

A garbled sound went through the train car that startled them momentarily. It was an electric, two-tone bell followed by a soft but authoritative voice.

"Passengers of the *Appalachia Arrow*," said the voice over the speaker system. "We have just crossed the West Virginia border. Welcome to the Mountain State."

Bindra nodded and looked back to her time travellers. "The train hits the bend at Rosbys Rock at 3:48. We have eleven minutes." The fourteen travellers circled again and each stared at their watches as Bindra counted them down.

"Five...four...three...two...one," she said, and their watches all beeped as they matched them with each other.

Bindra looked soberly up at the circle. "The next time we hear that sound, we'd better be off this train."

The task force pushed forward into the next dining car where they found themselves alone again, as Bindra expected. In her research on the disaster, she found the *Appalachia Arrow* had been built for long-distance, overnight runs but was eventually relegated to express trips. As such, most of the passengers and soon-to-be victims were in the forward coach cars, leaving the rear dining cars nearly empty. Against one side of the car was a narrow staircase leading up to what Bindra remembered as the kitchen compartment.

CHAPTER 43: THE APPALACHIA ARROW

"Zelda, Akande, Lumen and Marc, come up with me," she ordered. "The rest of you, keep to the main corridor."

Bindra led her team up the short stairway to the cramped kitchen hallway of the *Appalachia Arrow*. When they reached the doorway at the top, Bindra shoved her arm out and blocked Lumen.

"Do you feel that?" she asked him.

He paused and looked elsewhere and then met her gaze again. "Yeah. I feel it."

"They're here," she told the group.

"Who's 'they?'" said Akande.

"Thurmondites," said Zelda. "There's a reason he's been gathering followers. And trust me, they cannot be reasoned with."

The time travellers walked into the kitchen level. It was a small, simple space with a couple of tables against a window where the countryside flew by. On the other side was a counter with an attendant behind it.

"Hi!" the attendant said. "Can I fix anything for y'all?"

Bindra nervously tried to wave her off. "No, I think we're—"

The pressure change thwacked Bindra's ears and someone threw a chair at her. She ducked, but the chair hit Lumen. The attendant behind the kitchen counter screamed and hid. The Thurmondite chair-thrower grabbed another projectile—a coffee mug left on the second table—and chucked it at Bindra's head. Zelda materialized to catch it before disappearing and reappearing behind the Thurmondite, slamming the mug over his head.

"I think this'll be fun," she said, smiling at Bindra.

She hadn't quite finished the word "fun" when half a dozen more Thurmondites emerged into the moment. Bindra took advantage of their momentary surprise to punch the nearest Thurmondite—a young blond man with an almost-beard—right in the stomach. He doubled over and vomited, and Bindra ducked as people and chairs flew at one another. She rolled along the floor to avoid the bulk of the scuffle. When she could peer through the angry arms and legs of the fray, she saw Zelda holding her own, landing quick hits and knocks as she darted in and out of spacetime.

Bindra pushed her way toward Zelda, making herself small against the metal side of the train car. A wiry Thurmondite noticed her and grabbed her shirt by the shoulder, throwing a fist at her head. She dodged and the fist cracked against the wall. The Thurmondite roared with pain and released Bindra. She reached behind her back, desperately grabbing at anything she might be able to use as a weapon. Finally, her hands came upon a long, cold, metal object that, in her frantic mind, she imagined was a fire ax like the one her father had always kept in their house. She yanked it just as the injured and angry Thurmondite charged at her. Instead of giving way, the ax caught and clicked, and then Bindra was falling backward.

Bindra held fast to the metal bar as the dining car's emergency door swung open. The Thurmondite tumbled through the opening. He tried to stop himself at the last minute and fell too close to the tracks. He went under the wheels and was quickly cut in half.

Bindra hugged the emergency door as it swung all the way outward and slammed against the side of the train. Wind and noise battered her ears, and she concentrated on shutting out the landscape rushing by as she clung to the outside of the dining car. She placed one foot on the side of the train car and kicked so that the door swung closed. She almost lost her grip when strong hands grabbed her wrist and steadied her.

"Are you okay?" shouted Zelda over the noise of the train.

"I trust you not to kill me," yelled Bindra. "Don't let it go to your—"

A growl came from behind Zelda as a large Thurmondite shoved her through the emergency window. Bindra closed her eyes, and the deafening train noise ceased. She opened them again, fully expecting that this was probably the afterlife, but instead it seemed to just be a cramped, gray space with ugly carpeting and Zelda, crouched next to her with a look of tentative concern she'd never seen before.

CHAPTER 43: THE APPALACHIA ARROW

"Passengers of the *Appalachia Arrow*," said the voice over the intercom. "We have just crossed the West Virginia border. Welcome to the Mountain State."

Bindra and Zelda looked at each other and immediately reached for their wristwatches.

"Bought us some time," said Zelda.

"Yes, but be careful with that," said Bindra. "We have to know when 'too late' arrives."

She gestured to her wristwatch, and she and Zelda prepared to resynchronize.

"More time is always better than less time, and you're welcome, by the way, for saving your life."

"Hush, I'm doing math in my head."

Bindra whispered, "Five, four, three, two, one," and their watches beeped again. Knowing when they had arrived, they slowly stood up to figure out where they had arrived. They seemed to be situated behind the last group of seats at the rear of another train car, only this one was full of people. The coach car, Bindra surmised. She remembered this from Mr. Disaster's packet of papers. There were two coach cars at the front of the train where most of the passengers were sitting at the time of the disaster. Where the most fatalities would be.

Bindra looked around at the passengers to make sure she and Zelda had not been noticed, but all of them seemed occupied by one thing or another. There was an older man in a hat reading a newspaper. A teenager in all black with pink spiked hair listening to a cassette tape player. A middle-aged couple sleeping on each other's shoulders...

"We've got a few extra minutes before they arrive," said Zelda.

Bindra heard Zelda's voice, but it somehow seemed distant. She was too distracted by the passengers sitting peacefully along the train car.

"What do we have to do now, Bindra?" said Zelda, more forcefully this time.

"We're a car behind. There's another coach car and then the locomotive with a control cab."

Zelda nodded but noticed Bindra never stopped looking around at the passengers.

"And then what?" said Zelda.

Bindra shrugged. "Then we stop Thurmond from getting too close. Bar the doors, make sure the engineer drives the train all the way to Rosbys Rock."

Her eyes kept darting around the coach car. The attendant chatting with a smiling passenger. The woman writing in her diary. The mother pointing at the passing mountains with her son. She felt Zelda's hand on her shoulder.

"We have a job to do," whispered Zelda.

Bindra looked at her partner. She felt tears.

"A person can't bulldoze through a moment because it's inconvenient," said Zelda.

This reality is messy, tragic and unfair, the commissioner had told her. *The alternatives, however, are worse.*

You'd better be right, thought Bindra. She walked down the aisle with Zelda following cautiously.

"There's a vestibule between this car and the next," said Bindra. "But we might not have access from that car to the locomotive up front. We'll have to find a way around."

They received no notice from any of the other passengers as they made their way through the coach car. When they came close to the forward vestibule, a train attendant emerged from behind the front curtain and saw them.

"Hello," said the attendant. "Do you need any help?"

"We're fine," said Bindra curtly.

Unfortunately, Zelda said roughly the same thing at roughly the same time, which not only limited the effect of her terse response, but also made a somewhat suspicious impression. Bindra noticed a change in the attendant's face. Her eyes went briefly down to Zelda's hands. Bindra also looked. Her partner's knuckles were bruised and bloodied.

"May I see your tickets, ladies?" said the attendant with a smile but no sweetness.

Zelda almost started an answer when a noise distracted all three of them. It was a thumping noise from the car behind them, loud enough to be heard over the rolling of the wheels and noticed by some of the coach passengers. There was another thump followed by the sound of shattering glass. The attendant ignored Bindra and Zelda and walked toward the source of the noise at the rear of the coach. Quickly they rushed forward through the curtain and into the vestibule between cars.

"It's us," said Bindra. "We're fighting back there in the dining car."

"That means they're here too," said Zelda. "And we don't have time to go through another car. We have to get up there now."

Bindra closed her eyes and tried to remember every detail of the photographs and diagrams of the *Appalachia Arrow* she'd seen in Shaw and Kim's disaster report. She could visualize the rest of the train up to the control cab—torn, crushed and overturned in black-and-white photos with the engineer's body twisted and dangling from his seat. It was not a pleasant image. But it was the image they were there to safeguard. And it might be enough. Bindra held out her hands. "I have an idea."

They clasped hands and Bindra took them back in time. Just not very far.

"We're still here," said Zelda.

Bindra opened her eyes. She still held Zelda's hands, and they were both still standing in the cramped vestibule between coach cars. Zelda shook her head at Bindra. "What did you do?"

In reply, Bindra lifted a finger to the ceiling.

"Passengers of the *Appalachia Arrow*," said the voice over the inter-com. "We have just crossed the West Virginia border. Welcome to the Mountain State."

Zelda and Bindra looked to each other and frantically set their watches back again.

"Bought us some time," said Bindra.

"Yes, but be careful with that," mocked Zelda. "We have to know when—"

"Shut up. Follow me, as quickly as you can, and don't stop for anything."

With that, Bindra pushed open the door into the forward coach car and rushed down the aisle of seats. Zelda followed, and though the two women did attract some attention as they sped down the aisle, none of the passengers on the *Appalachia Arrow* did anything to stop them. Then Bindra came to the door to the next vestibule at the front of the coach and pulled it open. Only there was no next vestibule, just the stark, glinting metal of the locomotive in front and the roaring noise of the train as it sped through the mountains.

The passengers began to shout as intense wind and noise flooded the coach through the open door, but Bindra and Zelda ignored everything behind them. Bindra almost didn't think at all as she stepped out of the train and onto the coupler between the locomotive and the coach. She grabbed onto a railing protruding from the locomotive and peered around its left side. There she saw a narrow catwalk running along the side of the locomotive leading straight to the control cab, right where she expected it to be. She climbed around the left side of the locomotive and pulled herself under the railing and onto the catwalk, trying not to think too much about how easy it would be to slip and fall onto the tracks. Then she turned and helped Zelda onto the catwalk railing, careful to avoid her partner's long braid as it whipped around in the wind.

CHAPTER 43: THE APPALACHIA ARROW

A powerful arm snaked around Bindra's neck and yanked her back, away from Zelda, who slipped and nearly fell off the train before grabbing onto the railing and wrapping her arms around it. Bindra and the Thurmondite who was choking her both tripped backward. He fell onto the catwalk and she fell onto his considerable girth. Bindra kicked frantically and tried to pull his arm off of her neck, but he was far more powerful. Blue spots started to invade her peripheral vision, and she barely had enough time to do what she did best.

Bindra shut her eyes and launched herself and the Thurmondite into time, but she deliberately travelled neither upstream nor downstream. Instead, she halted them in the present. The speeding train appeared to freeze on the tracks. A few light, drifting snowflakes were now suspended in place over Bindra's head. She craned her neck and saw Zelda, frozen and still clinging to the catwalk railing. She heard the Thurmondite under her panting and heaving as the weight of time started to crush him. He resisted, trying to pull them back into the future, which was precisely what Bindra wanted. She knew she was stronger. She knew the present would crush him long before it crushed her. She knew the present was her weapon.

Soon enough, the Thurmondite's arm slackened around Bindra's neck and she could fully breathe again. She tumbled over him and released them both from the present. Time started again. The train once again careened through the mountains. Bindra scooted along the catwalk, toward the control cab, watching the Thurmondite stand above her on wobbly legs.

"What was that?" he said in a trembling voice.

"That was time travel."

Just then, Zelda's hand came from behind the Thurmondite, grabbed his ear, and slammed his head against the side of the locomotive. He collapsed onto the catwalk and Zelda walked over him, offering Bindra a hand.

"Sorry," said Bindra as Zelda pulled her up. "I got a little distracted."

"You can pay me back later," said Zelda.

Bindra and Zelda came to the end of the catwalk and climbed a short series of steps to the door that would lead to the control cab. Bindra twisted the door handle until it clicked and the narrow door swung open. There, on the other side of the cramped control cab, they saw the engineer slumped over in his chair with Thurmond standing over him.

Thurmond pointed something at Bindra and Zelda, limply, as if he was expecting them. His other hand was clasped around a black lever on the control cab dashboard.

"You're too late," said Thurmond over the noise coming through the open door.

"That's mine," said Zelda, nodding at the lightning gun Thurmond held.

"I'm happy to return it when we're done here," said Thurmond. "Please close the door."

Cautiously, Zelda closed the door behind them and she and Bindra both lifted their hands. Bindra nodded at the engineer's body. "Is he dead?"

"Just asleep," said Thurmond. "Perfectly fine except for being struck by lightning."

"He needs to die today," said Bindra.

Thurmond shook his head. "I'm sorry to see they've drilled so far into you, Bindra, that you would say such a thing. No one needs to die today. I've already slowed us down with the dynamic brake. At this speed, the train will coast around the bend at Rosbys Rock without incident. But if you need a disaster that badly, I'm happy to provide one."

Bindra's face quivered. "What does that mean?"

"Leave, Bindra," said Thurmond. "I don't want to keep fighting you, and I don't want to hurt you. Even after all this, you still mean something to me. But those folks you've brought with you? I can't fight every time traveller at once."

CHAPTER 43: THE APPALACHIA ARROW

He began drumming his fingers along the black dynamic brake lever.

"By now I think you've figured out that I built this train?" said Thurmond.

"Yes," said Bindra. "You hired Nathan Hocking and Continental Railways to build it using the material from the Jackson Park anchor point."

"Very good. But you might not know that I snuck in a design flaw for situations just like this. If I engage the automatic brake at the same time as the dynamic, the couplers connecting the dining cars with the rest of the train will release. The automatic brakes on the dining cars will disengage, and those cars, along with everyone on board, will hit the bend without being able to stop. Some laymen might die, but not nearly as many as will live. The only sizable casualties will be those you've brought aboard this train."

"Don't do that," said Bindra frantically. "I know you, and I know you don't want to kill anyone."

"Then you must let me do this. I can save lives today, Bindra."

"More trains crash because this one doesn't, Henry!" shouted Bindra. "More people die because these people don't!"

"I don't care," snapped Thurmond. "We have plenty of time to figure out the consequences, but right now I don't care, and neither do the people on board. This one, this train, not another train somewhere in the future, this train matters to them. It matters to me. And it's getting to where it's going."

"We can't change the past where and when it matters to us, Henry," said Bindra. "We can't decide fate for people."

Thurmond's hand left the black dynamic brake and hovered over another lever on the control panel. "I am fate. For the next three minutes."

In the close confines of the control cab, it was impossible for Bindra and Thurmond not to notice Zelda vanish without warning. They both snapped their heads toward the spot she'd occupied just a moment before,

383

and both of them paused as they tried to process what had happened. The only reason they noticed her reappear against the back wall of the cab was the frantic sound of her pulling the intercom handset off its hitch. Zelda held down the button and spoke in the most calm, American-accented voice she could muster under the circumstances. "Passengers of the *Appalachia Arrow*, the time is now 3:48 p.m. and we are nearing Rosbys Rock, West Virginia—"

She was lucky to get it all out before the lightning bolt struck her in the chest.

44

HARMONIC VIBRATIONS

"PASSENGERS OF THE *APPALACHIA ARROW*, the time is now 3:48 p.m. and we are nearing Rosbys Rock, West Virginia—"

The fight was coming to a stalemate in the dining car. In the upper level, Akande, Marc and Lumen had been able to subdue, with some difficulty, their adversaries. On the lower level, Romero and his troopers had blocked the vestibule to the next coach to prevent attendants or passengers from wandering into the fray. Then they began using anything they could find to fight off the remaining Thurmondites.

When Zelda's voice came across the speaker system, Lumen was almost to the staircase on his way to help the troopers on the lower level. He stopped himself, stunned at the fact that Zelda was telling them all it was 3:48 and therefore they should all be dead. He looked at his watch. It was still 3:45.

"Akande!" he shouted back into the kitchen compartment.

Akande was busy keeping the last Thurmondite in a chokehold. Next to him stood Marc, trying to nurse a bruised jaw.

"What is she talking about?" shouted Akande. "We've got three minutes!"

"Maybe they slowed the train down and we're around the bend already," said Marc.

"Or she's warning us to get off early," said Lumen.

Akande considered this and abruptly threw down the coughing Thurmondite. He stood up and started walking to the staircase. "Then let's get off early." He came to the staircase and shouted to the lower level. "Romero! Link up!"

Marc joined hands with Lumen who took Akande's hand. Hector Romero charged up the stairs and reached out to Akande. One by one the remaining troopers joined hands in a chain stretching from the upper level to the lower level. Marc looked to his side and saw the man Akande had been choking getting to his feet with a kitchen knife in his hand.

"Akande," said Marc. "It's time to go."

"Is everyone together?" shouted Akande.

The knife-wielding man charged.

"Akande, now!"

"Here we go!"

• • •

Zelda fell to the floor and Bindra ran at Thurmond. She shoved him into the dashboard and held fast to his arms. He dropped the lightning gun, but she was more desperate to get his hands away from the dashboard levers. There was no way of knowing whether the rest of the task force had heard, understood or heeded Zelda's warning. She imagined Lumen's broken body dangling from wreckage in a black-and-white photo.

Thurmond threw her off and Bindra landed on the floor next to Zelda. His hand clasped around her ankle and he started dragging Bindra back along the floor. Then the sheet metal was soft dirt and Thurmond was dragging her through leaves. He released her and she spun around with her back on the ground, hands and legs up in defensive positions.

There was no need. Thurmond was not attacking her. Instead he just stood over her, breathing heavy with his hands on his hips. He seemed tired. They were outside and the sun was high and bright. The air was cool and felt fresher than usual. Thurmond looked back at her with angry, disappointed eyes and started wandering away.

"When are we?" she said.

"1884," muttered Thurmond.

Bindra pushed herself off the ground and brushed leaves from her clothing. After the constant rumble of the train engine, the silence of 1884 was deafening. She looked around and saw nothing but trees. The geography gave it away. The ravine and the creek were just the same as they had been, the same as they were going to be. There was no bike path, no abandoned tennis court and swimming pool, but this was surely the place where Bindra first met Henry Zoller. She followed him through the trees, cautiously, but still hopeful. Henry was still there, still here, she was sure, in the place where they first met. Maybe she could still find him and carry him home.

"1884? One hundred years?" she said gently. "That makes you a centurion."

Thurmond gave a cynical laugh. "Yeah. Maybe I'll apply to the commissioners and get my red sash."

"I know that's a joke, but I really think you should consider it."

Thurmond nodded to himself and put one arm up to lean against a crooked tree. "I guess I should listen to my instructor."

He gave her a somber smile and stared out over the ravine. Bindra folded her arms and leaned against the tree next to his, careful not to make any sudden movements. She couldn't travel a hundred years and had no intention of being marooned. She couldn't afford to scare him off. Silently she followed his gaze across the wilderness that would one day be his home.

"I came here all the time," he said finally. "Remembering the last time I saw you. Wondering if you would come back."

He looked to the ground and slowly pulled something from his pocket, holding it up for Bindra to see. It was the red book she'd lost the night they met. "This is yours."

He handed it over but never looked at her. She turned it over and over in her hands, marveling at how old it looked now. She could not bring herself to open it, knowing that all she would find was Sean, still talking to her from the night he died.

"This was your evidence, wasn't it? Your proof that it was all real?" said Bindra. "This is what brought you here."

"You brought me here," said Thurmond.

Bindra nodded. Tears rolled down her cheek, but she kept her lips firm. "I'm sorry I didn't come back, Henry. I'm sorry I didn't teach you what you should have learned. I owed it to you."

Thurmond closed his eyes and sighed again. He was still tired, from the hundred-year jump, perhaps, or from sorrow. Bindra didn't know which.

"You didn't owe me anything," he said. "Nothing that happened after was your fault. You set me on the road and I'm thankful for that. Now I just wish I could get away from you so I can do what I know is right."

Bindra sank and the tears came faster. He still hadn't given up. He still hadn't turned away from interference. He was still going to go back. "Who's on the train, Henry? Why does this train matter to you more than the others?"

Thurmond breathed deep. "My father," he said vaguely. "My mother always told me about the train crash that killed him. She always wished he'd been around to raise me." He shrugged at the ravine. "So do I."

"Henry, you know what that would mean," said Bindra. "If you succeed, if you stop this train from crashing and killing your father, your life won't be anything like you know it."

"Good. I love a good paradox."

Bindra watched him bite his lower lip with determination, perhaps more to prove to himself that he was ready more than to prove it to her. She hoped as much. She hoped for any crack in Thurmond that might allow Henry to escape.

"I'm going to stop the crash, Bindra. I will fix this. And on the other side of all this, the way I see it, I will either be the same person I am—having saved seventy-two lives, leading the revolution against the old, oppressive theory of time travel—or I'll be another person entirely, or I will have never existed at all, never having caused the pain my life has brought upon others. It's what you might call a win-win."

"There's going to be pain, Henry," said Bindra impatiently. "Lots of pain and none of it your fault. But if you stop this crash, there will be more pain, more than there needs to be, more than either of us or anyone else can even know. And that pain will be your fault. If you want to be fate for the next three minutes, you'll be a terrible fate for people you don't know, for people who don't deserve it."

"You know that for sure?" said Thurmond.

"No, Henry. I have to believe the commissioners. I have to believe the laymen. I have to believe the people it will hurt, and I do. But it's not something I can be sure of."

"Let me tell you what I am sure of," said Thurmond quietly. "I've only loved one person and it was in my former life. And that life ended when his did in a way that was entirely preventable for a time traveller. So I spent most of my life trying to learn time travel, and when I finally did, I was told I couldn't do the one thing I wanted to do—the one thing anyone who becomes a time traveller wants to do. But still, I tried. I tried to stop a disaster. I tried to save peoples' lives. Not a terrible thing, you know? I tried over and over again, and every time, a trooper was waiting for me. Every time, the same trooper, there to stop me and send me back when I came from. I tried twenty times, but he was always there, and after twenty times, I was done. That was my limit."

Now he was crying too. Bindra was horrified. The determined traveller from Sean's story was Thurmond all along. The disaster that got Sean exiled to 2005, that put him on Thurmond's scent, that led the two of them to Mr. Disaster, to that night in the tunnels, to Sean's death. It all began with Henry Zoller learning about time travel.

It all began with her.

"I can never go back there again," said Thurmond through tears. "So I will go and stop this disaster, and the next, and the next. Or I will be reborn. My father will live, and everything will change, and maybe there will be no reason for Will Thurmond to be on Interstate 66 on the day of the crash."

He hung his head and tried to regain control. Bindra stepped closer to him and reached out, speaking in a high, weeping voice. "Henry…"

Thurmond slapped her hand away. He looked at her and smiled sadly. "I wonder if you'll remember me," he said, right before he vanished.

Bindra deflated and let her head fall to the side. "No," she said helplessly, to no one. "No, Henry, please…"

She crumpled on the ground and wept, loudly, angrily. She clawed at the ground where he'd been standing, crushing leaves in her fists. She was marooned in a foreign century, in the middle of nowhere. Zelda was unconscious, possibly near death on a supposedly doomed train.

Even if Thurmond stopped the crash, would he simply kill Zelda? And if Akande, Lumen, Marc and the rest had failed to get off the train, what would happen to them? All the people she'd dragged into this mess, including Henry, were careening to destruction.

All of it is my fault, thought Bindra. Thurmond held no monopoly on guilt.

She turned over and stared up at the sun. She no longer thought of the mission, as it were. Countless people, if Commissioner Sutton was to be believed, were now in danger because the past was about to be changed, time was about to be broken. But she couldn't bring herself to care. She allowed herself that amount of selfishness—that the only sadness she felt now came from those she personally knew and loved, those she'd personally put in danger. She was hopeless and raw. She would settle, were it possible, for being back on the train, next to Zelda, next to Lumen and Marc and Akande, to triumph or fail or die by their side. But more than that, she wanted to be back home. She wanted to be back in India. She wanted it all to be a terrible dream, an extension of the dream she'd once had when she first time travelled.

"Okay," she sighed to absolutely no one. "I really, really, really need to go back to my time now, please."

None of them deserved it, she thought, not even Henry. She brought them all onto that train—her friends, the Thurmondites, Henry. They were all there because of her. Dozens of people who weren't supposed to be there, dozens of people on a train that was going to crash.

She still thought it was going to crash. Why did she still think it was going to crash? Thurmond was there. The drunken engineer wasn't driving. The speed was down. They were going to go slow around the bend. But it didn't matter. She knew it didn't matter. Why didn't it matter?

"Harmonic vibrations," she murmured to herself.

That phrase was important, and she tried to remember why. It was something Mr. Disaster had said. Tiny, harmonic vibrations, building up between the train cars until the wheels come off the tracks, especially at curves like Rosbys Rock. It was the investigator Kim's theory. But Kim could never figure out what would have caused the harmonic vibrations...

"Weight," whispered Bindra.

The secret of the *Appalachia Arrow* disaster unfolded inside her head. Dramatic weight differences between the train cars. It was never the engineer. It was never the speed. It was the point at which everything went wrong. It was the weight.

"The train is going to crash," Bindra said aloud.

She jolted upwards with leaves still in her hair and shut her eyes in horror. The train was going to crash, and Thurmond didn't know it. It was going to crash with Zelda on board, with Henry on board. She could see the pictures in her head. They would all still be taken, but with new occupants. Henry and Zelda, possibly Akande, Marc and Lumen. All of them broken and mangled, twisted and bloodied in black and white photographs. They'd be unidentified, fodder for internet conspiracy theorists sharing the pictures of her dead friends far and wide. She needed to stop it. She needed to be on that train. She needed to be in 1984. But it isn't about years, it isn't about numbers, it's about moments…

It was about Zelda. It was about Zelda, dangling inside an overturned train car, autopsied for some US government report. That was her moment. It was a moment that had to be prevented. She had to interfere with the moment, just this one moment. The moment, not the disaster. Moments, moments, moments…

•••

Zelda was being dragged. But the thing that really brought her out of it was being dropped. Evidently whoever was doing the dragging had discovered something more pressing to deal with. Her upper body fell with a thud and she was fully awake as Thurmond stepped over her and walked back to the controls. Fully awake but still suffering too much pain and stiffness to move, Zelda watched Thurmond look over the dials and indicators at the front of the control car. That's when she started to notice the incessant shaking as if she were lying on a table with wobbling legs.

"Something's wrong," she heard him mutter to himself as he wobbled with the shaking train.

CHAPTER 44: HARMONIC VIBRATIONS

"Agreed," she said.

He turned to look at her. He was wiping his eyes. "We're at the curve now, Zelda. I don't suppose you've decided you want to see my side of things?"

"I never knew you as a kid, Thurmond," said Zelda. "So here's what I want."

Her head was still too heavy to lift, so she stared mostly into the diamond ridges of the sheet metal and the watch on her limp wrist as she spoke.

"I want to take you to that island. I want to see you sliced up and left for dead. I want to see you bake in the sun and learn what fear is. I want you to see all the things I've seen. But neither of us will get that chance."

By now the shaking of the train was so powerful that Thurmond's whole upper body wobbled as he spoke. "Why is that?"

"Because this train is going to crash," she said, laughing into her wristwatch. "And we are out of time."

Thurmond walked to the door leading to the catwalk. He pulled the lever and pushed it open to reveal mountains and forest rushing past. "I enjoyed our time together, Zelda. But I'm afraid it's over now."

He bent over and grabbed her wrists. She struggled as much as she could as he dragged her toward the door. The wind and noise from the open door were more than distracting, but still she felt the unmistakable change in the atmosphere when a fellow time traveller arrived.

Thurmond again dropped her as Bindra tackled him from the side. The two of them hit the back of the engineer's seat and fell to the ground. Zelda's upper body strength was back, at least, and she lifted herself up to look at Bindra who crawled over to her. She looked dazed, bleeding from the nose. *She must've come a long way for me*, thought Zelda.

"It's good to meet a fellow—"

"Shut up," snapped Bindra as she threw Zelda's arm around her shoulder and lifted. "We have to get out of here."

Bindra turned and looked for Thurmond. He stood wobbling with the increasingly unstable train, his hair blowing in the wind rushing from the open door. He was staring through the windshield. There, beyond the glass and coming up fast, was the bend at Rosbys Rock.

"It's still going to crash, Henry," Bindra yelled over the din. "It was the weight, not the engineer. You built this train out of an anchor point. It's too heavy; it was always too heavy. And when it hits that bend, the wheels will shake right off the rails!"

Thurmond said nothing. He didn't move. Bindra inched closer to him, pulling Zelda along.

"Bindra, we don't have time," Zelda whispered.

"You have to come with us, Henry," said Bindra. "This train is going to crash."

She reached out with her free hand and grabbed his. He looked back at her with tears and a smile that was not Thurmond's.

"It's my fault," said Henry.

Bindra shook her head. "No it's not."

"We have to go," said Zelda.

"I have to stay," said Henry.

They'd reached the bend, and Henry threw away Bindra's hand. Zelda launched them, but Bindra held firm. The world around them pinched and stretched and they were in the present.

Henry was frozen in time, and Bindra still tried to take his hand. The bend in the tracks came closer and farther and closer and farther. Desperately, Zelda tried to pull her friend into the future, but Bindra kept them in the present. Bindra was too strong.

"Bindra," she croaked. "We have to get off."

"I won't leave him," said Bindra.

"And I won't leave you," said Zelda. "Bindra, please."

Bindra looked at her friend, the friend whose moment had pulled her across a century. The friend whose face was nearly translucent now, with blue veins showing and red blood trickling over her lip. Still, her friend smiled and nodded to her.

"I trust you not to kill me," said Zelda.

Bindra nodded and wept and looked again at Henry. She let it go to her head, and she let go.

45

POINT OF
DERAILMENT

IT ALL HAPPENED REMARKABLY FAST.

That was something most of the survivors repeated to investigators after the fact. Looking at the photographs, said one survivor, you'd think it would take a lot of time to create all of that carnage. But it all happened in just an instant. One moment, everything was fine. Then came the next moment.

The NTSB investigators Shaw and Kim determined that the leading locomotive of Continental Railways Train No. 202, the *Appalachia Arrow*, made it around the bend at Rosbys Rock without issue. The second car, Coach #8842, which contained the most passengers and therefore the most casualties, was the one that actually jumped the tracks first and started tumbling down the mountain. Before the couplers broke, Coach #8842 pulled the locomotive down along with it. These two cars fell all the way into the ravine, taking down trees as they went, before coming to rest at the spot Shaw and Kim would label in their report as Site A. Sixty-eight of the victims died at Site A.

The next car—Coach #7373—was pulled from the tracks as well. The coach overturned and tumbled about halfway down the slope where it stopped at what became known as Site B. The remaining four fatalities occurred at Site B, along with a majority of the severe injuries.

The final two dining cars did not overturn at all and remained at the top of the slope, referred to later as Site C. Only first dining car, #3550, actually derailed, while the trailing dining car, #1120, came to rest not far from the POD, or "Point of Derailment."

There were seventy-two deaths in total. None of the survivors seemed to escape without injuries, but all of those who were injured ultimately recovered in local hospitals.

Shaw and Kim and their team of investigators struggled for weeks after the *Appalachia Arrow* disaster trying to identify the exact cause of the derailment. At the proper speed, the train should not have had trouble rounding the bend at Rosbys Rock. While Kim theorized about harmonic vibrations and hunting oscillations and searched for an explanation for the weight variances between the train cars, Shaw dug into the deceased engineer's background and discovered Continental Railways had previously reprimanded him for working while intoxicated. If the engineer had been drinking at the time of the derailment, this seemed to explain away the government's lingering questions about the accident.

Continental Railways, reeling from embarrassment, forced its president, Nathan Hocking, into retirement and enacted some of the strongest rail safety measures in the country. These measures not only included strict drug and alcohol policies for their employees, but also a comprehensive study of weight variance and harmonic vibrations in their rolling stock. As a result, eleven years later, the *Omaha Limited* made a routine run from Cleveland to Omaha without incident.

46

THE CENTURION

THE FINAL SOUND of the *Appalachia Arrow* disaster was a tall pine tree splitting and collapsing onto the overturned locomotive. After that, there were no more crashes and explosions, only moaning and screaming from the injured and then, soon after the last tree fell, fourteen wristwatches beeping in unison.

Bindra sat leaning against a pine tree with Zelda's arm still around her shoulder and listened to the beeping. One by one the members of the Independent Intercentury Interference Task Force turned their watches off and stumbled to their feet. Bindra stood as well and pulled Zelda with her. All around them was wreckage and fire and screaming. Bindra heard Zelda's weak, quiet voice next just beneath her ear.

"What do we do now?"

Bindra surveyed the area and remembered her father's stories about accidents and fires and stranded hikers in the forests and hills of the national park. She remembered him telling her about the hazards and terrain that hindered rescue missions during the critical first hours. It was impossible to know how long it would take rescuers to get to the crash site. It was impossible even to know if anyone knew there'd been a crash.

They were the only ones left who could help.

Then there was a gust of wind and she heard a noise behind her. Leaves were rustling and twigs were snapping on the ground. People were approaching, and someone was calling her name.

"Bindra Dhar?" yelled the voice through the trees. "Bindra Dhar?"

Bindra looked and saw the approaching group. Ten men and women pushed their way through the brush and the pine trees toward her. Their clothing gave them away as foreigners to the century. The one who was shouting was a tall man with tousled black hair and wearing a green vest. "Bindra Dhar?"

"I'm Bindra Dhar."

"We were sent to aid you," said the man. "By the Eighteenth Centurion."

Zelda regained enough strength to stand on her own and released herself from Bindra's shoulder.

"Percy?" said Zelda.

"No, m'lady. We are troopers of the Parallel Centurion."

Zelda had more questions, but Bindra spoke first.

"Help anyone you can," she ordered. "Get them up the mountain, then come back down and get our people out. There are dead time travellers on board, and we can't have any questions from the laymen authorities."

The parallel troopers moved without question, and Bindra turned to her task force partners.

"Lumen, Marc," she ordered. "You know this decade better than we do. Get to Rosbys Rock and send rescuers out here. Go now. As for the rest of you, these people need our help. Let's get them up the mountain."

And so, for the next few hours, the survivors of the *Appalachia Arrow* were carried up the mountain by people they could never identify and given first aid that investigators would later say saved many of their lives. The official NTSB report on the disaster does not dwell for very long on the scattered survivor stories of people in old-fashioned clothing treating their injuries, dismissing them as simple traumatic imaginings. The report also concludes that, although many survivors insisted rescuers arrived at Site A immediately after the crash, authorities did not reach the crash site until the early evening. This discrepancy was likewise explained away as the typical trauma survivor's misjudgment of time.

As one might expect, the report compiled by the Time Travellers' Guild is far more thorough than the one compiled by the laymen investigators.

That report details how laymen rescuers never found any bodies that weren't supposed to be on the train. Bindra Dhar made certain the bodies of those few Thurmondites who died in the crash were respectfully removed from the wreckage and spirited to Twenty-One. She was meticulous about ensuring that no foreign artifacts were left behind, and even as the sun began to set and the laymen rescuers started to arrive at the scene, Bindra Dhar ordered her task force and the troopers of the parallel centurion to scour the ground, searching for the lost lightning gun. They finally located it inside the mangled control cab, not far from Thurmond's body.

Bindra returned the gun to Zelda and told her to leave with the rest of the task force. She dismissed the parallel troopers back to Eighteen, and for reasons she did not articulate, Bindra Dhar volunteered to personally remove Thurmond's body from 1984.

When the laymen encircled the locomotive car, they found no reason to suspect anything unusual had just occurred, and certainly no reason to believe that time travellers had contributed to the *Appalachia Arrow* disaster and the survival of dozens of its passengers.

When all of this was read back to Bindra Dhar days later in the Clerk's office, it all seemed to flow through her mind without making an impact. Commissioners Sutton, Lee and Long were all there, Long and Lee staring at her with dour faces and Sutton reading another book with apparent disinterest in whatever the Clerk was saying. All of them looked a little older than she remembered. The Clerk was there, reading from an ancient, leather-bound book titled, *A Full Report on the Conspiracies and Misdeeds of the Time Traveller 'Thurmond' Committed in the Realms of the Eighteenth, Nineteenth, Twentieth and Twenty-First Centuries—As Investigated and Compiled by Commissioners Sutton, Lee and Long.* They'd outsourced printing of the report to Seventeen to avoid bias, so the language was flowery and the woodcut images didn't really capture the accuracy of many scenes. Still the commissioners insisted they'd spent years of their lives investigating everything thoroughly and came to the same conclusion.

"You've done excellent work, Bindra," said the Clerk.

She gave a cynical huff. "Have I?"

"You did what no one else could," said the Clerk. "You stopped Thurmond. You confronted a ripple and won."

Bindra rolled her eyes. "Ripples don't exist."

"Apparently they do," said Commissioner Long. Bindra was unaccustomed to hearing his voice.

"Excuse me?"

"The man on the train," said Commissioner Long, taking the book from the Clerk and flipping through its pages. "The first husband of Helen Zoller, mother of Henry Zoller, was not Henry's father. It appears his biological father was a man named Stephen Kenzie."

"Helen Zoller married Stephen Kenzie after her first husband was killed in the *Appalachia Arrow*," said Commissioner Lee. "Without the interference of a time traveller, Thurmond never would have been born."

"You're saying Thurmond created himself?" asked Bindra. "By accident?"

"He was a ripple, as he claimed," said Long. "It's how he was able to avoid our notice for so long."

CHAPTER 46: THE CENTURION

"We know it's a lot to digest," said Commissioner Lee. "But I assure you, we have researched everything—"

"Thoroughly," finished Bindra. "So I've heard." She looked around at each of them with a face she hoped would convey her disgust. "Everything is back to normal then?"

"I wouldn't say that," said Commissioner Sutton, who did not look up from her book. "We still haven't been able to locate Llewellyn and Ginnifer Listratta, Lupita Calderon still occupies the Twentieth Century, three hundred years are in political turmoil, and Thurmond's cult remains scattered across spacetime."

The rest of the room turned to Emily Sutton, who still refused to look up from her reading.

"Wow," said Bindra. "When you put it like that, Commissioner, it seems like perhaps I haven't done excellent work."

This, finally, drew Sutton's eyes from her book. She flipped it open to a middle page and tossed it onto the table for Bindra to see. The pages were blank.

"Excellent work," hissed Commissioner Sutton.

Bindra simmered and nodded. That was all that mattered to them, she thought. As long as the words only they could read never came to pass, as long as this reality never dipped into the alternates, the ones that were supposedly far worse, anything was worth it. She'd allowed—no, guaranteed—the deaths of seventy-two people on the mountainside at Rosbys Rock. She'd guaranteed that Henry Zoller learned about time travel, that he grew up to experience and create tragedy, that he rode that train to the end, that he stood in the control cab of that locomotive until it was torn from the tracks, that he flew into the windshield with such force that his neck shattered and his head dangled as she pulled his body from the wreck and brought it over century lines.

She had done excellent work.

"May I go?" she said. She wasn't even sure whom she was asking.

"Of course," said the Clerk. He had that voice that men sometimes have when they know they should feel sympathetic but they aren't quite sure how. "I know this has all been hard for you."

She waved him off. "It's the job," said Bindra Dhar, rising from her seat. "It's the profession."

She turned away from them and walked to the door of the Clerk's office.

"Trooper Dhar," said Commissioner Sutton.

She turned. She would let Sutton have the last word she clearly wanted.

"Commissioners traditionally don't care much for time travellers," said Sutton. "You've sensed that, I think. We can't do what you do. We're laymen. We're the ones who live with the consequences of time travel. We're subject, in so many ways that most of us never know, to the whims of adventurous time travellers. So having a traveller who would do everything you have done to mitigate that one-sided influence—to protect us—it means a lot. It really does."

If nothing else, Emily Sutton was sincere, and Bindra appreciated it.

"May I go?" repeated Bindra, this time directly to Commissioner Sutton.

"You may," said Sutton. "But in the future, we will discuss a very pressing matter."

"What pressing matter is that?"

"This report says you travelled one hundred years in a single journey," said Commissioner Sutton. "And we are in need of an Eighteenth Centurion."

• • •

Zelda promised Bindra she would make sure it happened, so she did, even though she didn't want to. She put on the white dress again, slung a bag over her shoulder, and walked through the woods with the commissioners, each of whom held a jar. Bindra couldn't bring herself to watch, saying she would say her goodbyes in her own way and on her own time. But she also didn't believe the commissioners would go along with it, so she asked Zelda to keep the pressure up until they agreed. It had, indeed, been a challenge. No one thought Thurmond deserved a proper traveller funeral. No one wanted to be there, least of all Zelda. But she had promised the woman who saved her life. She'd promised her friend and it was the least she could do.

So it was a reluctant funeral train of four who came through the forest to the ravine at Jackson Park one fall day in 1984. They stopped at the edge, and Zelda saw that a fifth mourner, one she did not expect, had joined them. There on the boulder where Bindra Dhar would one day meet Randall, stood Solomon Christie, dressed in white, without his centurion's sash.

Of course, thought Zelda. *Sol is Thurmond's native centurion.* A deposed centurion, a king on the run, as it were, but still it was his duty to bid farewell to his deceased citizen, even though attending this funeral represented a grave personal risk. Zelda allowed herself, however briefly, to admire him.

"'Tis good to meet a fellow traveller," said Sol.

Zelda waited for one of the commissioners in front of her to reply before remembering that they were not travellers. Though she wished she had their luxury of silence, she nevertheless did her duty.

"To make the road less lonely."

Sol nodded.

"We are gathered here today," said Sol, "to settle the matter of Henry Adam Zoller. His matter, which has burned to ash, we shall consign to this river in space, which is finite. His memory, which cannot be burned, we shall carry with us as we travel upon the river of time, which has no end. So it was, so it is, so it shall be."

Promptly, Sol Christie left his boulder. The three commissioners waded into the shallow water, and Emily Sutton released her beautiful voice.

"When death has come and taken our loved ones,
It leaves our home so lonely and drear,
Then do we wonder why others prosper
Living so wicked year after year."

The commissioners opened their jars and released the white ash into the creek. Zelda watched Thurmond swirl away and wondered for a moment what, exactly, kept her from becoming him.

"Farther along we'll know all about it,
Farther along we'll understand why.
Cheer up my brother, live in the sunshine,
We'll understand it all by and by."

Sol Christie hopped over a few rocks to reach Zelda's side of the creek. He stood next to her but said nothing.

"I have something of yours," she said as the ashes slipped away.

She reached into her bag and pulled out the lightning gun. She tossed it once onto her open palm so that the handle faced him. She looked again at the inscription on the barrel.

A gift from the Family Listratta to the Family Christie.

"You should keep it," said Sol, looking back to the creek. "I've never liked firearms."

Together they watched the ashes disappear. When their duty was done, the commissioners walked briskly from the creek and disappeared into the woods where the Clerk waited for them. Zelda and Sol were left alone with the sounds of birds, the rippling creek and Twentieth Century suburbia just beyond.

CHAPTER 46: THE CENTURION

"It's not safe for you to be here," said Zelda. "Lupita will not feel she has this century under her heel until she's captured you. You will be her highest priority."

"I have no doubt of it," said Sol. "Unfortunately for her, I have every intention of reclaiming my century."

Zelda laughed. "What makes you so confident that you can do such a thing?"

"Why shouldn't I be confident?" said Sol. "I'm with you, and you have that." He nodded to the lightning gun and walked away.

• • •

Bindra Dhar had spent so much of her childhood wondering about the old man who lived in her little village. And of course now, when she was an adult and a professional time traveller, the old man no longer lived there. Still, she saw him walking his usual walk up the road, along her family's fence, while she leaned against the doorway.

Bindra, having saved time itself, decided she deserved a vacation, so she returned home to India. To spare her family the shock of her sudden adulthood, she deliberately arrived a few years after she'd left home to become what her parents still believed was some sort of police officer. Her father praised her for dedicating her life to public service as he had. Her mother fretted over whether she was getting enough sleep.

She found her younger siblings were now teenagers and had concerns of their own—boys and girls and relationships, mostly. She understood. She kept a red book in which she wrote messages to Lumen, and a black book in which she received his messages. But in general she found herself thinking of him with diminished intensity, and she had a hard time listening to her siblings' complaints for long periods of time.

She returned to old habits. She found that her old sweaters, kept diligently folded, still fit comfortably. She proofread the pages that her mother furiously typed out—the beginnings of *Amrita's Revenge*. She visited the market often to buy coffee, which her family never kept in the house. Tea would no longer do; her time in America had ruined her in this regard. Almost every day she would walk to the national park, admiring the mountains and forests, the rivers and lakes, all the landmarks and sacred lands her father had protected over the years. She would find her first anchor point, the rocky outcrop not far from the road, and she would travel, upstream and downstream, hundreds of years at a time.

And then, back home.

She leaned against the door to the home she grew up in, wearing the sweater she used to love, drinking the coffee she could no longer live without, and watched Walter Brooks walk down the road. There was, of course, no other reason for him to be there except to find her. He came to the edge of their fence and leaned over.

"It's good to meet a fellow traveller," he said.

Bindra lifted her mug toward him.

"To make the road less lonely," she said.

She stepped off the porch. She felt compelled to come down and greet him, but she would show him none of what she was feeling inside. She wouldn't let him on to the fact that she'd taken a respite from the realm of the time travellers for a reason. He opened the gate to the fence and came into the yard, like the welcome guest he was. She held her mug out away from her so she could greet him with an embrace. *Why not?* she thought. He was her instructor. And besides, he was American. They hug all the time. It didn't have to mean anything.

But when she finally reached him, she promptly dropped the mug. It shattered on the ground, the coffee spilled into the leftover snow and she fell into Walter Brooks and wept. He held her tight and didn't try to tell her everything was fine, and she appreciated that. She was sure they stood like that for hours.

"You didn't teach me any of this," she said finally. "You didn't tell me any of this would happen."

"I didn't know," he said into her hair. "But, Bindra…"

He moved her so that she could look him in the eye and she saw he was crying too.

"You have done great work," he said, and he squeezed her shoulders with every word. "I don't think I could have done it."

"Did you know? When you picked me, did you know my legend? Did you know I would defeat Thurmond? Did you know they'd ask me to be a centurion?"

Mr. Brooks closed his eyes and hung his head.

"Bindra Dhar," he said. "All I knew about you when I learned your name was that you would make me proud, and you've done it. Instructing you has been the privilege of my life."

Bindra collapsed and sat cross-legged on the snow, gasping through tears. Mr. Brooks knelt on one leg, ready for her when she needed him. She had too many things racing through her mind. She'd lost Sean, lost Thurmond, lost seventy-two victims on the *Appalachia Arrow*. She'd almost lost Zelda, a moment that still haunted her. And there was Henry, who was still out there somewhere in time, not yet Thurmond. And there was herself, her future self, a self she couldn't escape, who had apparently sent troopers to help her save as many lives as she could.

"I have to do it, don't I?" said Bindra. "I have to be a centurion. No more ghamud dayim."

"Not necessarily," said Mr. Brooks. "We don't understand everything about how time works."

"We only know it doesn't work."

"It doesn't even exist. When will you learn?"

The two of them laughed through tears. Bindra sniffed, wiped away her tears and slowly pulled something from her pocket. She held up the old, ragged red book that Henry Zoller had carried for his entire life.

"I wish I could have said goodbye," said Bindra. "Or I guess I wish I'd never met him at all. I wish I'd never had an effect on his life."

Mr. Brooks looked down and fiddled with the grass peeking through the layer of leftover snow. "We're all just travelling through each others' lives, Bindra. But in the end, everyone makes their own choices. He made his, and they made sense to him. Now you must make the choices that make sense to you."

Bindra nodded. "I have to do it, don't I?" She stared down at the dirt and snow. "Not because of fate or destiny or anything like that. I have to do it because I have to do it."

Mr. Brooks sighed. "I can't tell you what you have to do, Bindra. I can only tell you this: you have been one of the most ambitious, impatient apprentices I have ever taken. So it seems only natural to me that you would carry your ambition to its logical extreme. But precisely because you have been one of my most ambitious, impatient apprentices, I know that your choices are your choices and your choices alone. It would be foolish of me to think that you would do anything that isn't your choice. So all you have to ask yourself is, 'What do I want?'"

Bindra nodded at the snow and rock. The mountain wind picked up, blew the hair from her eyes and dried her tears. Then she pushed herself off the ground and stood upright while Mr. Brooks followed. She laughed and smiled at the old man. He smiled back. She placed her hands on her hips and gazed around at the mountains and a familiar blue sky. She was a time traveller, and there was a whole century waiting for her.

ACKNOWLEDGMENTS

I STARTED WRITING *Fellow Travellers* in 2015, and in the time between then and now, a great many people have had one hand or another in helping this book along. Principally among them was my wife, Melissa, who devoured every chapter as I wrote it and always asked for more. My dear friends Emily Sirney, Nikki Lanka and Haylee Pearl read early drafts and asked important questions about the world I was trying to build. Mike Heslop and everyone else at Kafe Kerouac built the unmatched environment of warmth and creativity in which this book was born and matured. Carey Lynn O'Keefe read one of the later drafts and made me feel like I was on the right track. Terra Dalton tried her hardest to explain geology and physics to me so I could better describe anchor points and train disasters. I owe the final wording of the phrase "ghamud dayim" to Amel Khalife and Mimi Bekheet (with special help from Mimi's mother). Emily Hitchcock, Brad Pauquette, Shannon Page, and everyone at the Ohio Writers' Association and Bellwether took a chance on me and edited this book to its best possible version. Finally, I have to thank my parents and my family, who gave me plenty of pens when I was little, no matter how many ended up in the laundry.

411

JESSE BETHEA IS A WRITER and award-winning journalist born in Fairfax, Virginia. He is a graduate of Ohio University, a professional video producer, an amateur hiker, a recovering theater kid, a mediocre chess player and a semi-permanent denizen of Kafe Kerouac. He currently lives in Columbus with his wife and three cats.

Learn more about Jesse and keep up with his writing at
www.JesseBethea.com

Made in the USA
Middletown, DE
31 October 2021